THE MILAGRO AFFAIR

THE MILAGRO AFFAIR

D. G. HERNÁNDEZ

ARCHWAY
PUBLISHING

This is a work of fiction. All of the characters, names, incidents, organizations, and dialogue in this novel are either the products of the author's imagination or are used fictitiously.

Archway Publishing books may be ordered through booksellers or by contacting:

Archway Publishing
1663 Liberty Drive
Bloomington, IN 47403
www.archwaypublishing.com
1 (888) 242-5904

Because of the dynamic nature of the Internet, any web addresses or links contained in this book may have changed since publication and may no longer be valid. The views expressed in this work are solely those of the author and do not necessarily reflect the views of the publisher, and the publisher hereby disclaims any responsibility for them.

Any people depicted in stock imagery provided by Thinkstock are models, and such images are being used for illustrative purposes only. Certain stock imagery © Thinkstock.

ISBN: 978-1-4808-4158-1 (sc)
ISBN: 978-1-4808-4278-6 (hc)
ISBN: 978-1-4808-4159-8 (e)

Library of Congress Control Number: 2016920898

Print information available on the last page.

Archway Publishing rev. date: 3/14/2017

For

Sarah Frances

*"The gods envy us. They envy us because
we're mortal, because any moment
may be our last.
Everything is more beautiful because
we're doomed.
You will never be lovelier than
you are today.
We will never be here again."*

Achilles in movie Troy

CONTENTS

CHAPTER 1

The world's elite mingled in the crowds along the sun-drenched coastline of Monte Carlo, hopping from yacht to yacht, from party to party, sipping Dom Perignon, oblivious to the event that was unfolding before them.

The summer season of parties and charity balls had reached its zenith. Not since the arrival of Grace Kelly had so much excitement been generated in the Principality of Monaco. This, the final day of the summer party season, gave women one more chance to showcase themselves with the finest of jewels, fashion, and perfumes. The world's best fashion designers were present en masse, watching their art move about on the thinnest of bodies, not concerned about the models' often failing health. The very wealthy would soon leave for other parts of the world, where a new season of galas was about to begin. But none would leave before attending the auction of the *Milagro*, a yacht without equal. The *Milagro* was truly one of a kind and if there is one thing the very rich must have it's the one-of-a-kind possession.

My name is David Lorca, and this is the story of a man's dream to change the world.

I looked at my watch. Noon had finally arrived, and it was time to make the call.

"Alpha One, confirm location." I spoke into my secure satellite phone.

"*Milagro* control room," Alpha One responded.

"Bravo one, confirm location."

"*Milagro* control room, one meter left of Alpha One," Bravo One responded.

"Release retrovirus at eighteen hundred hours," I instructed them.

"Copy that," came the response from the *Milagro*.

I pushed the end button on my phone. I had waited ten years to make this call.

CHAPTER 2

"Hey David, come aboard." Colin yelled at me from the flybridge of his yacht. "Have something to show you."

I could barely see him as I looked up. The glaring sun shone brightly that afternoon in Monte Carlo.

"Love to join you Colin, but I can't," I told him. "On my way to meet with the reporter from the *San Antonio Chronicle*."

"Oh come on David, it'll only take a minute," he insisted. "Big surprise."

"Nothing you do surprises me, Colin," I yelled out, not bothering to look up at him. I started to walk away. Didn't want to keep the reporter waiting.

"I just bought a Picasso." I heard him yell. Many of the people within hearing distance looked up in amazement, as if wondering who it was that could afford a Picasso.

"That's the surprise?" I yelled up at Colin. This time I did look up. I didn't care about the blinding sun. "Are you kidding me? You have a Picasso on your yacht? Are you stupid or what?"

The same people that had looked up at Colin were now staring at me in disgust. I didn't care. I was too pissed off at Colin.

"Don't you know how stupid it is to have that painting out at sea? You're going to ruin it, you idiot! You know excellent painters. Have them paint you a replica—no one will know the difference. In the meantime, get that painting back on land where it belongs. Better yet, donate it to a museum where it really belongs."

I walked away knowing full well that Colin was not about to heed my advice. Colin can easily afford to buy several Picassos to line his yacht's walls, but that doesn't give him the right to ruin them. It's people like him that give rich people a bad name.

I put Colin out of my mind and continued my walk among the beautiful people. I had longed for this lifestyle ever since I was a kid. As a child, I wanted to be adopted by a wealthy family and be taken to the land of plenty, including a ranch with horses. I now found myself in the land of plenty, a bona fide member of the elite. Membership into this class has only one requirement: money, lots of it. Membership in country clubs is now an option exercised by me and not the clubs. My life will be different after today. And so will the lives of the rich people throughout the world. But more important, the lives of the poor will be forever changed.

I've enjoyed hanging around these people, and many of them have become dear friends, especially the young ones. I like their swagger; they really have it down. They depend only on themselves and their brains. Often referred to as the Silicon Valley Kings, these are the new oligarchs. Moore's Law is not a phenomenon to them; it's something they created and continue to perpetuate. These Silicon Valley Kings and others like them don't rape the earth. They make their billions by creating the unimaginable and bringing it to market. These Silicon Valley Kings are singlehandedly accelerating our evolution, bringing us closer to the singularity, the point at which artificial intelligence trumps human's minds.

"There you are." I heard a familiar voice calling from behind. I turned around only to have a beautiful pair of lips meet mine. The six-foot-tall Carolina stands an inch taller than me, and that's when she's not wearing her Jimmy Choo high heels.

"Missed you at my party last night, David. I really wanted to spend time with you, my darling. There were so many people at the party that we could've disappeared and nobody would have noticed," Carolina told me after our long kiss.

I met Carolina Nadal, a former Spanish supermodel, while she was still single. We dated on and off for a couple of years. She later married Daryl Kahn, a German billionaire and friend of mine. At her wedding, she told me she had tired of waiting for me to make up my mind. I never mentioned marriage, so I don't know why she thought I was busy making up my mind. I feel sorry for Carolina. When I met her, she was full of life and ambition. Nowadays she's a mere extension of her husband. Maybe I shouldn't feel sorry for her, maybe this is what she always wanted to be—a rich man's trophy wife.

"I'm sure your husband would have noticed if the two of us went missing. But in any case, I'm sorry I couldn't be there for you. As of late I've been too busy for parties."

"Daryl and I will be setting sail for Majorca tonight. But if you ask me nicely, I'll stay in Monte Carlo so we can be together. I'll make up some lame excuse. Daryl couldn't care less," Carolina pleaded.

"I really don't think that's a good idea," I began. But she wasn't listening. Before I could finish, she thrust her hand within inches of my eyes. All I could see was a huge emerald-cut diamond ring on her finger, its brilliance rivaling the sun that afternoon.

"Look at what I bought this morning," Carolina told me while still holding her hand to my face. "I woke up feeling depressed and disappointed at not seeing you last night. Spending money always makes me feel better, so I called the concierge and told him to send up a jeweler. I was shown several exquisite pieces, but when I saw this ring I knew I had to have it. My depression disappeared the instant I slid it on my finger."

"It's a gorgeous ring; I mean...what can I say?" I laughed.

"Tell me you love it," Carolina begged. "Paid half a million dollars for it."

"Half a million dollars? At that rate your husband will go broke in 2,400 days."

"Better up my spending. Don't know if he'll keep me around that long," the witty Carolina responded.

We said our goodbyes, and I promised her that I would see her in Majorca if I didn't get detoured. I knew I would; my detour had been planned for years. The countdown had begun, and there was no stopping us now. I had no intention of going to Majorca, I was leaving this life of opulence behind. I was less than six hours away from releasing the retrovirus.

CHAPTER 3

I hastened my pace. I was meeting Ignacio for my final interview and didn't want to keep him waiting. Ignacio proved to be the reporter I had hoped for, honest, direct, and unbiased. The first time I met him aboard my yacht, I thought I had made a big mistake by selecting him to write a feature story on me. He looked so young, too young to understand some of the many things I was going to share with him. I was wrong. He has allowed me to read some of his drafts, and I have to say, I'm impressed. Writing a feature story on anybody is difficult, but Ignacio has made it look easy. He has taken facts, my life story, and given it perspective. I don't believe that Ignacio sees this assignment as a job. I think he sees himself as being on a mission. Can't say what makes me think this, I just do. Hope I can help him accomplish his goal; many people have helped me accomplish mine.

"Hey David, think I could interest you in a yacht?" A shipbuilder asked me in jest as I walked by the thirty-five-meter *Azimut*.

"Think I'll pass." I waved and kept on walking.

The profits and commissions made by the sale of these floating castles are enormous, and so are the marketing budgets. The preparations for these extravagant yacht shows are unbelievable. The shipbuilders and their staffs laboriously go through photo files of invited guests, memorizing each guest's name, nationality, and any other information that might lead to a multimillion-dollar sale. These highly-paid crew members know the nuances of the rich, nuances that can be learned only by direct contact. Speak only when spoken to, don't look directly into a person's eyes, anticipate, yes always anticipate, know what their next request is before it is uttered. Once the prospective buyers begin to arrive, the yachts' captains communicate with their crews in silence, the well-choreographed show has just begun.

"Mr. Lorca. Over here, I'm over here," Ignacio Garcia, the young soft-spoken reporter from San Antonio yelled over the crowd. "Over here!"

"There you are," I said as I started walking towards him. "Heard you calling me, but I couldn't see you. This crowd is ridiculous."

"It's not so much the crowd, I'm just short, Mr. Lorca," Ignacio smiled as we shook hands.

"Glad to see you, Ignacio. Having fun in Monte Carlo, young man? And please call me David. I've shared so much of myself with you during these past few months that I feel you've earned the right to call me by my first name. Agreed?"

"Agreed."

"Instead of meeting aboard my yacht, let's leave the marina and go have coffee at one of my favorite places."

"I've never seen so many rich people, so much wealth, and all here for the *Milagro*'s auction. Any idea what it will sell for?" Ignacio asked me between breaths. I was walking at a pretty fast pace; I needed my coffee.

"You never know, never know how the bidding will go. The reserve is pretty high, so we'll just have to wait and see."

"The *Milagro*'s auction is six hours away, and the people are already in a frenzy. I'm positive that the winning bid will set an all-time record for the most expensive yacht ever sold. Especially after all the things I've heard people say about the *Milagro*."

"What are they saying?" I curiously asked.

"Well you know, that the *Milagro*'s onboard technology is more sophisticated than any military vessel in the world."

"Really? That sounds exaggerated, but tell me more," I insisted.

"I think it's what is not known about the *Milagro* that's causing such a stir," Ignacio said. "People are saying that it's so advanced it borders on science fiction."

"That last thing you said, what was it, science fiction? That's what all those rumors are, Ignacio, science fiction." I slapped him on the back, trying to change the subject. "Most rumors have an element of truth behind them, but in reference to the *Milagro*, the rumors are nowhere close to the truth. I know everything there is to know about the *Milagro*, and trust me, it's very ordinary in many ways. It floats on the water, gets you from point A to point B as quickly as possible, and is very expensive, just like any other yacht."

"You're about to taste some of the best coffee in the world," I told Ignacio after arriving at the Port Palace Hotel. I led the way to my favorite table out on the terrace. The reason I liked sitting at this particular table was because of the view. It encapsulated the lifestyle I had imagined as a youngster. The view was so spectacular, I took my sunglasses off; I didn't want anything to come between my eyes and the grandeur before me. I took one last look at my world of opulence, the world I had lived in for many years, before permanently telling it a final goodbye.

"I come here as often as possible, Ignacio, brings back old memories."

Ignacio took his reporter's pad and recorder out of his backpack. He looked at me in a strange way, and I noticed an alarmed look on his face. Ignacio looked at me as if he were seeing me for the first time. I didn't know what to make of his startled expression.

"Perhaps we should do this interview some other time," Ignacio said softly. "I know you've been traveling a lot. You must be exhausted. I don't mean to sound rude, but you look like you've aged ten years since I last saw you, which was only a few months ago. Don't mean any disrespect, sir. I'm just telling you this so that you can go get some rest. You'll be back to your normal self in no time, trust me, sir. Let's wait till you get back to San Antonio to wrap things up. Your health is much more important."

"No. We must do it now. Tomorrow is never guaranteed."

"No really, Mr. Lorca, I mean, David. This is too important of a day for you to spend answering my questions. I'm basically done with my story. I only have a couple more questions before I can call it a wrap. So let's just wait til you get back to San Antonio."

"No, I insist, let's do this interview now. I'll be fine, just a little tired, just like you said. Haven't had much sleep, too many things going on. And yesterday I lost my security chief. He died of an apparent heart attack."

"Sorry to hear that."

"Tragic story. Wish he were here today to help us solve a pending security problem, a problem that only he could have solved for us. I've tried to stay upbeat all morning long, tried to pretend that all is well, but it's obvious I haven't succeeded. The severity of the problem that remains unsolved is greater than you can imagine. But all I can do at this point is to remain optimistic and hope that my day ends better than expected. We'll miss him. Go ahead, Ignacio, start your recorder, let's get this show on the road."

"September 16, 2015," Ignacio spoke into his hand-held recorder. "Last interview for my feature story on Mr. David Lorca, Ignacio Garcia reporting for the *San Antonio Chronicle*."

I looked at Ignacio as he gently laid his recorder on the table.

"Mr. Lorca, can we keep it formal during the interview? It would help my objectivity."

"Sure, go ahead."

"Why did you name the yacht the *Milagro*?" Ignacio started the interview. "Any significance to the name?"

"Lots of significance. As a Spanish speaker, you know that *milagro* means miracle in Spanish."

"The miracle took place one summer day in northern Wisconsin. There she was, standing long and erect, lily white. She was the most beautiful thing I had ever seen. I forgot about the former Playboy Bunny at my side. I ran towards her ethereally. I had never experienced such a feeling. This must be a miracle; I'm in the midst of a miracle, I told myself. I only had eyes for her, the seductive mistress before me, begging to be boarded, but not by me. I reached out to her but didn't touch her. She wouldn't let me.

"Just like a kid, I ran and climbed up a set of temporary construction scaffolds that stood about fifteen meters away. I could now see the beautiful mahogany deck. It was immaculate, every seam lined up perfectly. Contemporary teak furniture brought the deck to life. I imagined people dancing on it as it sailed the seas. I was sure that the dancers wore nothing but the best of clothes, the best of jewelry, hell, the best of everything. A radar dish rotated high above the flybridge, never seeming to stop. The yacht's flags were fully extended by the vigorous winds that day. By the way, I now know how to read the flags on a dressed-up yacht.

"What kind of people own things like this? I asked myself. I don't care, I immediately told myself. This is what I want. This is what I've always wanted, I said as I gazed at the stunning yacht. A miracle took place in my life that summer day in Sturgeon Bay, Wisconsin."

"Wow, quite a story, David. I've been on your yacht and the deck is exactly the way you describe it on that yacht you saw many years ago. All seams line up perfectly."

"There are things in my past I like to keep around. Keeps me hungry. Any more questions? Because I really have to get going. I have one more deal to tend to, my masterpiece."

"Masterpiece? Hmm, sounds interesting. Anything you can share? We can go off the record if you'd like," Ignacio asked.

"Just a figure of speech, Ignacio. When the time comes to write about my masterpiece, you'll be the first reporter I call."

"Thank you, I would really appreciate the scoop."

"You're welcome."

CHAPTER 4

Port Palace Hotel
Monte Carlo
September 16, 2015
1:00 PM

"Since you insist, I'll proceed in asking my last two questions, and then I'll call it a wrap, I promise. I've saved them for the end, these last two questions, that is. Perhaps they should have been my first two questions, but sometimes I do my research backwards, more exciting, at least it is for me," Ignacio explained.

As much as David wanted to appear relaxed and ready to continue with the interview, he couldn't. The retrovirus's release was now only five hours away, and David still didn't know who was planning on stealing the racist gene research data. He couldn't help but wonder if his death was imminent.

"Go ahead, ask your first question, ask it last." David shook his head.

"How did you get started? I mean, how did you make your first dollar?" Ignacio sat up straight as he asked.

"Sold a patent I owned, sold it for $100 million." David burst out laughing, setting his worries aside, if only for a brief moment. "Sorry, that was not the question, was it? You wanted to know about my first dollar."

"A hundred million bucks? Was it the patent on the iPhone or what? That's a lot of money." Ignacio couldn't believe it.

D. G. HERNÁNDEZ

"I wish." David stopped laughing. "No, nothing as complicated or as advanced as the iPhone."

"Must have been pretty advanced stuff if you got $100 million for it." It was difficult for Ignacio to understand the vast sums of money the rich make on a single deal. David's world of affluence was as foreign as the moon to Ignacio.

"Nope, no cutting-edge technology. I developed and patented a system that made voting over the telephone possible. I can't remember when the idea came to me, but once it got a hold of me, it wouldn't let go. I thought of the many times I hadn't voted because of the inconvenience. You know, having to vote at your local school, library, fire station, or wherever your assigned polling place is located. And if you're out of town and didn't vote early, you can just forget it. You've just lost your right to vote.

"And even if you're not out of town, voting is not guaranteed. I've seen people give up and leave their polling place because the lines were too long. Working people don't have the luxury of leaving work early to go vote. There are children to be dropped off at the daycare or school, then do the reverse at the end of the day, and voting usually doesn't win out. Some states have recently instituted restrictive photo identification requirements. I tell you Ignacio, voting just keeps getting more difficult for the poor working class."

David took a sip of his now-cold coffee. Between questions, David kept asking himself, *Am I as good as dead? Who's coming after me and how?*

"Anyway, I showed proof of concept for voting via the telephone," David instinctually continued. "That was my only goal, developing proof of concept. This was in the early eighties, and the computer power to make voice voting possible did not exist. But I knew that the computer capabilities I needed were just around the corner. I figured that somebody with a higher IQ could take it the rest of the way. You know, have the engineers develop the actual product or products that would bring my idea to fruition. I simply wanted to make voting easier when I developed my concept. I wasn't thinking about making money. I didn't think it was right to make money off of voting. I would have given my patent away free of charge, noblesse oblige," David smiled.

"How exactly would voting over the phone work?"

"You simply call a toll-free number, and the computer recognizes your prerecorded voice pattern and opens up a ballot. You are now free to vote. It may be used in tandem with a computer, but it's not necessary. But first let me backtrack a little. Your voice patterns would be recorded when you register to vote. The required credentials to register your voice patterns would be the same as the ones that we currently use when registering to vote the old-fashioned way," David explained.

"But what if the computer makes a mistake?" Ignacio asked.

"Valid point, but like I said, all I wanted was to show proof of concept. The requisite technology would soon follow. The kinks could be worked out by people above my pay grade. Developing my proof of concept is now possible, the technology is now available. Today's technology has proven that voice recognition is as reliable as fingerprints. Don't know if you know this, but many financial institutions use voice recognition as the ultimate password. If the computer doesn't recognize your voice, you don't get into your bank account. USAA Financial in San Antonio, Texas, uses voice recognition instead of passwords and will soon move to facial recognition."

"How soon after you sold your patent was it developed? Because honestly, this is the first I've heard of it. But I'm sure it's being used somewhere in the United States," Ignacio asked.

"There's a very good reason you've never heard of voice recognition voting being used. My proof of concept was never developed into an actual voting system," David answered.

"Seriously? Do you mean to tell me that somebody paid you a hundred million bucks for a patent they didn't develop, a patent that could have made them billions of dollars? That's absurd! Who or why would anybody do such a foolish thing and sit on a patent that has such high earning potential?"

"That's a riddle I never solved. I never learned the buyer's identity. The entire deal was handled by lawyers and bankers. I signed several confidentiality agreements along the way, and that's it. The buyer wanted to remain anonymous, and to this day his wish has been granted."

"Well, you've certainly multiplied your first dollar many times over," Ignacio said. "And now for my very last question," he continued. "I saved it for last because I wanted to be on land when I asked it. I didn't want to be thrown overboard in the middle of the Mediterranean."

"Can't be that bad of a question. And besides, I've never thrown anybody overboard, although there have been a lot of firsts in my life."

"Nice to know," Ignacio smiled and took a deep breath before continuing. "My question goes something like this: You've received a lot of criticism from civil rights organizations for not doing much for your people. Your lack of involvement in political issues that affect Chicanos has been questioned. And of course, there's the issue of your wealth. You're criticized for not using your money to advance the plight of the less fortunate. You're criticized for hanging around with billionaires, with the rich and the famous. Others say that you've forgotten where you came from. Do you care to address any of these criticisms?"

"I can see why you saved this question or series of questions till the end. These are fair questions, Ignacio. And I'm glad you had the guts to ask them. Speaks well of you as a reporter."

"Thank you."

"Now, to answer your series of questions. During my college years, I was involved in the usual, ordinary kinds of political actions, demonstrations against the Vietnam War, marches supporting equal rights, a picket line around the Deans' office because of his lack of support for Chicano Studies. Don't forget, this was Madison, Wisconsin, during the sixties, a liberal hotbed of student activism. It was during my first few years at Wisconsin that I became aware of the politics behind our country's social injustices, foreign and domestic. Heretofore, I assumed, I thought, I believed, or whatever that injustices just happened. I didn't see the correlation between racist policies and the policymakers. Call me stupid, but I didn't see it. I guess I wasn't blessed with political discernment at a young age. I internalized the inequities; I blamed myself and people like me for all of our problems.

"The political landscape of the sixties afforded me an opportunity to gain a better understanding of the plethora of social injustices.

"Many people took to the streets, including myself, in protest of the injustices. There was always something to protest in Madison, protest du jour, as I called them. Don't mean to make light of the protests, but some were rather esoteric. But as a whole, the protests that took place across our nation did have a positive impact. Federal legislation was probably one of the best outcomes of the many demonstrations. The legislation gave the disenfranchised a tool, an instrument, if you will, in fighting discrimination. The Civil Rights Act of 1964, President Johnson's War on Poverty, Head Start Programs, and let's not forget, Affirmative Action Programs, whose most notable advocate was President Nixon, were all positive programs that came about because of people's involvement in the political process.

"However, the panacea was short-lived, if it ever had a life. Southern states chose to undermine federal legislation instead of embracing it. We must never forget former Governor George Wallace of Alabama and his famous quote, 'Segregation now, segregation tomorrow, segregation forever.' And for Governor Wallace, these weren't empty words. He actually stood and blocked the doorway to prevent two African Americans from enrolling at the University of Alabama at Tuscaloosa.

"Governor Wallace stepped aside from the doorway after being confronted by Deputy Attorney General Nicholas Katzenbach. Many in the minority community, whether liberal or conservative, saw this as a victory for all time. It was now time to move on with life because segregation was now a thing of the past, no more separate but equal, Plessy versus Ferguson had been overturned years prior. We had righted all wrongs, past and present. We could now go on living as equals.

"Sorry to say, this was not the case. Injustices and discrimination had not been eliminated. Legislation proved to be of little help in eliminating racism and its accompanying evils. The more I studied the issues, the less convinced I became that there was a people solution to a people problem. There can never be enough laws to rid the world of injustice, racism, and inequalities, I told myself. We can legislate til we're blue in the face, but we can't legislate equality. I cannot pass a law that says you have to provide me with equal access to success if you don't want to, and the *you* in this case is usually white males that run the world. People with racist tendencies can always explain, justify, or rationalize their reasons for discriminating. Defining injustice is subjective, just like an opinion, and opinions are based on personal morals. The question then becomes whose morality wins out? I'm sure you know the answer, Ignacio.

"The winner's morality always wins out, and to make matters worse, the winners get to write the official history of their conquest. The conqueror's morality always stands in stark contrast to the conquered's morality. A case in point is that of America's treatment of Native Americans. *Treatment* is perhaps too kind of a word to use. Perhaps we should see the treatment of the Native Americans as a failed attempt of complete genocide. The United States debated how best to expel the Native Americans from their lands to make room for the white settlers. Millions of buffalo were killed, entire herds, for the purpose of starving the Native Americans. I'm sure the white settlers thought they were being moral by not killing (although they did that, too) the Native Americans. The white settlers and the U.S. Congress put forth a classic straw man argument, arguing that it was better to starve the Native Americans into submission and into reservations instead of killing them outright, never arguing the real issue, the stealing of Native American lands.

"And would you believe that people that are taking a stand against discrimination and injustice are being labeled as un-Americans by people of certain political persuasions? How ironic. Chants of 'Let's take our country back' have also become popular in some quarters of American society. 'Take our country back from who?' is my question. Are those same people chanting 'Let's take our country back' going to honor the same request if made by Native Americans?

"We have a big racial divide in our country. Some might say that it's a new phenomenon, but it's not. What is new is that the racial divide is being made more evident by today's technology. Body cameras are showing what Chicanos in the *barrio* have been seeing for decades. We have video cameras in our cell phones that record instances of social and racial injustices as they occur in real time. That's why I say that the racial divide we see in America is not a new phenomenon; what's new is its exposure. And the exposure of this racial divide is not limited to the streets of North Charleston, South Carolina, Ferguson, or on the Texas-Mexican border.

"This racial divide is being promoted and pandered by some of America's illustrious leaders. Let me tell you of a case in point.

"At a private dinner featuring Governor Scott Walker from Wisconsin, Mayor Giuliani said and I quote, 'I do not believe, and I know this is a horrible thing to say, but I do not believe that the president loves America. He doesn't love you. And he doesn't love me. He wasn't brought up the way you were brought up and I was brought up through love of this country.' If this is not pandering to racist elements in our country, I don't know what is. Can you imagine this being said of a person who has dedicated his life to making our country a better place to live in and to raise our families? Our first black president is accused of not loving his country! It's beyond the pale.

"And now we have a guy by the name of Donald Trump who rises to the top of the Republican Party presidential candidates when he mentions that Mexico is exporting rapists and criminals into the United States. A few months ago, Donald Trump flies in to Mobile, Alabama, and tells the gathering that anchor babies are costing the United States billions of dollars, which is totally inaccurate, but his supporters believe anything he says. One of his supporters at that same gathering said, when interviewed by a local newspaper reporter, that he liked Donald Trump because he speaks his mind, just like George Wallace. His own supporter is comparing him to George Wallace, can you believe that?

"Perhaps you can see why I've become disillusioned and turned down many requests to serve on boards and commissions that serve as advocates for the less fortunate. But for the record, let me say that I did serve on several commissions, but it was business as usual, one study after another. Some years, affirmative action programs were popular, then there were years when they weren't. I decided that justice should not be at the mercy of political whims. Did I become a cynic? Maybe, but that's for others to decide.

"And as you know, Ignacio, I travel a lot. I think I have a pretty good global perspective. The United States does not hold a monopoly on injustice. There's injustice all over the world. I very much want to help solve the injustices of the world, racism in particular, but I will not waste my time on talk. I want us to identify the problem, its cause, and then cure it. We can no longer just talk. So of my critics I ask, 'Do you have a solution for the root cause of racism? Do you even know the root cause of racism?' I'm tired of watching people come together at town hall meeting after town hall meeting, coming together to talk about the latest shooting of a black youth by a white police officer, or when police officers are assassinated by thugs. They come together, talk about the problem, and leave in hopes that all will get better. Let me tell you, hope is not a methodology. Social scientists have not been able to solve the problems of racism because they have been looking in all the wrong places. I decided to look elsewhere for the cure, for the elimination of racism. I will share the results of my findings with the world before the day is over."

"Is this your masterpiece?" Ignacio asked.

"Can we go off the record?" David asked Ignacio.

CHAPTER 5

David sat alone in his yacht's stateroom. He sat in complete silence, assembling his thoughts, remembering the day, the day when the idea of the elusive gene first came to him. The gene he now so passionately sought. He could picture that day as clearly as he could picture the day President Kennedy was assassinated or when the Challenger exploded as it sailed into the heavens.

There was nothing special about that day in 1987, nineteen years ago. The day started out like any other. David arrived at his office, listened to his phone messages, answered some, and deleted others. By mid-morning he was ready to leave and get to the library. The autodidactic David was studying genetics, in particular, genetic diseases and disorders. Single gene disorders quickly captured his attention.

During his genetic research, he came across a very interesting syndrome, Williams Syndrome, a rare neurological disorder caused by the deletion of 28 genes from the long arm of chromosome 7. Individuals with the disorder experience heart problems, unusual facial features, widely spaced teeth, and a low nasal bridge. The symptom that stood out most for David was that children with Williams Syndrome were very gregarious and very much at ease with strangers. *How does a genetic disorder influence a social skill?* He asked himself.

With this question in mind, David sought to identify other social skills or disorders that are determined by genetics. If lack of certain genes from chromosome 7 makes people more gregarious, then the question becomes why? But better yet, he asked himself, what is the function of these 28 genes? Why were these genes present in the first place? David decided to look at the 28 genes whose elimination caused those with Williams Syndrome to become gregarious.

David observed the general population, not just the Williams Syndrome population, and wondered why some people were more at ease with strangers while others were not. In the Williams Syndrome population, he knew it was the deletion of about 28 genes, but what about the general population. What determined their varying degrees of sociability? Which one of these 28 genes is causing us to be less sociable and less comfortable with strangers? Are all 28 genes responsible for the social behavior or just one of the 28 genes? Is it possible that the social behavior is caused by a single gene? If it is a single gene that determines sociability, then why is it expressed in some and not in others? Why are some people very timid and some very extroverted? *Expressed or unexpressed gene,* the words kept bouncing back and forth like a tennis ball in David's mind. Do we have a choice in the matter, expressed or unexpressed? Of course not. Our genes decide for us. Some are recessive, and some are dominant. "That's it—genetics holds the answer," David told himself, suddenly realizing he had just come across the answer to an illness that had afflicted the world from time immemorial. "But I do need to be honest with myself. Maybe it's not genetically driven. Maybe it's just a crazy idea that popped into my head." He retreated. "But what if my hunch is correct?" David kept asking himself. "What if my hunch is correct?"

His ecstasy was quickly overtaken by panic. "Shit, maybe others have come up with the same theory, and if they have, they're miles ahead of me in making the discovery. Will I be wasting millions of dollars to finish second? I don't care if I lose everything I own; I'm going for it," David told himself.

He tabled all his other projects, concentrating only on genetics and genetic engineering. David read every scientific journal he could get his hands on. He needed to come up with proof of concept; otherwise his idea was dead in the water. He traveled throughout the world, trying to have his idea validated. Geneticist after geneticist shot his idea down, telling David that his idea did not have any scientific basis, that he needed to look elsewhere for the answer. On occasion, he did receive words of encouragement but was told that the required science and technology needed to show proof of concept did not exist, especially in the field of genetics. The dejected Don Quixote had no choice but to abandon his quest. Dulcinea would have to wait.

CHAPTER 6

It didn't take long for David's luck to change. He struck gold in 1990, the year the human genome project was kicked off and only three years after his epiphany. The US Department of Energy's Office of Health and Environmental Research, together with the National Institute of Health, initiated the $3-billion, fifteen-year project. Mapping the human genome breathed life into David's dream. His idea was one step closer to becoming a reality, albeit a very small step. Fifteen years was a long time to wait, but he had no choice.

David's dream really began to pick up steam on June 26, 2000, when President Bill Clinton and British Prime Minister Tony Blair jointly announced via satellite broadcast that the mapping of the human genome had been accomplished. Five years ahead of schedule. While not one hundred percent sequenced, it nonetheless gave David the science he needed.

David rose from his desk and left his stateroom. It was time to meet with the Race Group. His heart raced with anticipation, faster than it had during any of his marathons. He was about to make the most important business proposition of his life. David was about to reveal his brainchild, a secret of nineteen years.

The Race Group was waiting for David in his yacht's conference room, a well-appointed room with floor-length windows throughout.

The Race Group was a small, loose-knit group, just four members, one woman and three men, of which David was one. It was by coincidence that David became a member of the Race Group. He was running the Dallas White Rock Marathon in 1999 and had stopped by the expo to pick up his race packet. Two men that stood in line ahead of David were nervously talking about this being their first marathon. David overheard them telling each other that they would never again challenge each other to run a marathon. First-time marathoners. Hope they realize what they've gotten themselves into, David told himself. It didn't take long for the gregarious David to introduce himself to the first-timers. He shared with them the story of his first marathon and how terribly it went, but since then he had become a pretty good marathoner and would probably win his age-group category the following day. David told them which parts of the course they should respect, especially the Dolly Parton Hills.

They thanked David for his words of encouragement and asked him to join them for a spaghetti dinner that night, a carbohydrate-loading tradition among marathoners. And this is how his relationship with the Race Group began.

The Spaghetti Warehouse on N. Market Street, in Dallas, Texas, was overflowing with marathoners from all over the country. Chuck Zeigler, the Chairman of the Race Group at the time, briefed David on the Group's activities. David was especially impressed with the Group's nonprofit ventures. The Group dedicated many of its resources to helping people in underdeveloped parts of the world. The Race Group's approach to solving some of the world's most difficult challenges was incredibly unique; it was always long term. David listened intently as he was told of a particular village in the jungles of the Amazon River, a village in which the life expectancy was unbelievably low. The group brought in doctors to address the immediate medical needs, but what David found amazing was what he heard next. Chuck told him that they started a school for kids as young as six years old, which would become the village's future doctors in twenty years.

David couldn't believe it. What company or government initiates a twenty-year plan and actually brings it to fruition? The Race Group does, David was assured.

The Race Group resembled a think tank, but that's where the similarities ended. If after careful studies the Group determined that a certain policy was having detrimental effects, they would invest large amounts of money to bring about change. It really helped that all of the Group's members were billionaires, although being a billionaire was not a membership requirement. This turned out well for David since he was not a billionaire when he joined the Group.

Chuck, along with Marty Winzenried, the other Group member running the marathon, were both so impressed with David's business acumen and his meteoric rise in the stock market that by the time they finished their spaghetti dinner, David had an offer on the table. He had been asked to head their European business interests.

Immediately after the marathon, David and the other two exhausted runners boarded Chuck's jet and headed to Germany. Once in Germany, David decided to accept their offer, but under one condition. He told them he didn't want a salary. What he wanted out of the deal was to be a partner and be allowed to develop some of his own ideas.

David quickly became the apple of their eye; they teased him, telling him that he should change his name to Midas. David was making a lot of money for the Group, as well as for himself during those early years. It didn't take long before he was promoted from head of their European enterprises to Chairman of the Race Group.

David walked toward the waiting Group with much trepidation. He was about to propose to the Group that they undertake a research project. A research project that would find a cure for a disease that impacted the lives of every human being in the world.

He was within steps of the conference room when his satellite phone rang. He looked at the incoming number. There was a moment of hesitation, but he knew he couldn't ignore the call. David needed to pick up. He started to press the green button and allow the call to come through but stopped. The conference room door was now even closer. He reached for the door but didn't open it. He turned around and headed in the opposite direction.

CHAPTER 7

"What's wrong with you?" David yelled into his phone. "You know I'm about to make the most important presentation of my life and you decide to call?"

"Listen carefully David," the person on the phone told him. "Don't tell the group about the gene you're after. Concentrate on the retrovirus during your presentation and on the budget, but nothing else."

"You can't be serious. The purpose of the meeting is to tell them about the gene. I'm going through with my plan; I'm not changing anything."

"There's something you need to know. Maybe this will change your mind about telling the group about the X gene," the caller told David. "We've intercepted an encrypted message from your yacht. Even though it's a short message, we haven't been able to decipher it. I can't be more emphatic, David. At present you are not to trust anybody."

"Shit. Keep me posted."

David called Boden using the yacht's internal telephone system. Boden was in the conference room keeping the Race Group members company when the phone rang. He excused himself after he hung up and went to meet David on the second-level corridor.

"What's going on?" Boden asked.

"I just received a call telling me that an encrypted message, originating from my yacht, was intercepted moments ago. Where have you been for the past half hour?"

"Are you accusing me? Ask the Race Group members, they'll tell you where I've been for the last half hour."

"Right now everybody is a suspect, including you," David told his yacht's captain. "Now tell me, have you or any of the Race Group members been on the phone?"

"Did you hear that?" David suddenly asked Boden.

"Hear what?"

"Never mind," David said. "Answer me; have you or any of the members been on their phones?"

"No, I haven't, nor have any of the members. I would have noticed because we've all been sitting around the table, talking about nothing in particular, just waiting for you to join us and start the meeting. And besides, they couldn't have made a call. I activated the GPS jammers the moment we left the island. And as you know, once activated the jammers not only prohibit anyone from tracking us, but they also block telephone communications. So there's no way a call could have gone through unless the jammers were accidentally turned off. But I doubt it because it requires a password to deactivate the jammers. So whoever told you about a call leaving this yacht is totally off base."

"Who besides yourself has the password?"

"Albert, my first officer."

"Where is he?"

"Albert's up on the flybridge where he's supposed to be," Boden answered.

"Get him. And don't discuss what I've just told you with anybody. You got that?"

"Help!" Nick, the chef, yelled out as he ran towards David and Boden.

"What is it?" Boden yelled.

"First Officer Albert just shot himself!" Nick answered.

"He shot himself? What are you talking about?" David asked Nick.

"Yes sir, it was awful," Nick said. "He was standing by the outer rail and had a gun to his head. I yelled at him to stop. He didn't even look at me. The gun went off and he fell overboard."

"Take Nick down to his cabin. Now!" David yelled at Boden.

"What should we do about Albert?" Boden asked.

"Nothing."

CHAPTER 8

David opened the door and entered the conference room, apologizing to the Race Group members for being late.

"Tell us David. What's this big and secretive project of yours?" Rosalind, a charter member of the Race Group, immediately asked, not bothering to greet him. "We've rescheduled this meeting three times just so that we could all be present. Come on, David, if it's a vote you need, you could have done it by proxy. And one more thing, why weren't we briefed on the agenda? This is not like you at all, David. This is too weird. I hope the drama is worthy of your proposal, whatever the hell it is."

"And good afternoon to you also, Rosalind," David's sarcasm came through. The Group laughed and went about greeting David as usual. After several minutes of catching up on personal matters, the meeting began.

David stood as he addressed the group. "My project is worth every bit of the drama, Rosalind, and it starts with building the most sophisticated yacht ever."

"Over my dead body," Chuck laughed as he interrupted David. "Please tell us you're kidding. Heaven knows we've all had our share of expensive toys."

"I know, we've all bought and sold several yachts. But this yacht will be like no other, no one will ever build another like it. I'll fill you in on the purpose of the yacht as the meeting progresses," David assured Chuck and the rest of the Group.

The Race Group members had many things in common, but the one thing that stood out was that they had pledged to donate their entire fortunes to charities and foundations before dying. The Race Group had recently decided that Alzheimer's would no longer be tolerated and invested $10 billion in research that would rid the world of this heinous disease. The rich like one-of-a-kind things, and getting rid of Alzheimer's disease certainly fit the bill. But on that afternoon aboard his yacht, David was about to challenge his friends like never before. Some people dare not dream, but not David. David dared to dream and dream big. After all, dreams were all he could afford while growing up poor in the *barrio*.

"All of us here have accomplished much, some more than others, but none of us are short on success. This is what I want you to think about—success—as I present my proposal. I want you to think of the great contributions made by people like Einstein, Newton, Pasteur, Marie Curie, Rosalind Franklin, Richard Feynman, Alan Turing, Mario Molina, and others like them who have helped advance our civilization. Their inventions and discoveries have literally changed our world. Some of us in this room have made lots of money off their discoveries and inventions. What you will hear me propose today is on equal footing with what these men and women have accomplished. What I will be proposing is not about making money; it's about changing people's lives; it's about changing the world. But if successful, we're going to make a bundle."

"I like your proposal already," Rosalind said. "Let's hear it."

"The first thing I want you to understand is this: the project I'm proposing is going to be very expensive. The most expensive project we've ever undertaken. It's going to make our Alzheimer's project seem rather insignificant. If we commit to undertaking my proposal, you guys are going to have to trust me with a lot of your money."

"We've always trusted you. Why change now?" Marty said.

"Thanks. I also want you to understand that even though I will give you periodic updates, I will be in total control of the project. This project is not going to be handled by committee. I'll be working alone with my team of scientists and nobody else. Our research project will be one of the most clandestine operations ever undertaken in the world. Trust me, this is not hyperbole. That's why the less we communicate the better.

"With all of these caveats being noted, let me begin. I propose that we develop airborne retroviruses that can be used in gene therapy. The operative word is *airborne*. Can you imagine the impact of such a development on our healthcare delivery system? This is the future, guys, releasing an airborne retrovirus into the atmosphere, which then enters a person's DNA and alters a specific gene or group of genes."

"This is big, David. Being able to genetically alter people's DNA through an airborne retrovirus. Shit, if we pull this off, we can make gazillions of dollars. I move we accept David's proposal," Rosalind said.

"And there's one more thing. There's a gene I want us to discover and eliminate from our DNA"

Silence fell over the room when David told them of the gene he sought to discover and destroy.

CHAPTER 9

The young reporter could barely keep his eyes open as he was led into the office aboard David's yacht. He had not been able to sleep during the transatlantic flight in spite of having traveled in a private jet. He was too excited to sleep. He wanted to enjoy every luxury the plane and staff had to offer, including his first helicopter ride, a short trip from the Naples International Airport to the yacht.

"So you're the reporter from San Antonio, Texas?" David asked.

"Yes sir. My name is Ignacio Garcia, reporter for the *San Antonio Chronicle*," the nervous reporter answered.

"Happy to meet you, young man. I'm David Lorca," David extended his hand. "Hope you had a pleasant trip. I told my pilot to take especially good care of you. Told him that you're from my hometown."

"Both pilots were just great, sir. And Lucy made sure I had something to eat every minute of the flight. She's an awesome flight attendant," Ignacio blushed as he mentioned the very attractive flight attendant's name. "You have a beautiful jet," Ignacio added, trying to divert attention from his reddened face.

David's Gulfstream V jet was a thing of art in every respect. First was the jet itself, it had a range of seven thousand nautical miles and top speed of Mach .925, which easily accommodated all of his travel needs. David personally designed its interior, selecting the finest leathers for the sleek and contemporary seating. The geometric designs woven into the carpet were subtle yet impressive. Second, there was the art that hung on the main cabin's walls. Passengers often asked David if they were the real thing or reproductions. "They're reproductions," he would answer, never wanting to admit they were original paintings.

Sometimes when looking out his jet's window at fifty thousand feet, David wondered what we would look like if observed by aliens from outer space. He wondered if they would notice a difference in humans based on color or if they would be so advanced they saw only people, people with two legs, two arms, two hands, and a head on top of this mass we call a body. The aliens from outer space could easily determine that we are but a single specie with no important distinguishing features, David would tell himself. In his mind, David would play out different scenarios, wondering how we would be categorized and labeled by these aliens from outer space if they were on a research mission, traveling throughout the different galaxies. Labeling us in similar fashion as Darwin categorized the different species on the Galapagos Islands. David's thoughts went on for hours on occasion as he looked out his jet's window.

"Tell me David, what do you see out there? Can you see anything?" Brent Boller, his lead pilot would ask when he caught David in such reveries. David hated to be interrupted while staring out the window, but it was ok if Brent was the one doing the interrupting. They had deep yet lively conversations on just about any topic. But their favorite topics of conversation were science and politics.

"Of course I see something," David answered. "Over there I see dark energy, and over there I see dark matter. Do you know that seventy two percent of our universe is dark energy and twenty three percent is dark matter and I'm the only one in the world that can see both?"

This would be enough to start a scientific conversation between the men that would last almost as long as their transoceanic flights. This had always been David's favorite feature about his jet—the conversations it enabled at fifty thousand feet.

"Great, glad to hear you were well taken care of," David told Ignacio as he managed to get his mind off his thoughts at fifty thousand feet and back to the present.

"My editor couldn't believe it, I mean, you paying for everything," Ignacio said excitedly. "My last twelve hours have been so unreal, at least for me that is. First there was the limousine ride from my house to the airport, then I'm flown to Naples on a private jet, where I get on a gorgeous helicopter that brings me here, to your yacht. This is all so unbelievable. I don't know how to thank you and your pilot, Brent Boller. He was very accommodating, as well as informative. He explained the jet's capabilities as we flew over the Atlantic. Lucy brought me a cell phone in case I needed to make a call during the flight. I had to try it, so I made a phone call to a friend of mine from college. He couldn't believe my luck."

"Hope you can keep your objectivity. I don't want it to appear as if I'm paying you off. You know, writing only the good things about me." David smiled as he walked around his desk and sat in his leather chair.

"Oh no, sir, I assured my editor that my objectivity would not be compromised."

"Good, I wouldn't have it any other way," David said.

"Thank you, Mr. Lorca, for everything, especially for having chosen our newspaper to write a feature story on your life."

"Let's get started, shall we?" David asked.

"Yes sir," Ignacio said. "Interview number one, February third, 2015. I'm here with Mr. David Lorca aboard his yacht, Ignacio Garcia reporting for the *San Antonio Chronicle*." Ignacio spoke into his digital handheld recorder. Ignacio was about to enter a different world, one he knew nothing about but would soon learn.

"Mr. Lorca, you have definitely accomplished a lot. You are very well known in San Antonio. We know so much about you. We know of your exploits in the business world—those are well documented—but what I want to concentrate on are those things that people don't know about you, just ordinary things, whether they may have contributed to your success or not. Perhaps we can start with the mundane, things that seem unimportant but turn out to be the memories we never let go of, the things that define us. Family, neighbors, schools, classmates, teammates in sports, whatever you wish to share and talk about. Let's talk about things you never thought people would be interested in knowing," Ignacio said while placing his recorder closer to David.

"I've never been good at interviews. Difficult for me to open up. You know, always worried about reporters' hidden agendas," David mentioned.

"No hidden agendas here, sir. Just a straight-up story and nothing more," Ignacio stated.

"Good. Don't know if you know this, but I've never allowed anyone to write a feature story about me. Too personal. My immediate reaction when I received your request was to deny it. I told my secretary to prepare a letter denying your request and to have it ready for my signature that same afternoon. But the more I thought about it, the more I realized it was the perfect time for such a story. I've done a lot of things in my life, and I thought, why not? Let's put it down in writing. Can't hurt. I tore up the rejection letter and instructed my secretary to write a different one, and here you are.

"You know, Ignacio, as I anxiously waited for your arrival, I was reminded of how as a kid I could hardly wait for Saturdays to arrive because I was allowed to go downtown all by myself. Downtown was a huge magnet, and I was a tiny piece of metal. I can't keep Davy Crockett waiting. It's Saturday; he knows I'm coming. I need to hurry. These memories seem so recent, but they're not. It was 1957. I was seven years old and in the second grade."

CHAPTER 10

"*Levantate, mijo, ya amanecio.* Wake up, son, time to get up." My mother gently tugged at my arm. She was always gentle with me. Maybe it's because I was the baby of the family, the youngest of ten children, six boys and four girls. I don't know if I was an accident or not, but my mother, Sarah, had me when she was forty-three years old and my father Felipe was sixty. You probably know this, Ignacio, but for the record, I was born in 1950. My father was born in 1890 in Kyle, Texas, and my mother in San Antonio in 1907. My father and his family were sharecroppers in Kyle before moving to San Antonio in 1907. Coincidentally, the same year my mother was born. I found it embarrassing when my father told me they had traveled to San Antonio atop a mule-powered wagon. Actually it was a couple of mules that were doing the pulling. It was years later before I realized this was very common in South Texas in 1907, not just among poor people.

"*Levantate, mijo,*" my mother called out again. "I'm already awake," I answered, but I stayed in bed because I was too sleepy. Actually, it wasn't a real bed; it was a mattress on the floor. Sleeping on the floor wasn't so bad; it's the bed bugs that made getting a good night's sleep impossible. Their bite doesn't really hurt, but it's enough to wake you up. I couldn't see them in the dark, but I could feel them crawling on my body. Sometimes I got lucky and killed one as it crawled on me. I'll never forget the stench of a crushed bed bug, a smell like no other. Some mornings I would be so pissed off at them for having made my life miserable throughout the night that I would go after them with a vengeance. I would look for them in their usual hiding places, along the seams of the mattress and inside the pillow case. They didn't stand a chance once I found them. I would take them one by one and crush them between my thumbnails. It felt good getting even with them. Good to see my blood come out of their crushed bodies.

After doing battle with the bed bugs, I suddenly realized it was Saturday and jumped up from the mattress. I knew I was already behind schedule. No time for coffee, I told myself, can't keep Davy Crockett waiting.

Saturday mornings were definitely different than school days, but the one constant, regardless of the day, was my father's nagging cough. His lungs were victims of working at a mattress manufacturing company without proper protection. No government oversight during those years, no particle masks. His nagging cough continued until he had his morning coffee. I guess it soothed his throat. Even though my mother prepared all the meals, my father was in charge of the coffee. He carefully measured two scoops of H&H coffee into a pot of water and set it atop the stove to brew.

As it brewed, he washed up and shaved outside, at the rear of the house. We didn't have an indoor bathroom during those years, just an outhouse in the backyard. Fortunately, it was connected to a sewer line.

We brushed our teeth, washed our faces, and got our day going outside at the rear of the house. Our lavatory consisted of an apple crate that stood on its end with a small hand basin on top. A mirror with two large cracks hung on the wall. A water spigot to the right of the apple crate was our lone source of water. In later years when we had an indoor kitchen sink, our toothbrushes sat above it on the windowsill. I really thought we had arrived when we no longer had to go outside to brush our teeth.

While the coffee brewed, I would go outside and watch my father shave. Funny, isn't it, Ignacio? No matter their income levels, kids always get a kick out of watching their dads shave. To this day, I remember the brand of single-edged blades he used in his razor; *Blue Star* read the box with the blades. My dad and I never did anything together. Maybe that's the way it was back then, or maybe it was his age, don't really know. He did help me build a rabbit hutch for a school project once, but that's about it. I did hang around the house a lot and was with him as he went about his chores, but we didn't talk. He was quiet, went about his business, especially when he was training the fighting cocks. He couldn't work at a regular job because of his damaged lungs, so he started training fighting cocks for a living. Trainers received ten percent of the winnings from the fighting cocks' owners.

I followed him around as he trained the roosters, each one trained individually. I kept my distance, didn't want to get in the way. I didn't say a word. Back then, kids were not supposed to speak unless spoken to. My father never asked me to help him, so I just stood and watched. You know, there's a lot to the training.Physical training is only part of it. Diets are also important. My dad prepared special blends of grains, oats, and other food items I didn't recognize. I got to eat the leftovers. My favorite was the barley; it was my version of oatmeal. Along with the special diet, the roosters were also given prescription pills, some for stamina, some to prevent bleeding, and others for I don't know what. Each rooster received a handful of pills on a daily basis. This went on until the local pharmacist told my father he couldn't keep dispensing the pills without an official prescription. Don't know how the pharmacist got away with his errant ways in the first place. I guess that's a different story for some other time.

Early on, I learned how important it is for a rooster's wings to be equally balanced in reference to thrust, since the fighting takes place in midair. If a rooster is missing a feather on one of its wings, he will swerve slightly to his right or left and his spurs' thrust will be off target. To correct for the imbalance, my father sewed a perfectly matched feather to a proximate feather; the rooster's balance was now restored. The twice-a-day training for the roosters took most of the day. On Saturdays the roosters rested, and on Sundays they fought.

My favorite part of the training was the sparring sessions. Each rooster was put through a sparring session once a week. During the sparring sessions, the roosters' spurs were fitted with pads that looked like mini boxing gloves. The purpose of the pads was to prevent injury or possible death when they thrust their spurs into each other in midair. This is as close as I ever got to a real cock fight because they were illegal and I'm sure my dad didn't want me arrested. Although I don't think they would have arrested a kid. My dad never got arrested because he was always notified of any impending raids. He trained the sheriff's roosters.

Anyway, getting back to the sparring sessions. The handlers, with roosters in their arms, stood at opposite corners of the ring in our backyard. It was not a real ring like in boxing; it was a patch of dirt between the chicken coops. The handlers walked to the middle of the ring and allowed the birds in their arms to bite each other's bald heads. I think they were aiming for each other's eyes. They had bald heads because their wattles, earlobes, and combs had been removed. My dad used a razor blade to cut them off as soon the rooster reached a certain age. The fighting cocks needed a clear view of their target; they didn't need things hanging off their heads and face. Don't know if you've seen roosters fight, but they are vicious.

With their blood full of adrenaline and ready to kill each other, the roosters were released and allowed to attack each other. They raced towards each other, flying into the air, violently thrusting their padded spurs into each other. Feathers flew from the sudden impact, but both roosters landed gracefully on their feet, thanks to good training. The attacks continued. They stared at each other before each foray, eyes full of hate, neck feathers fully erect, both cocks wishing they had their deadly knives on their spurs. The knives they wore on Sundays.

Some roosters, the victors, made it back home alive on Sunday nights. The losers became rooster soup for dinner. Let me tell you, unlike hens, roosters made for tough eating. These were muscular athletes.

"Sorry, didn't mean to get sidetracked with the rooster story. I guess it's more about me remembering the moments my dad and I shared," David apologized.

"No need to apologize. Very educational. I knew about cock-fights but never knew the roosters were actually trained like athletes," Ignacio said.

"Saturday mornings," David said. "Yeah, once I woke up, my routine moved at lightning speed, starting with my bath. I had the routine down to a science, not a second to waste. I raced to the backyard, grabbed the small, galvanized tub, and brought it into the kitchen. The small tub held just a few gallons of water when completely full. However, I never filled it full because it would have been too heavy for me to carry it outside to empty.

"Once I forgot to rinse the tub before bringing it inside and found myself taking a bath with all kinds of insects that had made the tub their home during the previous night. Another good thing about the tub being small was that I didn't need much hot water to make it comfortable. It didn't take long to boil a pot of water on the stove. We all took our baths in the kitchen since it could be cordoned off with a bedsheet. There were no interior doors in our house, so I'd hang a bedsheet on the empty door frame.

"With my hair still damp, I applied a generous portion of Four Roses pomade, and off I went. But not before getting my bus fare from my mother and ten cents from my sister. My sister never went downtown in her entire life; she had club feet that made walking difficult. So her request was always the same, "Buy me popcorn or peanuts; here's a dime." That was her entire treat of the week, a bag of popcorn or peanuts, never both—not enough money. A bag of popcorn or a bag of peanuts sold for the same price. I had never thought about it until now, but I never felt tempted to indulge myself to any of her popcorn or peanuts on the way home."

"Mr. Lorca, please excuse me, but you have an urgent phone call," David's secretary interrupted.

"Who is it?" David asked.

"Your lawyer, calling from Madrid," she said.

"Tell him I'll call him later; tell him I'm in the middle of an interview." David said.

"We can take a break, Mr. Lorca. Go ahead and take your call," Ignacio told David.

"He always says it's urgent. Lawyers always say that, makes them feel important, makes them feel they can charge more." David waved his secretary away. "Back to the interview. Let's see, where were we?"

"Yes, you were on your way downtown." Ignacio said as he turned the recorder back on.

I always got off the bus at the same intersection, at the corner of Market and St. Mary's Streets. For no particular reason, just a habit I guess. I could have gotten off the bus at a different intersection, closer to The Alamo, but part of the fun was taking in the sights along the way. The downtown sidewalks were always crowded, especially on Saturdays. This was before the age of shopping malls.

Hundreds of airmen from Lackland Air Force Base stood out among the crowd. They wore their uniforms proudly. The young recruits had just graduated from basic training and were experiencing their first freedom in many weeks. Local Mexican boys ran through the crowded sidewalks with shoe shine boxes in tow, shouting out, "Hey soldier, shoe shine?"

Houston Street was my absolute favorite; it was the epitome of glamour. Exclusive shops lined the street for blocks, the best theaters, the best restaurants, the best jewelry shops, the best fashion stores, for both men and women. Houston Street was my Champs-Élysées. It transformed me. To me, Houston Street represented a lifestyle, one I longed for. The department store display windows were huge, rising high above the sidewalk. I noticed the anatomically correct female mannequins, displaying expensive clothing. I guess my hormones were starting to kick in.

San Antonio's premier theater, The Majestic, proudly stood on Houston Street. I always slowed my pace as I walked by the theater. I was mesmerized by the thousands of lights as I walked under the theater's portico. The rapid succession of the blinking lights brought everything to life. Never saw it at night; had to be home by then. But now that I think of it, the lights must have looked even more beautiful in the evening. I must have read the theater's marquee many times, but I can only remember one title, *Journey to the Center of the Earth*, staring James Mason. Funny that it's the only movie title I remember reading. Must be because of the scary-looking poster on display. But on second thought, it's probably the attractive looking Arlene Dahl that jars my memory. Perhaps the real reason I can still remember the movie's title is that I was a better reader by 1959.

The Manhattan Restaurant, a few doors down from The Majestic, was my second favorite attraction on Houston Street. Of course, I never ate at the upscale restaurant. Two large glass doors with large glass transoms above gave the restaurant an aura of wealth. The glass doors were tinted dark green, which made looking into the restaurant difficult, but I still managed to take a peek now and then when the doors slowly closed behind an entering or exiting customer. The restaurant's interior lights were neither bright nor subdued, just perfect, I thought. From then on, I equated this form of lighting with elegance. The waiters wore black suits, white shirts, and black bow ties. I so much admired the people who confidently walked in and out of the restaurant wearing fancy clothes, especially during the winter. Women wearing full-length fur coats and men wearing long black cashmere overcoats. Can't say I ever saw men with top hats and walking canes entering the Manhattan, but if they had, they would have felt right at home.

The Alamo finally came into view as I turned right onto Alamo Street. Pompeo Coppini's Alamo Cenotaph stood to the left of the Alamo. It was erected to commemorate those who died at the Alamo. On sunny days, which are most days in San Antonio, the cenotaph's white marble glistened as the sun shone on its surface. To the right of the Alamo was the Menger Hotel, where Teddy Roosevelt lodged while assembling the Rough Riders.

At last I reached my destination. Davy Crockett was expecting me, I was positive. Every visit to the Alamo felt like my first: breath-taking. The Alamo's entry doors were the largest I had ever seen in my life. I always made a point of touching the roughhewn wood doors with large nicks I imagined were made by bullets during the famous battle. I had never touched anything as old. As a kid, I thought everything in the Alamo was original. Never did it cross my mind that these were not the doors that kept the Mexicans out during the Battle of the Alamo. Thank god these thoughts never crossed my mind, for they would have ruined my fantasies.

Once I entered the Alamo, my focus intensified. There were no passing glances, only parallax views, the backdrop always being the same, the battle of the Alamo. Early on I would eavesdrop on the docent as she recited the Alamo's history. It was through her that I learned about the Alamo and its storied past. I never asked her a question because I assumed that with the answer came a fee and all I had was a nickel and a dime.

The parallax view that greeted me as I entered the Alamo served as an entry into a worm hole. Don't know if the term existed back then, but I felt I was traveling through a worm hole and into a different universe. I was entering a universe in which no one knew me, a universe in which I could become anybody I wanted.

The Alamo's cavernous sanctuary always scared the heck out of me. I was sure the Alamo's concrete ceiling was about to fall on me. I walked around, looking into the small prayer chapels off to the sides from the main sanctuary. Wrought iron gates kept people from entering, so I just looked from the outside. I stared at the various items in the display cases. Whether it was Davy Crockett's rifle or Jim Bowie's knife, I never tired of looking at the many artifacts.

The Alamo's gardens were beautifully landscaped with lush green foliage and imposing oak trees. The gardens were so relaxing, a Xanadu. As you well know by now, Ignacio, I love being around water. I know my love affair with water started at the Alamo. I loved looking at the mock acequias as they flowed through the Alamo's manicured lawns. I stood on the foot bridges, just inches above the acequias and stared at the slow-moving water below. It captivated me. The prismatic koi fish swam by slowly, looking up at me; I had never before seen such beautiful fish. They were not at all like the minnows in the stinky Alazan Apache Creek, a creek four blocks from my house.

My last stop at the Alamo was the barracks. I always wondered if this was the exact location where Davy Crockett slept the night before the heroic battle. It never occurred to me at the time that there was not too much sleeping going on the night before the battle. I stood in the middle of the barracks, pretending to be Davy Crockett, in full uniform. With an authentic coon cap, I grabbed Ole Betsy and readied myself to shoot at the Mexican soldiers as they climbed over the Alamo's walls. Sometimes I pretended to be Jim Bowie. I thought his knife was cool, but my pretending didn't last long. Reality set in after a while, ruining my role playing. The Mexicans won the battle. This signaled it was time to go home. Just one more stop: popcorn from Woolworth's.

CHAPTER 11

On the Saturdays that I stayed home, I didn't do much, but it was still a lot of fun. Saturday was a laid-back day, a time to relax and enjoy the neighborhood. I remember our neighbors' radios or record players blaring throughout our neighborhood. But nobody complained; that was life in the *barrio* on Saturday mornings. Kids would be playing in the alley, at no particular thing, just having fun.

The local barber shop was a busy place on Saturday mornings. The neighborhood men took advantage of their day off to pamper themselves with a haircut and a shave. Waiting to get their hair cut was not an inconvenience for the men; they relished the opportunity to visit with friends. These were many of the same men I saw during the week on their way to work, but there was something different about them on Saturdays. It's as if they had shed their subservient workday selves and become normal people. It was Saturday and a time for personal indulgence, even if it was only a haircut. A time for others to wait on them. It made me happy to see them happy. Listening to their sexually-oriented jokes contributed to my childhood sex education. Of course, I always pretended I wasn't paying attention to their jokes because I didn't want them to stop.

Wages for unskilled laborers were very low and kept the work-force living in poverty despite having jobs. I don't remember ever seeing men sitting around the neighborhood with nothing to do. Another reason why Saturdays were so festive is that it was the day after payday and time to pay bills and do a little shopping with any left-over money. It was easy to figure out if there was any left-over money because there were no ATMs, debit cards, or direct deposits. So if you had five greenbacks left in your pocket after paying bills, that was your net worth as well as your disposable income.

Jewish merchants in their dull and faded station wagons went door to door, selling their wares in the *barrio*. "*Mira, Mira, el Judio viene. Viene a collectar*. Look, look, the Jew is coming to collect." Some of the women on our alley clamored at the merchant, wanting to see the latest sale items. Others boasted, "*Mi esposo me dijo que puedo comprar lo que yo quiero*. My husband said I can buy anything I want." The Jewish merchants sold on credit, always growing their captive market. As much as the women thought they were splurging on themselves, they weren't. Most of what the merchants sold was basic clothing necessities, socks, underwear, t-shirts, work clothes, bedding, and not much of anything else. The weekly payments were usually in the two-dollar range. This I knew because I often overheard the negotiations between seller and buyer. My mother never bought from the door-to-door vendors.

"Did you enjoy school? Were you at the top of your class?" Ignacio asked.

"No and no." David laughed.

"Just kidding, at least about my not liking school. I did enjoy school very much, especially once I got to the seventh grade and started participating in sports. The one question I've never been able to answer is why I can't remember being in the first grade. I remember my days in kindergarten and second grade, but nothing in between. Don't know why my brain has blocked out that year. I know it's not because of the paddling, because I wasn't paddled until the sixth grade. I was paddled for speaking Spanish while walking to the cafeteria. Even if it was only one word that was spoken in Spanish, the punishment was always the same, a paddling. This might help explain why so many of today's young Hispanics don't speak Spanish. The spanking couldn't erase the Spanish from our brains, but it unconsciously prevented us from passing it on to our children."

"Interesting observation," Ignacio said.

Even though I loved school, I still enjoyed my summers. I lucked out one summer. My mother took me swimming. Getting to the pool was quite a journey. We had to take the Guadalupe bus line into downtown and wait for half an hour before boarding the San Pedro line that would ultimately take us to the San Pedro Park and swimming pool. This lengthy trip was torture for a kid that could hardly wait to jump into the pool at the shallow end; I didn't know how to swim then. My mother didn't come into the pool with me. She sat on a bench outside, watching me through the chain link fence. The only time I saw my mother in any body of water was when she was baptized, full-body immersion into the Rio Frio. She wore a white dress for the occasion.

San Pedro Park was established by Spain in the eighteenth century. It provided a great backdrop for the pool with its majestic cypress trees that encircled the pool. The San Pedro Playhouse with its Greek Revival architecture was another of the park's attractions.

Summers were great because I didn't have to wait til Saturdays to go downtown. Riding into downtown on workdays was very different than on Saturdays. The bus was full of people on their way to work. I heard many *buenos dias* on the bus, everyone appearing to know each other.

Riding the Guadalupe Street line into downtown was exhilarating; there was so much energy among the passengers. While not in uniforms, most men wore khaki pants and shirts. The majority also carried old black metal lunch boxes that held a thermos bottle inside. The women's clothing was more diverse. Some dressed in white starched uniforms. Perhaps a nurse, I thought or maybe a waitress. I knew maids also wore white uniforms so couldn't tell for sure during the morning ride.

By the time we reached downtown I really felt like an outsider. I had not contributed one word to the many conversations that had taken place all around me. Whether it was bragging about a new child, a grandchild, or a rosebush that was in full bloom, everyone appeared to be speaking at the same time, no listeners. Their energy was contagious. Every passenger had a smile, I swear, every single one.

There were days when I was on the return trip with workers on their way home after a brutal day of working in the hot sun. Not all worked in the hot sun, of course, but those are the ones I noticed the most, probably because of their body odor. The buses ran at capacity during the rush hour at the end of the workday. Standing-room only, with bodies packed in like sardines in the non–air conditioned bus. And to make matters worse, there were occasions when the bus had to wait for a train to clear the intersection. Without exaggeration, the wait sometimes lasted twenty to thirty minutes, and with a tanning company right next to the intersection, people became quite agitated and often cussed at the bus driver for not taking a detour around the blocked intersection. The stench from the decaying hides wafted through the hot and crowded bus and became nauseating. But the looks on the passengers' faces as they returned home from work and stared at the uncooperative bus driver were not angry. Their countenances told a different story.

The passengers' morning smiles were gone, and their faces looked lifeless. They looked straight ahead, zombie-like. I didn't really read too much into what I was seeing since I was only seven years old, but I do remember their appearance making me sad. On a lighter note, not only do I remember the horrible body odor of the construction workers on the bus, I remember others. Some smelled like onions; I figured they were cooks or waitresses. Some just smelled of cigarette smoke, but the ones that didn't smell bad were the ones I assumed were maids. Even though they looked tired, the maids' uniforms had survived the day; they were clean. I can now honestly say they were maids and not nurses because no nurse would have lived in the poverty-stricken *barrio*.

Can't believe the things I remember. Heck, I was only seven years old. That's almost 57 years ago. Remembering body odors—that's funny. You would think I would be describing the aromas of flour tortillas wafting throughout our house as my mother prepared dinner. Ah, those homemade flour tortillas, just thinking about them makes my mouth water.

One more thing about my bus ride memories. It didn't matter if I was headed downtown or back home, whenever the bus passed by Immaculate Heart of Mary Catholic Church, all passengers made the sign of the cross. With their right hand, all would touch their foreheads, move it down to their septum, and then to the left and right across their chests. Being a Baptist, I didn't know what was going on. I did know that people made the sign of the cross when they prayed or when a basketball player was attempting a free throw, but not during a bus ride. At first I thought they were praying because they were on their way to the free dental clinic that stood next to the church. I know I always prayed before being painfully treated at the same clinic. Actually, *treated* is not the right word. The clinic was in the business of extracting decayed molars or teeth.

I felt like an outcast, you know, everybody crossing themselves except me. So in the interest of being accepted, I started crossing myself whenever we passed by the Catholic Church, provided my Baptist mother wasn't with me.

CHAPTER 12

"Hearing you mention the San Pedro swimming pool brought back old memories to me as well. That was definitely the place to hang out, especially on Sunday afternoons. I've seen old pictures of the park in our newspaper's archives, pictures of swimmers frolicking in the pool while others enjoyed a picnic under large oak trees," Ignacio said.

"You're right." David said. "I keep forgetting that you're from San Antonio. I keep describing things that I'm sure you're very familiar with. But you're absolutely correct, Sunday afternoons at the pool were indeed special. As a matter of fact, it was on a Sunday afternoon at San Pedro swimming pool when I composed my first fiction."

"Are you serious?" Ignacio asked. "I thought it was later in your life when you wrote your first novel."

"Well, I didn't actually write it down, like writing a book. I merely composed a big story in my mind. A story I was reading out loud as I composed it. A story I composed to impress a girl."

"Sounds like you were a fun guy. Would very much like to hear the story you made up. We can go off the record if you'd like," Ignacio said.

"Nah, we don't have to go off the record. Funny story, that's all. Although it might embarrass my kids when they read about my youthful indiscretions."

"Actually it wasn't a Sunday, it was Labor Day, last chance to go swimming, school was starting the next day. Max and I were not about to miss this last day of swimming and gawking at girls," David continued, telling Ignacio about the first story he composed and read out loud to a group of three girls.

There was nothing special that afternoon, other than the fact that we would be entering the eighth grade the following day, so I guess I was fourteen years old. Max and I always hung out together. At this point we had been classmates for two years. We had similar interests. Both of us played sports and were in the school's orchestra. He played violin and I played the piano.

The swimming pool was very crowded, most crowded day of the year. It was impossible to swim without running into somebody, so I swam to the deep end of the pool where it was less congested. It was then that I saw three girls by the pool's edge. But it was the one in the middle that caught my eye. She was gorgeous.

"Hey, Max," I yelled at my buddy. "Bet I can score with those girls before you."

To us, the term *score* meant engaging in conversation and nothing more. As I said, I was only fourteen.

"No way, José," replied Max.

All I really cared about was the girl in the middle, I didn't care if Max flirted with the other girls. But this created a problem when he said he would take the girl in the middle.

We inched our way closer to the girls, pretending we had not noticed them. The crowded pool made it easy to conceal ourselves. I intentionally had my back to them as we got closer until I was within hearing distance from the girls. One of the girls was talking about the dress she wanted to wear to her senior prom. She went on and on describing every detail, the color of the dress and matching shoes, the length of her gloves, and the orchid corsage she hoped to get.

"I'll take the one in the middle," I repeated, hoping the girls hadn't switched positions while I had my back to them.

"No. I want the one in the middle," Max said as he started toward the girls.

"Wait," I said. I was getting desperate but managed to keep my voice down. "Look, Max, can't you tell they're older than us? Didn't you just hear them talking about their senior prom? They're in the twelfth grade. But I have an idea that just might work in making us appear older."

Not giving Max time to think, I turned around and faced the girls.

"Hi," I quickly said. "Are you girls from San Antonio?"

"What?" my target asked.

"Just wondering if you girls are from San Antonio," I said as I got closer.

"Of course, where else would we be from?" the other girl answered.

"How do you all like living here? Is it a fun city? Are there a lot of things to do here? Do you come here often? Is it always this crowded?" I asked in rapid succession, wanting to give them the impression that Max and I were from out of town.

Max looked at me and shook his head. But I knew my ruse was off to a good start when I heard the pretty girl in the middle ask.

"Where are you guys from?"

"We're from New York.... New York City," I confidently answered.

Why I said New York I'll never know, but I knew at this point that I was all in, point of no return. I knew that whatever came out of my mouth had to make us appear older. This was going to be my narrative.

I looked at Max, hoping he would play along. But how could he? Not even I knew where this story was headed. I liked jazz, but I had never heard of the word *improvisation*. But that's what I was doing that Sunday afternoon, improvising.

"Wow," the girls chimed in unison.

"I've never met anyone from New York," one of the girls added.

"Well, now you have. Now you know two people from New York. I'm David and this is Max." I can't remember their names; I was too busy concocting my story.

"This is our last day here. We're leaving tomorrow, going back home," I said.

"Why are you here? I mean, are you on vacation or what?" one of the girls asked.

"No, no vacation. Just work," I answered.

"What kind of work?"

"We're musicians; we performed over there last night," I said as I pointed toward the San Pedro Playhouse. And I wasn't totally lying; I had once substituted for my piano teacher when she was out of town. She played for a church group that worshiped there on Sundays. She was away one Sunday and asked if I would sit in for her, so I did.

"You guys get paid?" the pretty one asked.

"Of course. We're professional musicians," I answered.

"You guys look pretty young to be professional musicians."

"That's because we started taking lessons when we were little kids. Max on the violin and me on the piano."

I explained to them what key signatures meant, as well as time signatures, basic stuff like that. Just enough to make me sound legit.

"Have you girls ever heard of Dave Brubeck? He's a great guy, friend of ours. He also plays the piano, but he's really famous. His most famous song is "Take Five," which is written in a five-four time signature. You girls need to come up and visit us in New York. We'll introduce you to many of our friends. There might even be a ticker tape parade going on during your visit," I said.

"What's that?" They asked.

"A parade where people throw shredded paper from tall buildings," I answered. "A piano player was once honored with a ticker tape parade after he won the Tchaikovsky Piano competition in Moscow, Russia. His name is Van Cliburn. He's from Texas, lives in Ft. Worth.

I hear it's a nice town, but I prefer New York. I get to meet many famous people who also live in New York."

"Have you met movie stars?" one of the girls asked me.

"Nah, we mainly hang around with other musicians. Have you ever heard of Carnegie Hall?" I asked the pretty girl.

"Never heard of it, why?"

"Carnegie Hall is the most famous music hall in the world. Max and I have performed there. Only the best get to perform at Carnegie Hall," I told them.

I told them about Vladimir Horowitz, George Gershwin, George Shearing, and others. It was obvious they had never heard of the people I mentioned or of Carnegie Hall. What surprised me was that they were actually interested. I had never been to New York, so I couldn't go into detail about things. They were especially interested in the Statue of Liberty.

Occasionally I would look around the swimming pool, wanting to make sure I didn't see anybody I knew. I was too deep into my story; I didn't want anybody to ruin it. Max would look at me and then at the girls, not knowing how much longer I was going to continue. Heck, I didn't know myself. I didn't know how the story was going to end. Hadn't written the ending. I was doing pretty good just writing one sentence at a time. Making up the story was easy; I was always daydreaming about things that I had never seen. Whenever I took a pause, the girls would look at me as if saying, Don't stop. Keep going. We don't want the story to end. But like every story, it must have an ending, and so did mine. What didn't end were my dreams.

CHAPTER 13

The taxi slowly climbed the narrow, serpentine street. It was almost midnight when David hailed the taxi. It was time for him to meet the German geneticist. The driver became alarmed when David told him the address. "Are you sure *Señor, como se dice,* how do you say in English, you have right address? *Nada*...nothing up on mountain there. The place you look for gone...no exist anymore....closed...*muchos anos.* Take you to hotel better...ok?"

"Just keep driving" David told the driver in Spanish, "*Sigue adelante, sube la montaña.*" Suddenly the taxi jumped the curb and drove onto the sidewalk, barely avoiding a head-on collision with a speeding tour bus full of reveling tourists. The bus driver slammed on the brakes. The disgusting smell of burnt rubber accompanied the screeching halt. The embarrassed bus driver tried backing up and letting the taxi through. It was no use, the narrow street was full of traffic. Just like every night at this time, most of the traffic was headed down from the mountains toward the downtown district of Granada. The tourists had ascended the mountains earlier in the evening to the Sacromonte, the Gypsy section of Granada, where tourists enjoyed watching world-class gypsy flamenco dancers perform in manmade caves. The spectators sat along the caves' dirt walls, sipping on complimentary sherry or port, while the dancers performed within inches of them. Pictures of famous movie stars enjoying the dancers hung on the caves' walls. Pictures of Anthony Quinn and Sophia Loren were two of the more recognizable faces. The dirt floor did not provide good acoustics for the dancers' pounding feet, but their loud hand-clapping rhythms and the accompanying guitarist's singing were plenty loud.

The taxi proceeded past the last tourist attraction; the street was now nothing more than a dirt road. After a night of several performances, the tired dancers slowly walked along paths to their homes, their caves. David turned his head around and looked back towards Granada. The city lights grew faint as the taxi scaled the mountain. The taxi driver kept asking David, "*Estas seguro que queres subir?*" He no longer tried speaking English. "*Si, estoy seguro,*" David yelled back.

David was now traveling past the district of Sacramonte, an area he had visited many years before, in the late sixties during his Christmas break from college. Generalissimo Franco was in power, along with his much-feared Guardia Civil. On that occasion, David took the late-night train from Madrid to Granada. It was his first train ride ever; he excitedly jumped on board, stored his lone suitcase next to the others, and walked along the corridor to the second-class section of the train. David slid open the door of his assigned compartment and couldn't help but notice an attractive girl to his left. It was an easy decision; he decided to sit next to her even though there were other open seats. She didn't notice David, or at least she pretended not to by immersing herself in her reading. Not long after taking his seat, his skinny ass started going numb on the wooden seats, reminiscent of the church pews back home. The two pews per cabin sat opposite each other, with not much room to stretch his legs. And just like church pews, there were no arm rests.

With his ass now completely numb because of the wooden seats and his hands numb due to the cold cabin, David's excitement of this his first train ride was rapidly deteriorating. The blonde next to him was the only positive thing he had going. He was positive she felt the same way about him. Seated across from David was a priest, his clergy collar exposed through his partially unbuttoned overcoat. His pale face had a pleasant smile, which widened whenever he made eye contact with fellow passengers. As the train started to trundle out of the station, a middle-aged couple hastily entered the compartment and took the last available seats, the ones David had ignored. The woman's clouded bifocal glasses were beginning to clear as she took her seat and tucked her loose coat under her legs. She rubbed her gloved hands together while complaining to her husband about the cold accommodations. David finally decided to break the ice and speak to the girl next to him. He spoke to her in English. Good call—she was an American. She was studying abroad for one year at the University of Madrid and was vacationing in Granada during her Christmas break. After a few exchanges, they both became quiet as the other passengers started staring at them.

The lighting on the train was subdued and mysterious, reminding David of the movie *Murder on The Orient Express*. Despite the scarce accommodations, the walls throughout were made of dark wood panels. Silence ensued among the travelers after exchanging pleasantries and courteous greetings. The only person that didn't settle in for the ten-hour ride to Granada was a teenage boy. He sat next to the priest and was willing to engage in conversation with anybody that looked his way. The energetic boy tried keeping his voice down but wasn't very successful. The teenager told the priest about his vacation to Turkey and how he had single-handedly fended off a thief, saying it loudly in an attempt to impress the American girl.

One of the eight seats remained vacant throughout most of the trip. Its occupant was a chain smoker who hung out in the corridor where he could smoke in peace. He was very pleasant, probably in his early forties, and unusually tall for a Spaniard. After a somewhat short repose, the sleeping passengers came to life. The elderly nun that was sitting by the sliding door pulled out a bottle of wine from her satchel. David was surprised; he didn't know nuns were allowed to drink wine. She handed the wine to the priest and asked him, "*Padre, nos puede hacer un favor y bendiga el vino?*"

"*Obrigado*" the priest said after having blessed the wine and taken the first sip. He then handed the bottle back to the nun. She delicately took a sip and passed the bottle around for all to partake. David noticed that nobody bothered wiping the common bottle after they drank from it, so he didn't either. The middle-aged couple reached for the straw satchel they had brought on board. It was full of wrapped Christmas presents, but from the bottom of the satchel they pulled out a dark crusted loaf of bread. Following in the tradition of the wine, the bread was passed around for all to tear off a piece and enjoy.

"*De donde eres?*" The teenage boy asked David.

"*Soy Americano,*" David answered proudly.

"*Pareces Mexicano*, you look Mexican," The boy told him.

"*Yo, tambien, soy Americana,*" the girl volunteered.

David took several minutes and explained the history of Mexico and the fact that Texas was once Mexico. The passengers listened intently, proudly acknowledging the fact that Spain once owned and ruled the area that was now known as Texas.

"I see your country many years ago." The priest joined the conversation. "I was not old, I was...how you say, *joven?*"

"Young," the American girl answered.

"Yes, young, I was *mucho* young," the priest laughed. "I was in *la capital*, your capital, Washington, DC, no?" the priest continued. "Many people in *marcha*, how do you say, *manifestacion?*"

"Demonstration," the American girl answered once again.

"Yes, yes, demonstration. Black people want equal rights, street full, thousands *y* thousands of people, want to be equal," the priest said. "Why you Americans hate black people? They good, they work. God likes all *gente*...people I think you say it." He looked at the American girl.

She nodded.

"Not all Americans hate black people, I've been involved in several demonstrations that support equal rights for all people of color," David spoke to the priest in Spanish. "I agree, some people in the

United States do hate blacks and other minorities, but things are getting better."

"Yes, things better, no more slavery," the priest said sarcastically while practicing his English. "But things still not too good for black people."

The American girl decided that she had heard enough of a one-sided conversation.

"*Perdoneme, Padre*," she began. "I've been in your country for six months, not a very long time, but enough to notice a few things. First let me say, I've totally enjoyed my stay. Every Spaniard I've met has been very polite and kind. The Spanish family I'm living with is outstanding, I couldn't ask for a better home. But I'm very curious about one thing though, why are Gypsies treated....."

"They bad people," the priest yelled out before the American girl finished asking about the Gypsies. "All Gypsies bad. They smell bad, they steal babies. Nobody likes Gypsies...no can trust Gypsies. You no believe me, go to back of train, look at Gypsies in third-class section. You see they no good."

"You're just as...."

David quickly tugged at her arm, not allowing her to finish her comment. All conversations among them came to an abrupt halt. Fortunately, the train rolled into one of the many stations between Madrid and Granada at the exact moment of silence, giving all a reprieve from the awkward moment.

It was past midnight, but this didn't matter to the young Gypsy children who jumped on the stationary train. They quickly made their way from cabin to cabin, selling various snacks, drinks, and trinkets. Their clothes were tattered, their shoes well-worn, and none wore gloves. These children were the poorest of the poor, their future bleak, with no future in their future. They did brisk business in the second-class section; the first class passengers had a private dining car. The kids were very adept in sales and didn't easily take no for an answer.

"*No, no quiero nada*," David told the high-pressure sales kids.

He then turned to the American girl. "Excuse me, but don't you think it would be a great idea to stretch our legs. Plus I think you need a drink. Come on, the train won't leave without us."

They stepped off the train and walked into the freezing weather. The station's restaurant was closed, but its bar remained, passengers huddled at the bar and were quickly downing their drinks.

"I had to get you out of there. Looked like you were ready to tell the priest where to go, and it wasn't heaven," David told the American girl as they settled in on a small table by the window. "I'll have a glass of cabernet and the young lady will have a glass of..."

"*Lo mismo,*" she told the waitress.

"What's your name?"

"Cindy, what's yours?"

"David. Here on Christmas vacation, been here two days."

"I guess I should thank you for getting me out of there. That priest made me so damn mad. He looks down on Americans and implies we're all racists. I'm not saying there aren't racists in the U.S., but what gets me so stinking mad is that he's just as bad as any racist in the U.S. when it comes to Gypsies. He pretends to be such a saint. You've been in Spain for only a couple of days and haven't had a chance to see how the Gypsies are treated. Wait til you get to Granada. You're going to get an eyeful. At sundown, Gypsies are forced to leave the city and return to their caves up in the mountains," Cindy told David.

"He's a priest. Maybe he'll see the error of his ways," David told her.

"Don't bet on it."

"Relax, Cindy. Drink your wine. Let's talk about something else."

"Like what?"

"Like that admirer of yours, the kid seated across from us. I've noticed that he keeps staring at you and uses any excuse to talk to you. He's really having a great time flirting with you. Couldn't help but notice that he was in deep conversation with you when I got back from the restroom."

"Are you kidding me? He's just a kid, only fourteen years old," Cindy burst out laughing.

"Great, I got you laughing. For a while I thought the priest had ruined your vacation. But there's one thing you need to know. We Latino males are adults by the age of fourteen. So you better watch out."

"Don't worry about his intentions. He assumes you and I are traveling together, and I left it at that. It's safer for me if he thinks we're a couple." Cindy said.

"Great, now I'm being used." David smiled.

"You know I didn't mean it like that. I'm sorry, although now that I see you smiling, maybe I'm not so sorry. Anyway, I could care less if he's flirting with me because he's just a kid, regardless of what you say about Latino males."

Cindy took a sip of her wine. "He told me he's fourteen years old and his parents stayed behind, they're celebrating New Year's in Madrid. He was bragging about his parents being very high-ranking government officials."

"I was right, he's flirting with you. He's trying to impress you by telling you his parents are important people. He's so smitten by you."

David dropped the subject about the flirtatious boy and started to tell Cindy about his hometown and that he was visiting Spain for the first time in his life. It was an interesting conversation because they kept switching from Spanish to English, and then from English to Spanish. David found this strange because it was very unusual for a Spanish-speaker to speak in Spanish to an Anglo person in his hometown. He had always been taught that is was impolite to speak Spanish in front of Anglos because they usually didn't understand Spanish.

"Hurry, finish your wine. There goes the conductor and it looks like he's in a hurry to get going," David said as he took his last sip of wine.

"I wasn't going to tell you this, but..." Cindy started to say.

"Hurry, you can tell me when we're back on the train."

"Need to tell you now, before we board the train. Angel, the young kid's name, asked me if we wanted to stay at his house in Granada. Told me his parents will be away for the whole week and he would love to show us around the city. He also said we make such a nice couple. Can you believe that? I told him I would ask you and see if you'd be willing to accept his offer."

"Well, hurry up and ask me because I'm on a college budget and crashing at his parents' house would certainly help," David playfully said.

"We better decide fast because I'm sure he'll want an answer as soon as we get back on the train."

"I think you already know my answer."

"OK, it's settled," Cindy said as they boarded the train.

"Do we have to sleep together? I mean, I wouldn't want to blow our cover." David smiled widely.

"Don't push it, David. Maybe the same bedroom, but that's it." Cindy grabbed his hand as they headed back to the train. After all, they were traveling together.

David sat back and stared out the window as the train slowly left the station. Three Guardia Civil soldiers stood on the dock in their green uniforms and tri-corned hats. With carbines on their shoulders, they stared at the Americans as they rolled off.

Angel was proud to have "*los Americanos*" stay at his house, although David was positive that he was still a Mexican in Angel's eyes. Angel was the perfect host during their three-day visit, except for the fact that he was constantly hitting on Cindy.

On the second day, Angel decided to impress his guests with his driving skills and borrowed a friend's car for the day. After a few miles, it became obvious that the fourteen-year-old kid didn't know how to drive. Unfortunately, it was too late; they were halfway up the steep and snow-covered mountain road. Snow-covered tree branches were hanging low with the weight; some had broken and were strewn on the treacherous road.

Angel was driving way too fast as they approached one of the many switchbacks. Angel slammed on the brakes when he realized he was going too fast, but this caused the car to start spinning. The car hit the switchback's apex and bounced in the direction of the valley far below. David threw open the door and jumped out. The car started sliding down the side of the mountain. Cindy sat helplessly in the backseat of the two-door compact car. Angel was paralyzed, his hands glued to the steering wheel. David ran toward the car in a state of panic and grabbed the descending car's door handle, desperately trying to keep the car from sliding off the mountain. It was no use; the car was now dragging him down with it. In spite of this, David refused to let go of the door. He tried digging his feet into the wet snow, but it was useless. He couldn't gain any traction.

With the car leaning over the embankment and no hope in sight, the car suddenly came to a halt. There was complete silence, the snow quieted all sound. David was still holding onto the door as he yelled at Cindy and Angel to get out on his side but to do it carefully and without any sudden movement. With Cindy and Angel now safely standing on the side of the road, David let go of the door. He closed his eyes, expecting the car to fall off the side of the mountain, but it didn't move. David ran up toward Cindy and hugged her as hard as he could. Cindy started crying while in his arms as Angel watched from afar. "Thank you, David, for saving my life." Cindy gently kissed his lips.

David and Cindy returned home after their adventurous time together. David went back to Madison, Wisconsin, and Cindy to Madrid. David often thought of Cindy and wondered how things might have turned out between them if he had made an effort to continue their moment together.

CHAPTER 14

The taxi's front wheels fell into a deep rut in the dirt road, shaking David from his deep thoughts. Thinking of Cindy and Angel and their time together many years ago had made him relax, something he hadn't been able to do in a long time. Thinking of those carefree days when the only worry was making sure he had a place to sleep made him feel young again and full of ambition.

The taxi made a left turn onto an even smaller road. Complete darkness greeted them as the car came to a stop. "*No hay nadie aqui, vamonos.* There's nobody here, let's leave." The words flew out of the scared driver.

"*Espera, no tengas miedo.* Wait, don't be afraid..." David broke off mid-sentence when a silent, sudden burst of light hit the taxi. It was so bright and so brief that he couldn't determine its source. The startled driver slammed on the accelerator but the car stalled when the driver released the clutch without downshifting. David's satellite phone started beeping then went silent, its screen blank. The taxi driver frantically tried to restart the car, but after several tries he flooded the engine and the car refused to start.

A voice with a heavy German accent loudly instructed, "David, get out of the car." David complied.

"Come closer," the German voice instructed. David walked slowly toward the voice and was quite surprised by the man's appearance. It didn't match his voice. David's already heightened alert became more intense. He was here to meet with a German, and the man in front of him was not German.

"Stand still and don't make a move."

David obeyed without hesitation. The German voice told the taxi driver to leave and to keep his mouth shut if he knew what was good for him. David was surprised to hear the man with the German accent speaking Spanish.

"Don't tell him to leave. My briefcase is in the car," David yelled out.

"Then get it."

David rushed to the departing taxi and banged on the window desperately, trying to get it to stop. The taxi slowed down but didn't come to a complete stop. David reached in through the open window and grabbed his briefcase, falling to the ground as the taxi suddenly sped up. He slowly rose to his feet with briefcase in hand. Dusting himself off, he returned to the man with the German accent.

David's eyes had fully adjusted to the darkness, and the man before him came into focus. He was a large man, a little on the heavy side, probably weighing two hundred twenty pounds, but only five feet ten inches. His hair was more white than gray, just like his mustache.

"Now walk in front of me."

"Aren't you going to check me for weapons?" David asked.

"Don't have to. I have smart sensors along the road that can detect many things, including weapons."

They walked toward an abandoned nightclub about ten meters from where the taxi had come to a halt. The nightclub's facade was covered with faded murals depicting larger-than-life flamenco dancers, guitarists, waitresses serving drinks, and a bartender lighting a customer's cigar. The murals were no longer alive, pieces were missing, the colors were muted, and ivy had grown over the dancers' faces. The abandoned club's name stood above the entrance, El Secreto Club.

David carefully opened the door and entered the cave as instructed.

The Secreto Club was similar to the clubs David had visited during his first trip to Granada, similar in size and layout, but this is where the similarities ended. David found it hard to breath in the stale, dank, and moldy atmosphere of the abandoned club. Empty chairs and tables were scattered throughout the former nightclub. Empty whiskey bottles and glasses sat on the tables as if the club had closed for the night and never opened again. Why the sudden abandonment? Years of dust covered everything. An elongated bar with a mirrored back stood at the rear, the dust on it prevented focused reflections

"It's way past midnight and don't have much time, so tell me what's so important," the German voice demanded.

"Very impressive. That fireworks display of yours nearly blinded me. Do you always greet your guests with such fanfare?"

"You're the only guest I've ever had up here."

"Well, here we are," David told him as he laid down his briefcase. "I thought I was in deep trouble when I saw you. Your accent and appearance don't match. I thought I was here to meet with a German geneticist, a captain. Would that be you?"

"That's me."

"Is that your rank?"

"No, that's what I'm called. I'm known as the Captain, that's all you have to know. And don't read too much into my German accent. I'm Gypsy. Anyway, I'm sure you didn't come to Granada to talk about my accent, so tell me why you're here and what you want."

"You're right; I didn't come all the way to Granada to talk about your accent. But I'm still curious about your name. Why Captain? Were you a sailor in your previous life?"

"Would you rather my name be James Bond and speak with a British accent? Don't we have more serious matters to talk about?"

"Ok, ok, then Captain it is," David smiled, knowing he wasn't going to get any more information out of the Captain.

"Follow me this way," the Captain signaled.

The Captain walked behind the bar and slid the dusty mirror to one side, revealing something totally unexpected through a concealed entrance, a hidden cave within a cave. As the Captain disappeared into complete darkness, motion sensors immediately turned on the room's lights. The contemporary low-voltage lights brought the cave to life. David stood in awe of what he was seeing while the Captain continued walking into the expansive room and sat on a stool behind an elevated desk.

David took a few steps but stopped to admire a collection of Dutch paintings by Vermeer, Van Gogh, and Guys. David stepped closer to the paintings and examined them in great detail. He looked in the direction of the Captain, who was busy lighting a large cigar. The stale and damp air of the ante-cave was gone. Here, the stucco walls were painted in various pastel colors with an occasional accent wall painted in a darker hue. The large room and the corridors that led from it had their ceilings decorated with interlocking planks of maple. The marble floor with inlaid geometric designs was also a work of art. The Captain's cave was not typical of the Gypsy caves David had become familiar with. The only difference between the Captain's cave and a high-rise condo in Manhattan was the view overlooking Central Park. Off to one side of the main room lay an array of electronic equipment, but not your typical residential computer system. The electronic communication systems in the Captain's inner sanctum rivaled those of any CIA field office.

"I like your taste in art. But tell me, are they reproductions, because if they are I want to meet the artist. I know art and in particular some of the Dutch Masters. These particular paintings have not been seen in public for decades, so is it possible that they're the real thing?" David asked.

"Maybe yes and maybe no, but for now come have a seat and enjoy a cigar." The Captain said as he pointed toward the stool across from his desk.

"No, no to both, I don't smoke and I'd rather stand," David said as he walked toward the electronic equipment that was producing a current of warm air. As he got closer to the equipment, David recognized it. These sophisticated pieces of electronics were manufactured by his German company but only for carefully selected clients. David couldn't help but wonder how the Captain had acquired the powerful computers.

"Hope this meets your requirements as far as security is concerned. Your security person that arranged this meeting said you had concerns about meeting in a cave. I told him that you shouldn't worry. This place is as safe as it's going to get, I've made sure of that."

"It's a little too late to be concerned," David conceded, "so let's get down to business. I've been looking for a geneticist of your caliber for several years, and I think I've found him. You see, Captain, I came across your research by accident, a fortuitous event. Our German subsidiaries apply for patents pretty often, usually twice a month. Some time ago, one of my German companies applied for a patent, a patent we now own. As is customary, the patent office stamped our application, RECEIVED, dated it, and threw it into a basket full of other applications. A certified copy of our application and documents we had submitted were mailed to us. Very normal procedure, makes my application official, and states that the documents are under review.

"The large envelope sat on my desk for a few days before I got around to opening it. Guess what, Captain? The certified copy I received was not mine; it was a copy of the patent application you had submitted. Huge mistake. Here I was in possession of your application, but most important, in possession of your data. Couldn't believe it. There in front of me was your genetic discovery, a major breakthrough in genetics. The process you developed of isolating a gene from the DNA of one organism and transferring it into the DNA of another is pure genius."

"I didn't invent genetic engineering. Don't get carried away with the compliments."

"I know, but your isolation and transfer techniques are very novel and unorthodox. You're to be congratulated."

"Yeah, sure." The Captain rose from his stool and walked to the paintings David had been admiring. He got close to the paintings and slowly walked from one to the other as if inspecting them, wanting to make sure David had not damaged them by his mere observation.

"Let's cut to the chase, Captain. You know there's more to your patent than what you're letting on. Why did you withdraw your patent application two weeks after you submitted it? Why go through years of work and research only to abandon it?"

"I have something to tell you," the Captain interrupted.

"Wait, I'm not finished, Captain," David said. "Why did you submit your application under a false name? You used the name of a boy that died many years ago. A boy that would be exactly your age had he lived."

"Will you please shut up and listen to what I have to say?" the Captain said as he returned to his desk. In the middle of the desk sat a large, brown envelope.

"Does this envelope look familiar?" the Captain asked as he handed David an exact copy of the patent application documents he had received.

David opened the envelope and stared at its contents. "How did you get this from my office?"

"Don't worry, nobody's broken into your office. This is a copy of the original I had mailed to you. And just so you know, the envelope you received from the patent office was not a mistake. I intentionally had it mailed to you by my friends at the patent office. I occasionally do consulting work for the patent office, especially as it relates to genetic engineering techniques. So I called in a favor with some of my patent office friends and had the documents mailed to you."

"This doesn't make sense. Care to explain?"

"Because this is the only way I could communicate with you without getting caught. You know I'm under constant surveillance. Communicating with an American would have set off all kinds of alarms."

"You have my full attention. So tell me, why did you decide to contact me?"

"Some years ago, I was told by fellow geneticists that they had been approached by an American who wanted them to undertake a special project. The American wanted a certain gene discovered. A gene he was positive existed. At first, my friends thought he was kidding. But when he told them he wasn't kidding, they decided he was crazy. I knew you were dead serious about the research you wanted done, but I kept my mouth shut. I told my fellow geneticists that I agreed with them, that you didn't know what the hell you were talking about but to keep me posted.

"You're onto something, David, and it's not a wild goose chase. I've been conducting research that could very well work in tandem with yours. Thought you might be interested, and that's why I contacted you."

"Hell, yes, I'm interested."

"You may or may not know this, but I've been forced to work for the East Germans for most of my professional career. After the wall came down, I was still under the dictates of Neo-Nazis. They had me by the balls. These former Nazis and Neo-Nazis put me in charge of eugenics research. They evidently hadn't given up on Mengele's nefarious ambition of ethnic cleansing. Surprisingly, they had moved beyond the pseudo-science of eugenics and wanted me to discover a way of sterilizing people without their knowledge," the Captain said.

"Like what happened to Carrie Buck? Where the U.S. Supreme Court ruled that it was ok to sterilize Ms. Buck without her knowledge or consent?

"Not exactly. Hers was an actual surgical procedure, tubal ligation. What the Neo-Nazis wanted for me to discover was a way to sterilize people by changing their DNA with noninvasive procedures. They don't want people to know that they've been sterilized until it's already happened. Under this scenario, only the Aryan Nation would be allowed to propagate."

"This can only happen if there's a vaccine developed to prevent certain people's DNA from being changed, Captain."

"Exactly. If a Neo-Nazi doesn't want his DNA genetically altered, he has to be vaccinated. This presents a dilemma for them because it would be impossible to line up every blonde, blue eyed person in the world and vaccinate them without the world taking notice. And even if you could, it would be impossible because no such vaccine exists, at least not yet. This was just a crazy idea of my Nazi bosses. However, their craziness made sense in other areas of genetic engineering. So I took their idea and ran with it."

"What idea?" David asked

"Of wanting to sterilize people without them knowing."

David listened intently to the Captain's words. He knew exactly what the Captain was referring to, *an airborne retrovirus.*

"An airborne retrovirus?" David asked.

Without acknowledging David's question, the Captain continued. "The only noninvasive procedure that can alter a person's DNA is an airborne retrovirus. It can be customized to genetically alter a specific gene in our DNA."

The Captain walked back to his desk and relit his cigar. With his cigar in hand, he paced the room until David interrupted his deep concentration.

"Have you developed them, the airborne retroviruses?"

"No, not yet. I stopped my research a few months ago."

"Why?"

"My lab was audited and I thought they were on to me, so I destroyed all of the data relating to the airborne retrovirus. But I've recreated most of it since then and have it stored in my computers here, in my hideaway where it's safe."

"You were audited?"

"Yeah, a former Stasi officer showed up in my lab and kicked me out. He told me an accountant, whom I never met, was on his way to conduct an audit on my expenditures. The audit went on for several days, during which time I wasn't allowed to return. Shortly after the audit, I was placed under constant surveillance."

"Do you think they're onto you? Do you think they know about the retroviruses?"

"That's the only sensible answer. That's why I destroyed any evidence of my research. I was convinced they were onto me. But I gradually began to think that this was not the case. And let me tell you why. I make it a habit of downloading my retrovirus research onto a flash drive every day, right before I leave the lab," the Captain said. "That's why I came to the conclusion that they couldn't have found any evidence of the retrovirus. I leave nothing behind, not ever, not even the new file I started on your gene. The only data that exists today is in those computers." The Captain pointed towards them.

"Are you serious? You started a file on the gene I'm after without discussing it with me, without my permission?"

"I don't need your permission. You don't own the fucking human genome."

"You have to tell me, Captain. What else did you include in the file? I've got to know."

"Not much. Like you said, we haven't even discussed it. The only things I included in the file were the gene's name and some of my ideas as to where it might be located within our DNA."

"Anything else?"

"I wrote down a couple of notes. One was to remind me to tell you that the gene you seek is probably not acting alone, that it's likely working in combination with other genes. The other note was to make sure I told you that finding the combination of genes is what is going to make this research very expensive. That all that was in the file, just random thoughts, trying to get myself ready for this meeting."

"I can't believe you actually included the name of the gene I'm after in the file. Do you have any idea of the consequences if this information becomes public?"

David sat down, but not by the Captain's desk. He grabbed a stool and set it down against the wall. The Captain's words sent a tremor of fear through David. He felt weak; he closed eyes and sat quietly with his back against the wall. His hands were wet with perspiration despite the Captain's cold hideaway. David didn't know if what the Captain did was a major blunder, but he had to assume it was. What the Captain did was so fucking stupid, David told himself.

With his eyes still closed, David asked, "Do you think the gene exists?"

"Probably, but like I said, it's more than one gene we're after."

"Can we just refer to it as one gene for now? Less confusing for a nonscientist like me."

"I'll keep it as simple as you want. If the gene exists—there I've said it—from now on I'll refer to it as a single gene. If it does exist, we'll find it. I hope you're aware of the fact that this is going to be a very expensive undertaking. I'm talking millions."

"My calculations say that it might be in the billions." David paused. "Are you willing to work for me?"

David knew the answer before he asked the question. The Captain had contacted David for one reason and for one reason only, to become part of the team that would eventually make the discovery of the century.

"Will I work for you? I didn't go through all the trouble of meeting you just to tell you I'm not interested. But it's not as simple as just packing up and leaving. Those Nazis have a strong hold on me. Doubt they'll agree to let me go. No going away party for me, unless it's in a casket."

"I know you've been a virtual prisoner since your twentieth birthday. Want to talk about it?"

"Not today, David. There're more important things to talk about."

CHAPTER 15

"For now, can you agree to this?" David asked the Captain. "You go back to Berlin and pretend we never met. Don't change anything; keep working on whatever project you have on your desk. Don't do anything that will attract attention,."

"I think it's a little too late for that. You know my situation."

The Captain paced around in deep thought, not saying a word. He slowly walked towards David and stood within inches of his face. He grabbed David by the shoulders, stared into his eyes, and calmly asked, "Do you realize they're going to come after you with a vengeance?"

"What do you mean, come after me? What's that supposed to mean?" David asked.

"Just as I thought. You don't have a clue, do you? Don't you realize the danger you're placing yourself in by pursuing this research? If we discover a way of genetically altering the gene you're after, which I believe is your true goal, we will literally be able to change the world. If word gets out about our research, we might as well forget it, because powerful forces are going to come after us with all the fury they can muster. There's no way they're going to sit still and allow you to turn their world upside down. Their world, David, that's the way they see it. It's their world, not yours or mine, but theirs."

"I'm not afraid of them. Let them come after me. Let them expose themselves to the world for who they truly are."

"Do you honestly think that the guys that run the world are the ones that will actually come after you? Don't be foolish. They never do their own dirty work. They have goons for that. They have countless highly-paid operatives at their beck and call. Don't be surprised when the bullets start flying. Don't say I didn't warn you," the Captain said.

"So many good people have died in senseless wars, giving up their lives in vain. But if we're successful, and successful we will be, taking a bullet will seem so petty," David countered.

Though he didn't want to show fear, David knew that the Captain was right. One point that rang true was the Captain's reference to the world's power brokers. Many people use the term *power brokers* loosely. They say it without understanding what it really means, but not David. He knew many of the world's power brokers by name, and knew that in fact they did control the world. The fact that some people run the world is not a new phenomenon, David told himself. Aristocratic families have done it for centuries. These ruling families didn't just disappear like a lost civilization. These days, they just go by a different name. Their networks are beyond belief. There's no existing government that doesn't have their fingerprints all over it. There's a reason why these titans have dominated world affairs for centuries, thought David, and it's not because they're afraid of killing people.

"Listen, David. It's not just you they're going to go after. They'll go after your family. Walk away from this shit while you still have a chance. Leave it alone, and leave it to somebody who has nothing to lose other than their life. Because once you go down this rabbit hole, there's no turning back. Science is going to take a back seat to the world of espionage. The fucking games you're going to have to play in this strange world are going to drain you. They're going to take over your life. Here we are in the middle of the night, meeting in a cave. Doesn't that tell you something? This is the way it's going to be from now on. Always on the run, always in hiding, never trusting anybody, never having friends. Is this what you want?"

CHAPTER 16

"This is Ignacio Garcia reporting for the *San Antonio Chronicle*, March 14, 2015. This should have been my second interview with Mr. David Lorca, but after our first interview, I thought I'd try something new. Writing a feature story on any celebrity is always a difficult and challenging task. Giving perspective to a person's life is what makes the task most challenging. I want to bring to you, the reader, the raw data, if you will, and let you give it perspective. So the something new I want to try is the following. I asked Mr. Lorca if he would be willing to write a snippet of his life in the *barrio*. I assured him that whatever he wrote would be included verbatim in my feature story. He's been very gracious and generous with his time and has accommodated us with the following account. A story about a day in his life, as vividly portrayed by two nine-year-old boys."

A Day in the *Barrio*
Written by Mr. David Lorca
San Antonio, Texas, circa 1959

"*Seguro que si.* I'll buy the candy from you, but why should I pay you more than what you paid for it?" David asked Mauricio as they walked home from school. The fourth-graders were best of friends.

They loved sports and always made sure they were on the same athletic team because they were unbeatable when they teamed up.

"*Estas loco?* I bought the M&M's for a nickel, and if I sell them to you for a nickel all I'm doing is wasting my time because I'm not making any money. That's why you should pay me more." Mauricio answered emphatically.

"Just forget it," David said. "I'll just go to Romo's Grocery Store and buy the M&M's for a nickel."

"Go ahead," Mauricio replied. "But you'll be wasting your time because I bought the last two packages this morning."

"Maybe he got some more after you left."

"You know he only gets deliveries on Thursdays," Mauricio said.

"Yeah, I know, because sometimes he'll pay me twenty-five cents to help him restock the food shelves. I have fun working there, but right now I'm not having any fun, Mauricio. I mean, I help you with your homework and stuff like that and now you won't take a nickel for the stupid M&M's. Friends don't do this," David's voice became louder. "Next time my dad wins money at the cockfights, he's going to give me a dime and I'm going to buy two damn packages of M&M's. I can't believe you're doing this, Mauricio. How can you do it?"

David was too worked up to wait for an answer. "Remember when Juan's parents had their last baby and they couldn't afford to pay the lady that delivered the baby? Your dad and mine pitched in and paid her. They never asked to be paid back; they were just being good friends. The other day you told me that Father Solis at San Alfonso Church told you that you should do nice things for people— even strangers. Well, how about that? I remember you saying this because I told you our pastor also said we should be nice to strangers. That's when I told you we could be friends even if we go to different churches."

"Like I said, David, I have to make money. Six cents, *por favor*," a smiling Mauricio said.

"No, Mauricio, don't you understand? We have to help each

other! Your last name is Gonzalez. You're Mexican, just like me. It's our job to help one another. We can't be like other people. I heard that rich people don't help each other. To them it's always business. In our families, when somebody dies we all come together to pitch in and pay for the funeral. When rich people die, their families come together *tambien,* but they come together to split the money left by the dead person. *Por favor trata de entender.*" David looked away, searching his thoughts, wondering if perhaps he was wrong.

The two boys didn't say a word to each other as they continued walking home. David reached for his handkerchief from his back pocket and wiped off the perspiration that ran down the back of his neck. He knew that the M&M's were supposed to only melt in your mouth, but he wasn't too sure on that hot day.

David finally broke the silence. "Today I want candy, and I'm willing to pay you a nickel for it. Maybe tomorrow it will be the opposite. How would you like it if I charged you six cents? Remember when your older brother was thrown in jail because he spoke back to the police officer in Spanish? Hell, that's the only language he knew. He never had a chance to learn English like you and me. The policeman arrested him because he thought he was cussing at him in Spanish."

David continued. "It was my older brother who was home from the Marines that got him out of jail. You see, we have to help each other!

"You and I are lucky Mauricio. We're still in school. When your older brother was our age, he had to leave school a month early and get back a month late because your family went to Wisconsin, Michigan, and Washington to pick apples, cherries, or whatever food there was to pick in fields or orchards. Now you have to stay home with your mother because she's sick from all the stuff they sprayed on the fields from airplanes. Your brother flunked the same grade twice, and kids made fun of him because of this. He dropped out of school because he could no longer take it, being called dumb and stupid, not only by the other kids but also by his teachers." David's words were leaving an indelible mark on Mauricio.

"I know I'm going to college, Mauricio, and I know you don't know what that is," David announced trying to make his friend jealous.

"I know what a college is; do you think I'm stupid? It's the same as a school but you have to be real smart to go there. And also you have to pay *chingos de feria* before they let you in. So that leaves us out. Forget college and buy my M&M's," a teasing Mauricio said as he slowly and exaggeratedly lifted an M&M to his mouth.

"I know you're not stupid. You're just ignorant," David said, trying to be hurtful. He so craved the M&M's. "You might not have *chingos de feria*, but someday I will. Then I'll be able to afford college."

David found this to be the perfect time to share one of his most prized experiences.

"One summer after I had graduated from kindergarten, my mother said that if I didn't make my sister cry while she was at work—cleaning Miss Taylor's house—I could go fishing at the creek, the one close to Guadalupe and Zaramora streets. My mother had taken me to watch the older guys fish before, but this was going to be my first time all by myself. I had already cut bamboo from the edge of the creek. They just grow wild; you can use them as fishing poles. You can get as many fishing poles as you want, can you believe that? They grow everywhere along the creek; some are thick and some are skinny. You can cut down as many as you want. I think that if you are going to catch big fish, you need the thick ones. I cut down three thick ones and a bunch of skinny ones. When I got them home, I put them on the roof to dry," David's pace quickened as he continued with his story.

"There're no big fish in that stinking dirty creek," Mauricio laughed.

"Shut up, stupid, you're so ignorant. You don't even know what I'm going to tell you, so don't pretend to know things. Shut up and listen, maybe you'll learn something." David was not about to let his story go untold.

As if no animosity existed between the two, David continued. "Anyway, I told my mother to wake me up early because I had heard that fish like to eat breakfast, so I figured this was the perfect time to catch one."

"Who told you fish like to eat breakfast? Moby Dick?" Mauricio burst out laughing.

"Shut up, *pendejo*. You don't know anything."

"Alright, go on and tell me about fish eating breakfast," Mauricio said.

"If you say anything else, I'm not going to tell you anything," David said.

"I won't say a word. Now go on with your story."

"I thought no one would be awake this early, but my older brother was already having breakfast. He asked what I was doing up so early, so I told him as I got everything ready. I brought along the string I use to fly my kite. I took my rusty fishing hooks and my thick bamboo pole and left home. I was already on Guadalupe Street when I remembered I had forgotten to get some bait. I ran home and got some *masa* that my mother was using to make flour tortillas. I had seen some of the older kids use *masa* as bait.

"It was probably seven in the morning by the time I started fishing. I got bored after a couple of hours. Either fish don't eat breakfast or I was too late because I didn't catch anything. I started playing with a couple of turtles that were sunning on a mound of mud by the edge of the creek. One of the turtles ran and jumped into the water, but the big one didn't move. It let me pick him up. Maybe it was a girl turtle, I don't know, but it was heavy. I needed both hands to carry it. At first it pulled its head in, but after a while it slowly stuck its head out and was biting the stick I was using to touch its nose. I got tired of this and kept walking. I was getting farther from my house. It was fun walking along the creek. I was all alone. There was nobody around, but I wasn't scared. The bamboo is ten times taller than me. You can barely see where you're going, and nobody can see you either. I felt like I was in a jungle. I pretended to be Tarzan, but I didn't yell like him. All of a sudden the trail ended and there was a big lake in front of me. I had never seen this much water so close to me," David exclaimed.

"There are huge trees all around the lake. I think they are probably one hundred feet tall. I had heard some of our neighbors mention a *lago* called Our Lady of the Lake, so I figured this was it. The name of the lake didn't matter because I was afraid of it anyway. It looked so deep and I was afraid of falling in and drowning. What would I tell my mother?" David shrugged his shoulders.

"I kept walking towards the lake and I looked to my left. I saw this huge church with many buildings all around. The roofs of the buildings were very steep. It had pointed things on top of the roof that looked like spears. I don't know how the workers put the roof up without falling," David's attitude toward Mauricio softened as his memories came into focus.

"You should see it, Mauricio. Maybe we can go together if your mother lets you. I think it is made of huge stones. It looks kind of white. When I got back and told my mother what I had seen, she told me it was a college and that people go there to learn different things. I asked her what things, what things do they learn? She said anything you want! Can you imagine, Mauricio? I can learn anything I want!"

"Why can't I go?" asked Mauricio.

"Because I saw it first!" David remembered he was supposed to be mad at Mauricio. "They probably won't let you in anyway because they're kind of like a church and they expect you to do nice things like selling me the M&M's for a nickel. And you also have to be smart to go to college," David's animosity toward Mauricio had definitely returned.

"David, how can I sell you something and not make money?" Mauricio raised his hands above his shoulders. "You and the rest of the people in the neighborhood are very nice. If I ask them for a favor, they always help. But what happens when they don't want to help me and I don't have any money? If I sell the M&M's for six cents I'll have a penny left over and I can go to Doña Maria's store and buy two cookies for a penny. Also, don't forget about the time I hit the ball into the Garcias' front yard and broke their front window. Do you think they are going to help me if I need a favor? No!" Mauricio answered his own question.

"That's why we need to help ourselves whenever we can," Mauricio was now in control, "And besides, Father Solis told me that God helps those that help themselves. Let me tell you something else, David, people only help you if they like you. If they don't like you, they won't help you. Sometimes even relatives won't help. People only help you when they want something in return. Like the time we were invited to play ping pong at Father Solis's church. We showed up ready to play ping pong but they told us we had to go to some kind of Bible class first. You see, that's the way it works, David.

"I know you have six cents to buy my candy," Mauricio taunted David. "You don't know how lucky you are! Yesterday I was at Rodolfo's house and I offered him some of my candy, and do you know what he said? He said that he didn't want any because he might like it and he didn't have money to buy some. I think he's crazy. I can't believe he wouldn't take my candy."

"He never has any money, not even a few pennies," David answered. They're very poor. They don't even have gas or electricity in their house. *Pobre gente.* I know because he lives two houses away from us, right at the end of the *callejon.* He looks embarrassed when he walks in front of our house carrying a big can of kerosene. They have kerosene lamps and cook on a kerosene stove, so he passes by all the time, always struggling with the heavy can. We also buy kerosene but only in a one gallon jug, just enough in case the power goes out and we need to light the lamps. We also use it on cuts. Last time I stepped on a rusted nail my mother poured the kerosene into an empty sardine can, you know, those sardine cans that look like a flat football. Anyway, I put my foot in it and let it sit there until the bleeding stopped. Don't know how it works but it does.

"But the kerosene can that Rodolfo has to carry is big and must weigh a ton, especially when they buy fifty cents worth of *petroleo*. He has to take two or three rest breaks per block because he's not strong enough to carry the big can all the way home. He sits on the rusty kerosene can when he's resting and looks around to see if anybody is looking at him. I think he feels embarrassed when he's resting, but I don't know if he feels embarrassed because his family is poor and doesn't have electricity or because he's not strong enough to carry the can without taking a break. He gets a funny-looking smile on his face, you know, like when you're trying to hide something. I pretend I'm not looking at him but I'm sure he knows I am." David paused, taking a look at the package of M&M's in Mauricio's shirt pocket.

"I wonder what Rodolfo wants to be when he grows up because he never says anything when he's around. He does talk, but not about himself or his family. He's ok I guess." David said as he shrugged his shoulders. "His uncles, aunts, and the kids always go to *las piscas,* but not his mom and dad. They stay behind because they're always drunk and can't work. Everybody calls them *los winos*. His two uncles have big trucks. They cover the back of the truck's bed with a thick canvas and that's where they sleep when they go to Michigan or Wisconsin. I feel sorry for Rodolfo's older brother Gilberto. He's only fourteen years old, but sometimes he has to break up fights between his mom and dad. His parents get drunk and start beating up on each other. Sometimes we're playing football on Calaveras Street and we have to take a time out while Gilberto goes to break them up. You know, it must be hard to beat up your own father. I guess he doesn't have a choice. If he doesn't beat up his father, then his father winds up beating his mother," David said quietly

CHAPTER 17

"**Y**ou still haven't answered my question. Will you help me find the gene I'm after?" David asked the Captain.

"Maybe, but only if I we do it my way, and that means I'm in control of everything that takes place in the lab. I'll hire the scientists, geneticists, or whomever else I need. My lab is my lab and I expect you to stay out of my way. These are my terms, David. Take it or leave it."

"Of course, you'll have complete control of everything that takes place in the lab. You can hire and fire anybody you want. But you have to understand one thing. If you ever have any questions or concerns about anything, I want you to ask me and only me. Is that understood?"

The Captain nodded.

"And where exactly am I going to conduct this research?" the Captain asked.

"At your inn. After today you'll be the proud owner of the Pines Inn."

"What I need is a lab, not a fucking inn."

David knew that secrecy was at the top of his list when it came to protecting his research project. Conducting his research in the United States was not an option because it would be difficult to conceal his lab in a country with so much security. It would be next to impossible for foreign scientists from around the world to frequent a lab in the

US without NSA scrutiny. His lab needed to be situated in an isolated location yet needed to be close to a large cosmopolitan city with a major airport.

After careful analysis, David settled on Germany since one of his companies already had a presence in Europe. David found the perfect spot within Germany, the Pines Inn. Situated only two hours from Berlin, the Pines Inn met all of the requirements. The inn had been in business for many years and was situated in a very secluded pine forest. He immediately bought the inn through a trust company to avoid identification of ownership and started building the lab under the guise of building underground walkways to accommodate the inn's guests during the harsh winters. The state-of-the-art lab was built thirty feet below the inn.

"That's what I'm giving you, a lab. It just happens to be underground and situated directly beneath the inn's lobby. There's only one way in and out of the lab, very secure. Plus the inn provides a perfect cover, Captain. Your researchers and scientists will check in and out just like any other guests without ever arousing suspicion. I've spent a lot of money building this lab; let's put it to good use. But I do need to tell you one very important thing: your cover will be that of an innkeeper. You're going to make a great innkeeper."

The normally-reserved Captain did not like the idea of having to pretend to be an innkeeper and mingle with the guests. But he knew David's idea made sense.

"I'll need to hire top-notch researchers and import sophisticated lab equipment from different parts of the world. I'll be doing this through third-party dealers that know how to keep their mouths shut but are very expensive," the Captain explained. "And one more thing."

"What's that?"

"I'm going to need the best encryption expert in the world; our computers must be hacker-proof, no getting around this."

"Have anybody in mind?"

"Yes. I don't know his name but he's the best hacker in the world," the Captain said. "But you don't have to worry. He's a good guy, always on the right side of the law."

"Sign him up."

"There's something you need to know about him before you decide to sign him up," the Captain said.

"Tell me."

"He hacked into my lab's computers in Berlin and found the airborne retrovirus research data. But instead of exposing me, he congratulated me and offered to help me if ever the need arose. Well, I think the need has arisen."

"What else can you tell me about him?" I asked.

"That he is young. Told me he was respectful of me because I was old enough to be his grandfather. I call him the kid."

"Get a hold of him. Sounds like we need him."

"I'll do my best."

"Anyway, I think you'd better get going. Daybreak is almost here," the Captain continued. "You'll have to get down to Granada on your own. Walk down to the entertainment district. It's a long walk, but you'll find a taxi there."

"You're right. But before I leave aren't we going to discuss your salary requirements?"

"How much do you think I'm worth?"

David walked towards the Barcelona chair to get his briefcase, grabbed it, and unlocked it.

"You're worth a lot, Captain. That's why I know you'll be a very rich man by the time this is over. This is just a down payment. Go ahead, open it."

"This is a lot of money," the Captain said staring into the open briefcase.

"A million dollars," David said.

Both men shook hands and were saying their goodbyes when they were suddenly startled by the piercing sounds of the activated alarm system. The annunciator panel by the cave's front door came to life with pulsating lights. The Captain rushed towards the panel. Its warning lights were on full display. The word *INTRUDERS* was blinking on the Captain's computer monitor.

"Doesn't look good," the Captain said.

Both men stared into the computer's monitor. A Hummer with its lights off was racing up the mountain. The smart sensors and cameras with night vision lenses were transmitting every detail. The Hummer's heat signature showed six heavily-armed occupants. The Captain's prophetic words were being fulfilled: *Don't be surprised when the bullets start flying.* But neither of the men had expected the attacks to come so soon.

The Captain and David continued looking at the computer, knowing that the Hummer was only a couple of minutes away.

The Captain's irreplaceable retrovirus research data was now being threatened by the rapidly approaching Hummer. Years of research were now within minutes of being destroyed. The Captain raced toward his desk and from behind it he pulled out a couple of clear plastic bottles. They were not labeled, but David could see they were filled with a green liquid. The Captain tossed David one of the bottles.

David caught the bottle in midair as the Captain yelled, "Pour that shit on the computers! We don't have time to remove the hard drives or to erase the fucking data."

"What is it?"

"Don't ask! Just pour it on every computer once I download its data."

"Is it...?" David pointed at the Captain's phone.

"Yes, it's encrypted," the Captain answered, staying a step ahead of David and downloading the computers' data to his satellite phone.

Multiple rounds of gunfire rang loud and the monitor went blank. Gone were the Hummer and its assailants from the screen. The sensors and cameras had been shot and destroyed.

"Damn it, Captain, let's just get the hell out of here. This whole place is about to blow up, including the computers."

"Fifteen seconds, fourteen, thirteen...." the Captain counted down. "There, I'm finished downloading my research data. Now let's get the hell out of here," the Captain shouted at David.

"Are you crazy? We can't run out there. We'll run straight into bullets." Damn it, never meet in caves or basements, David repeated to himself.

The Captain held his phone in his left hand and punched at the keys. Suddenly a concealed trap door hidden within the geometric marble floor design opened. David could now see a metal ladder leading into darkness. He hesitated, not knowing if he was getting into a worse situation by descending deeper into the cave.

"Are you just going to stand there?" the Captain yelled out.

David grabbed his briefcase and followed the Captain down the ladder and into a dark tunnel. With the pushing of a few buttons on the Captain's satellite phone, the trap door closed and became invisible once again. The tunnel was small but large enough for the men to stand erect.

With the trap door securely closed behind them, both men hurried down the tunnel. David tried pushing the pace from behind, sometimes stepping on the Captain's heels. The tunnel descended sharply through a series of switchbacks. Water seeped from the tunnel's walls and accumulated in deep puddles, making their escape route extremely treacherous. The Captain's breathing was becoming more labored by the minute and he had to stop numerous times to catch his breath.

David's frustration with their slow progress was starting to show. He yelled at the Captain to pick up the pace, refusing to accept the Captain's obvious physical struggles.

Several minutes into their escape, the Captain's pace slowed down to a crawl and stopped. With a terrified look on his face, the Captain looked back at David, grabbed his chest and fell.

"Captain, Captain...what's wrong?" David asked as he pulled the Captain's face out of a puddle of water and rolled him on his side.

"What's wrong, Captain. Can you hear me? Say something, Captain," David shouted. But the Captain remained unresponsive.

David dragged the Captain by his shoulders and sat him up against the wall. The Captain desperately tried to move his right hand up toward his chest, but his hand made it only halfway up before it fell back down and the Captain's head fell on his chest. With his eyes still closed, the Captain tried using his left hand. This time his hand reached his inside coat pocket before it also fell. David immediately reached into the Captain's coat pocket and found a bottle of sublingual nitroglycerin tablets. In one quick motion, David opened the Captain's mouth, lifted his tongue, and jammed a tablet underneath. David looked at the Captain, looking for any positive signs, but there weren't any. Other than having a pulse, the Captain appeared lifeless.

David looked at his watch, knowing that it was only a matter of time before the armed men came barreling down the tunnel. The dim tunnel loomed ahead. He had to make a choice: leave the Captain behind or stay with him and get killed. David looked down at the Captain, ready to leave, when he noticed the Captain's fingers twitch. He grabbed the Captain's hand. It was cold. David took off his coat and draped it over the Captain's shoulders and sat next to him. Minutes passed. The tunnel was eerily quiet.

"Say something, Captain," David said in desperation.

There was no response. David kept vacillating, leave the Captain behind or stay. David was about to make a run for it when the Captain suddenly coughed. With his head slightly up, the Captain tried to say something but after several tries gave up. David changed his mind about leaving and dejectedly sat down next to him.

"I'll be ok, just let me rest," the Captain whispered without moving. "Just let me rest."

"We don't have time, Captain. They're coming after us. We don't have time for you to rest."

"No, just wait. I tell you, I'll be ok. I just need a few minutes," he said between breaths.

"Where does this tunnel lead to?"

"Granada," the Captain said softly.

"Are you saying Granada, as in the city of Granada? That's miles away!" David exclaimed.

"I know."

CHAPTER 18

Island of Capri
Aboard David's Yacht
June 20, 2015

"This is Ignacio Garcia, reporting for the *San Antonio Chronicle*. My editor in San Antonio read "A Day in the *Barrio*" as written by Mr. David Lorca, and guess what? He asked if Mr. Lorca would be willing to indulge us just one more time. Much to my surprise, the very busy Mr. Lorca has once again given us a profound insight into his young life. I'll remind the reader that this story as incorporated into my feature story is written verbatim; these are Mr. Lorca's exact words. In his last story, he was in the fourth grade. In this story, he is in the ninth grade and ready to move on to high school. "Meeting Myself," a story about David and his catharsis, as told by him and his friends. An emotional read. Enjoy it."

Meeting Myself
Written by Mr. David Lorca

Place: San Antonio, Texas
Date: April 1966
David's Age: Sixteen Years Old

"Why did you walk off the job?" Rudy asked David as they sat outside Neto's house that spring afternoon. Neto's house was the usual hangout for the ninth-grade boys, who had known each other since the sixth

92   D. G. HERNÁNDEZ

grade. It was the boys' last year at Cooper Junior High School before heading to Sidney Lanier High School just down the street. They could hardly wait for their rite of passage to high school and getting to meet new girls. Two of them, Rudy and David, were athletes and were always challenging each other, both on and off the court. Neto's mother enjoyed having the boys hang out at their small house. She always served them fresh flour tortillas as snacks. As is the case with most teenage boys, they wanted their privacy, so they usually hung out in the backyard around an old picnic table. Cell phones were still decades away, so when the guys sat around and talked, they really were interacting with one another.

"Change the record, man. I want to listen to Herb Alpert," David yelled at Neto, who was inside the house gathering another round of tortillas.

"Don't change the subject, David. Why did you walk off the job?" Rudy insisted.

"Don't you understand, man? I just had to walk off the job. The parade had just started and I had just sold two sodas when I saw Virginia and Becky. You know them; they're in our English class. They were walking on the opposite side of the street, but I'm positive they saw me. It never occurred to me that somebody from school would see me selling sodas at the parade. I was on Broadway and Jones Streets when I saw them." David spoke to Rudy and to the other guys around the table.

"I was so embarrassed. I waited for a break in the parade and crossed the street and ran over to where they were. I made up a story, told them that a friend of mine got sick and couldn't work so I was filling in for him as a favor. I told them he really needed the money and I couldn't say no when he asked for help. I was talking so fast I'm sure I sounded stupid. I even told them that I going to give every penny I made to my friend in hopes of giving the impression I didn't need any money. I don't know if they believed me, but I had to make something up. I'm glad they didn't ask me who my friend was."

Fiesta Week, San Antonio's premier weeklong celebration, was in full force when David was spotted selling sodas at the Battle of Flowers Parade, the largest daytime event during Fiesta Week. The parade was typically held on Friday, the second-to-last day of Fiesta Week. The Battle of Flowers Parade was such a big event in San Antonio that it was an official holiday for most San Antonians. Schools throughout San Antonio closed so that all students could either participate in the parade or be one of the hundreds of thousands of spectators.

The big event at the beginning of Fiesta Week was the King's River Parade, so named by the Texas Cavaliers. The Cavalier organization was composed of Anglo men from affluent cities to the north of San Antonio. Once a year, the Cavaliers anointed a king from within their ranks who was given the title King Antonio. The symbolic King of Fiesta was actually afforded valuable privileges. He never had to stop at a red light—police escorts made sure of this. The King's public investiture took place in front of the Alamo but was preceded by a secret ceremony inside the Alamo. King Antonio would visit many of the local schools; however the Edgewood Independent School District once spurned the King's visit in protest of the Cavaliers' discriminatory and exclusionary practices. Shortly thereafter, the Texas Cavaliers became a little more inclusive.

Extravagantly decorated barges floated down the meandering river as thousands of spectators lined its banks. During the Spanish colonization of the area, Spanish priests established a series of Catholic missions along the river. The most famous of the missions was the Alamo, made famous by the battle that took place within its walls, between General Santa Anna and the Texas rebels and made even more famous by the movie *The Alamo* starring John Wayne.

Fiesta week was filled with more activities than one could attend. The other major events during Fiesta week were the Flambeau Parade, the Band Festival, Royalty Coronations of the various Fiesta Queens and Duchesses and the downtown carnival.

The Battle of Flowers Parade was special for students like David. High school marching bands from throughout the city participated.

Visiting military bands from around the country added glamour to the three-mile-long parade. Beautifully decorated floats carried the Queen of Fiesta and her royal court and the various duchesses.

There was a particular float that caught David's attention during one of his many years of watching the parade. It was titled, "Children of Texas." There were over thirty children on the float. David wondered why there were only Anglo children on the float.

The reviewing stand was situated in front of the Alamo. Bleachers were erected days in advance, awaiting San Antonio's privileged. Local politicians and commanding officers from the area's military bases basked in the reviewing stand that hot April afternoon. With no awning to protect them from the sun, many of the women sought solace beneath their parasols.

The stratification of San Antonio's population was evident by the seating patterns along the three-mile parade route. Parade spectators along the first half of the parade were mainly middle-class and upper-middle Anglos, with a sprinkling of middle-class Mexicans. The majority of spectators along the second half of the parade route were Mexican. The seating along the second half of the parade route was on a first-come basis. Many came early to stake out a good spot. Some brought lawn chairs; others sat on the concrete curbs along the sidewalks. Kids sat on their dads' shoulders, trying to get a good look at the passing parade.

Street vendors did very well along Broadway Ave. Most of the street vendors were Mexican-American boys that worked for various vending contractors. Getting a job as a vendor was easy—just show up at a vending contractor's sidewalk location and sign up. The kids were given a nail apron advertising a local hardware store to use as a money apron. If the vendor was selling sodas, he would be given a shallow metal tray with twenty-four individual compartments that held the twenty-four cups of sodas: twenty Cokes and four Seven-Ups. As soon as the vendor sold out his inventory of drinks, he would return to the contractor's station and pick up a full tray and start selling again. The kids got paid two cents for every soda they sold. Selling popcorn and peanuts was more profitable; kids got paid five cents for every bag they sold. David noticed that the older boys with more seniority got to sell the lighter-weight popcorn and peanuts. This didn't make sense to David. The sodas weighed more, so he figured the older and stronger boys should be selling the heavier products.

David's memory had every fiesta event indelibly recorded: the colorful floats, the mouth- watering aromas of delicious foods, the sweet smell of cotton candy as it spun around, the sounds of the marching bands, the screams of riders as they were whirled about in the scariest of carnival rides. However, the one Fiesta experience he wished to forget was the one that shaped his life.

"David, people have to work. There's nothing bad about having to work," Rudy told David.

"Don't you think I know this, Rudy? People work, but not at something as demeaning as selling Cokes during the parade. The girls probably think I'm too poor to take time and enjoy the parade."

"There's nothing wrong with selling Cokes at the parade. A lot of guys do it."

"I know. But I still felt embarrassed."

"*Chingao bato!*" Neto chastised them. "You guys still talking about the same shit? I went in, changed the record, came back outside, and you guys are still talking about walking off the job or whatever."

"Look, David," Rudy pointed out. "I know you're cool. But don't forget where you live. You're one of us. We've been together since the fourth grade. Nobody is better than anybody else here. But I have to tell you, man, sometimes I get the feeling that you would rather be somewhere else. When we're out here laying on our backs on this picnic table, not saying a word, just looking up into the sky, listening to music, you seem to be in another world. I don't know. I know you don't think you're better than us. You never put us down. You're cool. But I can tell you want something that's out there. I don't know what that something is, but I can tell you want it."

David reminisced as he listened to Rudy. David remembered his mother saying, "No one will ever make fun of my son." She always told him to sit up straight at the dinner table, even if it was just wooden crates that he sat on instead of regular chairs. She also told him to put both feet on the floor as he ate and not to cross his legs while at the table. "No one will ever make fun of my son." Yes, she was also telling me to get a good education, David thought. Nobody ever makes fun of an educated person. I will learn music, math, and science. Nobody will ever make fun of me.

No one will ever make fun of my son. *That's it!* David realized. She was not giving me a set of rules to live by. She was just pointing the way! Neto and Rudy won't understand if I tell them what's going on in my mind. David never shared his mother's words with anybody.

"My dad took me to buy fireworks on New Year's Eve and there were only *Americanos* working," Rudy told David.

"I saw them, too, when I went last year, but there is a big difference. These guys don't have to work. They just do it for fun. Their dads probably own the fireworks stand."

"If you hadn't walked off the job, you'd have money to buy Delia a *raspa* next time you walk her home. I know she likes *raspas*."

"Even if I had made money, I wouldn't buy her a *raspa* because she'd want to know where I got the money. What would she think of me if I told her I had sold sodas at the parade? There were thousands of people at the parade. I'm sure there were other people from school that saw me. I wouldn't be surprised if the whole school knows by now. I know other kids from school sell stuff at the parade, but I just see it differently. Maybe I should confess and admit I was selling Cokes at the parade so I could afford to go to the carnival." The reality was that David could never see himself admitting this.

"Look, man, Delia likes you. She doesn't care if you sell sodas," Neto reminded David.

"Yeah, David, she really loves you!" Rudy quipped. "*Mira bato,* she knows all about you. She knows you live in a rundown alley, full of potholes and no sidewalks. She's seen you in pants with holes in them, not lately, but when we were in the sixth grade. She knows there's shootings and stuff like that where you live, but she still likes you. She's pretty, and you know that. She always has her hair all teased up and dresses nice. She could go steady with anybody she wants, but she goes steady with you."

"Shut up, Rudy! I know she's pretty, and that's why I like her. That's why she can't find out that I sold two lousy sodas at the parade."

"What is your problem, David? There is absolutely nothing wrong with selling Cokes at the parade!" Neto's voice was full of frustration. His short temper and hulking body would have caused fear to many, but he always looked out for David.

"Come on guys, I know there is nothing wrong," David said. "I know that many guys do it. It's just that I feel embarrassed because people probably think that I'm dumb or stupid, that I don't know how to do anything else except sell drinks at the parade. Some of the vendors can't read or write, especially the older ones. They see me as somebody that is going to grow up and become an old street vendor and nothing else. Some of the older men don't know that some people make fun of them behind their back, probably because they don't understand English. They just go on selling Cokes, beer, popcorn, or whatever. I don't want to be like them. You know, I wouldn't mind selling anything as long as I knew I was respected. But who's going to respect us when the rich people who live on the north side of town see us on television being arrested for whatever. The television always shows the bad stuff, never the good things." David had never heard himself speak so forcefully without being angry.

"Anybody who knows you knows that you're not dumb or stupid," Rudy told David. "I enjoy hearing about the articles you read in *Life* magazine, *Look* magazine, and *National Geographic*. You probably think I'm not listening to you, but I am. You know a lot of things. People would be impressed if they heard you talk. Remember the time you said, 'What I wear to school is more of a refinement rather than a difference to a degree of what I wear when I play'? You see? You read stuff and you remember what you read."

"Yeah, I remember when you said that shit about what you wear to school," Neto couldn't hold back. "I laughed when I heard it. I made fun of you, told you to repeat it so I could laugh again. But I wasn't really making fun of you. I don't know, man, sometimes it just makes me feel good to make fun of things," Neto said.

"When was the last time you asked the soda vendor to tell you his life story before you bought a drink from him?" David asked sarcastically. "No matter what you guys say, I'm still hoping that the girls from school didn't see me at the parade. Embarrassing, man!

"Do you guys ever wonder why you feel a certain way? When I get embarrassed I feel...like...like kind of sad," David added.

Not waiting for a reply, David continued. "I had this same feeling when I thought I was a Boy Scout. I registered at San Alfonso Church to become a Boy Scout. They gave us a book, I think it was called *Boy Scout Handbook*. It had the motto, *Always be prepared*. It also had pictures of how to make knots with ropes. Once I signed up, I went to all the meetings. They were a lot of fun. Most of the guys were older than me, but it didn't matter because I was one of them, a Boy Scout.

"One night after the meeting, the Scout leader told us to make two lines. We faced each other as we stood in line. We were about six feet apart. One of the guys had broken a scouting rule so he was made to walk slowly between the two lines. I think they called it a gauntlet. We were supposed to hit him or kick him as he walked between us. This was his punishment. Some guys would hit him really hard. If he tried walking fast they would make him start again. He didn't cry or anything," David told his friends.

"I was really having a great time learning so many things. It was fun looking at all the badges you could earn. We learned how a tent was supposed to be put up. I had never seen a real tent before, only on television. It wasn't very big. We put it up over and over again, trying to get faster every time. A statewide Boy Scout convention was coming to town and we were told of the various events and competitions that were going to take place. All I cared about was the competitions, especially the tent competition. I knew there was nobody faster than us in setting up a tent. I was positive we could win. I had a red Boy Scout handkerchief that you put around your neck. My mother bought it for me as a gift." David could taste the bile in his mouth. The bile tasted exactly the same as it did that day, the day of which he spoke. How can memories have tastes? David wondered.

"Our Boy Scout leader told those of us that didn't have a Boy Scout uniform that we could still go to the convention and participate in the competitions as long as we wore our red handkerchiefs. This made me feel really good because I knew there was no way my mother could afford to buy me a uniform.

"The day of the convention finally arrived. It was a Friday, and I ran home as soon as I heard the last bell ring. I had been looking forward to this day for two months. My mother wished me luck when I left the house and told me I looked real handsome with the red handkerchief around my neck. She had managed to buy me the least expensive part of the uniform. We eagerly gathered around the church van, ready to be transported to the Scout convention. Just before we started to board, our leader told some of us that we couldn't go because we didn't have a uniform. He said he was sorry but those were the rules from the higher ups.

"I felt funny when he said this. I didn't go home right away. I told my mother I really didn't want to go to the Scout convention. I never went back to the Scout meetings." David's voice tapered off, almost to a whisper. I guess you really can taste memories, he told himself.

"Do you think you're better than other people? You must really think you're better than other people. Otherwise you wouldn't feel embarrassed, David," Rudy yelled out as he paced around the picnic table.

"*Otra vez bato?* Leave him alone. Maybe walking off was something he had to do," Neto said, wanting to change the subject.

"No, man, he has to listen to us. You know I'm right, Neto," Rudy told him.

He then turned to David and continued, "Look, David, we all have to work doing something. Some people work at restaurants as cooks, waitresses, busboys, dishwashers. Others work as bus drivers and janitors. Some work on the river barges downtown. They're not embarrassed—it's honest work. They make money to buy what they need. Remember last week? Ruben told us he got a ten-dollar tip just for carrying a man's luggage to his room. We all teased him, told him that he probably did more than carry the man's luggage for ten dollars!" Rudy laughed as he remembered.

"Ruben knows we were just kidding," Neto interrupted. "Hell, he has more girlfriends than all of us put together. He's tall, probably six-feet-two and can date those tall girls we shorter guys can't. He can also afford to buy nice clothes, don't forget that."

"I'm only a couple of inches shorter than Ruben," David did not consider himself short.

"*Por favor batos,* can we move on?" an irritated Rudy demanded. "We all know Ruben is tall, handsome, and popular with the girls, but that is not the reason I brought Ruben up."

Rudy was getting frustrated with David, realizing that he was not about to change his mind about being embarrassed at selling sodas at the parade, but he still forged ahead.

"Other than the big tip, Ruben also told us that it's hard to get a job as a bellboy at the hotel because the older men never quit their jobs. They make good tips, and they work there til they get old. They then bribe the bell captain to hire their sons as bellboys, so you see there's hardly a chance to get these good jobs."

"And don't forget Hector's father. He works at a downtown hospital parking cars. Shit, he makes good tips parking the doctors' cars all day long. That's how he bought Hector that almost-new Mustang. Hector should ask his dad to get him a part-time job parking cars during the summer. I don't know what's wrong with you, David," Rudy said.

David was very familiar with the stories Rudy spoke of. Hector's father was a great person. He was always in a good mood and was very nice to all of Hector's friends.

"I like Hector's father. He's always telling us about the nice cars he gets to drive, especially one that he said cost ten thousand dollars. Can you imagine that? A ten-thousand-dollar car?" David asked.

David's mind drifted back to thinking about Ruben and the great money he made at the hotel. Tips were always good, and besides, the hotel gave him a clean uniform every week. David looked up to Ruben. He was the best math student in school. But he didn't get good grades because he never had time for homework, which counted for twenty percent of the grade. "Why do you miss school so often?" some of his friends would ask. They knew the reason but overlooked it because of all the nice things he owned. On occasion, he would buy lunch for several of his friends.

Mr. Navarro, Ruben's father, got Ruben his job at the hotel and immediately started to teach him the trade. He took much pride in mentoring his son.

"Always be courteous, these are very important people, they know lots of things. Always say 'yes sir,' even when they are wrong. Make sure you put their suitcases on the luggage stand and hang their clothes in the closet. Show them where the light switches are and how to adjust the thermostat. Ask them if they would like the ice bucket filled. Ask if they would like a wakeup call in the morning. Tell them your name so they can call on you when they need something. Keep asking if there's anything else you can do until he reaches for his wallet. Once he reaches for his wallet, don't say anything, don't over-sell. He's going to give you a tip. Keep your mouth shut. Thank him and use his last name when you thank him. He'll appreciate the fact that you remembered his name— makes him feel important." Mr. Navarro felt so proud that he could offer his son such valuable advice. "I want the best for my son, and I'm going to teach him everything I know. He's going to be better than me," the proud father boasted as he told the story to David and his friends every time they ran into each other. David and his friends knew the story well.

"Maybe you're right, Rudy," David offered. "Once Delia's mother said that I was a proud person. Do you think she said that in a bad way? I thought being proud of who you are was a good thing.

"Do you think people should worry about what other people think of them?" David asked. "If what other people think of you is incorrect, do you have an obligation to correct this misconception? And when there is an incorrect perception, is it a problem for the person who has an incorrect perception or for the person who is being perceived incorrectly? How can there be two different realities of the same person or object? What causes differences in realities?" David shot the questions in rapid succession.

"It must be context! When a stranger sees me, all he sees is a person who lives in a certain part of town, speaks with a certain accent. He sees me working as a non-skilled laborer, assumes that my parents are not educated. I fit the stereotype he has of people that look like me, his erroneous stereotype." The guys listened to David.

Context is a very valuable tool. If we hear the roar of a lion while camping out in the wilds of Africa, our brain puts this roar in context and we scramble to safety. But if we hear this same roar while watching a Tarzan movie, our reactions are different. How can I override my context so people can see who I really am? Is it possible to remove myself from one context and insert myself into another? Of course! It only takes money! I won't change—my context will, and this will change others' perception of me! David became overwhelmed with excitement as these thoughts raced through his mind.

Maybe I am related to Moctezuma! I'm a descendent of an Aztec Emperor. David recalled the many laughs he and his mom often had concerning this topic.

Flashback

Richard and David walked hurriedly, making their way to the

carnival. They were carefree. This was years before David would be too embarrassed to be a street vendor.

"Walk faster, Richard. The lines of people waiting to get on all the rides must be long by now!" They had decided to walk the three miles to downtown in order to save the five-cent bus fare. Walking back home provided a total savings of ten cents, enough to buy a hot dog.

The carnival was the thing most people from the *barrio* looked forward to. It provided fun for people of all ages. The children rode miniature cars on fixed tracks that went round and round. The mothers proudly watched their children, exhorting them to hold on tight to the steering wheel. The children were equally proud, for they thought they were in fact steering real cars.

David had saved two dollars, and Richard one dollar and eighty cents, three quarters and a nickel. "We can get on at least ten rides each and have money left over for something to eat." Richard planned their day as they walked toward the carnival.

"I know," David said in agreement. "Let's get on all the scary rides and not waste money trying to win prizes. Some of the guys spend all their money trying to win a teddy bear for their girlfriends. They must be crazy!"

"The girls are so lucky because their boyfriends pay for the rides. My mother said that the man should also pay for the food and drinks." Richard looked forward to becoming a man.

"I know, my mother says the same thing," David told Richard. "Although I don't know if it's that cool being a girl. The women have to do all the cooking, washing clothes, having babies, and changing diapers. It smells awful! My mother said she never wants to see me changing my kids' diapers, that it's not a man's job.

"Last year I won a white coffee cup with just three nickels," David continued. "I knew my mother was going to like it a lot. She set it on top the refrigerator and doesn't let anybody use it. She always tells people I won it for her. You have to figure out where the nickel is going to bounce, that way you know how hard to throw it"

"Did you see the guy with all the medals on his uniform?" Richard asked as they walked through the crowds in awe of all the action around them.

"Yes, he's in the Junior ROTC. That's like being in the Army even though you're still in high school. I think they teach them how to shoot a rifle. You have to learn how to march and stuff like that."

"Do you have to pay to be in the ROTC?" Richard asked.

"No. They give you a uniform, and you have to wear it to school every day. You also get to march in the parade."

Richard and David took a break from the carnival to watch the parade. David's favorite entry was the Marine Corps Band. Actually, it was the crowd's favorite as well. Many of the guys from the *barrio* enlisted in the Marine Corps. The thousands of spectators along the parade route would give the Marine Band a standing ovation as they marched by. The crowd rose to their feet and then sat back down again, creating a scene similar to the "wave" one would see at sports venues years later.

"If you wear the uniform to school every day, you save money and people won't know that you can't afford new school clothes." Richard listened intently as David spoke.

"I know what I'll be wearing when I'm in high school," Richard interjected.

"Look, that guy won a huge teddy bear and is trying to win another one. I bet he is putting saliva on the dimes. I've heard that sometimes you can do it and not get caught. Be careful if you try," David warned Richard.

"Yes, I've also heard that if you smoke before putting saliva on the dime it makes it more sticky," Richard knew what David was talking about.

CHAPTER 19

"Hi, Ignacio," David said. "Sorry I had to leave for a couple of days. Hope I didn't cause you to miss any deadlines. Don't want to make your editor mad."

"No missed deadlines, and don't worry about my editor. He told me to take all the time I need. But he also said, now these are his words, 'It better be a damn good story,'" Ignacio said while readying his recorder.

"In that case, let's get started on this damn good story." David sat down.

Ignacio spoke into his recorder. "This is Ignacio Garcia reporting for the *San Antonio Chronicle*. June twenty fourth, two thousand fifteen. My editor and I can't thank you enough for the two stories you have written."

"You're welcome," David interrupted.

"In the first story, you were around age seven, and in the second, you were in your early teenage years. Why don't we continue with this sequence and talk about your late teenage years, high school years, and perhaps other events that were important to you during these years."

"I'll try, Ignacio, but I'm not promising anything. Hopefully the editing process will take care of the timelines. I'm not always sequential. My mind has been known to drift," David said and then continued.

"My high school years, fun times. I had a steady girlfriend, an afternoon job that paid for nice clothes, and I was running great, qualified for the Texas Relays.

"'Remember guys,' our track coach told us. 'This weekend you'll be representing our high school at the Alamo Heights Relays. You all know what this means, and I'm not talking about the running. People will be watching you guys. You need to be on your best behavior. I don't want you to go out there and act like a bunch of Mexicans.'

"This is almost an exact quote, Ignacio. Hard to forget, the coach's pep talk centered on behavior and not running. We were very well behaved at school, so I knew he wasn't talking about behavior in its normal context. No, he was telling us something else, something that applied to him as well. Our coach was Chicano.

"This was not the first time I had heard a coach tell me how I was supposed to act when traveling to an Anglo neighborhood or school. It must have been in junior high school when I first heard such words. It was during this time that I first traveled outside my neighborhood to compete at athletic events. My coach's subtle words didn't go un-heeded, but perhaps their true meaning went unnoticed. 'Being on our best behavior' meant 'Don't forget who you are and how you're supposed to act.'

"I can't remember the first time I heard that people in Alamo Heights didn't like Mexicans. I do remember my father telling my older brothers not to go into Alamo Heights after dark. 'Don't go past Hildebrand Street if you're driving on Broadway.' It was not just my father saying it; I heard other grownups say it. I don't know if such warnings originated in our DNA, but they were so ubiquitous that I obeyed them.

"How did San Antonio's memes originate? I don't know. I was not thinking about such things while in high school."

"I don't think too many high school students are concerned about memes either," Ignacio interjected.

"You're probably right, Ignacio. But I'm no longer in high school, so let me tell you, the most insidious thing about a meme is when it becomes part of our DNA. I kid you not: memes can actually become part of our fixed DNA. That's when the meme defines who you are. And do you want to know what's even more insidious, Ignacio? It's when the mutated gene is passed on to future generations.

"Anyway, getting back to my high school years and Alamo Heights. I lived on the poor side of town, and the rich lived in Alamo Heights. But the differences between the two communities were not just about money. The differences went far beyond. When I thought of Alamo Heights, it was an all-encompassing thought. To me, Alamo Heights was much more than a tiny city within the City of San Antonio. It represented an ideal that was to be emulated. A place to buy a home and raise a family. I had heard that Mexicans were not allowed to buy houses in Alamo Heights, but I was young and thought it was a money issue. I had never heard of restrictive covenants.

"One of my sisters and her husband would periodically take me for a drive along Broadway Street on Friday evenings. It was a glamorous street, leading from downtown San Antonio to Alamo Heights. I stood in the car, behind the front seat, awestruck by the bright lights along the grand corridor. My brother-in-law would make a U-turn on Hildebrand Street, head back into downtown, and start the tour all over again. We never ventured into Alamo Heights. My sister would tell me about the beautiful houses with lush gardens located north of Hildebrand. She described Alamo Heights in vivid detail. I never bothered to ask her how she knew of which she spoke. I even remember the bus driver at the Inman Community Center once tell us kids, and this are his exact words, 'When it rains in Alamo Heights you can walk on the street and not get muddy. It's not like here in the *barrio* where the alleys are full of water and mud for days until it finally dries up.'

"Anyway, I was sold on Alamo Heights. That's the place I wanted to live. Heck, it had the best of everything; why wouldn't I want to live there? The smartest and the brightest students lived in Alamo

Heights and the vast majority of them were Anglo. And so by extrapolation, I believed Anglos were inherently smarter.

"No, Ignacio, I had never heard of such a word as *extrapolation*. My young brain just worked out the faulty logic on its own. I didn't question the logic; results proved everything to me."

"What do you mean when you say results proved everything?" Ignacio asked.

"Results as in who owns everything and wins all of the time. I noticed that the Anglos owned everything that was worth owning in San Antonio: the banks, law firms, accounting firms, large construction companies, and retail stores. I also noticed the names of elected officials, from school board members to mayors, from municipal court judges to federal judges; they were all Anglo last names. Were there a few minority office holders at the time? Sure, there were, but none could be elected without the blessing and explicit approval of the Anglo power brokers. So when my young and naïve brain made these observations, I assumed that these men had risen to the top because they were smarter. Then it must follow that they were better because they had accomplished more.

"I didn't see any inequities; that's just the way it was. I assumed they were better because that's what I assumed. I guess it's similar to somebody trying to explain his or her faith. At the end of the day, all a person can say is I believe because I believe.

"What were the cues that prompted my beliefs? Again, I didn't know. I was only a kid. But cues existed. I remember hearing people say things like, 'Your baby is so pretty and light complexioned, she looks Anglo.' 'Your baby's eyes are gorgeous. They're almost blue; hope they never change.' I was hearing these words spoken by Mexicans and not Anglos from the north side of San Antonio. My neighbors not only complimented the light-complexioned babies, but went out of their way to put down darker complexioned babies. *'Pobrecito, el niño de Maria nacio tan prieto.'* Remember what I said of insidious memes becoming part of our DNA? Who taught us our memes before they became part of our DNA?

"The television programs 'The Adventures of Ozzie and Harriet'... 'My Three Sons'... 'Leave It to Beaver' and other television programs symbolized the ideal American family. And Alamo Heights was my local version of the ideal American life and family.

"There were nights when I laid on my mattress, imagining what rich people's houses looked like, especially on the inside. Laying there on the floor, I looked at the baseboard, only inches from my face. This is where my imaginary trips to my imaginary house always started, at the baseboard. My imaginary house had hardwood floors without imperfections, no wood slivers to penetrate my bare feet. With my socks on, I was able to slide on the highly polished and waxed imaginary floors, just like the kids on television. Having decided on hardwood floors for my imaginary house, I would proceed to the walls. I usually landed on pastel colors for the walls, nothing too bold. But then I would return to my selection of flooring materials, maybe carpet, wall-to-wall carpet, I contemplated.

"My imaginary house had nice windows, and when they broke, I insisted that they be replaced with glass and not a piece of cardboard. Oh, and my house was warm in the winter, nice and toasty.

"I pictured myself having my own bedroom; it was upstairs, just like the Beaver's. My bedroom had a bed; the mattress on the floor was a thing of the past. My bed had store-bought sheets, not empty flour sacks that had been sown together to be used as sheets. Even though an empty flour sack was the perfect size for a pillow, I still insisted on store-bought pillow cases.

"And just like I had seen on television, I found myself racing my brothers down the stairs of my two-story house. I would always beat my brothers because I slid down the curved handrail.

"The kitchen was special. It had all of the modern conveniences, and at the top of the list was an electric mixer. On the kitchen counter I would also have an electric toaster and a spice rack, and the family would gather around the kitchen island. My imaginary house had a dining room table with matching chairs. Wooden apple crates would no longer be used as chairs. Oh, and I insisted that my house have a doorbell. I lay there, embellishing my house until my mother turned off the lights and came to bed, on the mattress next to me. It didn't matter that the lights had been turned off; my imagination worked in the dark."

"Sorry to interrupt, Mr. Lorca. You have an important call from the Pines Inn," David's secretary said.

"We'll have to finish this later, Ignacio."

CHAPTER 20

Granada, Spain
December 5, 2006

David and the Captain finally made good on their escape as they exited the primitive tunnel. David was surprised at his new surroundings. The tunnel had led them into the basement of an upscale hotel on the outskirts of Granada. Without hesitation, the Captain immediately walked toward the opposite end of the cavernous basement. He looked around before pressing his thumb against the keypad of a large metal door. The keypad recognized his thumbprint and the door automatically opened into a dimly-lit mechanical room. David noticed a lone suitcase lying on its side. The Captain grabbed it, walked out of the room, and shut the door behind him.

With suitcase in hand, the Captain climbed up a set of stairs that led to the lobby. David clutched the briefcase with the million dollars tightly as he followed the Captain up to the lobby. The lobby was eerily empty and quiet. A lone ceiling fan in the middle of the lobby with its humming vibration was the only thing that could be heard. The two slowly put one foot in front of the other, afraid of walking into an ambush. Memories of the Hummer racing up the mountain were still fresh in the men's minds. They looked toward the front desk, then toward the concierge's desk. They were both empty.

"*Quien es?* Who is it?" A woman's voice reverberated throughout the cavernous lobby.

David looked around but didn't see anybody.

"*Soy yo.* It's me," the Captain responded.

A tall and attractive woman suddenly appeared from an adjoining room and walked towards them. The light-complexioned woman with dark hair was dressed in a dark blue pant suit. Without looking at her, the Captain immediately headed to the computer behind the front desk. David stayed behind, ready to run out the front door in case of trouble. The Captain started to punch a series of numbers and letters on the computer's keyboard. David couldn't believe what appeared on the screen.

"*Elena, ven....pronto.* Elena, come here...hurry," the Captain commanded. She ran around the front desk and joined the Captain at the computer, pushing David aside.

Top Secret
United States Government - CIA

David stood in silence. The geneticist he had just hired was hacking into U.S. government computers, CIA computers. The monitor kept blinking as the Captain went from one document to another, making notes on a hotel ledger as he read the documents. David was close enough to hear their conversation. The Captain and Elena were trying to determine who from the CIA had authorized the bombing.

"Do you notice anything strange about any of the communications between here and Langley?" The Captain now spoke to Elena in English.

"Can't tell. We haven't been able to decipher the encrypted messages. But I bet we'll soon find out. The kid agreed to help us." Elena spoke confidently.

David looked at the Captain when he heard Elena say, *the kid*.

"You know how to reach the kid?" the Captain asked her.

"Of course," she answered.

"Anyway, why the CIA?" the Captain asked Elena.

David had a similar question. How did the Captain know it was the CIA?

"The Cold War is still going on sweetheart..." Elena answered the Captain.

"What did she call you?" David asked the Captain.

The Captain didn't answer.

"You asked if there was anything strange about the communications," Elena continued. "Shit, it's not only strange, it's very strange. None of the communications are going to the top. All of the talking is taking place between mid-level career operatives. They're leaving the CIA Director out of the loop," Elena added before walking back to her office.

"Or it could be that he knows but is being protected. Directors sometimes want to claim ignorance rather than guilt. But my best guess, and this is only a guess, is that these are CIA rogue agents that are moonlighting. Making a lot of money on the side," the Captain said.

"Let's get the hell out of here, I'm running very late," Elena said.

"Aren't you forgetting the suitcase?" David asked.

"You mean the empty suitcase I use as a prop?"

"What?" David asked.

"Get it for me, hurry."

They exited the hotel and got into an awaiting black Mercedes. The driver didn't wait for directions.

"What the hell is going on? Those were real bombs, Captain. Somebody tried killing you."

"Me? Are you crazy," the Captain yelled. "It's you they're after."

David sat silently in the back seat. He knew the Captain was right; it was him that they were after. It only made sense. If killing the Captain was the objective, they could easily have killed him in Berlin.

"Relax, David, I know it got kind of scary back there, but I don't think they really wanted to kill you. They just wanted to scare you. Otherwise they would have detonated the explosives inside the cave and not outside by the door. They're just sending you a message. What

I haven't figured out is why just a message. Are they underestimating you, thinking that you'll run at the first sign of danger? Hard to figure out. This whole fucking bombing operation doesn't make one bit of fucking sense."

"I have a question: How did you know it was the CIA that came after us? I mean, you immediately went to the hotel's computer and hacked into the CIA's computers. You must have had a reason for putting the blame on them," David asked.

"I noticed the weapons' outline against the assailants' heat signatures. These are sophisticated weapons that are only available to the CIA. Israeli commandos might have them, but I doubt it. Anyway, this is how I knew it was the CIA."

"So if I'm the target, where does that leave you? Do you get a free ride? Why just me?" David asked.

"Because nobody knows I was up there. Not one fucking person knows I'm the person you were meeting with. On the contrary, they knew it was you up on the mountain. You were probably being followed the moment you got off your jet. They knew you were meeting with somebody when they set off the explosives, but they sure as hell don't know it was me."

"How can you be so sure?" David asked.

"Because nobody saw me leave the hotel. The tunnel works in both directions, David. See you later, I'm off. I have a flight to catch. I'm sure that the goons that keep me under surveillance are wondering why I'm running late. They're probably thinking I got lucky with one of the local girls. They think that's the reason I come here. If they only knew."

"Don't forget, Captain, keep a low profile. I'll keep in touch with you through intermediaries. If you need to communicate with me, do it through them. Never communicate with me directly. By the way, what did you do with the data; where did you transfer it to?" David asked.

"I'll tell you next time we meet," the Captain said as he exited the Mercedes.

David opened the car's window and yelled at the Captain as he walked away. "Don't you want this?" David pointed at the briefcase.

"Keep it for now," the Captain yelled back.

CHAPTER 21

Hans walked into the Hard Rock Cafe and requested a table by the large windows overlooking the canal. He was in need of a strong drink. His flight from Berlin encountered severe weather, leaving him rather traumatized. In spite of his military training, Hans had never been able to overcome his fear of flying. He ordered a double scotch on the rocks but immediately changed his mind and ordered hot tea instead. It was imperative he stay sober.

Hans Friedrich was born in London, England, in 1954. His parents fled Germany immediately after World War II, narrowly avoiding arrest and prosecution for their war crimes. Escaping with art stolen from wealthy Jews, they lived the life of luxury in London. Unscrupulous art dealers paid the Friedrichs millions of dollars for the entire cache. Their new-found wealth gained them entry into London's upper class and its accompanying social networks. If asked about their background, their answer was always the same. They couldn't stand Hitler and his atrocities, so they packed up and left their dear Germany with broken hearts.

On his sixth birthday, Hans was enrolled in one of the most exclusive prep schools in London. His parents departed to Argentina within hours of having dropped him off at school, narrowly avoiding arrest once again. The young boy was left in the care of the boarding school and his extended family that lived in Austria, where he spent his summers in solitude, always wondering why his parents had abandoned him, always wondering what he had done to deserve a life without parents.

Hans grew into a well-defined athletic body, a muscular six-foot-six body. The handsome individual with blue eyes and blond hair would have occupied the front and center position of any parading army. Beautiful women were always more than willing to accommodate the distinguished-looking German's sexual appetite and prowess.

His early years would never have predicted such an outcome. He was a sickly boy, spending many hours at the school's infirmary, never seeming to get well. The school's nurse could not make sense of Hans' constant lethargy. No elixir seemed capable of helping the depressed youth. "I don't understand why my parents never come and visit. Can't figure out what I did to make them hate me. I guess it doesn't matter because I hate them, too, for having abandoned me," Hans would contemplate. After three years of living a tormented life, Hans was summoned to the Head Mistress's office, where she gently told him that his parents had died in a car accident.

With high academic credentials from Eton College and then Oxford, the now-independent Hans renounced his British citizenship and made Germany his home. All Hans knew about Germany was what his parents, and in particular his mother, had told him. He fell in love with the stories, always wanting to hear more, especially about Hitler and how great a leader he was. The now-adult and zealous German immediately joined the army. His love of Germany had never waned, unlike his love for his parents.

Hans' intellect and physical abilities gained him admission into East Germany's elite intelligence agency, the Ministry for State Security. The young Stasi officer moved up quickly through the ranks because of his unequalled abilities in counterintelligence. The fearless operative with a death wish always volunteered for the most dangerous of assignments. He came close to having his death wish granted during a covert operation in West Germany. He never saw the enemy nor the knife that cut across his face and almost cost him his right eye. Hans never answered when asked what became of his assailant. Word of his exploits spread throughout the agency. He quickly became East Germany's marquee neo-Nazi.

Hans' top security clearance gave him access to Germany's most secret and sensitive documents. In these documents, Hans came across information that ignited an inextinguishable fire in him.

That was years ago. Hans was no longer a Stasi officer; today he was his own man.

Moe walked in and sat opposite Hans at the small table. He wore a red baseball cap and dark sunglasses. His long-haired wig touched the scarf he wore around his neck. Moe looked menacingly at Hans while taking a cigar from his coat pocket. He chewed the tip off the Cohiba and put it in his mouth.

"You made it sound like an emergency," Moe said. "Hope you didn't drag me here to tell me about the Middle East opportunity because it's too late, I'm already in on that deal. They're repeat customers."

"Yeah, and don't forget who got you those repeat customers," Hans said. "My reason for dragging you here today is not about the Middle East. I got something that will make all of our previous deals seem like child's play."

"I just sat down and you already have me pissed off, Hans. You're always exaggerating things, always trying to squeeze more money out of me. And as far as deals go, I've put plenty of big deals together, so don't fucking say they're child's play. I'll be the one to decide if you have a hot deal or not, so let's start again. What do you have for me?"

Hans ignored Moe's comments. The deal he was about to propose was too big to get sidetracked by personal insults.

"About two-and-a-half years ago, I conducted an audit on a geneticist that goes by the name of Captain. He's been working at the behest of former Nazis and neo-Nazis, friends of mine, in Berlin for most of his adult life. His handlers happen to be friends of mine.

The reason for the audit was because his handlers thought there was something fishy going on in the Captain's lab but couldn't figure out what it might be. So I was brought in," Hans said.

"Stop," Moe said. "You said *the behest*. Do you mean forced?"

"Yes, forced by former Nazis," Hans answered. Anyway. What I found out during my audit was that the Captain has been fooling his handlers since day one. He's been conducting secret research behind their backs. The only reason the Captain, a Gypsy, has been allowed to live this long is because of his work on some shit that allows women to have twins or triplets. Some shit like that.

"The Captain hated his neo-Nazi handlers, but he had no choice in the matter. Shortly after receiving his doctorate in genetics and biochemistry, he was awarded several prizes for his work in genetic engineering by the German government. The Captain became the talk of the town, the youngest scientist ever to receive such awards. The year was 1956, the year the Captain turned twenty-two years old. His parents had been victims of Hitler's atrocities. They were among the half-million Gypsies that were murdered at Auschwitz and other concentration camps. The Captain was only three years old when Josef Mengele joined the Nazi party, but he would learn everything there was to know about the Angel of Death by the time he was a celebrated geneticist. The Captain swore vengeance, but it was not until he met David Lorca that he discovered how he would serve it."

"So I guess it's adios Captain, now that you've uncovered his lies."

"No. I gave the Captain a clean bill of health, a clean audit."

"What?"

"I told his handlers that the Captain was clean. I told them that the Captain was starting to show signs of dementia, but other than that they had nothing to worry about. I suggested that if they still had doubts about his loyalty they should put him under surveillance. They took me up on my suggestion and hired me to oversee the Captain's every move. So I retired from my job as a German intelligence officer and now work for myself."

"I've been sitting here, being very patient, listening to this interesting story about a Gypsy geneticist. But what the hell does this have to do with me? I'm an arms dealer, remember?" Moe said.

"I know you're an arms dealer," Hans said. "I also know you like to make money and you don't care how you make it. We're two of a kind, Moe. We have no scruples. We go after any deal, no matter how dirty, as long as it makes us money."

"This deal of yours, is it the reason for the clean audit?"

"Yes," Hans answered.

"I'm game. Now tell me, how I can make money on this deal?" Moe asked.

"During my audit, I found a crumpled piece of paper in the Captain's trash can," Hans said. "I needed to get rid of my chewing gum, so I reached for it. I unfolded the piece of paper to place my gum, but was startled by what was written on the paper."

CHAPTER 22

Amsterdam, Netherlands
Hard Rock Cafe
January 17, 2007

Hans leaned across the table and handed Moe the crumpled piece of paper. It read. *Don't forget to download racist gene research data to flash drive and don't forget to delete data after download.*

"Don't forget to download racist gene research data to flash drive," Hans repeated in a whisper.

"Racist gene. Is this your idea of a joke?" Moe smirked.

"Laugh all you want, but the idea of a racist gene goes back a long time. But nobody, that is until now, has ever taken it seriously. Prominent geneticists have not ruled it out, but they have refused to research it for several reasons—one of which is that going after the racist gene is too political. It begs the question that racism is real, not a popular topic. Another reason for geneticists not going after the racist gene is the lack of funding for such a project. There's no money to be made by discovering the racist gene."

"A few minutes ago you said this is about money. Now you tell me there's no money to be made," Moe said. "Will you make up your mind?"

"I know you can figure out the money angle. Think hard; you'll get it," Hans said.

Hans knew Moe had friends in high places, citizens of the world, who profited from the very people David wanted to help. Hans also knew that there was no way to morally or ethically put up a fight

122   D. G. HERNÁNDEZ

in favor of racism once the gene was discovered. The discovery of the racist gene and its eventual elimination from people's DNA had become personal for Hans. The elimination of the racist gene would mean the end of his beloved Aryan Nation.

"While you're thinking, let me continue," Hans said. "So I sat on this information for these past two-and-a-half years while observing the Captain's every move. Including midnight runs to Potsdam. I'm positive he knows he's under surveillance, but he hasn't changed his routine. Anyway, I gave him enough time to continue his racist gene research in hopes that I could cash in on any discovery at a later date because I was positive he hadn't made it yet. The reason, only a hunch, that I doubted the racist gene had been discovered was because of the wording on his note. *Don't forget to download racist gene research data to flash drive.* The word *discovery* is nowhere to be found in the note. If I had made a discovery, especially one as important as this one, I would have used the word *discovery* as many times as possible.

But things suddenly changed. A CIA friend of mine told me that an American had contacted the Captain and scheduled a meeting in Granada, Spain. I panicked. I thought I had miscalculated and that the Captain was about to sell his discovery. I immediately went to Granada and waited for them. The Captain arrived in Granada as scheduled and checked into his hotel. I had my men hang out at the Granada airport to monitor all arrivals, especially from the U.S. They called me around nine in the evening and told me a private jet with no markings landed and stopped at the end of the runway. Without turning off its engines, the jet's door opened and its ladder dropped. A man in a suit walked out, ran along the tarmac, and headed toward a private hangar. Nothing happened for a few minutes, until suddenly a black Mercedes raced out of the hangar. My guys followed the Mercedes from a distance, where they observed the man being dropped off at a downtown restaurant. With so much secrecy—a jet with no markings and dropping off a passenger on the runway—I am positive that this is the American the Captain is meeting with. Are you listening to me?" Hans asked, noticing that Moe was looking out the large windows and down at the canal.

"I'm listening. But I was just wondering: If the neo-Nazis have such control over their geneticist, why is he allowed to leave the country?"

"Early in his career, the Captain was allowed to go visit relatives in Granada, but that turned out to be a hoax. He was actually going there to visit prostitutes. When his handlers found out the true nature of his visits, they just looked the other way. They decided it wasn't a threat, so they've let his visits to Granada continue to this day. Anyway, around midnight the American left the restaurant and took a taxi to the Sacromonte, the Gypsy section of Granada, up in the mountains. At this point, we have the American going up the mountain to Sacromonte but no sign of the Captain. The Captain never left the hotel."

"Are you shitting me? The Captain travels to Spain, an American is let off on the runway by a jet with no markings, but they never meet? Do you think they noticed they were being followed?"

"Hard to tell, but I doubt it because the American did meet with somebody," Hans said. "If the American even suspected he was being followed he would have aborted the meeting, but he didn't. The American definitely met with somebody, but I haven't been able to find out who he met with."

"How do you know he met with somebody?" Moe asked.

"I saw him get in a taxi and..."

"Did you follow him?"

"One of my men did."

"Well then, he should have seen who the American met with."

"What he describes is weird. He told me that the taxi came to a stop in front of an old abandoned nightclub, a cave. After that, he says he didn't see a thing because as soon as the taxi came to a halt in front of the abandoned cave, a sudden burst of light lit the whole fucking side of the mountain, like lightning during a thunderstorm. He said the lighting was so bright that it blinded him for a split second. He freaked out; he thought it was something from outer space because the lightening was not accompanied by thunder or rain. Hell, it was a clear night. He couldn't believe it, an explosion without sound.

"The scared fool rushed down the mountain, but then regained his courage. He pulled off the road and waited for them, knowing that sooner or later they would have to descend. After a few minutes, he saw the taxi coming down. He followed it for a while and noticed that the American was not inside. He pulled the cab over and inspected the taxi, and sure enough, the American was not inside. My guy pulled out his gun and told the cabbie he better talk. The cabbie said a man with a German accent was there to meet the American, but that's all he knows. The moment my guy radioed and told me this, I immediately sent up my men to flush them out of the cave. My men set off explosives by the cave's entrance, but nobody came out of the fucking cave."

"Are you stupid, Hans," Moe yelled.

People within hearing turned around when they heard Moe yell. The waiter rushed to their table. Moe smiled and reassured them that everything was fine, that they were just having a lively discussion.

"You set explosives; you let your target know he's being watched. How stupid is that? Jesus Christ, can't fucking believe you actually bombed the fucking cave. You're nothing but a spoiled kid that was raised among the blue bloods in London. You don't know shit about surveillance. You're always trying to be this super Nazi, always trying to prove yourself, especially to your deceased parents," Moe said, trying to keep his voice down.

"Leave my parents out of this."

"Well, tell me, what the fuck were you thinking when you set off the explosives?" Moe was so pissed off at Hans that he felt like punching him in the face.

"I was positive that the Captain was on the verge of selling the racist gene data. I waited two-and-a-half years to get my hands on the

Captain's discovery, I was not about to let it slip out of my hands. I was not about to let any fucking American beat me to it. That's why I did what I did," Hans said.

"That's bullshit. You know the real reason why you did what you did."

"I just told you why," Hans leaned in towards Moe. Hans tried to sound convincing, but he knew he wasn't fooling anybody.

"I want to hear the truth. I'm only going to ask one time and if I don't hear the truth I'm walking out of here." Moe's voice was level and cold.

"Ok, ok, it's just that I thought I could do it myself, you know, not have to bring you into the deal. I was wrong, ok? I fucked up. I should have come to you first."

"You fucked up, and now you want me to clean up your mess? Did you honestly think you could do this all by yourself? You leave me out of the deal, and now you want my help. Is that it?" Moe asked.

"I have to start looking out after myself. That's why I didn't come to you in the first place. I always give you valuable information that makes you millions, and I get shit compared to you. When do I get to make big money?" Hans asked.

"Well why don't you take your fucking valuable information elsewhere and see how far you get, you piece of shit."

"All I want is my fair share," Hans said.

"I'm a businessman, you asshole. I know the value of things. If it's as big a deal as you say, I'll take care of you. Now tell me, who was the American meeting with?"

"I already told you. Nobody came out of the cave. We had to leave because all kinds of cop cars started racing up the mountain. They must have heard the explosives," Hans answered.

"This deal sounds pretty fucked up. There're so many unknowns. Don't know if I want to get involved in this bullshit."

"This is not bullshit, and I'll tell you why," Hans said.

"No, my mind is made up. I'm leaving."

Hans reached across and grabbed Moe's forearm.

"Get your fucking hand off of me," Moe yanked his arm from under Hans' hand.

"You've got to listen to me. Two weeks ago, the Captain announced his retirement and told his handlers that in two months he was taking a job as an innkeeper at the Pines Inn."

"Are you talking about the most exclusive resort in Germany?" Moe asked.

"Yes, but do you really believe he's changing jobs to become an innkeeper? From distinguished geneticist to innkeeper? I don't think so. This is a bunch of shit; he's moving his research to a lab that's hidden below the inn."

"How do you know all this shit?"

"I have my sources."

"Interesting."

"That's why we have to strike now. Once he moves his lab to the Pines Inn, we'll never be able to get the racist gene data. It'll be impossible to break into a lab that sits underground."

Moe tried to hide his excitement at having learned about the racist gene. He knew exactly how to make money off the deal. Step one: he would contact his usual clients, the world's power brokers. Tell them of the racist gene's potential discovery and its implication. Moe's clients were smart enough to figure out that once the racist gene was discovered, its elimination would be the likely progression. Fighting the elimination of the racist gene would be futile. The gene's discovery had to be stopped now.

Moe was not stupid; he knew he couldn't guarantee his clients that the gene's discovery would never happen. This was a major problem for Moe. Nobody was going to pay him billions of dollars for a temporary fix. The more he thought about it, the more he was coming to the conclusion that this was not a good deal after all. Science is progressing at an exponential rate. If the gene is out there, it will be found with or without the American or the Captain.

The fearless Hans had always been afraid of Moe. He acted like a scared puppy whenever the two met. The only reason Hans kept coming back to Moe was because of the money. Moe paid top dollar for information and always paid on time. Hans knew other arms dealers, but they rarely paid on time. And when they did, they wanted to renegotiate the terms, something Moe never did.

Moe stopped listening to Hans; he was too busy putting a list of prospective clients together. Names of clients who would be all too happy to put billions of dollars in Moe's hands.

"This racist gene shit just might have some money-making potential," Moe said. "But goddammit, Hans, why are you so positive this operation is all about discovering the racist gene? Which I'm not convinced even exists," Moe demanded.

"Have you forgotten the note I just showed you? The Captain wrote it, reminding himself not to forget to download the racist gene data to the flash drive. It's so important that he wrote a note to remind himself. Plus there's the underground lab. What kind of research requires such secrecy? Even multibillion-dollar pharmaceutical companies have physical addresses, but not the Captain's lab.

"Come on, Moe," Hans continued. "Don't you get it? Because I do, and this is what I need. I need to put a team together that will help me break into the Captain's lab and steal any and all racist gene data. Once we get the data, we can sell it for a shit load of money."

"We need to do more than steal the data. We also have to destroy the fucking lab and everybody in it. Including the American and his geneticist. Nobody is going to pay us when there's a possibility those Bozos will try doing the same thing all over again," Moe added.

"I'll do whatever you say."

"Do you think you can pull it off?" Moe asked.

"Damn right I can. But we have to do it now, before they sell the data themselves."

"How much will this escapade cost me?"

"Maybe... half a million euros," Hans answered. "This mission is complicated; it's full of risks, Moe. They have all kinds of security. For sure I'll need a helicopter, which I'll have to buy on the black market. This operation is pretty chancy, Moe. People can and probably will get killed."

"Don't make a move until I tell you. I have to line up my buyers."

"I won't make a move until I get the half million euros."

CHAPTER 23

San Antonio, Texas
June 10, 2009
5:30 AM

The Gulfstream V came to a halt inside a private hangar at the San Antonio International Airport after an all-night flight from London. Catherine and David had not slept much during the flight; they had been too busy going over last minute details for David's stealth entry into Mexico.

"Welcome to San Antonio," Brent spoke into his headset's microphone. "San Antonio has been having great weather, hot and dry. Sun should be coming up in about an hour."

"Funny," David said as he looked over at Catherine and smiled.

"Brent does have a way with words," she told David. The thirty-two-year-old French woman was accompanying David to San Antonio, her first visit to Texas. Catherine tried hiding her apprehension, but she wasn't having much success.

"Ok, let's review one more time," David told Catherine as they waited for the customs officials to arrive at the hangar.

"I take the Number 68 bus from downtown to the *barrio*," David started to recite his clandestine trip's details. "I get off the bus on the corner of Guadalupe and Calaveras Streets. Once I get off the bus, I should easily blend into the *barrio*. If I'm being tailed by anybody other than a Mexican, he will immediately stand out and I will instantly switch to plan B, which is to return to downtown San Antonio. If not, I continue with plan A. I walk west on Guadalupe and take a right on

Zarzamora Street. I head north on Zarzamora Street to a Bill Miller Bar-B-Q Restaurant on the corner of Commerce and Zarzamora Streets. In the parking lot, I'll find a white Volkswagen Jetta with its key taped to the underside of the left windshield wiper. I get in the car and drive to Uvalde, Texas. Did I get it right?"

"Yes, perfect," Catherine said. "But I still don't understand why it has to be him. Why Warren? I know the Captain needs the best encryption expert in the world, but I'm sure there are others besides Warren. There has to be somebody just as capable, somebody who's not hiding in Mexico."

"He's not hiding in Mexico. That just happens to be where he lives."

"I helped you plan this trip, David, and we both know that a lot of things can go wrong. And to top it off, you'll be traveling during a full moon; you'll be visible a mile away in that barren desert. I know I keep repeating myself, but I'm really worried about this...this clandestine operation. This whole thing could blow up in your face; you could wind up in prison, David. In a Mexican prison."

"We're already here, Catherine. We're only 150 miles from the border, and I need to at least meet Warren. I don't know if it's because the Captain believes in him, but I'm positive he's our man. There's no North Korean, Russian, Chinese, or Ukrainian hacker that comes close to Warren. But if I get bad vibes, I'll thank him and get back here as quickly as possible," David said.

"I just don't want anything to happen to you, David."

"Nothing is going to happen to me. I know my way around."

"Why are you being so stubborn, David? Is this trip really about Warren, or is it about your ex-wife? You could have flown directly into Mexico. Why did we have to fly into San Antonio? Is this why we're here, so you can see her?"

"I can't believe you just said that. You of all people should know that it's not about my ex-wife. I wouldn't have divorced her if I still loved her."

"Then why do you sometimes call out her name in the middle of the night? Heaven knows what you're dreaming about when you call out her name. How would you like it if I called out my husband's name during my sleep?" Catherine asked.

"At least I'm divorced. All I ever hear from you is that your divorce is right around the corner, that it should be finalized soon. It's always soon, there's always just one more document to sign, but your divorce never happens."

Catherine's substantial fortune was one of the largest in Europe. The French citizen and descendant of European royalty inherited vast land holdings in Hong Kong, Belgium, and South Africa at the tender age of twenty-six. The inheritance made her one of the few billionaire women in the world. However, her wealth made her the target of unscrupulous men, including her estranged husband. He was receiving a hundred-thousand-dollar-a-month allowance from Catherine during the divorce proceedings. He was in no hurry to finalize their divorce.

David met Catherine on his yacht while hosting a dinner party for the winner of the Monaco Grand Prix. David's post-race parties had become a tradition among the racing elite. As usual, the excitement of the just-completed race always spilled onto David's yacht within minutes of the checkered flag. The winning Formula One driver, his entourage, and other celebrities clambered aboard the mega yacht, all too anxious to start the celebration.

David welcomed his guests and turned the microphone over to the winning driver. After a few banal words, the driver started showering the crowd with champagne. All roared with laughter, not concerned about being soaked with the bubbly. David noticed the attractive and beautiful Catherine as she tried to avoid the spewing Champagne. David ran toward the helpless woman, grabbed her hand and whisked her up to the flybridge. David was at her side the rest of the afternoon and into the evening.

It didn't take long for David and Catherine to start dating and vacationing together. Neither of them had any inkling that their sexual attraction would evolve to love. The strong-willed Catherine filed for divorce from her husband within months of having met David.

"We've had this conversation before, and we know how it always ends, so let's not go there. We're here; we need to stay focused," David said.

Riding in a limousine, David and Catherine headed south into downtown San Antonio on Highway 281. Catherine looked out to her right as they drove past Trinity University.

"I'm sorry, David. I'm sorry I brought up your ex-wife. I know better. You've never given me a reason to question you."

"We're under a lot of stress, Catherine. You don't need to apologize."

"Stress is no excuse."

"I have an idea, let just change the subject. Now's not the time for distractions."

"Good idea." Catherine immediately took David up on his offer. "I've been going over every detail of your trip. But there's one thing we haven't covered."

"What's that?"

"Do you have any idea why Warren decided to make his home in Ciudad Acuña? Are we missing something. Are we overlooking something? Could it be that you're walking into a trap?"

"No way. Like I told you earlier, that's his home. He's been living there since way before I ever thought of contacting him. Maybe he likes living in solitude, alone where he can do his thing in peace. But I really have no clue. But it does remind me of a quack that used to live in the same area. Actually, the quack lived in the city, the former Villa Acuña, now named Ciudad Acuña. Dr. Brinkley, the quack's name, was banned from the radio broadcast business in the United States because of false advertising. Obviously he was not a real medical doctor; he bought his degree. I guess there were college mills back then, just like today. Anyway, he took to broadcasting from across the border, to avoid any regulations. He advertised that he could cure impotency by implanting goat testicles into impotent males. He was the quintessential charlatan. Maybe there's something symbolic to Warren making his home in the same area as Dr. Brinkley."

"That doesn't make sense," Catherine said. "Warren's no charlatan. He goes after the bad guys, remember?"

"Whatever the reason, it must be good because I would never want to live there. Many years ago, I lived in Barksdale, a small unincorporated area, just north of Uvalde. Several times I traveled past Del Rio and into Ciudad Acuña, and let me tell you, it is awful. Nothing but wastelands," David said as they arrived at the Hilton Hotel.

Catherine opened their room's curtains after having settled in and stared at the San Antonio River far below.

"This is a two-day operation. I'll be back before you know it," David said as he hugged her. "But in the meantime, be very careful. I don't want you to open the door for anybody, and don't answer the hotel phone. If I need to get a hold of you, I'll call you on your satellite phone. And don't forget; don't call me unless it's an emergency. I've also arranged for room service. Only two people are authorized to respond to any of your requests. Their names are Sylvia and Eva. I took their pictures; I'll email them to you. Make sure you can see their faces through the peephole before letting them in. Promise me you'll be careful, Catherine. Don't let anything happen to you; don't leave the room for any reason."

"You don't have to worry about me. You're the one who's placing yourself in danger."

"I'm sorry for putting you in this situation, for placing you in this hell. But you're the only one I can trust. You have to believe me; I never wanted to get you involved."

"I want to be involved, don't you get it? I want to be relevant in your life, David. That means getting involved in every aspect of your life and not just the glamorous life aboard your yacht. I want all of you, and if that means placing myself in danger, then so be it. I'm not a little girl, David. I knew what I was getting into the moment I...the moment I..."

"Stop, Catherine. Leave it alone, at least for now."

"Please, David, don't let anything happen to you." She reached up and kissed him.

"I won't."

CHAPTER 24

David drove to Uvalde Texas to meet the coyote. He exited Highway 90 West and drove north on Getty Street to the assigned meeting location, a Mexican taco restaurant. The nondescript taco joint's wall clock confirmed that David was running on schedule; it was eight o'clock in the evening. He walked into the restaurant wearing clothes that were very foreign to him and his usual wardrobe. His cowboy hat was slightly tilted to one side and showed years of use, including sweat stains. Faded denim pants with a tucked-in cowboy shirt completed his disguise. David made sure the secondhand boots were comfortable before buying them at the local Goodwill Store in downtown San Antonio. The store's employees stared at the newly transformed man as he exited the fitting room. The pants were loose so he added a belt with a large cowboy buckle to his purchase. The Goodwill Store manager thanked David for the donation of his expensive designer clothes he left behind in the fitting room.

David looked around the empty taco restaurant for a few seconds before proceeding to a small table by the front window. In keeping with local custom, David didn't remove his hat as he entered the restaurant.

David ordered coffee and a potato-and-egg taco.

"More coffee?" The waitress asked long after David's cup had gone empty.

"No. No thank you."

"We'll be closing in ten minutes. You sure you don't want anything else?" The waitress asked again as she laid the bill on the table.

"No, *es todo*."

David looked at his watch; it was almost nine and still no sign of the coyote. He had been told that the coyote was a muscular six-foot-four-inch Hispanic male that went by the name of Miguel. That's all he knew about the man. No recent pictures of the coyote existed. The waitress walked towards the door and reversed the open sign. The black sign with red letters now read *closed*. David looked at his watch. It was nine o'clock. The door opened and in walked an imposing Hispanic male. He appeared to be in his mid-fifties, with a gray mustache and a cowboy hat over his shoulder-length hair.

"We're closed," the waitress told him as he approached the serving counter.

"All I need is coffee."

"*No le hace*, we're closed," she insisted.

"You're going to throw that coffee away," the man told the waitress as he pointed at the half-full glass decanter. "Here." He threw a ten-dollar bill down on the counter. "Keep the change; just give me a cup of coffee to go."

"*Sigueme*," Miguel called out to David as he walked out the front door.

David immediately rose from his table and followed him outside to the rear of the restaurant. It was dark, but David could see an old pickup truck parked by an overflowing trash dumpster. The driver's side door opened and burly man stepped out. He handed the keys to Miguel and walked away.

"Get in," Miguel instructed David.

David walked around to the passenger side of the pickup and opened the door. On the seat was a Glock 42. David grabbed the holstered gun and tucked it into his pants at the narrow of his back. With the pickup's lights turned off, they drove down a narrow alley for two blocks. After a couple of turns, they were on Getty Street, heading towards Highway 90 West. Once on Hwy 90 West they drove for half an hour before taking the Bracketville exit and onto Ranch Road 693.

Miguel pulled off the deserted road and brought the pickup truck to a complete stop. With its lights and engine turned off, both men sat in complete darkness. Within minutes, a pair of headlights appeared in the distance, about two miles away. Neither of the men said a word as they watched the lights get closer and brighter.

"Get out," Miguel said.

David could now see that the approaching lights belonged to a large pickup truck with sidelights, bringing the black gooseneck horse trailer it was towing into sight. The truck stopped on the opposite side of the road, but its loud diesel engine kept running. The driver, a Mexican with a straw cowboy hat, got out of the truck and walked to the rear of the two-horse trailer. He threw open the squeaky metal doors and led out two black quarter horses. He saddled them and handed the reins to Miguel.

After inspecting the horses and the saddles, Miguel handed the Mexican driver a canvas satchel. He opened it, counted the bundles of one-hundred-dollar bills, and put them back into the satchel. Without saying a word, both men tipped their hats and walked away. David and Miguel got their backpacks from the bed of their pickup and mounted the horses. Both men were surprised as a woman exited the Mexican's pickup, walked towards Miguel's truck, started it, and drove away.

"Are you good on a horse?" Miguel asked David as he handed him the reins to his horse.

"We'll soon find out. But in the meantime, you might want to put these on as we head into the dark desert." David handed Miguel a pair of what appeared to be ordinary sunglasses.

"Don't need them. Brought my own sunglasses," Miguel said.

"These aren't sunglasses. Put them on and tell me what you think," David said.

"Holy shit!" Miguel shouted out as the dark desert suddenly came to light.

One of David's companies had recently developed the most sophisticated night vision lenses ever. David called the ordinary-looking night vision glasses Chupacabras after the urban legend. He claimed that the nanotechnology incorporated into the night vision glasses enabled him to see the legendary blood-sucking creature. But on a more serious note, he loved the science behind the night vision glasses. The emerging field of nanotechnology enabled the miniaturization of the former bulky and cumbersome night vision goggles. David made sure that his glasses were never referred to as night vision goggles.

"Told you they're not sunglasses. I call them my Chupacabras. The nanotechnology that's incorporated into my glasses allows me to see Chupacabras in complete darkness."

"I don't know too much about you, David. But you sound like an interesting person. I mean, I've never heard anybody use the words *nanotechnology* and *Chupacabras* in the same sentence."

They rode for a short distance before leaving the road and proceeding into the vast darkness, the full moon hidden behind thick clouds. David followed Miguel, safely staying two horse lengths behind. David remembered a friend of his, a Vietnam War Veteran friend, telling him to never stay too close to the point man; snipers always take them out first.

Getting into Mexico before daybreak was imperative. Both men were well aware that the remaining forty-mile trek was the most treacherous. Their tight schedule was dependent on good horses. Fortunately, the obedient horses' brisk pace and stamina were proving their quality breeding.

The clouds were starting to break, and the full moon was now starting to shine brightly. After a few minutes, the clouds disappeared and the moon was in full view. The dark desert night was gone. The men were now fully exposed and could now be seen from miles away.

In spite of the full moon, both men decided to keep their night vision glasses on.

David's horse suddenly bucked at the sound of a rattler. Unable to keep its balance, the horse fell on its side, landing on David's leg. The rattlesnake leaped into the air, striking the fallen horse on the neck. The horse tried getting up, but it was no use. He had a compound fracture on his left hind leg. Miguel pulled hard on the left rein, turning the horse around and back towards David

"Where's the snake? Can you see it?" Miguel yelled out as he tried to keep his horse under control.

"I can't see shit," David yelled back.

"Shish, quiet... don't move. I hear something," Miguel whispered. Then suddenly Miguel yelled out, "Behind You.".

David didn't have time to react. A mountain lion sprang from the darkness and lunged at David, straight for his neck. It missed its target, but the impact knocked David to the ground. The mountain lion pounced as the helpless David lay on his back. David grabbed the attacking lion's throat but couldn't protect himself from the vicious claws. The lion escaped David's grip, roared, and was about to dig into David's throat when a loud shot rang out. Blood splattered on David as the dead animal fell on top of him. Miguel quickly turned off his flashlight and ran towards David with his gun pointing at the lifeless animal.

"You could have killed me," David said as he tried getting up from under the dead lion.

"Would you have preferred the mountain lion killing you? Get up. Let me take a look at you. Any bites?" Miguel asked as he helped David to his feet.

"No, I don't think so," David said.

"If he bit you and was rabid or carrying rabies, you're in deep shit, my friend."

Miguel searched David's body for any signs of bites. There weren't any. All he saw were bleeding scratches, deep scratches.

"No bites. That's good," Miguel said, "but I need to take care of those scratches."

Miguel reached into his backpack and pulled out a first aid kit.

"Is that a syringe in your hand?" David asked.

"Yes, now pull your pants down," Miguel told David.

"Damn it, Miguel, I hate shots. Do you have to?"

"Yep. Now wash those scratches real good with this peroxide and then spray them with the Neosporin. Hope they don't get infected. Those cats carry a lot of bad shit on their claws," Miguel said as he handed him the aerosol can and a bottle of hydrogen peroxide.

"Wish we could have saved the horse," David said.

"Me too. It was no fun shooting such a beautiful animal."

"Where's your horse?" David suddenly asked.

"Fucking ran off. Got spooked by the mountain lion."

"Are you shitting me? There's no way we're going to make it to the border before daybreak without at least one horse. Fuck!" David yelled out in frustration. "I can't believe our luck. First a rattlesnake and then a mountain lion. What are the odds?"

"Long odds," Miguel half smiled.

"No time for jokes. Think hard, Miguel. How can we make it to Mexico before daybreak?"

"I don't have to think very hard. There's no way."

"That's not an option."

"You hired me to get you into Mexico, and that's what I intend to do, so listen. We passed a canyon about two miles back. We need to get our asses back there as quickly as possible and hide there till midnight at which time we'll try this again."

"Are you crazy? That's not for another twenty hours. I don't have a day to lose. Do you hear me? You got to do your job and get me into Mexico now." David paced around the dead horse.

David and Miguel made it back to the canyon and found a hiding place below an outcrop, hoping it would provide enough cover from the eyes of roaming border patrol agents.

"I can't believe we're here wasting a full day, a day I don't have," David said as he took out his satellite phone to give Catherine the bad news.

"You know something, David? While you were on the phone, I was thinking. A rattlesnake causes your horse to buck and fall down on your leg, which could have led to its amputation or at least maimed you for the rest of your life. You're attacked by a mountain lion that could have easily broken your neck had he not missed. But instead of counting your blessings, you stand there complaining about wasting one fucking day of your life. From where I stand, losing one day sounds pretty compared to the alternative. Consider yourself lucky, my friend."

"Hope our luck holds out," David said sarcastically.

"Here," Miguel handed David an energy bar. "Have something to eat."

"Thanks."

"Sit down. Save your energy. You'll need it when we head out tomorrow night," Miguel told David.

"I'd rather stand. Don't want to get bitten by snakes," David said.

"I've seen rattlers jump ten feet into the air, so unless you're floating ten feet off the ground, standing won't keep you safe. Forgot you city boys don't know much about how to survive out here. And I suppose you also don't know that the snakes are now in hiding, hiding in a cool crevasse. Maybe in that crevasse above your head," Miguel told David.

David jumped from under the small outcrop that stood two feet above him. The alarmed David suddenly smiled when he realized Miguel was having a good laugh at his expense.

"Are you sure about what you said, about the snakes?" David asked, wanting to know if Miguel was kidding or not.

"*Estoy seguro*," Miguel smiled.

Though it was only two in the afternoon, the men's hideout was becoming very uncomfortable. Temperatures were already above one hundred degrees Fahrenheit. Birds flew high above the small canyon. Some noticed the men and flew in for a closer look at the intruders. Ants and scorpions went about their business without the slightest interest in the two men. David refused to let his guard down throughout the day, reacting to every sound and moving object.

"Have you been a coyote for a long time?" David finally broke their hours of silence.

"Long enough."

"You don't say much, do you? Are you always this quiet?"

"You didn't hire me to talk."

"True."

Miguel sat with his gun at his side, the brim of his hat shading his wide-open eyes. No time to take to take a nap. He was on the job.

"Why are you paying me so much money to smuggle you into Mexico?"

"Some things are better left unsaid, and this is one of those things, Miguel."

"Good enough for me."

"Heard you were once a Border Patrol agent. What made you change sides?"

"Like you said, some things are better left unsaid," Miguel answered. "Now be quiet and let me think because I'm still trying to figure out why an American is paying me so much money to get smuggled into Mexico. You don't look or talk like a criminal. Anyway, it should be a lot easier getting you into Mexico than getting you back to Uvalde."

"Have you ever lost human cargo?" David asked.

"Hell, no. I've never lost anybody."

Miguel stood up. Something about David's question caused him to become agitated. With squinted eyes, he looked out into the desert. He stepped out of their hiding place for a few minutes before returning.

"I saw several people last night. They were *narco traficantes*, well-organized drug traffickers."

"I didn't see anybody."

"You don't know how to look. They saw us just before the rattle-snake and mountain lion incident, when we still had our horses. They were probably wondering why we were headed south," Miguel said.

"I wish you would have pointed them out to me."

"What for? I'm your coyote. I'm the only one that needs to be on the lookout."

"Why didn't they come after us?" David asked.

"Why should they? We're no threat to them. We're not law enforcement officials. Their job last night was to transport drugs and nothing else," Miguel answered.

"Wonder if they made it. I mean, got the drugs to their destination."

"I'm sure the *mulas*, drug couriers, made it," Miguel said.

"Yes, I know what *mulas* are."

"The *mulas* looked like they were on schedule. They were about eight miles from the highway when I saw them. The exchange of the drugs and money usually takes place somewhere within a mile or two of the highway. The *mulas* deliver the drugs to the American couriers and return to Mexico before daylight. By now, if my timing is correct, the drugs are somewhere between Waco and Dallas."

"Appears you know a lot of what goes on around here," David said. "Does it bother you to see all of these drugs going into the U.S.?"

"Not as much as what goes on with human cargo. I've seen many dead and decaying bodies out here. Thousands of nameless people have died on their journey into the United States. I'll never forget the first time I came across human remains. I started throwing up. Wild animals were feasting on a dead man's body. They didn't deserve to die; they didn't want to die. They wanted to live, to live a better life in the U.S. They were in search of jobs, good-paying jobs so they could support their families back home. They lost their lives in search of a job and not handouts as so many politicians would want you to believe.

"Many have made it across the border only to die at the hands of the coyotes that smuggled them into the U.S. When they find themselves in danger of being caught, those cowardly criminals flee and abandon their human cargo locked in vans, left to suffocate in the blistering heat of summer with no means of escape.

"Women are especially vulnerable when crossing the border, the constant threat of rape by their coyotes," Miguel continued. "The sex trafficking is deplorable. Young girls being forced into prostitution. You asked why I left law enforcement and changed sides. I'll tell you why. I have two young daughters and I swore that as long as I was alive I would never allow sex traffickers to exist. I've never killed any of the sex traffickers. I just tie them up and call the Border Patrol. If the U.S. wants to eliminate sex trafficking, then legalizing prostitution would be a good first step. In the meantime, I'm going to continue my one-man battle against sex trafficking."

Night finally arrived, and both men headed toward Mexico once again. This time they were successful, arriving safely and without complications at the border.

"Thanks for getting me this far, and thanks for telling me why you do what you do. Sounds like you're a good guy, Miguel. Sounds like you like helping people."

"Guess so. I'm helping you."

"Yes, you are, Miguel. More than you'll ever realize. I'll see you on the flipside," David said as he started his lone trek into Mexico.

Miguel stayed on the U.S side of the border. His job while waiting for David's return was to find a safe location for David to cross back into the U.S.

CHAPTER 25

David walked into the dilapidated garage after an all-night walk that started with a short swim into Mexico. The lone mechanic was busy repairing a flat tire in the first of the four bays. From the most distant bay, the mechanic glanced up and saw David walking toward the garage but didn't acknowledge him. The ringing telephone didn't fare any better in getting the mechanic's attention. David nervously stood by the garage's front door and waited. As David started to leave, the mechanic yelled out and asked him to wait, that he would be with him in a few minutes. The mechanic lazily rolled the fixed tire towards a car whose front end was being held up by a floor jack.

"*Que onda? Que necesitas?*" The mechanic asked, wiping his hands on a rag, not bothering to look at David. David didn't answer the stranger. "Where in the hell is my contact?" David kept asking himself. He couldn't decide whether to answer the mechanic. "Is this the guy that has a motorcycle waiting for me?" David wondered.

"Are you the *Americano* that was supposed to be here yesterday?" the mechanic asked in English.

David was now positive that he was being set up. The mechanic before him hadn't uttered the password. David walked backwards, refusing to take his eyes off the mechanic.

"What's the matter, did you lose your tongue. Why don't you answer? Are you the *pocho* that was supposed to arrive here yesterday?"

the mechanic asked again as he continued wiping his hands with a shop towel.

"Yeah, yeah, that's me," David happily answered. The mechanic had uttered the password, *pocho.*

"You're late, man, a whole day late. I had to come in on my day off just to make sure I was here in case you made it. I thought something happened to you and the deal was off."

The mechanic finished cleaning his hands and finally looked up at David.

"Holy shit, something did happen to you. Look at you, man. Is that blood all over your shirt? Go wash up in the back and I'll get you one of my shirts. If the police see you in that shirt you'll be in a heap of trouble. Man, looks like you were in a knife fight and lost."

David walked to the rear of the garage and thoroughly washed off any evidence of blood. He cleaned his wounds, re-bandaged them, and slipped into a clean but oil-stained shirt.

"Here you go," the mechanic said as he pushed the motorcycle out of the garage. "It doesn't look like much, but it'll go."

Catherine had made sure David memorized the directions to Warren's house; Miguel would not be around to guide him. Getting to Warren's house was proving difficult since many of the landmarks that he had been told to use as guides were not very evident. Take a right when you see an old house with an old wood shack in the back. Shit, every other house fits that description, David told himself as he drove down deserted dirt roads.

After a while, he was just guessing as to which way to proceed. The one landmark David thought would be totally useless turned out to be the most valuable. He was about to make a U-turn and try another road when he saw the tractor. Catherine told him that he was to get off the road and head directly toward an abandoned tractor in the middle of a pasture. A motorcycle instead of a car now made perfect sense to David. The native grass was knee high but still manageable. From where the tractor stood, he could see the arroyo he was to follow the rest of the way. It led straight to Warren's rusty and abandoned-looking mobile home.

"Anybody home?" David asked as he knocked on the torn screen door that was not capable of keeping bugs from entering at will.

"Come in," Warren yelled out.

David opened the door and cautiously entered. He took two steps into the mobile home and stopped. Warren, with a lit cigarette hanging from his mouth, was busy on one of several computers that sat on a long table in the middle of the mobile home. The lanky computer genius's long hair almost touched the keyboard as he typed at lighting speed. The sparse mobile home was nothing more than one big room, no interior partitions, not even a restroom. Behind the row of computers was a futon with two pillows and a blanket. Electrical extension cords were strewn all over the floor in a messy array but all came together in an orderly manner before exiting the mobile home through one of the windows. The extension cords were all plugged into a noisy propane generator at the rear of the mobile home.

"Have you always lived such a Spartan lifestyle?" David asked.

Warren was too busy on the computer to answer David. Actually, he was now busy on three different computers, rolling on his desk chair from computer to computer.

"Jesus Christ, was there a sale on band-aids?" Warren stared at David. "You must have over a hundred of them all over your arms. Are you ok?"

"Other than being in the brush for two nights and doing battle with a mountain lion, I'm perfectly fine. Anyway, I'm David."

"Yeah, right. I'm Warren. Elena told me you were coming."

"Not hard to believe you ran into a mountain lion. I see them around here quite often. But I'm surprised it attacked you," Warren said.

"Trust me, this one attacked."

"Hope it didn't have rabies."

"If you see me foaming at the mouth in three weeks you'll have your answer. Just kidding, I'll be ok; it didn't bite me."

"Never know. Let's hope your mouth stays dry. Anyway, what can I do for you? Elena told me you were coming but didn't provide me with any details. Said she wasn't privy to them."

"I need you to come work for me," David said abruptly.

"You certainly don't waste time on small talk."

"Don't have time to waste. I'm already a day behind schedule, so let's cut to the chase. I need you to develop encryption software, employing the best quantum mechanics has to offer and combining it with your talents. And while you're at it, I also want you to develop algorithms that will help me with my computer modeling of future social trends. I'll give you a hint: my computer modeling has to do with race relations."

"Why me?" Warren asked.

"Because the Captain wants you on our team. You do know the Captain, don't you? I'm sure you remember hacking into his computers. He thinks highly of you, and so do I. The Captain will be conducting very sensitive and highly classified research. Only a few people in the world will be aware of our research; you'll be one of them. Other than the algorithms and encrypting the Captain's research on a daily basis, I also want you to make our computers hacker-proof. Heard you know a thing or two about hacking."

"I've heard the term," Warren said.

"Well, will you come work for me?"

"Whoa, let's slow things down a bit, shall we? I don't even know you. I mean, I know a lot of things about you but not you the person. I'd like to get to know you before going any further. Plus I don't need a job, much less a boss."

"You'll be your own boss. I just told you what I need from you, and that's it. There's nobody in the world that can direct you or your work because what you'll be working on doesn't exist. Sure, there'll be deadlines, but you look like the kind of person that always gets things done ahead of schedule. The Captain said I can trust you, and that's all I need to know."

"What else?" Warren asked. "What else can you tell me about the job?"

"That your life will never be the same. This is not about a job, Warren. This is about you being part of a dream, a dream of mine. My jet is in San Antonio; we leave in two days. If you decide to accept my offer, be there. Go to the Southwest Airlines curbside check-in and wait for me to pick you up and take you to my private hangar. Two days from today at ten in the morning."

"Let's go outside; let's go for a walk," Warren said.

"Do I look like I need to go for a walk?" David smiled.

David followed Warren. They walked around to the rear of the mobile home and sat on the tailgate of Warren's pickup truck.

"Haven't been out this way in a long time. Way before I got married," David said.

"How long have you been married?" Warren asked as he lit a cigarette.

"Recently divorced."

"It was pretty gutsy, you know, crossing into Mexico illegally. Hope your return trip is less eventful. Stay away from mountain lions," Warren laughed.

"Mind if I ask you something?" David asked.

"No, go ahead."

"Why do you live out here? Why this desolate place?"

CHAPTER 26

"It's a long story, and I know you have to get going," Warren said. "It doesn't matter. I'm already a day behind schedule. So go ahead, I'd love to hear why you live out here."

"It's really not a long story. I guess I just say that when I don't want to talk about things. Some things I like to keep to myself."

"Sounds just like me, I use the same phrase. 'It's a long story,' I tell them when I don't want to answer."

"We fell in love with the area, living out here in this desolate place was our dream. Luke's and mine," Warren started.

"Who's Luke?"

"Luke was my partner. He was murdered almost two years ago."

"Sorry to hear that," David interrupted Warren.

"Luke and I had always dreamed of coming down here, to settle down," Warren continued. "We had visited several areas in Mexico, but we liked the proximity to the border. You know, being able to drive to San Antonio and Austin. Especially Austin; it was Luke's favorite city in the whole world. We had so much fun there, getting drunk and partying on Sixth Street with many of our friends. They knew how much Luke and I loved each other. They told us we were going to live the rest of our lives together, that we were going to grow old together. That's all we wanted."

"How did it happen, the murder?" David asked.

"I'll get to that in a second, but first let me tell you a little about

Luke and me. Not often I get to tell our story. Don't get many visitors out here."

"Love to hear it."

"Luke was from Alabama, from Mobile. Luke's father worked in the shipyards and his mother was an elementary school teacher. They were so proud of Luke when he was accepted at MIT. Especially since it was in Boston, their home before having moved to Alabama. This is where Luke and I met, at MIT. I was just a kid then. I was sixteen and he was eighteen. That was ten years ago."

"You look a lot younger than twenty-six."

"Thanks. I guess looking younger is better than the alternative. Anyway, Luke and I were on our way here when he was murdered. What you saw inside the mobile home is exactly the way it was when Luke last saw it. We had all kinds of plans. First we were going to build a house up on the hill, close to the tractor you used for navigation purposes. Then we were going to become self-sufficient by growing all of our food, including raising chickens and goats. I love roses and Luke promised me the most beautiful rose garden in the world. The list goes on and on, but the sad part is that we never had a chance to start our dream together because of what happened.

"We were planning on leaving Mobile early in the morning, but we just lollygagged. We were having a difficult time saying our good-byes. It was noon before we loaded the last suitcase and hit the road. We were so happy—not a worry in the world. Luke's parents gave us a going-away party. They invited so many of their friends. It was a special day. Luke's parents had finally accepted us as a couple.

"As we got close to Houston, Luke decided to take a detour to Austin to visit friends. So we got on Highway 290 and headed west. We didn't hang out in Austin very long—just a quick visit to tell our friends about our plans—plus it was getting late. We were driving south on Interstate Highway 35 when Luke told me he needed to take a leak, so I exited the highway and pulled into a rest station. We got out of the car and headed to the restroom. Luke and I were holding hands as we made our way.

"'Hey fags, you wanna have a good time?' We turned around and saw three guys running towards us. We didn't have time to react. It wouldn't have done any good. Two of them had baseball bats. I don't want to say any more, other than that they killed Luke and almost killed me. I lay unconscious in the intensive care unit at the Baptist Hospital in San Antonio for several days," Warren said.

David couldn't get himself to say a word. He knew there was nothing to say.

"Don't look so gloomy. I'm taking you up on your offer. I'll see you in two days," Warren told David as they walked toward the motorcycle.

"You won't regret it," David yelled as he rode off. "Get ready to live the dream!"

CHAPTER 27

"My god! What happened?" Catherine asked David as he slowly walked into the hotel room.

"When you called me, you made it sound like it was nothing, but look at those scratches. You need a doctor." Catherine looked over David's shoulder as he took the bandages off his arms and chest.

"All I need is a long hot bath and a comfortable bed."

"Aren't you going to tell me what happened?" Catherine asked.

"Yes, of course. Warren is going to join our team. Just like I told you. We're not going back empty-handed."

"I'm talking about those scratches," Catherine said.

"I was attacked by a mountain lion the first night out, miles before we reached the Mexican border. A doctor won't be necessary. Miguel gave me some antibiotics and gave me a shot on my ass. I'm not trying to be short with you, Catherine. It's just that I haven't slept for days. I'm in no mood to go into details. Please forgive my rudeness."

"I'll never believe anything you tell me over the phone, David. What you just told me is a far cry from having been bucked off by your horse when it got spooked by a rattlesnake."

David slept for several hours before waking up and finding himself in a large and comfortable bed.

"Are you ready for me to give you a tour of San Antonio?" David asked as he joined Catherine. "But before we do that, I need to grab a bite to eat. I'm famished."

"I was wondering if you were ever going to eat," Catherine said. "You told me you were hungry, but by the time I called room service you were already asleep. I've never seen a sober person pass out so fast."

"Did I snore?"

"Yes, you always do."

"You should have poked me or whatever to make me stop."

"Why? It's the middle of the day. Anyway, I couldn't hear your snoring because I was out on the balcony reading *The Old Man and the Sea*. The only time I heard your snoring was when I came in to get a glass of iced tea."

"That's right. Forgot it's the middle of the day. My sleeping pattern is totally out of whack."

"The San Antonio River is quite an attraction. While you were gone, I sat out on the balcony and watched people walk up and down the river walk all day long. The steady stream of tourists never stopped. Do the restaurants down there serve good food, or would you say it's too touristy?"

"Everything sounds good right now. But I'll defer to you. What do you feel like eating?"

"Mexican food of course," Catherine immediately answered. "But I want the real stuff. I want what the locals eat."

"Are you sure? Have you ever had real Mexican food?"

"Probably not. And that's why I'm counting on you," Catherine smiled.

"I was going to take you to the Alamo, to the River Walk, to the Mercado, and grab a bite to eat along the way. But you just gave me a terrific idea when you said *the real stuff*." David smiled back.

"And what would that idea be, Mr. Lorca?"

"It's a surprise. Can't tell you, Ms. Dubois," David said as they exited their room.

David drove west on Commerce Street and took a left onto Colorado Street.

"That's the high school I went to." David pointed out Sidney

Lanier High School to Catherine as they passed it. He took a right turn onto Guadalupe Street.

"I can't believe the bellboy let you borrow his car," Catherine said.

"First of all, he's making money on the deal, and secondly, I had to borrow it because taking a cab to where I'm taking you would look very conspicuous," David said.

"Can hardly wait to get to wherever you're taking me."

"Have you ever had a puffy taco?" David asked.

"What is a puffy taco?" Catherine asked. "Is this a joke, like a *knock, knock, who's there*, joke?"

"No joke," David laughed. "The shell of the taco is made of corn dough, or *masa de maíz* in Spanish. When it's deep fried, it expands, makes it puffy, hence the name, puffy taco."

"Let's go have a puffy taco," Catherine said.

"This is a pretty eclectic place," Catherine said as they entered Ray's Drive In. "Let's look around the place before we sit down. Do you think they'll mind?"

"I doubt it."

"Look, David. There're pictures of your high school basketball team hanging on the wall behind you."

"Those are pictures of the Lanier High School Basketball team when they were state champions. They won the state title a couple of times during the 1940s, a little before my time," David laughed.

"Look over there, David. Isn't that altar just amazing? There are more than twenty pictures and statues of the Virgin Mary. There's nothing fancy about the makeshift altar, but it's so full of life. Those framed paintings and statues of the Virgin Mary and that other saintly lady remind me of my first trips to Rome. I was a little girl when my parents took me to St. Peter's Basilica. The cherubs were my favorite of all the statues in the Basilica. Anyway, getting back to the altar, who's that saintly lady next to the Virgin Mary?"

"That's *La Virgen de Gualdalupe* in the middle of the altar. She's the patron saint of Mexico. She appeared to an indigenous man—his name was Juan Diego—in 1591. The apparition took place at the hill of Tepeyac, which is a present-day suburb of Mexico City."

"Look at the sign by the street, *Ray's*; it's rusted. It kind of goes with the restaurant's interior motif. Although I don't know what I would name the motif. Let's see, there's an antique pickup truck in the middle of the dining room, then you have a Pac Man game machine and an altar to the Virgin Mary and La Virgen de Guadalupe. I guess I was right when I said it's eclectic. I like this restaurant."

"It's not a restaurant, it's a drive-in," David laughed. "People can eat in their cars if they so desire."

"How did you find out about this place?" Catherine asked.

"This is my neighborhood, Catherine. Born and raised just a few blocks from here. I'll show you the exact spot as soon as we're done with these puffy tacos," David said as the waitress brought them their food and lemonade.

"Well, what's the verdict. How do you like your puffy tacos?" David asked her halfway through their meal.

"They're delicious. Doubt I'll find them in Paris. And this lemonade is incredible. It must be made with real lemons." Catherine reached over and held David's hand. "I'm so glad you brought me here. It means a lot to me."

"This isn't exactly the Noma in Copenhagen, Catherine. But I'm curious, why do you say it means a lot to you, the fact that I brought you here?"

"It's difficult to describe because it's a feeling. Being here with you makes me feel good. Makes me feel good because you're letting me see another side of you, one I hadn't seen. You've told me about your childhood, but words can never describe what you're showing me. This is the reality that you were born into. This is what formed your innermost thoughts and memories, the things that define who you are. Your past has suddenly become real to me. By bringing me here you're not only telling me but showing me, this is part of who I am. You're telling me, this is my past and I want you to see it. Just like two lovers who decide to share their sexual past, not caring what the other will think. Both lovers standing completely naked before each other, both knowing that there can be no intimacy with secrets. Both lovers telling each other, this is my past, can you accept me? Both lovers now stand at the mercy of their love. I love you, David."

David remained silent as he listened to her every word. Especially the words that kept ringing true. *There can be no intimacy with secrets.*

They walked out of Ray's Drive In and got into the borrowed car. They exited onto Guadalupe Street and drove east. David turned right on Calaveras Street and left onto Montezuma Alley.

"Close your eyes," David told Catherine.

"Why?" She asked.

"Because we are about to turn onto Montezuma Alley," David said. "Where I was born and raised."

"Ok." Catherine said.

David took a left turn onto the narrow alley and stopped.

"Ok, you can open your eyes now," David told her.

Catherine opened her eyes. She looked straight ahead. The alley was full of potholes, no sidewalks. A mangy dog slept in one of the potholes. Catherine's eyes didn't blink. She didn't say a word. Scabrous houses appeared on her left and on her right. Decades-old layers of lead-based paint were peeling off the decayed wood below. The roofs were patched with different colored materials. The empty spaces between the houses were overgrown with weeds. As a gust of wind picked up a cloud of dust from the alley and sprayed it on the windshield, an overcast fell on Catherine's view. The few trees that existed were trash trees, no oak trees, no elm trees, no weeping willows. Window air conditioning units stuck out of three houses, but they were no match for the hellish summers. An old and rusty pickup truck without tires sat in a backyard, a restoration project that would never be funded.

"Tell me," David looked at Catherine. "What's your first impression?"

"I have many," she answered.

"But if you had to pick just one," David asked, "what would that impression be?"

"This is poverty, David."

"Yes. But mine was a genteel poverty." David tried to lighten the moment. "You're getting too serious—smile."

"I can't, David. Not right now."

CHAPTER 28

David and Catherine exited the Hilton Hotel, made a right turn, and headed toward La Villita Arts Village. The previous night had not been kind to David. It had deprived him of much-needed sleep. The racist gene research consumed his every waking moment, and now it was starting to consume his nights as well.

With the addition of Warren to his team, David now had his starting lineup. His dream of improving the lives of the disenfranchised was now one step closer. This accomplishment, while small in comparison to what lay ahead, should have made David feel good about how things were progressing, but this didn't turn out to be the case. The pursuit of the racist gene had taken a toll on David's personal life. A personal issue kept nagging at him, and he knew it had to be resolved before he could allow himself to feel good about anything. He had to tell Catherine the truth.

David held Catherine's hand as they walked around La Villita Arts Village, serving as her tour guide. He struggled to act interested in their surroundings as he described the architecture and history of La Villita. David halfheartedly told her that La Villita was San Antonio's first neighborhood on the south bank of the San Antonio River. Originally settled by Native Americans, La Villita later became home to a series of brush huts that were called *jacales*. The *jacales* housed Spanish soldiers stationed at the Alamo, David added. Years later, European immigrants moved into the same area in the nineteenth century and gone were the brush huts of the Spanish soldiers. New and well-constructed houses appeared. La Villita neighborhood became more cosmopolitan as German, Italian, French joined the local Mexican population in settling the area. The neighborhood flourished, businesses appeared, and buildings arose to meet the growing demands, the buildings that now housed the present La Villita Historical Arts Village.

David's tenure as a tour guide came to an end at La Villita's outdoor theater, known as the Arneson River Theater. It was named after Edwin Arneson, who was the regional director of the Work Projects Administration (WPA) and who oversaw the construction of the theater. The WPA was a public works program created by President Franklin Delano Roosevelt in 1935 in efforts to combat unemployment during the Great Depression.

David and Catherine sat on the grass-covered stepped seating. They silently sat next to each other, staring at the empty stage across the narrow river. Neither appeared interested in breaking their silence, particularly David.

"When you get this quiet, I never know what to expect. But I do know this: it's usually bad. So go ahead and get it over with, David. Tell me what's on your mind. I'm a big girl. I can handle whatever is causing you to act this way."

David leaned toward the stage, placed his elbows on his legs, and propped his head on his hands. Several times he started to say something only to stop before uttering a word. The ball was on his side of the court and he knew it.

"Catherine, you know I love you and that I care about you more than I can adequately explain."

"Oh, David. Will you please stop with the disclaimers and get to the point."

David slowly turned his head and faced Catherine.

"When we were at Rays Drive In yesterday, you said something, something that I haven't been able to get out of my mind. You said there can be no intimacy with secrets, or something like that. I've never heard those words, but when I heard you say them, I knew what you were saying was true. When you said there can be no intimacy with secrets, I suddenly realized what has been nagging at me. I knew something wasn't right, but I couldn't put my finger on it. Something kept me from loving you the way I wanted. I now know what that something is. That something is the truth. I've kept it from you, the truth about my divorce. I didn't divorce my wife because I didn't love her. I divorced her in order to protect her."

Catherine took a deep breath, held it, and then let out a big sigh of relief. Relief at hearing the true reason for David's divorce. Catherine had suspected all along that there was more to the divorce than what David had let on, telling her that his wife had been unfaithful. This is why Catherine had never understood why David's wife, an unfaithful wife, had received eighty percent of his wealth in the divorce settlement. It now made perfect sense.

"I guess this is where I'm supposed to start yelling at you, cussing at you, slapping your face, and telling you I'm leaving. Is this what you're expecting me to do? Is this why you've avoided telling me the truth about your divorce?"

"You have every right to be angry at me, Catherine. If you want to slap me, cuss at me, or whatever, I won't stop you. I should have told you a long time ago, but I couldn't. The timing wasn't right."

"The timing wasn't right to tell the truth, but it was perfect timing to tell a lie? I've never come across such perfect timing."

"I didn't know I was going to fall in love with you, Catherine. That's why the timing, to tell you the truth about my divorce, wasn't right in the beginning of our relationship. But as we both know, things have changed and we're in love. Keeping the details of my divorce secret from you was keeping me from becoming intimate with you. That's why I have to tell you the truth, Catherine. I want to be intimate with you. Telling you that I loved my wife when I divorced her is not easy. Telling you that I divorced her in spite of loving her is not something I expect you to understand. I couldn't understand it myself, but it was something I had to do. It would have been so easy to divorce her if she in fact had been unfaithful, but she never was. She was the perfect wife."

"Wow, the perfect wife. You really know how to make me feel good, don't you, David?"

"I can only tell you the truth."

A river barge full of tourists waved at Catherine and David as they passed by, not noticing Catherine's tears.

"If you decide to leave and end our relationship, I'll just have to accept it. But before you leave, you need to know everything that went down and why I made the decision I made."

"Telling me the details will not influence my decision, David. But if confessing your sins makes you feel better, go ahead and confess."

"When I met the Captain, he warned me of the danger I was getting myself into by pursuing my dream. His warnings did make me feel apprehensive, but it was nothing compared to the apprehension I felt when he told me of the dangers that awaited my wife and family. He was absolutely correct. Within minutes of his forewarning, we were under attack. I decided, then and there, that I had to fly solo. This was my mission and mine alone. I couldn't tell my wife about my research because this would definitely put her in a very precarious position. I thought it would be easier on her if I told her I had fallen in love with another woman, so that's what I did. It must have torn her apart, but I couldn't let anything happen to her or my children."

"Can we back up a little? Did you say you came under attack, like somebody trying to physically harm you? Since when has genetic research become a dangerous profession?"

David had one more confession. He spent the rest of the day telling Catherine about the racist gene research and its political implications. And the dangers that came with it. The more he told her about the gene, the more interested and intrigued she became, repeatedly interrupting him with questions.

"You're such a good liar, David. You had me convinced it was the intelligence gene you sought to discover," Catherine smiled.

"I'm sorry, but..."

"I know, the timing wasn't right."

"I can't begin to tell you how good it makes me feel now that you've told me about the two most intimate things in your life. I know it's difficult to forgive yourself for what you did to your wife, but you shouldn't punish yourself for the rest of your life. You did what was in their best interest. You did what every good husband and father would have done."

Catherine leaned closer to David and rested her head on his shoulder. She had never seen him in such a melancholy frame of mind. Gone was the gregarious and enthusiastic David. David appeared so remorseful, yet his voice was full of determination. The idyllic setting along the banks of the San Antonio River stood in stark contrast to David's turmoil. He had one last thing to tell Catherine.

The sun had set behind the theater stage when Catherine suggested they head back to the hotel. David started to rise and get going but immediately changed his mind. He knew he had to tell her now, otherwise it might be too late. After several clumsy attempts at telling her his intentions, he gave up and decided to try a different approach.

"When I first saw you aboard my yacht after the Grand Prix of Monaco, you looked sad or scared. Maybe these are not the right words, but you didn't look very happy. Your beautiful brown eyes looked around as if looking for an escape hatch. Seeing you like that made me want to come to your rescue, but I didn't know what you needed to be rescued from."

"I was very insecure when I met you," Catherine said. Maybe that's the look you saw in me. I couldn't figure out why I felt that way. I was and still am worth several billion dollars, well educated and as you call me, *chula*, so I really had no reason for feeling insecure."

"Do you still feel insecure?"

"I don't know. There are times I feel in complete control of my life, then I have my bad days."

"We all have our bad days, and I'm having a very bad day and it's about to get worse."

"On that note, why don't we leave and make sure things don't go downhill. You've told me about everything I need to know. Let's leave all that behind and enjoy the present."

"It's the present that we need to talk about, Catherine. Don't you realize the danger I'm placing you in now that you know about the racist gene? I cannot let anything happen to you. Please understand…" David started to tell her what had to take place.

"No, David. Don't go there. Please don't tell me what I think you're going to say. Don't do this to me."

"I have to, Catherine. Don't you understand? Damn it, I can't believe I told you about the racist gene."

"Stop."

"No, Catherine, listen to me. I was not willing to put my wife's life in danger and neither will I put yours. I should have never gotten you involved."

"I'm involved, so get over it."

"No, Catherine. There's no getting over anything. I've decided that we both need to go our separate ways and that's final."

"It's not up to you to decide what I want to do with my life. You can't just pick up and leave me. You can't keep running away from people that love you just so that you feel better about yourself. Just so you can tell yourself you did the right thing. I love you, David. Now do the right thing and ask me to travel with you the rest of the way. Let's take this journey together."

"Let me tell you one more thing before you decide if you want us to take this journey together," David responded.

David told her in great detail of his plans to not only discover the racist gene but to eliminate it from humans' DNA. He told her about the retrovirus.

CHAPTER 29

Moe didn't waste a minute. As soon as he finished his meeting with Hans in Amsterdam, he boarded his jet and flew straight to London. His exuberance was difficult to control as he envisioned the exorbitant fee he could command by suppressing the discovery and elimination of the racist gene.

There was no doubt in Moe's mind of the cataclysmic effect the racist gene's discovery and eventual elimination would have on the world's richest people. *These people, the world's power brokers, do not take things lying down—they take control. They determine the state of affairs; they determine the distribution of wealth throughout the world. And they only distribute the wealth among themselves, the chosen few, the self-anointed ones. I couldn't care less about the injustices they create. I'm not going to get into the morality of the shit they're about. I need to stay neutral; don't talk politics. All I care about is making money. I've made millions by protecting and enhancing their power throughout the world. There's no reason to change my strategy. I'll use the same sales pitch: "I'm here to protect your interest and to ensure you maintain your world dominance."* Moe kept rehearsing the presentation he was about to make to James Morgan, the most powerful of the world's power brokers.

Moe exited the taxi and hurriedly entered Harrods Department Store through one of its many canopied entrances. The store's aisles were at capacity with Saturday shoppers and tourists. Hundreds of people patiently waited in line at the base of the Egyptian Escalator to take pictures of the altar erected in memory of Princess Diana and Dodi Al-Fayed, one of the few places where picture-taking was allowed.

If ever there was a store that could proclaim itself as a one-stop shopping location, it is Herrods. From pianos to washing machines, from televisions to Persian rugs, from chocolates to twenty-four carat gold satellite telephones, all can be found at Harrods.

Moe sat at his favorite table at the Georgian Restaurant on the fourth floor, enjoying the talented pianist's music while waiting for James. Taking tea at Harrods was a favorite indulgence for Moe whenever he found himself in London. Relaxing in the opulent and elegant restaurant reinforced his sense of success and accomplishment. Moe's Faustian deal had afforded him a life of luxury. A far cry from his humble beginnings.

"Thanks for agreeing to meet on such a short notice. Didn't mean to cut into your vacation, but you being in London made it very convenient for both of us," Moe said as James joined him at his table.

The tall and thin American was vacationing with his wife in London when Moe came across the information of the racist gene's discovery. James had inherited his fortune from his father, who in turn had inherited it from his father, an industrialist and oil magnate. James' parents didn't spend too much time with him. His father was too busy making money and his mother was an alcoholic, so James was left to the care of his strict and sadistic nanny.

As soon as he came of age, the young boy was shipped off to Deerfield Academy, where he was groomed among other members of his privileged class. In spite of James being a mediocre student, his father made sure he was accepted at Dartmouth College where he went on to become the editor of a very conservative student tabloid. By the time James received his graduate degree in his mid-twenties, he had acquired the necessary skills to fulfill his life's preordained role.

James was now ready to take the baton from his father and become the leader of the worlds' power brokers.

"Look, Moe, I don't like you or people like you. And I especially don't like to be seen with you in public, so let's get this meeting over and done with as quickly as possible."

"James, James, why are you being so harsh? You and I both know that we're two of a kind. We feed at the same trough. We're both dirty, James, but you like to play games and pretend you're not. You go to church on Sundays where the Cardinal personally greets you and thanks you for your more-than-generous donation for his new residence. After church, you go to the country club for a scrumptious brunch, again pretending to be somebody you're not. You spend hundreds of thousands of dollars for your daughters' debutant balls, making sure they meet the right guy, making sure they marry into the right class—your class, the wealthy. You donate millions of dollars to worthy causes and sit on boards of well-respected charity organizations. You like to stay clean while playing a dirty game, and that's why you hire people like me. I do your dirty work. You need me, James. That's why you're here even though you hate me. Yes, James, we're two of a kind, so let's keep our morals out of this conversation. Let's not stand in judgment of each other."

Moe's lips were almost trembling with hatred as he spoke to James. Moe didn't care about James's morals and nefarious dealings. What he didn't like was that people like James always played a zero-sum game with the rest of society. As unscrupulous as Moe was, he still had a sense of fairness. He hated the fact that James and his gang always won. However, the astronomical fee he would soon receive temporarily tempered his sense of fairness.

Moe had been James' go-to guy for many years in spite of the fact that Moe hated James. Moe's loyalty was one of the reasons James always sought him out to do his dirty work. Once Moe accepted a client and assignment, he could not be bought out by a higher bidder. And one more thing, Moe knew how to keep his mouth shut. Early

D. G. HERNÁNDEZ

in his career, he served three years in prison, a prison term he could have avoided had he testified for the prosecution in a federal case. His client never spent a day in jail, thanks to Moe.

In the early years, James and his associates used Moe to deliver weapons to unsavory rebels whose sole purpose was to topple duly-elected governments. Once the rebels took control, they were free to plunder their countries' natural resources and sell them to James at below-market prices. This pattern of helping to overthrow legitimately-elected governments continued for many years, but now James and his cadre of American power brokers had something bigger in mind, the United States of America.

James's father and others like him had started their anarchy-leaning movement by the middle of the 1900s. By the end of the century, they had poured millions, if not billions, into creating conservative propaganda machines that went by the name of think tanks. The think tanks were created to legitimize their distorted views of democracy, advocating for a small and limited government. These antigovernment-regulation zealots disguised their true agenda—making more money by freeing themselves of government regulation—by spreading lies and distorting the truth. They especially made hay by spreading fears and rumors that President Obama was on the cusp of doing away with the second amendment of the U.S Constitution when he suggested universal background checks for prospective gun owners.

James and his consortium's plan to take over every legislative body in the United States required an operative of high intelligence and ambition. Without hesitation, James decided that there was only one person he could trust to carry out their ruthless battle plan, and that person was none other than Moe. The arms dealer was now being contracted to manipulate political elections by the various think tanks' CEOs. Moe's business diversification was adding millions to his bottom line. His net worth was approaching the billion-dollar mark. His meteoric rise was a result of making sure every activity was in keeping with the power brokers' mission of taking over government at every level. The meticulous Moe made sure there was no wasted motion in any of his undertakings. He micro-managed to the point of making sure any of the think tanks' names met his approval. *Their names must always give the impression that their members are ordinary people fighting for personal freedoms*, Moe consistently said. The think tanks' names also had to sound patriotic and nationalistic.

In spite of Moe's genius, James and his consortium were not without ideas of their own. They realized that in order to legitimize their perverted agenda, they needed to enlist the help of the academic community at major colleges and universities. However, they also realized that this was an almost impossible feat, so they came up with an ingenious plan. They approached major universities, including the Ivy League universities, and offered to underwrite new fields of study. Hidden in these generous offers was their agenda: infiltrating the intelligentsia and giving themselves instant credibility. Suddenly appearing on conservative television and radio shows were disciples from the various university programs that James had funded. It was no accident that the disciples had learned the conservative agenda they preached well. They had been taught by handpicked professors, and James had done the picking. The strategy of infiltrating the universities finally put James' agenda on the map by giving it a semblance of fairness and respectability. These Stepford disciples that were presented on national television as experts were nothing more than mouthpieces for James.

"Enough of this bullshit!" James shouted at Moe. "I called a few of my friends after we spoke on the phone yesterday, and they are just as pissed off as I am. We're not about to let some fucking geneticist, a geneticist we don't know shit about, fuck things up for us. Do you understand?"

With his hands raised slightly above the table James, stared at Moe, expecting an immediate answer, but none was forthcoming.

"Don't just look at me. I'm asking you a question. Do you understand?" James repeated.

Moe smiled and nodded.

D. G. HERNÁNDEZ

James continued, "I want to leave here knowing full well that you're going to take care of this problem, that you're going to make it go away. I don't care how you do it, just get it done. There will be no regime change under my watch. The fucking American and his geneticist don't know who they're up against."

James and the rest of the world's power brokers were running scared. They were well aware of their impending doom should the racist gene be discovered and eliminated. They could see the writing on the wall, and they were prepared to blast it down. Nothing was going to stop James from keeping and augmenting his power. James was born on third base but thought he had hit a triple. He could ill afford to be sent back to first base.

Moe recognized James predicament and was more than ready to seize the moment. Moe's thoughts started at the beginning, tracing back previous dynasties and rulers. Dynasties had ruled the world since the dawn of time. The Hapsburgs, the Ottoman Empire, the Roman Empire were all dynasties that had come and gone but had been replaced by new generations of rulers. The difference between yesterday's rulers and today's was very evident to Moe. Previous rulers were easy to identify; their wealth was on constant display. The kings and queens lived in castles with moats around them to keep enemies out but also to show their power and invincibility. However, today's rulers are very subtle and learn early on to hide their wealth from view. Today's rulers hire the best accountants money can buy to veil their every penny. The average citizen never gets to see James' multi-million-dollar jet, nor his yachts. That's the difference: the working classes' master is invisible to them, for they rule with an unrestrained invisible hand. By controlling the international banking system, today's invisible rulers control every facet of people's. *These guys will never relinquish their power, and this is where I come in,* Moe thought as he sat opposite James.

"I'm glad you feel this way. And don't look so depressed, James. Enjoy your coffee. It's not the end of the world."

"It could be unless you put a stop to this shit," James replied "We paid you $120 million to buy out David Lorca's voice voting patent some time ago. I'm afraid to ask; how much are you're going to take us for this time?"

Moe looked at James and smiled, remembering the easiest 20 million he had ever made. Laying his cards on the table before receiving a retainer was not something Moe ever did. But because of the magnitude of his proposed fee, he had no choice.

"Wasn't paying $120 million to buy Lorca's patent worth it? Didn't you and your business associates around the world profit by not allowing people to vote over the telephone? How much did the Citizens United case cost you? And how much is it costing you to keep it in play? You power brokers and kingmakers travel to places like Indian Wells, Jackson Hole, and other places to plot your next move. I sure would like to be the fly on the wall when you powerful men meet.

"You know, James, I can't help but wonder, what can be so secretive that you confiscate cell phones, laptop computers, iPads, and any type of recording device from all of the guests before entering your clandestine meetings. I don't think I've ever seen a billionaire's cell phone confiscated. What can be so secretive, James? It can't be that you're discussing the virtues of democracy, because information is the currency of democracy. It's very obvious that your secretive meetings are not about sharing information. You know as well as I that there is no price you guys are not willing to pay to maintain your world dominance. So answer me, wasn't spending $120 million to keep people from voting worth it?"

"Of course..." James started to answer.

"It's a rhetorical question, James. You know damn well that voter suppression around the world has lined your pockets way beyond the price you paid. That's why I know you guys are going to like my proposal."

"Don't be so sure."

"I normally don't share my solution to a problem with my clients until I obtain a handsome retainer," Moe continued. "But the magnitude of the situation you find yourself in requires I make an exception. So here it goes. Just like I told you on the phone, an American is funding a German geneticist and his team of researchers to discover the racist gene. My sources tell me that the discovery has been made. I haven't verified this, but for now let's assume they made the discovery. I want to make this assumption to make a point. And the point is this: the discovery of the racist gene is going to turn your world upside down. And do you know why? Because they are not stopping at the discovery. I strongly believe that they are now working on how to eliminate the racist gene from our DNA."

"They can't do that."

"Oh yes they can, and let me tell you why. The American and his geneticist didn't spend billions of dollars and years of their lives just to marvel at the racist gene through a microscope. They have an agenda, and that is to eliminate the gene from our DNA. I've done extensive research on the American and I'm positive that he really believes that he was born to change the world. What better way to change the world, your world in particular, than to eliminate racism?"

"Who is this American you're talking about?"

"James, what kind of businessman do you think I am? If I decide that you need to know who he is I will let you know. But not until then, so let's get back on track. If the elimination of the racist gene proves successful, you will no longer be the ruthless son of a bitch you have been all of your life. Your racism will be gone, and you will never again be able to intentionally harm a person of color."

"Are you implying that I'm the only racist in the world and that only white people have a racist gene in their DNA?"

"Of course not. If the racist gene exists, it exists in everybody's DNA. But does it matter if a person of color has a racist gene in their DNA?"

"It sure as hell matters because it proves that people of color are racist, too."

"So what if people of color are racists? They can't hurt you with their racism."

"They can lynch me," James protested.

"Interesting choice of words. But let's be serious, James. You need to look at the big picture. You need to look at racism from an institutional point of view before you decide if a person of color can hurt you or others like you. So answer me: can a person of color determine how high a white person can move up the corporate ladder?"

"He most certainly can," James shot back.

"Oh yeah, well then let me ask you this: How many minority CEOs of multinational companies do you know? How many people of color do you guys have on your boards? Can a person of color deny you membership into your local country club? How many people of color does the Augusta Country Club have? Can a person of color determine how much money is spent on your education? There's no way that the poor, or people of color, or the disenfranchised can hurt you with their racism because they're powerless. They don't have anything you want or need, except for their labor, of course. So you see, you're safe. They can't hurt you even if they wanted."

"I don't know about that."

"Sure you do, James. People of color who seek justice can riot in the streets, burn a building or two, overturn a car, and set it on fire. But after a night of rioting, they get out of bed in the morning and go to work at one of your companies. You still don't get it, James. Their racism can't hurt you. The only positive thing about racism is that it makes a lot of money for you. That's why people like you have to keep racism hidden in the depths of the social sciences, where you can give it lip service all day long. That's all you guys want to do in reference to racism. You just want to talk about it and not solve it. You guys should be pretty worried right about now because racism has now been elevated to the realm of the empirical sciences. The talking is over, my friend. Game, set, and match, you've had it."

"I've had it? What is that supposed to mean?"

"Now that the racist gene has been discovered and soon to be eliminated, people will finally become free from your oppression. A while ago you said people of color are capable of hurting you, and I disagreed. My disagreement, however, is based on the premise that the status quo remains in place. Right now you guys sit at the top of the food chain. You don't have any predators. And it is my job to make sure it stays that way. It's my job to make sure you retain your world dominance."

"And how are you going to accomplish this?" James asked.

"My immediate goal is to contain the situation, just like an oil spill. I need to get my hands on any existing research data and destroy it. I also have to make sure that the American and his cadre of geneticists never again attempt to discover the racist gene. But I do need to be upfront with you. What I'm proposing is only a temporary fix."

"A temporary fix? I'm supposed to pay you for a fucking temporary fix?"

"I don't earn my money by selling my clients a bill of goods." Moe explained. "I earn it by explaining all of the possible outcomes. That's what I'm doing with you. I'm making you aware that what you're buying is not a permanent solution."

"Ok, I get it. Now go on."

"I just told you. All I can do is get rid of the American and his geneticist, as well as the data. I can promise you they'll never set foot in a lab again, but I can't possibly prevent future geneticists from undertaking similar research."

"So how much is this temporary fix going to cost us?"

"How much is it worth to you?" Moe asked.

CHAPTER 30

"Keep your fucking money. I never want to see you again!"

The high-priced prostitute yelled at Hans as she slipped into her scanty dress. No time to delicately adjust her garter belt, no time to slide her long legs into her black fishnet stockings, no time to tighten her provocative corset, her escape reigned supreme.

"Take the fucking money and get the hell out of my life," Hans repeated. "This is who I am...I can't change." Hans continued muttering to himself, not making sense in his drunken stupor.

Heather had heard the familiar refrain, and it always signaled trouble. The routine was always the same, heavy drinking followed by rough sex. Even though she could have done without the bruises he left on her, she went along. The money was good; Hans was very generous. Being Hans' wet nurse and indulging him in kinky sex didn't sit well with her, either, but it was included in her job description. *It's only a job,* Heather repeated to herself while pandering to his sexual proclivities and peccadilloes.

But things had changed over the course of several months. Hans had not gotten drunk during those months and had managed to stay in control. His penchant for rough sex had subsided, and Heather could not have been any happier. This change in Hans coincided with her feelings toward him. She was falling for Hans.

Heather felt so good about their romance that she decided to take their relationship to a new level. She decided to break her self-imposed rules as a prostitute and spend the entire night with him. And in the morning, she was hoping that Hans would take her along on his assignment, checking up on the famed geneticist he had under surveillance. Heather had no clue what Hans meant when he said "under surveillance."

Early in their relationship, Heather didn't know what to make of Hans' drunken confessions about his occupation. She didn't know if he was bragging about being a spy to impress her or if he was really telling the truth. She debated the issue and decided not to believe him. After all, she reasoned, a real spy would never make such claims. But that was in the beginning; Hans was now sharing actual details of his work. "I don't want to hear any more details," the scared Heather told him. But that didn't stop him. As a matter of fact, it was during one of his drunken escapades when Hans told her about a geneticist he had under surveillance at a place called the Pines Inn. A geneticist that had made a major discovery in genetics. Hans bragged to her that the discovery was worth millions of euros and he was about to get his hands on it. Hans described the inn and the surrounding majestic pine forest to her in great detail, but more importantly, he told her of the secret lab hidden meters below the inn.

Now that Heather was falling for Hans, she overlooked some of his indiscretions, including whatever he was up to with the geneticist. She was convinced that she could change Hans with time, that love would solve all problems. Heather thought that going with Hans to the Pines Inn and giving him the best sex ever was a good first step in his rehabilitation.

Such were her thoughts and plans earlier in the evening before Hans got drunk and out of control. Heather couldn't believe what was happening, Hans was relapsing to his old self. Hans' rough sex was going beyond agreed levels of sexual gratification. Beyond anything she could have ever imagined. He refused to stop in spite of Heather yelling out her safe word. The more the handcuffed Heather pleaded for him to stop, the more aggressive he became. In frustration of not being able to sexually perform, Hans clumsily removed the handcuffs from her wrists and ankles and threw her to the floor. Hans tried jumping on top of the helpless Heather but slipped and fell to the floor beside her. The fall momentarily immobilized him, giving Heather but a few seconds to escape.

Hans woke up with a terrible hangover and a bump on the back of his head, not remembering a thing of what had occurred the previous night. The handcuffs were hanging from the bedposts, but Heather was not in them. The money was still sitting on the nightstand. He knew something bad had happened, he just couldn't remember what it might have been. Hangover or no hangover, he couldn't afford to miss the eight o'clock train.

Hans was now only minutes away from the village and his prey, the Captain, but he couldn't keep his mind off Heather. Throughout the train ride, Hans kept reminiscing about his first tryst with Heather. Heather looked exactly like the girl he had described and requested from the local madam. "She must be tall, young but not too young. She must have blonde hair, blue eyes, and large but firm breasts. Must be a wet nurse and willing to try adventurous sex." Berlin was not the only city in which he had made such requests, but this is where he met Heather. I must get these thoughts out of my mind, Hans demanded of himself as the train came to a stop. *Hitler, Hitler,* he remembered Heather screaming out her safe word. As hard as he tried, he just couldn't remember any of the events of the previous night. What could have gone so wrong that Heather had to use her safe word?

The inn lay deep within the pine forest, invisible from the road below. A long and treacherous gravel road that led up to the inn gave no indication of its exclusivity. The winding road seemed more like a maze as it cut through the thick forest, not giving new arrivals a sense of direction as they made their way up to the towering inn. From high atop the tower, the innkeeper could see an approaching intruder with ease. The road was also lined with hidden cameras capable of observing any moving object, day or night.

The Pines Inn's main building was massive. While only a one-story building, it stood forty feet tall. Its steep slate roof seemed to disappear into the tall pine trees that encircled the majestic structure. Guests entered the lobby through massive timber doors that seemed capable of stopping large caliber bullets.

The inn's colossal lobby was breathtaking. Massive chandeliers hung from the forty-foot-high ceiling. The front desk ran the entire length of the lobby and was decorated with intricate carvings of exotic game. The concierge's desk sat off to one side, almost hidden behind a wall of indoor plants. Two long corridors led from each side of the lobby, one to the dining room and the other to an impressive library. The lobby's roughhewed floor planks seemed strong enough to support a parade of elephants.

Hans was escorted to his cabin the moment he arrived at the inn. His mind was still on Heather, but he had a job to do.

As was the custom, a bellboy walked through the lobby, ringing a small bell. Announcing that dinner was served.

Hans entered the inn's dining room and chose to be seated at a distant table toward the back. He surveyed the room as he was led to his table but didn't notice anything unusual. Several guests gathered around the circular fireplace in the middle of the dining room while others enjoyed a glass of wine at their tables before being served their dinner.

Trays full of local cheeses were laid out on an elegantly decorated table with an ice carving of an elk with its head down, ready to attack. Other guests that weren't ready for dinner sat around a piano bar, listening to the lounge lizard sing. Across the dining room's walls hung large elk mounts, evidence of the beautiful animals that once roamed the area before being hunted into extinction.

Hans stayed at his table long after every guest had left. The bartender came to his table, thanked him for the generous tip, told him good night, and left for the evening. Hans now sat all alone, thinking of Heather while staring at the empty wine bottle in front of him.

Hans looked up and was startled when he saw the Captain standing in front of him.

"Sorry, Masseur Friedrich, if I knew you were staying behind I would have asked the bartender to keep the bar open. My apologies, sir, I'll make sure it doesn't happen again. I would also like to apologize for not having had a chance to introduce myself in a proper way. Mind if I join you?" The Captain sat down before receiving an answer. He stretched out his hand across the table and introduced himself to Hans.

The ebb and flow of the fireplace's bright flames created movement throughout the room. The Captain observed the scar on Hans' face, on the right side. The scar started above his right eye and continued an inch below. The flickering flames cast a shadow on Hans' face, making the scar appear as if moving from right to left and then left to right.

"If there is anything we can do to make things better, please let us know. My inn is known for its privacy, and we intend to keep it that way," the Captain said.

The Captain was slowly easing his way into confronting Hans. Hours earlier his bartender summoned the Captain, "Sir, can I see you for a moment? We seem to have run out of rum."

"Impossible, we received a case just last month," the Captain hurriedly approached the bar, not believing what he had just heard. The bartender mouthed an exaggerated *shsssh*. He started to whisper as he showed the Captain the empty rum bottle.

In a whispered voice, the bartender continued, "I think we have a problem, sir. The man sitting at table number two is a German spy."

"A spy? What the hell are you talking about?" the nervous Captain asked.

"Follow me to the cellar," the composed bartender instructed.

"I didn't recognize him at first," the bartender began once they reached the cellar, "but that scar on his face is very unusual. It starts above his right eye and continues below it, yet his eye is intact. Anyway,

I do remember him staying here some time ago. I believe it was soon after we arrived. He kept to himself. Well, almost. A girl from the village down the road came looking for him shortly after his last stay. I was in the lobby when she ran in, headed towards the dining room, looked around, and ran across to the library. It was at this point that I decided to stop her. She was causing quite a scene. At one point she almost dropped the baby she was carrying. She was hysterical, so I took her to the kitchen to get her out of sight. She was demanding I tell her where she could find him. She was convinced I knew who he was. I told her that if she wanted me to help her find the person she was looking for, she was going to have to tell me about him. I needed to know his age, height, color of hair, and other significant details. The moment she started to describe him, I realized who she was talking about. There's no doubt in my mind; that scar on his face is hard to forget. 'I remember him well, but he hasn't been here in several months,' I told her. After calming down, she let me know she was pregnant with his child. She went on with her sad story, telling me that her baby was only eighteen months old and that she couldn't afford to have another child."

"Did she believe you? That you didn't know anything about him?" the alarmed Captain asked.

"I think so. I gave her a cup of tea to help her relax. The girl noticed the harsh stares she was receiving from the annoyed kitchen staff, so she unbuttoned her blouse and started nursing the crying baby. She told me that all she knew about him was that he was an agent or spy in the German Army; she didn't mention if it was East or West Germany. He told her about him being a spy while drunk, so she didn't know if it was true or not. She also told me that he beat her after they finished having strange sex. She buttoned up her blouse, held the baby up with its head on her shoulder, and started to make her exit, but not before saying something strange."

"What did she say?"

"Every time Hans came to see me my child would have to cry himself to sleep, I was not able to nurse him."

CHAPTER 31

"Tell me, Hans—if that's your real name..." The Captain couldn't contain himself any longer. "Why are you really here? And don't tell me it's to get away from the big city and relax."

"Sounds like you have it all figured out," Hans said.

"Maybe," the Captain said. "One thing I know for sure is that you're a spy, or should I be more formal and call you a Stasi officer? Found out this about you from a local girl, a very pregnant local girl who has been looking for you. Seems you got her pregnant during your last visit, but I'm sure you couldn't care less. But let me offer you a little bit of friendly advice: get the hell out my inn because she's coming back. She's not giving up until she finds you."

"That's very thoughtful of you, looking out after me, very generous indeed. But I really doubt your benevolence."

"Enough with the charade!" the Captain yelled at Hans. "I've worked for people like you, and I know the exercise well. I'm used to people like you coming into my laboratory whenever the hell you want, at all hours of the day or night, snooping around. The girl calls you a spy, but she doesn't know that everybody is a spy where I come from. You can never trust anybody. Your audits, as Stasis call an interrogation, became pretty routine after the war. I don't have anything to hide, so go ahead and do your job. Start your interrogation or audit, whatever you want to call it."

"Well, well, well," Hans said. "I should have known better. You old-timers seem to know everything. You're right, Captain, about the audits, that is. Let's call this an audit and nothing more. I've been assigned to audit many people throughout my career and I've gotten pretty good at it. Some say I'm the best auditor. So good, in fact, that I can tell when people are lying. Can you believe that, Captain? I can tell when people are lying to me."

"Good. In that case, you'll see right through me and get this shit over in a matter of minutes."

"I don't think so. I think we have a lot to talk about. I'm curious about a lot of things that seem to be taking place here. So let's relax and enjoy our time alone. We're all alone. Nobody to monitor our conversation. Just me and you."

The inn rested quietly. The fire had abated. With stoker in hand, the Captain remained quiet for a few moments, trying to calm himself down. In spite of having been interrogated by the Stasi many times during his stint in East Germany, the Captain felt very threatened by the imposing German before him. As much as the Captain tried to make himself believe that this was just a routine visit by the Stasi, he couldn't convince himself. While he prepared himself to answer the usual questions—Have you been approached by known enemies of the state? Have you been offered money in exchange for any sensitive information?—he realized that this was definitely not a routine visit. He wondered why a senior officer like Hans had been assigned to investigate him. Most of the routine inspections at his lab had been conducted by officers half Hans' age, kids straight out of training.

This is no idiot in front of me, the Captain told himself. *He's in no hurry. He's giving me enough time to hang myself. He knows what he's doing, he definitely knows what he's doing,* the Captain repeated. *I got it,* the Captain arrived at his conclusion. *Hans is here to confirm information, not to gather it. He must know about the lab.*

"You may have all night, but I don't. I have an inn to run, so go ahead and do your duty to your country or whoever you work for."

"You make things sound so official, Captain. Relax... relax. I'll tell you what, we'll just talk, and if along the way I think of a question, I'll ask, ok? I know you've been through audits, and I have to assume you've despised them, so let's make this as civil as possible. Let's behave like normal people."

"Like normal people? There's nothing normal about this interrogation."

"I suppose you're right. Maybe this isn't a normal interrogation. And the reason for this is that you're not a normal suspect, Captain. You're a very smart man, the type that can make up a believable story, one that can convince me and send me on my way. That's why this audit is very difficult and complicated even for a person like me. So that's why I decided the hell with it, why don't I just get to know the guy? After all, he's some kind of a celebrity, so why not get to know him? It might be fun. You don't have to tell me about your exploits as a geneticist; I know all about that. But the one question I feel compelled to ask is why you never married. I'm sure that with your fame as a geneticist, you could have easily gotten just about any girl you wanted. I like women, Captain, and as far as I know, I have never heard about you having any male lovers, so I'll assume you're not gay, but I'm still intrigued by your personal life."

"Don't know why my personal life would intrigue you. It has nothing to do with why you're here."

"I know it doesn't. Your personal life doesn't have anything to do with why I'm here. I guess I'm just curious. You know, Captain, sometimes it's lack of information that arouses my curiosity, like in your case. I couldn't find out anything written about your personal life. Why is that, Captain? There is much written about your scientific work, about your patents, about certain discoveries in genetics. But absolutely nothing about you, the man. It appears that you have deliberately decided to live a life of isolation, a life without friends. How sad."

"I'm a boring person, not a fucking movie star. What do you expect, the paparazzi chasing after a boring geneticist?"

"A boring geneticist? I highly doubt it." Hans laughed out loud. "The great German geneticist is a boring person, now that would make a wonderful headline."

"You give me too much credit. 'The great German geneticist.' I don't see it that way. Hell, as a kid I never even heard the word *laboratory*, much less aspire to be a great geneticist. If I had seen a beaker as a kid, I would have used it to drink water and used a pipette as a straw. But now I'm called a distinguished scientist by the German government. Can you believe that? A distinguished scientist. There's nothing distinguishing about being a scientist. It's what scientists do with science that distinguishes them. And we as scientists should always use science to improve people's lives. That's what I believe; we're here to enrich people's lives through our discoveries. You said you wanted to know me personally, well now you know how I feel about being a scientist. And there's something else that I feel strongly about."

"And what would that be?"

"That I will no longer be about making discoveries that line people's pockets. Pharmaceutical companies make billions of dollars off discoveries we scientists make. I'm not saying that they shouldn't get a return on their investments, but enough is enough. From now on, I'm taking my discoveries straight to the people. No pharmaceutical company is going to make billions off my work."

"Are you telling me you're still conducting research? I thought you retired."

"You're right—it was just a figure of speech. I keep forgetting. Retirement is hard to accept."

"That's what I've heard other retirees say," Hans said.

Their privacy was suddenly interrupted by raucous screams. A woman ran into the dining room and raced by Hans and the Captain. She held on to her see-through nightgown tightly as she ran out the back door and into the cold night. Her husband gave chase, threatening her, commanding her to return to their cabin.

"Never...never will I accept you having a fucking mistress, you asshole!" she yelled as she ran further into the dark night. Her husband, not fully dressed, apologized to Hans and the Captain as he gave up the chase. He reached for an extra chair in hopes of joining the two but sensed he was not welcome. He apologized again and left.

I can't stand this Nazi, but what I can I do? If I seem too anxious to get rid of him, he'll guess that I'm hiding something. If I engage in conversation for too long, I might fuck up and say something that will give me away. Either way, I'm screwed. I can't fuck up the project. David will kill me and I'll never forgive myself, the Captain told himself.

"So much for privacy. That ruckus made me forget, where were we?" Hans broke into the Captain's thoughts.

"Science and quality of life," the Captain answered.

"Has science improved your quality of life, Captain?"

"It depends. Quality is a relative term," the Captain said. "But it doesn't matter—we all wind up dead. What happens between the time we are born and die is mere passage of time. Some people are fortunate and have a great life while others are not as lucky. But what gets me really pissed off is when kids never get a chance at life. They should never be deprived of their potential or happiness."

"Did you have a happy childhood, Captain?"

"Are you serious? You're here to talk about childhood?"

"Just wondering," Hans answered.

"I can't believe what I'm hearing! A Stasi officer wants to know if I had a happy childhood."

The Captain thought about telling Hans to screw himself but decided against it. He immediately realized that he could buy more time for the guys down in the lab that were feverishly trying to wipe the computers clean of any racist research data. The Captain kept thinking about his researchers down below, hoping that his text had been received and obeyed.

"Hurry!" the Captain's assistant yelled across the lab. The two geneticists that were working late into the night looked up, startled by the assistant's loud command. "The Captain texted me just now.

He's up in the dining room with a man he thinks is part of the team that previously tried breaking into his lab. The Captain can only stall him for so long, so get going! Transfer all data from the computers to the mobile devices, then delete data from the computers.

"If they make their way in, let them look around. Don't put your lives in danger. Do everything they tell you. Give them total control of your computers if they ask. Answer their questions truthfully. Tell them you're geneticists, working on privately-funded research. Your research involves isolating the Y chromosome from the rest of the DNA. If they ask you why you deleted the data, tell them you were just trying to protect data from being stolen. Tell them there have been previous attempts at stealing our data."

"If this Nazi wants to hear my story, the Captain thought, "I'm going to give him the long version."

"A happy childhood is something I know absolutely nothing about," the Captain began. "All I can say is I was once a kid, but I never had a childhood."

"You sound so negative, Captain. I thought scientists were optimists. You've accomplished a lot, so it couldn't have been very bad. The way I see it, it looks like you had a good upbringing."

"Good upbringing and happiness aren't the same thing. My parents provided me with the best upbringing they could, but that doesn't mean I was happy. Do you know what it's like to be hungry, day in and day out, always hungry. I guess I should feel lucky that my brain developed in spite of the shit we ate."

"Now you're talking. These are the type of things I was referring to when I said I wanted you to tell me about your personal life," Hans said. "Didn't know a thing about you being raised in poverty."

"And I suppose you don't know I'm a Gypsy either. And I suppose you also aren't aware of the fact that Hitler sent thousands of us to die at Auschwitz and other death camps. Nah, you're too smart—I'm sure you've always known that Hitler didn't discriminate between Gypsies and Jews when it came to murder. Hitler took not only my childhood away but also the childhood of thousands of Gypsy children like me.

"Although I have to admit, there was a moment when things weren't so bad. When I was five years old, we were living with my aunt and her non-Gypsy husband. He had a small dairy farm that served the local community. My dad helped with the milking and other chores in exchange for our room and board. I didn't do much, but I did get to go with them on deliveries. It was during the deliveries that I discovered a new world, the world of the rich. We would make deliveries to wealthy people that lived in beautiful homes with acres of gardens all around. I even got to go inside some of those homes and see rich kids playing and laughing. I saw these kids who had everything, an abundance of luxuries, and wondered why they were so lucky. They even had servants that obeyed their every command. How is it that the rich control everything, especially people? Why is it, Hans? Why do rich people have to control every fucking thing?

"Anyway, my uncle died and so did our brief respite. My parents and I walked from town to town in search of money and food. As we walked along the sides of the roads, people would yell obscenities at us and tell us to go back to where we came from. Hell, we'd been born in Germany. Our vagabond lives continued. My parents had enough of the obscenities, so it was up to the mountains. That's the way it was during those years, hiding from Hitler and trying to exist on food that was not fit even for vultures.

"My parents would descend into the villages at daybreak," the Captain continued, "always leaving me behind, probably because they didn't want me to see them begging for food. Didn't want to be humiliated in front of me. From the moment they left to the moment they returned, I was scared shitless, so I just sat in one spot, not wanting to make a sound. It was always a challenge trying to keep my mind occupied and away from my hunger pangs. *Don't think about food,* I would tell myself, this will only make you more hungry," the Captain said while tapping the side of his head with his rotund index finger.

"A cold brook was never far away. I was never thirty, so I guess I should have counted my blessings. As a matter of fact, my parents would tell me to drink a lot of water, that it was good for me. It was only a ruse. They also told me that eating too much food would make me fat. Hell, I wasn't worried about getting fat. I would have settled for a few morsels.

"As if being alone during the day was not bad enough, there were some nights I slept alone because on moonless nights my parents often got lost on their way back. I was so terrified, I don't know how the hell I fell asleep. But my parents were always at my side when I woke up, ready to feed me. I felt like a tiny bird in a nest, too young to fly but old enough to be hungry. Sometimes the food was good, but most of the time it wasn't fit for a vulture. But I didn't care. I was too hungry to care. I ate the fucking food. Food poisoning was never out of the question. I hated the vomiting that sometimes lasted for days. The good thing about the vomiting is that it made my hunger seem petty. This is the first time I wondered why food decayed."

"Couldn't you tell that the food was no good?" Hans asked.

"When you're on the run, you settle for whatever you get. If all you get is shit, then that's what you eat. I can see my parents now. They always looked so tired, so haggard. They were trying so hard to make things easier for me, but it was useless.

"However, one day much to my surprise, my parents returned with still plenty of daylight left. And what was even more surprising was the feast they brought with them. A full loaf of bread—not just crumbs—a banana, an apple, a piece of fried chicken, and a handful of raisins. I thought my stomach was going to explode with so much food. This went on for three days. I couldn't believe the luck my parents were having. The food kept getting better, and to top it off, they said I could go with them the following day. I was so excited, I could hardly sleep that night. I just couldn't figure out why my parents were not as excited as I was. They kept telling me how good a son I was, that I was the best thing that had ever happened in their lives. They kept focusing on everything positive about me. I started to feel embarrassed by their constant praise. They started to reminisce, detailing the few fun times we had as a family. But after a while, I stopped listening. I was too excited about going into town the following day.

"Morning finally arrived, and without saying a word, we immediately started our hike down the mountain. You should have seen the huge smile on my face as we made our way down. We were halfway down the mountain when my father slipped and fell into a shallow stream with jagged rocks. He let out a loud grunt. It really scared me. For a moment I thought that's it, our trip is over. After not moving for a few seconds, he slowly pushed himself up. His left knee was bleeding, but no broken bones. He limped but continued down the mountain as if nothing had happened. I felt good again;, my trip into the village was still a go. My father's leg must have felt better because he started to pick up the pace.

"By mid-morning we arrived at the village. You'd be surprised to hear what I first noticed about the village. It wasn't the people or the shops that lined the narrow street or the two cows that were being hauled on the back of a truck. No, it wasn't any of those sights. It was the difference in the temperature. I wondered why it was cold up on the mountain and warm down in the village. I didn't know science then."

"I didn't know science as a child either," Hans said.

"Without any hesitation, my parents and I quickly made our way to a modest house at the end of a narrow street. The house was not new but appeared to have been recently painted. As a matter of fact, now that I think of it, it looked like a gingerbread house. My father lifted his hand, but before he could knock a man and his wife opened the front door. We were ushered in without saying a word. I looked up and noticed that the couple was staring at me. I was hoping that seeing me in my tattered clothes would not cause them to change their mind and ask me to wait outside. I followed my parents further into the house."

D. G. HERNÁNDEZ

The Captain stood and walked to the bar. In deep thought, he stood motionless for a few seconds before grabbing a bottle of merlot and returning to the table.

"On the living room wall hung a picture of a boy sitting on a huge fallen tree. He had a big smile on his face, as if to say he was responsible for the tree's fate. Other than that, he looked very ordinary, about my age, which was six by this time. After the initial greetings, we just stood there in the living room. Nobody said a word. The lady finally took me by the hand and led me to the kitchen. Her hand was very soft and smooth, very different from my mother's calloused hands. After sitting me at the table, she walked toward one of the many wall cabinets and pulled out a beautiful looking bowl, white with blue artwork. It looked very expensive. She served me porridge along with a freshly-baked muffin. I was eating as fast as I could because I didn't know how long my good fortune would last.

"Through the open kitchen door, I could see my parents in the living room. They were busy signing papers that sat on the coffee table. The husband, whose name I didn't know at that time, watched as my parents signed the papers. Once finished, my parents handed the papers to the man without looking at him. They walked towards the kitchen, entered through the opened door, and stood next to me in complete silence. My father finally spoke and told me to stay and finish my breakfast. He told me they would return later in the day, but in the meantime, I was to behave and be obedient. My mother asked me to stand so she could give me a hug. The hug lasted so long I thought my porridge would get cold. As you may have guessed by now, that was the last time I saw my parents."

"Very interesting story, Captain. Wish I had more time to learn about your childhood," Hans interrupted the Captain. "But I think it's time we get back to business. You mentioned that you were audited shortly before you retired to come here. Did they find any unusual activities or, in your case, any unusual research?"

"Of course not. Do you think I'd be here if they had?"

"I have friends in a lot of places, one of whom served as a high-ranking Stasi officer," Hans explained. "Some time ago he told me about an audit he conducted on an old Gypsy geneticist. He told me that his former Nazi bosses had lost trust in him and wanted to know what he was up to. Is this starting to sound familiar, Captain? He found out you weren't conducting the research you had been directed to undertake. When I learned about the audit's results, I became more intrigued; especially the part about the retroviruses, vector viruses, or whatever they're called. You thought nobody would ever know about the retrovirus, but you made a huge mistake. The auditor found a computer in your storage room that you had discarded without destroying the hard drive and all of its stored files, including the retrovirus research file. He told me about the retrovirus data he found but didn't think it was anything important, so he gave you a clean bill of health. But I became very curious when he told me about your retrovirus research.

"And do you know what I found out? There's a lot of money to be made with these airborne retroviruses. Notwithstanding the greedy person I am, I decided against taking immediate action. I decided to back off and observe you from a distance. I decided to give you time to complete your research, to make your discovery, and to make me a lot of money."

"What do you want from me?" the Captain asked.

"Just like I said: make a lot of money. Pharmaceutical companies will pay billions for these airborne viruses you've discovered. These airborne retroviruses can be used to deliver vaccines, shall we say, through thin air. You can inoculate an entire city by merely releasing the retrovirus from an airplane flying at low altitudes. You didn't really think you could keep this discovery all to yourself, did you, Captain? Of course, you can always say no to my proposition of us becoming partners. But if you do, I'll have to go back to Berlin and tell them a terrible mistake was made on your audit. I would be forced to tell them the truth. I don't think they would be too thrilled to hear you lied to them. I'm sure they wouldn't hesitate killing you. So what's it going to be, Captain?"

"Maybe getting killed is best. I'm old. I don't have many years left. They'll be doing me a favor."

"Perhaps I need to sweeten my proposition, Captain. What if I were to tell you that once I found you up here in this luxurious inn, I found out that you're not an innkeeper at all. In fact, you've never retired. You're still doing research, right below us. I'll tell your handlers in Berlin that you are about to become a very wealthy man by selling the retrovirus. Can you imagine how pissed off they're going to be, knowing that you spent their money developing the retrovirus and now you're going to sell it. Knowing this would really get them pissed off. I'm sure they would torture the hell out of you before putting a bullet through your head."

"All right, all right, I'll do it. I'll partner with you," the Captain yelled out. "Now will you leave me alone? I'm very tired. We can talk about it in the morning. I'm not going anywhere."

"Why wait till tomorrow? This won't take long. We go down to the lab, I make copies of the data, and I leave. I'll sell your discovery and split the money with you. Is that a deal?"

"I have years of documents and research. Do you want all of it?" the Captain asked.

"I just remembered something, Captain. There's something else I almost forgot to mention. All of your guests recently came down with influenza. You demanded that they stay in their cabins and avoid any contact with each other. You're not a medical doctor, yet you were the one that tended to them. This perplexed me. Why would you risk getting sick. Why not call a doctor? After all, you're the one that is telling people to avoid contact, to quarantine themselves in their cabins.

"As I traveled to this remote place, I kept getting more curious by the minute," Hans continued. "I kept wondering why a smart person like you would not take his own advice and avoid contact with others. I couldn't solve this riddle as I journeyed up here in the slowest of trains. I kept wondering why you would endanger your health to an unknown culprit. I laughed out loud as the answer hit me. You were never in danger of getting sick! You've discovered an antibiotic or perhaps a vaccine, haven't you, Captain? You never took ill even though you were in constant contact with the sick. What was in the syringe that miraculously healed them? Tell me, Captain. What drug did you administer?"

"I didn't give them anything other than an intravenous saline solution because they had become extremely dehydrated. You must believe me, Hans. The illness left on its own just like any other virus. And you're wrong, Hans, I haven't discovered any antibiotic or vaccine."

"Stop lying, Captain. Stop bullshitting me! It doesn't matter what you've discovered. I don't care if it's in food science, medicine, or germ warfare. I just want you to be honest and tell me what you're working on. Tell me what's really taking place in the lab below us. This is the last time I'm going to ask: have you made any kind of discovery?" Hans demanded.

"Yes, I've made a discovery. There, I've said it, I've made a discovery."

"See, Captain, it wasn't that difficult telling the truth. Now all you have to tell me is what you discovered."

"You already know. I discovered a process of developing retroviruses. What the auditor found in my computers in Berlin was only theoretical. I hadn't actually developed the living retrovirus. Before I could make any discovery, I first had to find a reagent that would allow the chemical reactions that I needed to react. Naturally occurring elements don't always want to combine. Sometimes you have to add energy for the reaction to proceed. Sometimes you put them in a medium that will allow the reaction to take place. Some chemicals don't like company and repel each other, while others are very gregarious and like company. I guess you could say I found ways of changing their attitudes. I got them to become friends and combine to form new reagents. These new reagents allowed unprecedented chemical reactions to take place, thus allowing me to develop retroviruses. This is where my experiment went awry. Some of the retroviruses I had genetically engineered accidentally escaped from my lab downstairs. Every guest could have died, including myself. What saved us was that the DNA of the genetically engineered retrovirus did not replicate, it became harmless.

"When people started to get sick, I thought I had just killed the inn's guests, every one of them. I knew of two terrorist groups that were working on accomplishing the same thing, but they wanted to use the retroviruses as weapons. They didn't care if an antidote existed. The only way I could develop the antidote was to grow cultures of lethal microbes that could be carried by the retrovirus. This is why it was important that I discover the antidote as well. If I discovered the antidote, no one could ever use them as weapons." The Captain stopped to catch his breath, happy to know that Hans didn't know genetics.

"Enough. I've heard enough of your gibberish. First you talk about retroviruses, then you speak of terrorist groups that are also conducting the same research. You say you almost killed all of the inn's guests because you haven't discovered the antidote. You're insane, Captain."

"As a scientist, I don't always make sense with words. Perhaps if I slow down a little I may make more sense. I'm sure you wouldn't be making sense if you had come close to killing as many people as I almost did. Please try to understand.

"I can explain everything but get off my back," the Captain continued. "My preliminary research was very ordinary. But one day I accidentally discovered how to drive chemical reactions in novel ways—just like I told you. Based on chatter I came across on the Internet, I realized how dangerous it was if other people made similar breakthroughs. As a matter of fact, I think these terrorists I mentioned are on to me. I don't know how they could have found out about my research, but they must have because they tried stealing my data. The bastards broke into my lab, but we were able to fend them off. But trust me, they'll be back. They're not about to give up. And do you know why I know they'll be back? Because they probably haven't been able to figure out how to make the retrovirus self-replicate but assume that I have, that I have discovered a way of enabling the retrovirus to self-replicate. Their assumption is correct, Hans. I have discovered the reason why the retrovirus didn't self-replicate, and they're willing to kill to get this information. I'm not stupid. I know my life's in danger, so I'm asking you for help. Maybe we can become partners, but only if you're willing to protect me. I also want you to give me your word that I get a share any profits you'll be making off my discovery. I know there's a lot of money to be made by weaponizing my retroviruses."

"You're good, Captain. You haven't told me shit. You've wasted several hours of my time with this fucking mumbo jumbo scientific explanation, but what the fuck have you actually discovered?"

Hans left, leaving the Captain alone in the dining room.

From his isolated cabin, Hans spoke into his satellite telephone. "Nothing to worry about, David. I couldn't get shit out of the Captain. I tried every trick in the book, but he held strong. I thought I had him when I told him of the audit, the audit you told me about when you hired me. I mentioned the retrovirus, just like you described, but it didn't faze him. He just continued lying, talking about terrorists. I couldn't get him to confess or divulge any information about the true purpose of the discovery. I have to hand it to the old man, he held strong. He talked in circles all night long. I'm the best in the business, and if I couldn't break him, nobody can. He's too fucking committed to the project to sell out. He'd rather get killed than talk."

CHAPTER 32

Hans arrived at the Gare du Nord train station and took a taxi to the Pizza Visuvio Restaurant on the Champs-Elysees. His meeting with Moe was still an hour away, but he couldn't wait. He was hungry and decided to order lunch. While Hans looked at the menu, the waiter brought him an espresso. "Compliments of the gentleman behind you, sir," the waiter told him.

Hans turned around and saw a man wearing a Real Madrid jersey, sunglasses, and a long beard.

"Come join me at my table."

"How long have you been here?" Hans got up from his table and joined Moe.

"For a while," the disguised Moe answered. "Wanted to make sure you weren't being followed, so I just sat and waited for you to arrive."

"I don't think you have to worry about me being followed."

"Why have you been avoiding me? Haven't heard from you in several months. Anything wrong?" Moe asked. "Do you want to tell me how you managed to fuck up such a simple burglary? You fucking idiot."

"How the fuck was I to know that the helipad was structurally unsound. How was I supposed to know from the satellite photos that the shit was worthless? The motherfucker collapsed within seconds of our landing. Two of my men and the pilot were shot and killed as we escaped from the burning chopper through the left door. Carl and I ran toward the woods. We were receiving heavy fire as we ran further into the forest. One of the bullets hit Carl in the head. I was the only one to make it out alive."

"Are you telling me that I gave you half a million euros for nothing?"

"You don't have to tell me I fucked up. I know I messed up. But let me tell you the good news."

"Are you serious, you fucked up and this is good?" Moe asked.

"Yes, that's why I haven't contacted you in months. I have been busy trying to finish what I started. And this is the good news. You are now looking at the head of security for Mr. David Lorca."

"David Lorca!" Moe exclaimed.

"Yes, do you know him?"

"Of course not, how would I know him?"

"Don't know, it's just the way you pronounced his name. In any case, he's the American that's behind the Captain and his research. He's a billionaire who lives in Monte Carlo but is originally from San Antonio, Texas. The same guy that flew to Granada to meet with the Captain. I'm on the inside. Can you believe this?"

"How did you pull it off? How did you get your ass to be head of security for this...Mr. David Lorca?"

"Lorca decided to increase the level of security after my failed attempt at breaking into his lab. He was so pissed off at his security detail for having allowed a helicopter get as close as it did that he fired all of them the moment he brought me on board."

"You still haven't answered my question: how did you pull it off? Why did he hire you?" Moe asked.

"David needed to hire somebody to replace his soon-to-be-fired security personnel so he asked his contacts in the intelligence community if they knew of somebody that might meet his security requirements. Guess who got recommended by his own intelligence circle? Me. It pays off to have friends on the other side."

"Just like that he hires you?" Moe asked.

"He interviewed me on two separate occasions. I told him about my experience in law enforcement, in particular with underground crime syndicates, and that did it," Hans said.

"Since I hadn't heard from you in months, I thought you were dead."

"Well tell me, who's willing to pay us to destroy the data and to get rid of Lorca and the Captain?" Hans asked.

"It's none of your fucking business. Got it? You don't get to ask questions. Your job is to sit and wait for my instructions. I have to get going." Moe stood up and started walking to the exit.

"I found out something else that I think is significant," Hans said.

"What's that?" Moe asked as he returned to the table and sat down.

"I'll tell you, but it's going to cost you."

"How much?" Moe asked.

"A lot."

"Let me be the one to decide."

"Lorca is building a yacht," Hans said.

"That's it? That's what you found out? That Lorca is building a yacht?" Moe shook his head.

"It's not just a regular yacht. Brought you a miniature set of plans; they're here in my briefcase. Review the plans in detail; you'll be impressed. So make sure that my fee reflects the information I just gave you. You know where to deposit the money."

"Are you fucking crazy?" Moe asked. "You want money for a fucking set of plans?"

"Don't forget to make the deposit," Hans said as he got up and left.

CHAPTER 33

Moe opened the door and walked out onto his room's balcony. It was a warm and sunny day, too pretty of a day to be indoors. He leaned on the balcony rail and gazed at the hundreds of tourists atop the Arc de Triomphe. A knock on the door immediately broke his brief repose.

"Damn, you look good," Moe told Beth as he let her into his room. "It's always a pleasure looking at you, or should I say it's always a pleasure seeing you."

Beth, whose impressive resume also boasted of her reign as a former beauty queen, walked passed him, not taking time to thank him for his coarse compliments and greeting.

"Do you mind telling me who in the hell is building this thing, because it's certainly not a pleasure yacht," Beth said as she removed her designer sunglasses. "I've been studying these plans since you gave them to me four months ago, and I don't know what to make of them. Where did you get them? Because based on what I've seen, these plans are definitely top secret material. I sure as hell hope I'm not walking into something I won't be able to get myself out of."

"Sorry, I can't answer either of your questions."

"I've never seen anything like this. If this ship ever gets built, I want to be there for its christening. As a matter of fact, I wouldn't mind being on its maiden voyage."

"I thought you'd be impressed," Moe said. "My sources say that the yacht is being built as we speak. But as far as you being a passenger on its maiden voyage, those are long odds, my dear. Anyway, getting back on track. I have an idea of the yacht's capabilities, which I assume are many, but I have no idea what's all in the plans. I see steel doors, hatches, air systems, a wine cellar with special equipment, engine rooms, a radar room, et cetera, but I'm not an expert in this area. I can see what's on the plans, but I don't know what I'm looking at, and that's why I hired you. So tell me, what did you find?"

"Aren't you going to offer me something to drink before I brief you on my findings?"

"Why of course, I have champagne on ice for the lady."

"You flatter me by remembering that champagne is my drink of choice."

"You're going to love this vintage Krug I picked out especially for you," Moe said.

"You're too generous, Moe."

"How was your flight from JFK?"

"Too damn long. I don't care that I flew first class, it's still a seven-hour flight. I sure as hell miss the Concorde."

"Here's your bubbly. To what shall we toast?" Moe asked.

"To making money. What else is worth toasting?" Beth raised her glass and took a sip. "Ooh, this Krug is so special. You're spoiling me, Moe."

"A lady like you deserves to be spoiled."

"Enough. Now let me show you why you're paying me so much."

"I'm paying for secrecy."

Beth took out an enlarged set of plans, consisting of at least one hundred sheets, from her suitcase and unfolded them on the desk. The plans didn't show who had designed or engineered the Milagro. Several areas on the plans were highlighted in red, the rest of the pages remained untouched.

"What did you find out?" Moe asked. "Anything interesting?"

Beth Morris was born and raised in Boston. Her father retired as a Rear Admiral in the United States Navy and her mother was a former journalist for the *New York Times*. The University of Michigan graduate had earned degrees in Marine Engineering and Nautical Engineering. The free-thinking Beth did a short stint in the Navy but soon got bored and left the military. She decided to freelance and opened a consulting firm. Her boutique practice was very specialized. It only had one client: the United States Navy. She spent most of her days at the Pentagon, consulting with her client on top-secret projects.

She soon got bored with her consulting work as well and decided to travel. Beth traveled the world but tended to gravitate towards the Middle East. It was during one of her trips to Jordan that she met Moe. That's the day Beth went rogue.

"I found out a lot about the *Milagro*. That's the name that appears on the plans," Beth said. "Let's start with the easy stuff. The yacht—let's call it that for now even though it's more like a naval ship—the plans call for it to be equipped with mini nuclear reactors. Can you imagine the cost associated with this? When was the last time you boarded a nuclear-powered yacht? Or a nuclear-powered submarine?"

"Submarine?"

"That's what I said, but first let me tell you something else. Having nuclear reactors requires a lot of upfront costs, but you can't beat the advantages, one of which is that the *Milagro* can stay out at sea for at least four years without refueling.

"Now to answer your question," Beth smiled at Hans. "Remember those transformer toys that became popular during the eighties? Surprise—the *Milagro* can transform itself into a submarine."

"Are you shitting me?" Moe asked.

"Hell, no. Look, look carefully at this section of the plans and notice how the yacht's exterior seams are joined. These are not weld joints. The *Milagro*'s exterior shell can be unfastened. And this is how they are unfastened. Do you see what I see?" Beth asked as she flipped to the structural section of the plans.

"Damn, those are blasting caps," Moe said.

"Your knowledge as an arms dealer is showing, Moe. Not too many people would have recognized these caps. Electric blasting caps with boosters that lead to the plastics. With a strong burst of an electrical current to those caps, the *Milagro* sheds its exterior and, bam, you now have a submarine."

"Being nuclear powered makes even more sense on a sub because you don't need oxygen and there is no exhaust," Moe interrupted Beth. "However, and this is a very important however, the reactors have to be cooled. Seawater is used to keep them cool, which is great except for the fact that the sub leaves a thermal wake. When this thermal wake reaches the surface, it creates a thermal scar because of the warmer water's lower density. The thermal scar then becomes observable through thermal imaging devices. This is not good if you want to be completely invisible," Moe said.

"Never took you for a science nerd," Beth laughed. "But you are only partially correct, because the *Milagro*'s engineers have a solution for eliminating the thermal scar. Besides, maybe they don't care about leaving a thermal scar. Maybe it's not important for them to be stealthy. I tell you, Moe, whoever is building this ship is not your average Joe.

"Now let's flip back to this other page on the plans," Beth continued. "The mechanical section back here. This room, what they call a wine cellar on the floor plan, is really an advanced science lab layout. It has its own purified air filtration system that feeds the lab's clean room. Look at these fume hoods and the protective gear that is required to be worn by anybody entering the lab. It says it right here in the notes. This is a Biosafety Level Four lab, similar to the type of lab that is required when conducting Ebola virus research. Why in the world would you want this type of lab on a yacht? Doesn't look like a wine cellar to me," Beth said as she flipped from one page to another in the set of drawings.

"Anything else?"

"Yes, and it's right here on this page. I almost missed the most important part of this fucking yacht. When I first looked at these," she pointed at the plans, "they looked like ordinary electrical conduits, no big deal. But as I was about to turn the page, I noticed something strange. It's one long continuous conduit with no joints whatsoever. This continuous conduit is made of carbon fiber with a glass-lined core. These conduits originate in the lab and go all the way up past the flybridge. Now tell me, Moe. Why would you go through all the trouble of making the lab so secure, Biosafety Level Four, only to have an open exhaust to the exterior? This breaks every safety protocol in the book. Doesn't make sense. This is too important of a feature to overlook. If I were you, I would definitely look into this. This rabbit is worth chasing."

"Well, Beth, you've done a wonderful job, as usual," Moe said, cutting her off. "How much do I owe you?"

"I'm not finished. There's one more thing that is unique about this yacht," Beth said.

"Why does this not surprise me?"

"It has an airlock system on the ventral side, on its belly, if you will."

"Like I said, all I saw was a series of doors, rooms, and hatches. I would never have guessed that it was an airlock system."

"You can go in and out of the yacht through its underside."

"Now why would you want to have that on a yacht?" Moe asked.

"This is not a yacht, Moe. This vessel is beyond anything I've ever seen. When I was in the business of designing and building naval ships, the first question I asked my clients was, 'What's the mission of this ship you want me to design?' I sure as hell would like to know the *Milagro*'s mission."

"So would I."

CHAPTER 34

The Captain looked around the small pub as he waited for Warren to arrive. The Captain had demanded that Warren meet him there for a private meeting. The pub was nearly empty. It was still early, and the local dairy farmers would not be arriving for Happy Hour until the last cow was milked. The bartender and the lone waitress were behind the bar, carrying on a quiet conversation.

Warren found the Captain's request rather strange but decided not to ask any questions.

"You're late. I said six o'clock and it's six-twenty. I don't like to be kept waiting," the Captain reprimanded Warren.

"Relax. Chill out, Captain. What's wrong with you? It's your fault that I'm late, dragging me all the way out here. I wouldn't have been late if we had had this meeting at the lab. So tell me, Captain, why are we meeting here? Why meet in a public space if our meeting is supposed to be a secret? The lab is much more secure than this joint could ever be."

"I wanted to get away from the lab. Thought it might help me be more objective with what I want to talk to you about. I want to speak freely, and it's difficult to do this back at the lab."

"We always speak freely, even when David is around. This is absolutely not cool, Captain," Warren objected. "I came here thinking that this was just a social meeting; you know, just to have a few beers and relax, but I'm getting a sneaky suspicion that this is not the case." Warren pulled out a cigarette as he continued chastising the Captain.

"I didn't ask you here so that you could lecture me, ok? There's no way to sugar coat what I'm going to tell you, so I'll just say it. I strongly believe that David is not going to release the retrovirus."

"Is this what this meeting is about?" Warren yelled out as he took a long drag on his cigarette.

"You guys need another beer, Warren?" The bartender asked, hearing the commotion from Warren's table.

"No, I was just talking to my friend."

"Keep your voice down. And yes, Warren, that's why I asked you to come here, to tell you that I don't believe David is going to release the retrovirus."

"We've dedicated years of our lives to this project and now you're saying it's not going to happen. You're crazy, you know that Captain? You're crazy!" Warren yelled out, again getting the bartenders attention.

"Don't you know how to keep your voice down?"

"Not in times like this. This is absolute nonsense. David has more invested in this project than the two of us combined. This is his brainchild, Captain. He's been working on this project since the mid-eighties. It's ludicrous to think that he's not going to release the retrovirus. You're bordering on the insane; you need to get a grip. Looks like stress is taking a toll on you. You need to take a vacation and get your head straight."

"Working around the clock to meet deadlines has nothing to do with what I'm telling you, so listen. Remember when I discovered the racist gene and then a year later I finished developing the retrovirus that would genetically alter it and render it useless? Remember? That was four years ago. I had the retrovirus ready to go but David said no. He directed me to find a way to reverse the altered racist gene back to its original state. Do you know how crazy that sounded to me? My staff of researchers and I had spent six years of our lives on discovering the racist gene and how to get rid of it, but that just wasn't good enough. David decided to add four more years to this project for no good reason. Are you listening, Warren? We find a way of neutralizing the racist gene only to have David tell us to find a way of activating it again. Does this make sense to you... does it?"

"Of course it makes sense, Captain. I was at the meeting when David instructed you to find a reversal process. It made sense to me then and it makes sense now. If in neutralizing the racist gene we negatively impact some other part of our DNA, we simply reverse the process. I know this would reintroduce racism, but we'll just keep working on finding another way of neutralizing the damn gene. I totally get your point, but David is only practicing good science, that's all he's doing. Don't forget, we're dealing with cutting-edge technology and science so David has to be overly cautious, overly careful, that's all. I understand your passion, but you're not the only one with skin in the game. So cool it and don't get paranoid on me, Captain. You're seeing things that don't exist."

"Is this what I get for trusting you? A slap in the face?"

"It has nothing to do with trust. I trust you and I've always trusted your judgment. But you're wrong this time. David has every intention of releasing the retrovirus. The *Milagro* is built and ready to do its job. The *Milagro*'s auction is scheduled for September 16 of next year—that's only ten months away. On that day, you'll see David keep his promise to us, but more importantly to himself."

"Maybe you're right, maybe I am getting paranoid. But to this day I still don't see why we had to find a reversal process. Genetic engineering is being used in various treatments for genetic disorders without having to have a reversal protocol. You don't get rid of cancer just to reintroduce it at a later date. I'm still not convinced that David will absolutely release the retrovirus."

"That's your choice. You can believe whatever you want, but that doesn't make it real. The only thing you can point to in buttressing your view is that David made you discover a reversal process. I need to hear more evidence of what you're alleging, otherwise I'm sticking with my opinion, which really doesn't mean shit because this is David's project. He can do whatever the hell he wants."

"You do what you want, Warren, but I'm releasing the retrovirus."

"You say that, Captain, because you know you are not capable of releasing the retrovirus by yourself. For you, releasing it is only a hypothetical question. You know the protocol when it comes to releasing the retrovirus. You know that it all comes down to David making the call. He's the only one that has the code that will allow us to activate the release mechanism. Without him entering the code remotely, the retrovirus isn't going anywhere. Consider yourself lucky that you don't have to make the call. I can't imagine the balls it takes for anybody to make the call."

"I could do it"

"Perhaps, but that's not your job. Your job was to make the discoveries, and you've done it. You have a lot to be proud of, Captain. You have discovered the genetics behind racism. I don't know if you realize what you and David have accomplished. You guys came together—whether by fate, accident, or whatever—for a purpose. Eradicating racism in our lifetime will literally be a miracle, and you guys have accelerated evolution by millions of years. You're the scientist here. You know darn well that it would have taken millions of years for the racist gene to disappear from our DNA on its own. You and David are about to free billions of people from the atrocities of racism. Take pleasure in knowing that future generations will be about caring for one another, about uplifting each other and not tearing each other down."

The Captain was right. It had been four years since David had directed him to find a reversal process for the altered racist gene. He and his research assistants had worked around the clock, giving it their all. The demands that came with making the additional discovery were taking a heavy toll on the Captain's health. He would go to bed only to rush back to the lab and conduct a new experiment, an experiment that might yield the desired results, but none were forthcoming.

After four miserable years, the Captain gave up. With a heavy heart, the Captain went to David and told him. *"I have finally discovered the reversal process."*

CHAPTER 35

"They've discovered the racist gene, but that's not all!" Hans yelled out as he rushed into Moe's hotel suite.

"Fuck, fuck, fuck …I knew it!" Moe yelled out. "I knew they were going to discover it sooner or later, but not this soon. I'm fucked, I'll never get my money back. Can't believe I bought into this shit. The American and the Gypsy are probably at the American embassy right now telling them that they need to talk to the president."

Hans took his coat off and threw it on the sofa, but not before removing a DVD from its left pocket. A DVD video and audio recording of the meeting between the Captain and Warren at the pub.

"That's not all, Moe. They've discovered how to genetically engineer the racist gene away."

"This shit is getting worse by the second. Any other bad news?"

Moe was right all along when he told James Morgan at Herrods that once the racist gene was discovered it would only be a matter of time before its elimination. But being right was now meaningless. The opportunity had passed him by. He could not now even offer a temporary fix to his clients. The racist gene had been let out of Pandora's box only to be eliminated.

"You were right about what would happen once the racist gene was discovered, but you're absolutely wrong about them going to the American embassy. Take a look at this," Hans said as he handed the DVD to Moe.

Moe sat in silence. He couldn't believe what he had just seen on the video.

"Just like you said, we're fucked. We have nothing to sell your clients. In ten short months they're going to release the retrovirus, and that's it, checkmate, game over. The only way to stop the release is to blow up the fucking lab with everyone in it, including David," Hans said.

"Do you think I'm stupid?" Moe asked. "Why would I want to kill them and prevent them from releasing the retrovirus?"

Within minutes of receiving the bad news, Moe had constructed an ingenious plan. A plan that could make him more money than he could have ever imagined.

"Because if you don't stop them it means the end of the Aryan Nation and I'll never let that happen," Hans responded.

"You're the most racist person I know, Hans. You think you're better than blacks, Hispanics, Jews, and all people of color."

"I know I'm better."

"Your racism is going to make you a very wealthy man, Hans." Moe looked him straight in the eye.

"I just told you that in ten months the retrovirus will be released. I don't care about any fucking money. All I want is to protect my Aryan Nation from becoming extinct. As it is, interracial marriages have ruined the purity of our race. But that is nothing compared to what the retrovirus will do. We white people cannot let this happen, Moe. We have to do something, we have to stop them."

"What if I were to tell you that there is a way to preserve your Aryan Nation and still make a ton of money," Moe replied.

"I just told you, I don't care about the fucking money. This is personal, Moe."

"I understand your loyalty, but you should make some money because there are risks. And you also have to consider that we might not be able to stop them. In which case, you'll be a non-racist, but a rich one."

"I'm getting the hell out of here, I'm going to stop them while I still can."

"Aren't you going to listen to what I have to say?" Moe asked.

"There's nothing you can say that will change my mind."

"Shut your fucking mouth and listen to what I have to say. Listen carefully because this is our last chance to make more money than you can ever imagine. What I heard in the video is that a retrovirus will be used to enter people's DNA and genetically get rid of the racist gene, right?"

"Yes."

"This means that if we can get somebody to discover a vaccine against the retrovirus, we're back in business."

After listening to Moe, Hans quickly left as he had promised.

CHAPTER 36

"What's with you and this afternoon tea routine?" James Morgan asked as he joined Moe at his usual table at the fourth-floor restaurant.

"I would think a multi-billionaire like you would take time to enjoy a cup of tea now and then. You know, show a little class."

Moe's emergency meeting with James was taking place in London, not to accommodate James, but because meeting in New York was not an option. Due to an outstanding warrant for his arrest, Moe was not about to set foot in the United States. He had refused to appear before the U.S. Senate Intelligence Committee and testify about his involvement in the Rwandan genocide. He was not about to spend the rest of his life behind bars.

"Things have gotten a hell of a lot more complicated since we met. Alarmingly complicated."

"Just fucking tell me; stop beating around the bush," James scolded Moe.

"The geneticist and his team have discovered the racist gene, and just as expected, they've discovered how to genetically engineer it away."

"There's no fucking way we're going to allow this to happen. You need to get your ass out there and put a stop to this shit. Do you hear me. Don't just sit there, get your ass moving. Now!" James' shouting caused some of restaurant's guests to leave.

"For a person who hates being seen with me, you sure are attracting a lot of attention."

"We paid you a substantial fee to make this problem go away, but you didn't deliver." James continued with his tirade. "Nobody fucks us and gets away with it, especially you. Jesus Christ, I can't believe this is happening. Fuck, I can't fucking believe what you just told me. Don't they know they can't fuck with us without getting hurt? Who do they think they are, God? They're fucking with nature. If God wanted people of color to run the world, it would have happened a long time ago. I don't know about you, but if we're going down, we're taking a lot of people with us. Tell me where this fucking lab is located, which country? We'll blow the bastards out."

"Are you finished? Are you finished ranting?"

"You haven't heard the last of me. I'm getting the hell out of here. If you can't take care of this shit we're getting somebody else." James threw his napkin on the table, stood up, and started to leave.

"Sit down, James. I can fix this, but you need to sit and listen to what I have to say."

James remained standing in spite of Moe's request. He shook his head and started walking away. Moe jumped to his feet, ran toward the departing James, and threw his body in front him, stopping him in his tracks.

"Don't let your anger get in the way of making a sound decision, James. Now please, let's quietly walk back to the table. I have a solution to this terrible situation, but you have to be willing to listen."

"Ok, I'm listening," James said as he sat down.

"This is what's going to happen. On September 16, 2015, the airborne retrovirus is scheduled to be released from a yacht named the *Milagro*. This airborne retrovirus will enter your body just like any flu virus and make its way to every cell in your body."

"Is this a science lesson?"

"Please listen. Let me continue. The retrovirus enters the nucleus of every cell in your body and attaches itself to your DNA. Once it does this, the retrovirus starts doing its job of genetically engineering your racist gene away. This retrovirus is self-replicating; you won't be able to stop it. As a matter of fact, once it gets in your system you'll be spreading the retrovirus to others. You become a carrier."

"I thought you said you had a solution. All you're telling me is that I'm about to get fucked."

"I have a solution for you, your family, and the rest of you people that run the world. But it's going to cost you."

James didn't respond. He sat with an empty look on his face, staring straight ahead but observing nothing. Hundreds of scenarios were racing through his head, but none were offering a way of maintaining his world dominance. The world's power brokers had met their match in David, and he was taking them down. September 16, 2015 loomed ten months away, and there was nothing he could do.

"Are you listening to anything I'm saying? Look at me, James. I need for you to look at me and pay attention to what I'm saying."

"I was just thinking, that's all."

"Good, because I need for you to think about my proposal, but more importantly to think about my fee."

"Let me hear your proposal first."

"Nice try, James. But I'm not telling you shit till I get fifty percent of my fee upfront. Once you do this, I'll set my plan in motion and let you know what's taking place."

"Ok, then tell me your fucking fee."

"I've always wondered what it feels like to be the richest man in the world," Moe said.

"What the fuck does that have to do with your fee?"

"Because I'll soon find out how it feels to be the richest guy in the world. I'll find out the moment you pay me my fee."

"You're such an asshole, Moe. This discussion has just ended. Hope I never have to see your face again. I'm taking matters into my own hands."

"Go ahead, see how far you get. And besides, what will your business associates around the world think of you when they find out you passed up the deal of a lifetime? You get to keep all the power in the world for how much, $80 billion? You guys are worth somewhere between three and four trillion, according to my latest calculations. Trillions of dollars that you guys have stashed away in offshore banks. Do you know how insignificant $80 billion is compared to your trillions? I thought so, you know my fee is the deal of a lifetime."

"I'll let you know."

"Don't take too long, the retrovirus could be let loose any day. Perhaps it's already out there."

CHAPTER 37

"**R**elax Captain. I'm not going to waterboard you. I'm much more civilized than Dick Cheney. Besides, waterboarding doesn't' work," Hans said as he walked into the Captain's lab.

"Who let you into my lab? You're not authorized to be here," the Captain yelled at Hans.

"I let myself in. I'm the head of security; I don't need your fucking permission."

"I don't care what your title is. Now get the fuck out."

"I can go anywhere I please, old man. Don't ever forget that."

The Captain continued working while keeping a close eye on Hans as he walked around the lab, opening office door after office door, making sure the researchers had left for the day. The Captain continued centrifuging several test tubes as Hans inspected the offices.

"Looks like we're all alone," Hans told the Captain as he closed the last office door.

"And soon you'll be all alone because I'm leaving as soon as I finish putting these things away. You'll be free to snoop around all you want, but don't forget to lock up after you're done. I'm sure you have the code."

"You're not going anywhere, Captain."

The Captain was not impeded by Hans' threats and continued with his last task before leaving the lab for the day. He adjusted his safety goggles before attempting to pour a bronze-colored liquid from a tray of test tubes into two Florence flasks. In spite of the Captain's warnings of standing too close, Hans hovered nearby as the Captain carefully emptied each test tube. The flasks were half full as the last test tube was drained of the bronze liquid. The Captain grabbed the flasks by the neck, turned around and was about to put them in the refrigerator when one slipped out of his gloved hand. The flask shattered as it hit the floor and spewed some of its contents on Hans' shoes. Hans quickly grabbed his handkerchief from his back pocket, leaned down, and was about to wipe his shoes when he heard the Captain yell out.

"Stop, don't touch it!"

The Captain rushed towards Hans with the one remaining flask in his left hand. Hans looked up, but it was a big mistake. The second flask slipped out of the Captain's hand and shattered on the floor. Much of the bronze-colored liquid splashed on Hans' face and eyes. The Captain grabbed Hans' upper arm and led him to the emergency eye wash station.

"Don't rub your eyes. Just keep them open and let the water do its job."

"What the hell was that? What got into my eyes?" Hans asked as he leaned over the emergency eye wash faucet bowl.

"Nothing that will kill you."

After a few minutes of flushing his eyes, Hans dried his face and walked back towards the Captain's lab station. The Captain didn't bother looking up. He continued locking his lab station's drawers. The sting in Hans' eyes was unbearable, but that didn't keep him from reaching into his coat pocket and pulling out a small plastic bag. Inside the bag was a lone strand of hair, a black strand of hair. Hans stared at the bag, smiled, and handed it to the Captain.

The Captain looked at it but didn't see anything. He was about to throw it back at Hans but decided to take second look. He took a step to his left and stood directly beneath one of the many ceiling lights.

He held the plastic bag up to the light with both hands. He rotated it slowly and was carefully examining it when its contents suddenly came into focus.

With his shoulders slouched, the Captain slowly dropped onto his lab stool. His glazed eyes stared blankly at the floor, remembering the many times he had had to run DNA tests on hair samples from dead Gypsies whose bodies had been exhumed from areas around Hitler's death camps. He was just a kid when half a million Gypsies were murdered by Nazis.

"Who does this strand of hair belong to?"

"You're the world's premier geneticist. I was hoping you would tell me."

"Don't fucking play games with me. You know where you got this sample. Now tell me, who does it belong to?" The Captain threw the bag across the lab table at Hans.

"It belongs to your son, Captain. The one you've been protecting all these years."

The Captain got up from his stool and walked towards Hans without saying a word. He moved slowly but with a steady cadence. Hans retreated, walking backwards without taking his eyes from the approaching Captain. Hans pulled his gun from his shoulder holster and aimed it at the Captain, ordering him to stop or he would shoot. The Captain kept walking towards him. "Stop," Hans yelled out again before firing his weapon in the Captain's direction.

"Is he dead? Tell me, you son of a bitch. Did you kill him?" The Captain lunged at Hans but missed as Hans jumped to one side.

"Move back, you old man. Turn around and start walking. I won't shoot to miss next time."

The Captain slowly turned around and started walking toward his lab station.

"Is he alive?"

"Yes, and if you want him to stay alive, you'll do as I say."

As much as he wanted to believe that he really had a son, the

Captain decided to run a DNA test on the hair sample. He picked up the plastic bag from the floor. After a few hours, he had his answer: he did have a son.

"What do you want from me?" the Captain asked Hans.

"A vaccine. I want you to develop a DNA-based vaccine that will immunize people against the retrovirus," Hans told the Captain.

"Impossible. It can't be done."

"Isn't there an old adage that says the moment a scientist says it's impossible, he's already made his first mistake?"

"I mean it's impossible for me to create a vaccine. You're asking me to do something that's beyond my expertise."

"I know you'll get it done, Captain, I'm not worried."

"Ok, I'll do it but it's going to take a long time. I have to get the right people, equipment, and who knows what else. I'm a geneticist—I don't know anything about vaccines."

"You don't have time. I want it now."

"Be reasonable; I need time," the Captain begged.

"I'll be back soon, and for your son's sake, don't disappoint me."

CHAPTER 38

"Why won't you let me love you, Hans? Tell me, Hans. Tell me. why won't you let me love you? "Heather cried.

It was late in the evening when they arrived back at their hotel after a spending a glorious time together. Hans had taken her to dinner at one of the finest restaurants in Berlin, in celebration of nothing in particular. Throughout their dinner, Heather shared stories of her adolescent years, telling Hans how she always thought of herself as being the ugliest girl in school. They laughed as she told Hans about classmates making fun of her long legs and skinny arms. The enamored couple held hands as Heather went on and on with her childhood memories. Halfway through dessert, Hans looked at his watch and suggested that it was best they head back to the hotel because he had to get up early the next morning. Heather knew what getting up early meant. Hans was about to leave on a mission and didn't know when he would return.

Hans gazed out the open window of their hotel room, not wanting to see Heather's tears as she hugged his naked body with hers. Seeing her in tears was not something that would have caused him any consternation a few months earlier. Hans couldn't have cared less about Heather's tears or any other prostitute's tears in previous encounters, but tonight it was causing him great grief. Heather's childhood memories and stories, while happy ones, had left Hans yearning for something he had never had. As Heather described her years of innocence, Hans pictured the little girl with braided hair playing in the schoolyard or taking her turn at the swings with her braids flying through the air. Heather was now more than she had ever been in Hans' psyche. She was not just a prostitute. She was a real person.

"It not just about sex anymore, don't you get it?" Heather begged as their naked bodies separated. "That's what I was trying to tell you the night you went crazy and wouldn't stop when I cried out my safe word. I kept yelling it out but it's as if you were in a trance...you wouldn't listen. I had to run, I was too scared to stay."

"Stop. Stop it, Heather. Stop torturing me. Don't you think I regret that night? I don't know what got into me. I was so drunk I don't remember a thing. I know I must have done something so terrible, so bad that it made you run away. I never want to hurt you again. I never want to make you run away in fear. And the only way I can guarantee that it never happens again is by me leaving and never returning."

"Neither of us is leaving until you tell me what's going on. I know you have a lot on your mind, Hans, but that's no excuse for blowing me off. You and I came across each other by chance. If it weren't for my madam, we would have never met. It was all about sex when we met, but things changed with time. It got to the point that I hated leaving after we had finished having sex. I could hardly wait for you to call again. I would phone my madam in the middle of the night, asking her if you had called, wondering if you had called and requested a different girl. I became so jealous that just thinking about you with another woman made me sick. I've never felt this way before. I've never had feelings like these in my life. Don't you get it, Hans?"

"Please stop, Heather."

"No, I won't stop until I finish saying what I want to tell you. Do you think I haven't noticed a change in you, too? We've both changed, Hans. It just happened. Neither of us planned it, it just happened. We've fallen in love."

"What makes you think we've fallen in love? How can you be so sure?"

"I just know. And you know it too. I might not be able to explain it, but I know what I feel. Isn't that what love's about, feelings?" Heather slowly walked back toward Hans and stood in front of him.

Hans held her in his arms without saying a word, wondering if his eyes were capable of tears. He reached down, cupped Heather's face with both of his hands, and gently kissed her. She put her arms around Hans as he carried her to bed.

The morning sun filtered through the flowing curtains. Hans slept for two hours before being awakened by the sounds of blaring auto horns and by the clanging of trash dumpsters as they were emptied. Heather and Hans embraced each others' naked bodies, making love before either said a word.

"Do you have to leave? Can't you stay one more day?" Heather asked as she got out of bed and pressed the brew button on the hotel's coffee maker. "It would be splendid if we could spend the whole day in bed."

"Impossible."

"Why?"

"I have to leave. I have something I have to take care of. Plus, we said a lot of things last night. I need time alone to think about what I said. I want to make sure I'm sure about what I said, especially about loving you."

"Are you getting sentimental, Hans?"

"Perhaps, but I want to be absolutely sure about loving you. I've never been in love, Heather. I don't know what it's supposed to feel like. However, I do like what I feel, that's for sure."

"Ah, how sweet."

"You must be right, Heather. Love is about feelings, there's no other way to explain it." Hans said as he sat on the bed "I always made fun of people when they told me they were in love."

"Why would you make fun of such a nice thing?"

"I don't know. But anyway, when they told me they were in love I would ask them one question: 'How do you know you're in love?'

They answered by telling me they couldn't describe it, but they knew it was love because they could feel it. That's when I would burst out laughing. I would tell them that if it was true love, they would be able to describe it. Now I know I was wrong."

"I love you so much, Hans. Please don't leave."

"I have to, Heather. Please try to understand."

"Understand what?" Heather said.

"Forget it, let's talk about something else," Hans said.

"I know what, Hans. Let's talk about us. Let's talk about our future together. Let's talk about where we want to live. I've got it, let's talk about building our dream home. It's going to be lovely. It'll be huge, and we'll fill it up with kids."

"I've never thought about having children." Hans reached out and laid his hand on Heather's exposed leg. "I think we're getting ahead of ourselves. Maybe we should talk about kids some other time. We need to get to know each other, inside and out, before having kids."

"You sound so serious, Hans. Having kids will just happen, just like falling in love. Children will add so much to our lives. It'll be so much fun, seeing you with a baby in your arms."

"Stop," Hans yelled out.

"What's wrong? Does having children scare you?"

"I never want to have a child, I mean…an unhappy child."

"Oh, Hans. Why would you say such a thing? Our children will be the happiest kids in the world."

"I didn't get much sleep last night." Hans laid the empty coffee mug on the nightstand as he spoke. "Couldn't fall asleep. I kept thinking of you and, well I don't know, I've never trusted anybody. But last night as I lay awake, I realized I had changed. I realized that I had finally found a person I could trust, trust with my life."

"Your life? You sound so morbid. Just kidding, I know what you mean. And I also trust…"

"Please, let me continue before I change my mind. There's something in my past that nobody knows."

"I love you, and that's all that matters. I don't care about your past. We all have a past we don't want others to know. Don't forget how we met."

"Yes, it matters. My past matters a lot, Heather. My life as a kid was pretty screwed up. I hated my parents, I wished them dead." Hans said.

"Lots of kids hate their parents. What's so bad about that?"

"Not just as a kid," Hans continued. "I hated my parents for most of my life. Up until the moment I found out the truth. I hated them for having abandoned me in London. I was only six years old, six years old and all alone. Stuff like this really screws up your mind. My parents packed up and left, told me they would come for me as soon as possible. From one day to the next, they were gone. I had two aunts that would come visit me every once in a while, and some summers I would spend time at their house in Austria; they're the only family I ever knew. They told me that my parents would soon return for me. They lied. It never happened; they never came for me."

Heather leaned toward Hans, but he pushed her away. He looked straight ahead with his eyes glazed over. Heather had seen Hans retreat into his own world on occasion, but she felt he was now retreating into a hell hole by the look on his face. His face became contorted, his body stiffened, and he appeared to have taken a new identity, as if possessed by an evil spirit.

"Do you know why they never came for me? They couldn't. They couldn't fucking come and get me because they were wanted for war crimes. They were on the run. First they escaped to London and then to Argentina. I hated myself when I found out the truth. My parents left me behind to protect me; they wanted a new life for me. Can you imagine? I hated them with all my soul and all they were doing was protecting me. They loved me and wanted the best for me," Hans said.

"What are you talking about, Hans? What war crimes?" Heather asked.

"Yes war crimes. You never heard of war crimes? It was all a bunch of bullshit; my parents never committed any fucking crimes. They were loyal Nazis that were fighting a necessary war. And do you know what else? Do you know what else? I lost my twin brothers, all because of some fucking assholes at IBM. They fucking screwed up their punch cards. My brothers would be alive today if not for their fucking mistake," Hans said.

"What mistake, what punch cards?" the frightened Heather asked.

"I'll tell you what fucking mistake—my parents were labeled fucking Jews, IBM's punch cards fucked up, shit I don't know. All I know is that my parents were loyal Nazis; they weren't no fucking Jews." Hans slapped at the empty mug on the nightstand, breaking it into tiny pieces as it flew against the wall.

"Their fucking mistake cost my twin brothers their lives. Fuck, I didn't even know I had twin brothers. I had twin brothers that were killed, all because of IBM's fucking mistake."

Hans continued. "My parents and twin brothers were sent to Auschwitz. They were thrown in there with all the fucking Jews, all because of IBM's fucking mistake. My brothers died because of some fucking experiment. Mengele thought they were Jewish twins. It wasn't his fault; it was the American company that made the fucking mistake. Somehow word got back to Hitler about my parents' detention at Auschwitz, and he intervened and made sure my parents were immediately released. But it was too late; my twin brothers were dead. The war came to an end, but it signaled the beginning of my parents' lives as fugitives. During the Nuremberg Trials, they were found guilty, in absentia, of war crimes for rounding up Jews in Paris. I didn't know any of this shit until later in my career, when I had a higher security clearance. I came across some documents in old archives, original documents showing my parents' involvement with Hitler. This is when I learned why I had been abandoned."

"Oh Hans, I'm...."

"Quiet, don't say anything, don't say a word. Let me finish. There's something else I must tell you."

"What is it Hans?"

"Listen carefully. Remember I told you about a scientist that is conducting genetic research. You know, the one I went to visit in that little remote village," Hans said.

"Yes, of course I remember. The safe word night, how could I forget?" Heather said.

"I haven't told you the whole story or the truth. I'm working with the same group that the geneticist works for. I'm the head of security. The guy in charge of everything is an American named David Lorca. Several years ago, he hired the Captain to discover the racist gene."

"The racist gene? The Captain? What are you talking about?" Heather asked.

"The geneticist I've told you about, he goes by the name Captain. The group made a big discovery in genetics and genetic engineering. They discovered the racist gene and how to genetically engineer it away. This whole project is so secret that they use quantum encryption."

"What's that?"

"It's the most advanced encryption system in the world. It can't be broken. A young guy by the name of Warren is in charge of the encryption."

"What's going on, Hans? You've told me stuff before, but this is really scaring me."

"Don't be afraid. Just do what I tell you and everything will be fine," Hans said.

"Do what?" Heather asked.

Hans was positive he was in love with Heather. He was positive he could trust her, but the stakes were too high. The vaccines that were being developed would protect his Aryan Nation and give rise to the Fourth Reich. Hans pictured himself as its leader. Sharing this information with Heather was not possible for Hans, but he had to tell her something. Moe always took care of his operatives, and if anything happened to them, if they got killed during a mission, he took care of their families. This was no different. Moe had requested that Hans provide him a contact, a person who would receive Hans' share of the money should anything happen to him. Hans decided that he would tell Heather a half truth, that his mission was to steal the racist gene and nothing else.

"I've been offered millions of dollars to steal the racist gene research data. We're going to be so rich that we'll be able to buy anything we want. Our lives are about to change, Heather, our lives will never again be the same."

"I don't like it, Hans. Nobody pays you millions for no good reason. Please don't do anything stupid. Let's grab our suitcases and get the hell out of here. Let's go to some distant place, where nobody knows us. We don't have to be rich. We can get a job, any job. All that matters is that we be together. But please, Hans, let's leave now."

"We'll leave when I say so, do you understand? I'll tell you the whole story when we've left the country, but for now let me tell you this. If anything happens to me, you will be contacted by a man named Moe. He'll give you the information you'll need to access my share of the money. Remember the names of the people I mentioned. You might need to know them in case I don't make it."

"No, Hans. Please don't leave me alone, I'm begging you."

CHAPTER 39

Moe sipped champagne as he waited for James Morgan at Le Café Marly. He stared at the Louvre pyramid as it rose in the Cour Napoleon, mesmerized by its beauty and grandeur. The overhead clouds dissipated, forcing Moe to move to a different table to avoid the sun's rays that were bouncing off the glass pyramid and into his eyes. Moe accepted James' best offer, $20 billion—considerably less than his request—but with one caveat: Moe would receive fifty percent of his fee up front. Hours before arriving at the Le Café Marly, Moe verified that the money had been deposited in his offshore bank accounts. With $10 billion safely ensconced in his accounts, Moe readied himself to meet James.

"Don't know if you like the world of art, but I've always loved it here," Moe said as he stood up to welcome James. "Looking at the Louvre with all of its majesty and splendor makes me think of days gone by. Makes me think of the days when kings and queens ruled with absolute power. But then again, some things never change." Moe's blunt words didn't seem to sit well with James. "Have a seat, I've ordered a bottle of their finest champagne."

"I'm not here to celebrate anything."

"Maybe I should first tell you what I intend to do to save your ass. Perhaps then you'll feel like celebrating."

"Whatever your plan is, we want everything to look like an

accident. We don't want to see pictures of bullet-riddled corpses in newspapers around the world, do you understand?" James warned Moe.

Moe looked down at the multitude of people as they entered the Louvre through the glass pyramid. The pyramid reinforced Moe's belief that some things never change. Moe's brain raced through history. First, he told himself, there were the Pharaohs, that ruled the ancient world with an iron fist. The modern-day pharaohs rule with an invisible hand. The ancient pharaohs wore collars of gold and precious gems; today's pharaohs wear neckties and business suits. The modern-day pharaohs sit on boards of the largest multinational banks in the world, which in turn control the world's economy. The modern-day pharaohs have created the largest income inequality the world has ever known, and along with the income inequality comes political inequality. These were the words Moe had intended to share with James, but he shortened them by merely telling him, some things never change.

"If your expectations are that somebody go in like John Wayne and start shooting up the place, you're looking at the wrong person. You could have hired some two-bit hoodlum to do that. I can't believe what you just said, James. Do you honestly think I would propose such a stupid plan, shooting up the place, and expect a $20 billion fee? I was positive you thought more of me than that, James."

The waiter refilled the champagne flutes and placed the bottle back in the ice bucket. Neither man said a word until the waiter left the table.

"If September 16 is the scheduled release date of the retrovirus, we're almost out of fucking time. No fucking time left to stop them."

"Who said anything about stopping them?"

"That's not funny." James looked away.

"I'm not trying be funny. I told you I would tell you my plan once I received fifty percent of my fee. I've received it, so I'll tell you how I'm going to save your ass. But please don't interrupt me until I'm finished, ok? When I'm done, you can ask all the questions you want."

"Just tell me what the fucking plan is."

"Step one: I develop a vaccine that will inoculate you against the airborne retrovirus. Step two: I make sure the retrovirus is released five days after the scheduled date."

"That's the plan?"

"That's it, plain and simple. This two-step plan will make sure you guys rule the world until—I guess until you get tired of ruling. The first time we met I told you I couldn't guarantee you a permanent solution to your impending doom, the discovery of the racist gene. But I told you I could at least provide some breathing room. It was during our second meeting that I told you things had taken a turn for the worse. I told you that the racist gene had in fact been discovered, but more importantly, so had the process of eliminating it. This spelled the end of the world for you powerful people. I explored thousands of scenarios by which we could make this problem go away. And do you know what I found out? There weren't any solutions to your problem. Trying to stop the elimination of racism now that the racist gene has been discovered is like trying to stop evolution. We can't. Evolution proceeds without our permission.

"Once I acknowledged this fact, that we couldn't stop the elimination of the racist gene and racism, I doubled down. Through my sources, inside the American's circle, I learned that the racist gene is a primitive gene, but a very important gene before humans became civilized. The racist gene served as a defense mechanism and nothing else. It could have easily been labelled the "survival gene." If a Neanderthal or whatever type of creature that existed in ancient times saw somebody that didn't look like them, they attacked it. Very simple response mechanism: you don't look like me equates to you being the enemy. As we evolved, we no longer needed this primitive gene because we developed language. By talking we could differentiate between friend and foe.

"This being said, can you imagine the advantage you would have over others by retaining the racist gene in your DNA? If you think you and your buddies have an advantage over every citizen of the world today, wait til they lose their racist gene and you get to keep yours. I bet your mouth is starting to water. Am I right, James?"

James did not utter a word. He was indeed having a hard time understanding the ramifications of eliminating the racist gene from people's DNA. *Doubling down*, the words kept ringing in his mind. "Moe is right," thought James, "we're going to beat them at their own game. If the racist gene is eliminated, people's attitudes will be softened, and they will not see us as the enemy. Gone will be the battles for equality, minimum wage, equal education. Heaven knows we spend billions of dollars fighting these nagging problems, but they just don't seem to go away. People of color will from now on give us the benefit of the doubt because they won't see us as an enemy, just like Moe said." Thinking of all the possibilities of how we come out ahead on this deal made his head spin.

"The vaccine will guarantee that you're the only racists in the world. The racist gene will survive in your DNA. And guess what? You will pass on the racist gene to your offspring. Your dominance in the world will continue forever. Having the racist gene will prove more profitable than having a superior intelligence gene in your DNA—which, mark my word, will soon be discovered."

"I'm speechless. I don't know what to say. I mean, how in the fuck did you come up with such an idea? This is pure genius!" exclaimed James.

"I should have held out for more money, but what the hell, we're not going to take it with us."

"But will it work, the vaccine? What happens if the fucking vaccine doesn't work?"

"In a few weeks we'll be conducting clinical trials."

"You mean you already have the vaccine?"

"Yes and no. We have it, but we have to make sure it works. That's why we're getting ready to run the clinical trials. But I'm positive that everything is a go with the vaccine, that it's going to work as advertised. I say this because we got lucky and had the same geneticist, the one that developed the retrovirus, also develop the vaccine. You see, James, when you already know the complex molecular structure of the retrovirus and how it attacks, developing a vaccine to fight it becomes less challenging. It would have taken years to develop the vaccine had we not had the services of this geneticist. Setting that aside, let me continue. If the clinical trials prove unsuccessful we will need more time to refine the vaccine. So if the vaccine is not ready by September 1, we go to plan B."

"Which is?" James asked. "And why the five-day delay?"

"Why a five-day delay? Because we need—or rather you need— five days. Three days to start delivering and administering the vaccines to everybody you designate, plus two days for everyone to develop the antigens that will protect you from the retrovirus.

"Now to answer your first question," Moe continued. "Under plan B, which is implemented if clinical trials prove unsuccessful, we sabotage the release of the retrovirus until we have time to develop the vaccine. The ultimate release of the retrovirus is a must, so I have to make sure I don't destroy their capabilities in the process of delaying the scheduled release. But we still need the five-day window under either plan. In my business, I often tell my clients, trust me. People continue to hire me because they have learned to trust me, just like you have. So I'm telling you once again, trust me. I'm going to make sure nobody fucks with your world." Moe got up and left.

CHAPTER 40

Hans rushed into the lab, pushing several researchers out of his way as he made his way to the Captain's office. Hans was not alone; he was accompanied by Bodashka.

Well aware that he was not capable of confirming the Captain's vaccine trial results, Hans immediately turned to his friends and former East German agents for help. Without hesitation, they directed Hans to a young geneticist that was always willing to conduct clandestine research—for the right price. Hans immediately flew to Ukraine to meet the young geneticist. Satisfied that Bodashka was capable of verifying the Captain's claims and could also be trusted to keep his mouth shut, Hans hired him. Within days, Bodashka was transported to the lab at the Pines Inn.

Without knocking, Hans threw open the office door, startling the Captain and causing him to drop a folder full of research data he was reviewing. The Captain looked up and noticed Bodashka as he picked up the last piece of paper from the floor. In an instant, his body filled with a surge of adrenalin. The Captain was positive the young man in his office was an assassin, and he was the target. Bodashka had a smile on his face, but it was not a sinister smile. He looked much too young to be a professional assassin, but the Captain's mind was made up. He was about to die.

With resignation, the Captain shook his head and picked up a stack of computer printouts, including diagrams, charts, and schematics of the retrovirus from his desk and handed them to Hans. He then turned around and from his credenza picked up another stack of computer printouts that contained the vaccine's trial results. Thinking that he was about to speak his last words, the Captain spoke as slowly as possible, wishing to extend his life if only by a few seconds as he briefed Hans on the results. The Captain handed Hans photographs of what the actual results looked like under the electron microscope.

Bodashka listened intently as the Captain briefed Hans. He couldn't believe what he was hearing. Bodashka hadn't understood why he was being paid such a large sum of money to merely verify a vaccine's effectiveness against a virus. He now knew why. Without much fanfare, the Captain ended his presentation by telling Hans that the vaccine had proven to be effective against the retrovirus.

"Wonderful presentation, Captain. But do you really think I'm so stupid as to believe you? I brought my own expert." Hans pointed at Bodashka. "He's here to verify your claims. For your sake, let's hope he concurs with your opinions and claims."

The Captain couldn't believe his luck. He wasn't going to die after all, at least not now and not at the hands of the young man before him.

"Let's get to work, and if I can verify what I just heard, you're a genius," Bodashka told the Captain. "First you discover the racist gene, then you develop a retrovirus that can do away with it, and now you develop a vaccine that fights the retrovirus. All I can say is, wow."

"I didn't bring you here to praise the Captain. So get going on what I brought you here for. We don't have all night," Hans interjected.

The Captain led Bodashka into the lab and left him alone. The young geneticist approached the electron microscope and immediately started on his task at hand. He started by observing the before and after markings on the DNA strands taken from the trial's participants. On several occasions, Bodashka asked the Captain questions, making sure the Captain had not doctored the results.

Bodashka left the electron microscope, walked over to an empty lab table, and instructed the Captain to bring him the files he had earlier handed to Hans. Bodashka went over every detail in the files, turning each page slowly and deliberately, making sure there were no errors in the interpretations of the vaccine's effectiveness. Several times he flipped back to pages he had already reviewed. "Fuck, this kid is good, perhaps too good," the Captain whispered to himself.

With a startled look on his face, Bodashka suddenly looked up from the notebook he was reviewing. He abruptly stood up, tipping the lab stool over in the process, and rushed out of the lab and into the Captain's office. There, Bodashka picked up one of the notebooks he had already reviewed and brought it back into the lab with him. Without saying a word, he placed both notebooks next to each other. He stared at them, his eyes shifting from one notebook to the other.

The Captain knew what was happening. Bodashka had discovered the vaccine's limitations. Bodashka stood up and walked over to the electron microscope. He turned around, hidden from Hans' view, and looked directly at the Captain. There was no doubt in the Captain's mind what the intense stare meant, and it was not good.

Bodashka returned to his lab stool and reviewed a few more notebooks of data before signaling to Hans that he was done. With a wide smile on his face, he gave Hans two thumbs up, indicating that the vaccine was ready to go.

Bodashka reached out and shook the Captain's hand and said thank you. The Captain looked at Bodashka and asked him if he had ever been to East Berlin. Only once, Bodashka said, "while in my mother's belly."

Hans immediately interrupted the two men and personally ushered Bodashka out of the lab and to a waiting car. Bodashka was rushed to a private airstrip and flown back to Ukraine.

"Are you sure it only takes two days for the vaccine to work?" Hans asked after having made his way back to the lab.

The Captain nodded.

"I see you really love your son," Hans said as he walked toward the Captain.

"Fuck you."

"Is that any way to thank me for saving your son's life. That's right, Captain, your son was as good as dead when I found him. I don't mean it literally—he wasn't in some dungeon—but his life was not his. The moment you left Berlin and came out here, your handlers didn't give a shit about keeping your son alive. I convinced them to tell me where they were keeping him, told them I could put him to good use. I told them he could still be of help to the Aryan Nation. I was right—you came through with the vaccine. Thanks to you, racists like me will continue to exist."

"I did it to help my son, not to help you and your fucking Aryan Nation."

"And you're still not done. There's something else."

"Let him go. I kept my part of the deal, now you keep yours."

"Not so fast, Captain. There's more to the deal than I've told you. So listen. I need you to prepare two thousand individual dosages of the vaccine, enough to immunize all of my associates and their families."

"Are you crazy? Do you have a fucking clue what you're asking me to do? Two thousand vaccines? I suppose you think I can merrily walk out of here with two thousand syringes of the antivirus vaccine without anybody noticing. Are you fucking crazy? Here, you're welcome to take these, but not two thousand."

Hans grabbed the last three remaining syringes containing the retrovirus vaccine from the Captain's hand and put them in his suit pocket.

"On September 16, you and Warren will be inside the *Milagro* downloading all of the data from your lab's computer's to the *Milagro*'s. According to David's plan, a refrigerated truck carrying the retrovirus will arrive at the marina, ready to be unloaded. David has specifically ordered that Warren personally unload the truck. He is to take the canisters to the lab and hand them over to the technician who will immediately hook them up to the dispersing pumps. The technician will then hand over control of the pumps to the computers aboard the *Milagro*. At this point, only you and Warren will have control over these computers and, ultimately, control over the release of the retrovirus. Anyway, getting back to how you're going to get me the vaccines. Warren knows the plan but has no clue as to the number of canisters that are being transported. He'll know that he's unloading a shit load of canisters but will never know that half of them are carrying the antivirus vaccine, all two thousand doses. This is how you're going to get me the two thousand syringes of the vaccine without anybody noticing."

"You have it all figured out, don't you? You fucking Nazi," the Captain yelled at Hans.

From his coat pocket Hans pulled out a package of gum and opened it. With gloved hands, he carefully pulled out all five sticks and laid them on the Captain's lab table. The Captain stood on the opposite side of the table as he observed Hans skillfully unwrap two of the sticks of gum. Hans gently rubbed a white powder into the gum before rewrapping them and perfectly lining them next to the undisturbed sticks. He had done a masterful job. "Nobody will ever be able to tell that two of those have been unwrapped and laced with poison," Hans told himself as he walked to the sink to flush the remaining powder. The Captain was so close to the sticks of gum he could smell the bitter almond scent of the potassium cyanide.

With a smirk on his face Hans walked back toward the Captain and the sticks of gum on the lab table. The obsessive Hans noticed that the sticks on the left side were not perfectly lined up with the others so he gently pushed them, bringing the errant two into a perfect line with the others.

"I must be slipping. I thought I had perfectly lined up all five sticks of gum," Hans said.

"You evidently didn't," the culpable Captain answered.

With his brilliant work now complete, Hans removed his surgical gloves.

"At exactly seventeen hundred hours give these two sticks of gum to Warren," Hans said as he picked up the two sticks from the left side of the perfectly-lined row. He's so addicted to his cigarettes that he'll gladly accept them since smoking is strictly prohibited aboard the *Milagro*. An hour later, when the *Milagro*'s auction begins, my men will enter the *Milagro* through its dorsal airlock door to retrieve the canisters containing the syringes of the vaccine. Got it?"

"Do you really think I'm going to kill Warren?"

"Have you forgotten that I'm holding your son? Your son is not off the hook until this whole game is played out. Understand? But don't worry, I've made it easy for you. You don't have to kill Warren. The gum doesn't contain enough poison to kill him, but it will certainly make him very sick. He'll get as sick as you got when as a kid you ate the shit people gave you. Warren will be so sick he won't be able to put up a fight against my men. Hell, he won't even be able to pull out that little pistol he carries on his ankle holster."

"I should have poisoned you a long time ago," the Captain yelled out at Hans. "I probably won't last much longer, but if I do, I'm coming after you, with or without my son."

"Stop making threats, you old man. Now shut up and listen, I haven't finished giving you instructions. Once my men retrieve the vaccines, the retrovirus, and the research data, you are to immediately call David. Tell him some of the canisters weren't properly sealed and the retrovirus has been contaminated. Tell David that it will take you at least five days to sort out the problem. Let him know you can't release the retrovirus until then because you can't guarantee its effectiveness. You will also tell David that no one is to board the *Milagro*. Tell him you have to isolate the retrovirus from any additional outside contaminants. Tell him you and Warren have everything under control."

CHAPTER 41

David waited in the most unlikely of places. He did as instructed: "Drive to the address I've given you on Bismardkstraße. Park your car two blocks away and walk the rest of the way. Once I see that you have entered the porn shop and you're not being followed, I will meet you inside. Pay for the movie that is showing in booth number four. If it happens to be busy, go to booth number five. I will be watching you by this time, so I'll know which one you're in. Instead of knocking on the door, I'll merely scratch my fingernails on it. This way you'll know it's me. Open the door, but be careful. I don't trust anybody." David had memorized the woman's sensually spoken words. He didn't know how she had gotten his satellite telephone number, but he knew he was about to find out.

He entered the porn shop and immediately noticed that it was no different than walking into a department store. The aisles were wide, the lights were bright, the floors were clean and highly polished. The countless racks of adult movies were categorized by sexual preferences, some by names of famous porn actors or actresses and some by the name of the film studios. Past the movie section were shelves and racks of colorful adult toys of every size and shape. Sex toys for every fetish: whips, handcuffs, even penis-shaped lollipops. A young couple giggled as they went about deciding which of the many toys to buy. Some customers were single women who knew what they were shopping for and didn't need much time to decide. The older men with reading glasses examined the movie covers in detail, making sure their selection met their sexual proclivities. The cashiers' counter was circular and situated by the entrance. Every entering or exiting customer had to pass by the two cashiers working that night. David panicked, suddenly realizing he had only a credit card and no cash. He knew that the moment he used his credit card to pay for the movie it could be traced to an exact location, in real time. David couldn't believe his oversight and stupidity. He searched his coat's pockets again, and again came up empty-handed. He was about to give up and leave when he remembered Brent slipping some euros into his coat's ticket pocket. "Tip money," Brent told him as he left the airport.

The cashier took David's money and handed him the key to private viewing room number four. With a severe limp and with the aid of a cane, David slowly walked toward viewing room number four. The charade was for Heather's benefit—she had never met him. The cane was made of highly polished dark wood and adorned with a silver serpent slithering its way up the slippery cane. Even though David had been involved in a cloak-and-dagger style of life during the previous ten years, he was still not accustomed to its nuances.

David reached the private viewing room and opened the door with the key fob that had been handed to him by the cashier. *High tech doesn't escape any industry*, David smiled. Continuing with his disguise, he limped into the room. His eyes quickly adjusted to the small room's subdued lighting. A tall cocktail table with two barstools stood opposite a thin-screen LED television that hung on the wall. No sooner had the movie started than he heard the scratching.

David made two quick steps toward the door, no longer having to pretend to walk with a limp, and opened it carefully. A voluptuous woman's silhouette appeared on the doorway. The dark-haired and elegantly-dressed woman walked into the room and headed toward the cocktail table. A teardrop-shaped diamond on a gold necklace hung from her long neck. There was no doubt in David's mind that the woman before him was accustomed to the finer things in life.

He looked down at her French-tip fingernails that had so sensually scratched the door. David's eyes immediately shifted to the large diamond and emerald ring she wore on her index finger.

Without saying a word, she gracefully pulled out one of the bar stools and sat down with her back to the television. From her purse she took out a cigarette case and pulled out a joint. She casually lit it and set it on the glass table top. She then lit another joint and did the same. The no smoking sign on the wall didn't seem to apply to her. She obviously didn't play by the rules.

"The sign reads, Do Not Smoke," David told her, "especially a marijuana joint. Are you deliberately trying to get us in trouble? What's wrong with you? Put those damn things out."

Not listening to a word David was saying, she lit a third joint and placed it on the table next to the others. She instructed David to not say a word and to stand by the door, told him she knew what she was doing. He didn't particularly believe her, but he wasn't about to walk out. He needed to know who this woman was and how she had obtained his satellite phone number. Smoke started to fill the small room, and within seconds the smoke detector was activated. David stood frozen by the door, looking at the relaxed woman sitting within feet of him. She looked at her watch, and as if on cue, all hell broke loose.

The sirens of the approaching fire trucks and their sudden stop in front of the porn shop brought panic to the customers. They scrambled toward the exit, throwing down the movies and sex toys on the counter, all leaving emptyhanded. The men looked down as they exited, avoiding the security cameras' stare. The firemen ran towards the private viewing rooms, looking for the source of the fire.

"Follow me," the woman told David as they exited amid the chaos. "Walk slowly and get rid of that cane; leave it behind."

When they reached the street, she pointed at David's rental car. "Unlock it and get in. No, the other side. I'm driving," she told David.

They drove past the porn shop as they drove away and noticed that a crowd had gathered around its entrance. The firemen were walking out and ridding themselves of their heavy firefighting gear. With one hand on the wheel and the other reaching toward the back of her head, the woman transformed herself from brunette to blonde, tossing the wig out the window.

"Tell me about the Pines Inn," Heather told him.

"What about the Pines Inn? I've heard about it, but what does that have to do with me?" David asked.

"I'm sure it has a lot to do with you. It's not by coincidence that the moment I mentioned the inn you immediately agreed to meet."

"Tell me what this is about or I'll jump out of the car, I swear I will," David grabbed the door handle. "I'm serious, tell me now or I'm out of here."

"You'll know soon enough," she said as she sped up.

She drove David's car into a public underground garage. Inconspicuously, they walked up two flights of stairs and exited onto Spandauer Damm Street. She locked her arms around David's left arm, leaned on his shoulder, and walked two blocks before entering a busy hotel lobby. They rode the elevator to the top floor and entered a lavish penthouse suite.

"I need to talk to you about Hans," she started.

"Who's Hans?" David immediately interrupted.

"Let's not play games. I know who you are, as well as the Captain and Warren. And just so you know, my name is Heather."

"You obviously know mine," David remarked.

"Yes, I know your name but not much more. I've gone to a lot of trouble to tell you what I'm about to tell you, so listen. I met Hans some time ago. I was a high-priced call girl at the time. It was fate, really, the way I met him. My madam told me of a special client, a client requesting certain sexual proclivities, including me being his wet nurse. She asked me if it was something I might be interested in, but I immediately told her no. My madam persisted, told me I could make a lot of money with this guy. I had just had a miscarriage, so I said, yeah, why not? Anyway, the details are not important. What's important is that I have fallen in love with Hans. He tells me that our love is mutual. Don't know if it's true, but I'd like to believe it."

"Ok, so you know Hans. Now tell me, how do you know Warren and the Captain?"

"I didn't say I know them. I've never met them. Hans has mentioned their names, as well as yours, but that's it. I don't care to know any one of you. All I want to know is about your discovery—you know, the one you made at the Pines Inn."

David sat down across from Heather. He couldn't feel any part of his body. He was in shock. "If Heather knows about the racist gene, I have to assume she's not the only one. How could I have been so stupid and placed so much trust in Hans? I trusted him with my life, for God's sake. How did I miss it, how could I have been so blind? How could I have been so stupid? Why did he do it, why would he have told his hooker about us?" David was frozen in his thoughts.

"Are you ok?" Heather asked. "You look like you just saw a ghost."

David managed to get to his feet and slowly walked toward the window. He had not had a panic attack in years, but now he suddenly found himself in the middle of one. He knew how debilitating their effects were. Panic attacks always left him incapacitated for days. Knowing this caused his attack to become even more severe.

"Can I get you some water?" Heather asked the pallid David.

David didn't respond. His panic attack was now in full force.

"Here, now drink it. Maybe you're just dehydrated." Heather placed a bottle of water in his limp hand.

David took a small sip, knowing that there was nothing that was going to make his panic attack go away.

"If you don't want to listen, then don't," Heather said, "but I'm still going to tell you what I know and why it's urgent that I talk to you."

"Hans is in great danger," Heather continued. "He's plotting with somebody to steal your racist gene research data."

David desperately fought the attack, but it wasn't doing any good.

He felt like running out of the room but held back in confusion. The inability to make decisions was one of his greatest fears when in the middle of a panic attack.

"There, I said it," Heather said. "Didn't you hear what I just said? Hans is plotting to steal your racist gene research data."

Heather walked to where David was standing. Looking at him with tears in her eyes, she said, "You have to help me. You have to help Hans. He doesn't know what he's doing."

Heather gently hugged David. He could feel her body shaking as she cried. David remembered his ex-wife hugging him when he was experiencing a panic attack. His ex-wife wouldn't say a word; she would just hold him.

"I feel so damn miserable. I wish I had never gotten involved with Hans and his mysterious world," Heather said while still hugging David. "I can't remember when Hans started weaving this web because he did it very gradually. He would give a piece of information and then nothing for months. He told me about a geneticist that had made a major discovery, but he left it at that. Months later, he added that the geneticist was a Gypsy who went by the name of Captain and also mentioned a computer whiz kid named Warren. After telling me nothing for a long period of time, he suddenly laid out all of his cards. This is when I panicked and knew I had to contact you for your help."

Heather gently let go of David and started pacing the room.

"I've heard him talking on the phone, saying, 'in a few months we'll both make millions of dollars.' I can tell he's afraid of the person he's communicating with. I can hear the fear in his voice. This whole mess is driving me crazy. Hans is dealing with a bad person—his life is in danger. I don't want to see him get killed."

"Killed?" David asked.

"Yes, David, killed. He told me that if anything happens to him, I will be contacted by somebody named Moe. Moe is to give me access codes to bank accounts where I can find Hans' share of the money."

"Why?" David asked.

"Why what?" Heather asked.

"Why is he stealing..."

"Why is he stealing your discovery?" Heather finished.

David nodded.

"Money. It's all about the money. Didn't you hear me say that he plans on becoming a millionaire? He's told me the same thing but says he's doing it for me, for us, but he must have decided to make money long before he met me because he was already spying on the Captain by the time we started hooking up. But even if he did plan to steal your discovery before he met me, it doesn't matter, people change. I want to believe that it's no longer about the money."

"I still don't get it. Why is my discovery so valuable to somebody out there?" David asked as he fought his attack.

"I don't have any answers. All I know is that you have to help Hans. Please, David, you're the only one that can do it. I'm not a scientist; all I know about the racist gene is what Hans told me. He told me you've discovered ways of getting rid of the racist gene, or alter it or whatever, by means of a retrovirus. If this is true, you have to use your discovery to help Hans."

David's mind starting drifting before he responded to Heather's request. *None of this makes any sense. Hans tells Heather that he's being paid millions to steal the racist gene research data, yet doesn't say anything about destroying the retrovirus. If somebody wants to keep us from ridding the world of racism, they need to destroy the retrovirus.*

"Are you serious?" David asked. "You want me to help him, a person that is hell-bent on stealing from me? A person who has no scruples, a thief."

"Please help him, David. If you help him, there's no way he'll go through with his plan. You know I'm making sense, David. You have to help."

"Let him get killed. That's all I have to say."

Heather's voice quivered as she spoke. "Hans' parents were Nazis that bought into Hitler's eugenics and Aryan Nation propaganda. In his efforts to propagate the perfect Aryan nation, Hitler instituted youth camps where he brought in teenagers that passed the race test, meaning they had blonde hair and blue eyes. Here they were encouraged to have sex and have babies, perfect Aryan babies. This is where his parents met. His parents weren't as young as some of the other Aryan kids. They were old enough to play larger roles in the Nazi party. Everything was perfect for the young Nazi couple until something went terribly wrong."

"What happened?"

"While snooping around in secret war files—don't forget that as a Stasi Officer Hans had high security clearance—he found the birth certificates of twin boys with the same last name as his. Nothing unusual, but then he noticed the twins' parents' names. Same as Hans' parents' names. Hans learned of his twin brothers he never knew he had. He found hundreds if not thousands of other such birth certificates. Hans noticed that they all contained a series of numbers on the bottom right of the certificates. Nothing strange if each certificate were to be looked at individually and apart. But when Hans looked at the complete box of birth certificates, he noticed something very strange. All the numbers on the bottom right of each certificate were in sequential order. He suddenly realized there was only one possible reason why these birth certificates were labeled top secret and all newborns had been assigned sequential numbers. No other German birth certificates contained such numbers on the bottom right, much less in sequential order.

"At this point, Hans was more intrigued than ever regarding his family roots, so he delved deeper into Hitler's eugenics experiments. The more he learned of his family's history, the more enamored he became with the Aryan Nation bullshit. He kept delving deeper, only to find out that his twin brothers were killed by the Nazis—they had been subjects in some experiment. He told me that an American company IBM screwed up with their punch cards and labeled his family Jews. And what is incredible, David, is this. He doesn't blame Hitler or Mengele for the twins' murder; he blames the American company."

CHAPTER 42

"I think this is all very stupid. You bringing her here, to my lab of all places." the Captain said as they waited for Heather to arrive.

David arranged for Heather to meet the Captain at his lab, a risky but necessary next step. The probability of Heather being caught inside the Captain's lab by Hans was very real, but David was willing to gamble. He wanted Heather to put her neck on the line in order to prove her trustworthiness. At first Heather rejected David's insistence on meeting at the lab but acquiesced after realizing she had no choice. David made it clear to her that even though he was the boss, he was not moving forward on her request to help Hans unless the Captain was on board. David was giving her one, and only one, chance to make her case to a reluctant Captain.

The elevator doors closed behind her as Heather entered the lab. The corridor she found herself in was separated from the lab by a thick glass wall. Off in the distance, she noticed two men wearing long white lab coats over blue scrubs. Heather wasn't positive if one of the men was David since they were both wearing skullcaps and goggles, but she was positive David wasn't the short and overweight man. She noticed the men scrutinizing a test tube under a fume hood, carefully shaking it every few seconds. The shorter and heavier of the two men removed the test tube from the fume hood and placed it in a small refrigerator. The taller, slender man turned around and noticed Heather.

"Don't worry, we're not contagious," David told Heather as the men removed their lab coats, caps, and goggles. "Follow us down to the break room."

"Listen, Heather, I brought you here so that you can convince us that you're telling the truth because as far as we know you could be in cahoots with Hans," David said. "So give it your best shot. How you go about convincing the Captain and me to help you is totally up to you. So choose wisely because if your story doesn't add up, this is what I'm prepared to do: I will have your tongue surgically removed if we catch you lying. And after I have your tongue removed, I will make sure you receive the best medical care so that you will not bleed to death but survive to live a prosperous life—albeit, a life without a tongue. How does that sound to you? Does not having a tongue make you want to tell the truth?"

Heather had never heard David speak such menacing words. She remembered their first meeting, David had been polite and courteous. This other side of David terrorized her.

She had no intention of lying, but the thought of making a mistake as she laid out the facts terrified her. Heather knew how Hans had a habit of twisting her words and making her sound like a liar even when she was telling the truth. She had no doubts that David was just as capable.

Heather looked out the break room's window and into the sterile lab, looking every bit like an operating room. Bright lights glared down on a large stainless steel table in the middle of the lab. She suddenly saw herself strapped down on an operating table as surgeons with razor sharp scalpels removed her tongue. She was about to burst out crying but regained her composure.

"Hell, it appears I suddenly find myself in a no-win situation," Heather forced herself to say. "If Hans finds out I've been here to see you, I'm screwed, and if you decide I'm lying, I lose my tongue. And what have I done to deserve this? All I've done is warn you that your discovery is about to be stolen. And this is the thanks I get."

"You're here because you want me to help Hans. You couldn't care less about my discovery being stolen."

"Ok, you're right, but this doesn't mean we can't help each other."

"I'm not about to help any fucking Nazi," the Captain yelled at Heather. "David told me about Hans' intentions, and I told him the same thing. But I told him I was willing to hear you out and see what you had to say. But I've suddenly changed my mind; I'm out of here."

"Wait Captain," Heather yelled out. "Please hear me out before you leave, Captain. That's all I'm asking—hear me out before you say no. I can't possibly know how it feels to be you. You have every right to hate Hans and people like him. Hans has told me all about Hitler's experiments and of the unspeakable shit they did to Gypsies."

"Fuck Hans, he doesn't know shit. Yeah, he knows what he read in the archives, but he doesn't know shit about how the experiments actually went down. He thinks he knows, but there're only a few of us that know the details of what took place under Mengele. I've come across several files that never left Auschwitz, personally handwritten by Mengele. I'm the only living person that knows what's in the files."

"Damn it, Captain, why are you refusing to help?"

"I'll tell you why I refuse to help. I was born and raised in what later became East Germany. I became somewhat of a celebrity because of my work in the field of genetics. Those East Germans were desperately trying to revive their dream of establishing themselves as the perfect race, so they came after me. Those neo-Nazis kidnapped me in the middle of the night. I was kept blindfolded and in solitary confinement for days. I was constantly beaten while tied to a large wooden chair. That's where these scars came from," the Captain said as he raised his hands and showed her his scarred wrists.

"After having been tortured, I was taken to a vacant building where I was told I had a son. I was told that the woman I had lived with for a short period of time, I believe it was seven months, had borne my son. I had no way of knowing whether it was true or not because Angela left me two days before I was kidnapped. She didn't even have

D. G. HERNÁNDEZ

the decency of leaving a note behind to tell me she was leaving. I really thought she loved me, but what can I say, she fucking left. But the fact that she suddenly left made me wonder if they had also kidnapped her, part of their plan to control me. So whether it was true or not, I couldn't take a chance. If indeed I had a son, I had to make sure nothing happened to him. I had no choice; they had me by the balls, which was their favorite way of torturing me, literally. From then on I was theirs.

"I did everything they asked of me. They even had me working with the East German athletes in preparation for several Olympic games during the seventies. I had them all juiced up. Didn't you notice the medal count?

"So there I was, stuck in East Berlin, held captive by neo-Nazi criminals, just like the ones that murdered half a million Gypsies at Auschwitz and other death camps. These people never go away; they never disappear. Nothing was going to stop them in their pursuit of the perfect race. Nothing was about to get in the way of the Aryan Nation, not their defeat in World War II nor the loss of their hero, Hitler. They knew I was a Gypsy, but they needed all of the scientists they could get their hands on.

"They were planning on killing me from the beginning, but I convinced them that I was close to making a genetic engineering discovery, in particular, how to manipulate the DNA so as to allow the Aryan women to conceive twins and triplets. They wanted to multiply their supposedly perfect race as quickly as possible, so my plan enticed them. They were thinking beyond Germany. They wanted the Aryan people to rule the world, and this required a large number of Aryans. Plus, I told them they were on the right track in reference to the retrovirus."

"Stop Captain, that's enough," Heather interrupted. "I know that the Nazis put you through hell. But I beg you, Captain, please help Hans. He's a victim of the racist gene, just like you."

"Don't fucking compare me to that Nazi. His kind massacred millions of people."

"You're right," Heather told the Captain. "I can't deny that, but the hate in him is killing him. His racism is embedded in every cell of his body. Every cell in his body is infected with this disease. Nobody wins in a racist society; we're all losers."

"Hans truly believes he's part of the perfect race," Heather continued. "I've tried to convince him that there's no such thing, but he won't listen. Please, Captain, you have the ability to help Hans; you can cure him. You mentioned Mengele. I'll tell you something. Hans has a direct connection to Hitler's eugenics and Mengele's experiments. Hans' twin brothers were murdered by Mengele. Hans found out about his twin brothers in documents at the Institute of Anthropology, Human Heredity, and Eugenics in the Berlin Dahlem archives. This is where he found out his family's history. His parents had never told him of his twin brothers or of their murder. Can you imagine finding pictures of your murdered brothers? Hans' mind really got screwed up after that." Heather looked at David in despair.

"We don't have time to lose, Captain," David said. "Helping Hans is our only hope of finding out who is after our discoveries. But more importantly, we might be able to find out why somebody is willing to pay millions for our discovery because right now I don't have a clue. If the thieves behind Hans want our racist gene data so they can use it for the same purposes we have in mind, they could simply let us proceed without costing them a penny. I tell you guys, this planned theft doesn't make one bit of sense. Right now I can identify only two reasons why somebody wants our data. One reason would be that the thieves want to claim the fame of being the ones to rid the world of racism before us, but that's an expensive claim to fame. The other reason is that they don't want to rid the world of racism, in which case they could simply blow up the lab together with all of us in it and save a lot of money. I've run out of ideas. How about you, Captain, do you have any ideas?"

"No I don't. But this is your project, David. You can do as you please. You have asked for my consent out of courtesy, but I suggest you make the call. If you feel strongly about helping Hans in order to find the perpetrators, then do it. I work for you and I'll support any decision you make. And by the looks of it, you've already made up your mind, otherwise she wouldn't be here. So let's get started and see where it takes us."

"Thank you, Captain," David replied.

"Follow me," the Captain told Heather.

David and Heather followed the Captain out of the break room and back into the lab. Instead of going to the Captain's office, they turned left and walked into a refrigerated room. The room was not particularly cold, perhaps forty-two degrees Fahrenheit, but cold enough for Heather to ask for a lab coat. David walked to a stainless-steel cabinet, pulled out a plastic bag with a new lab coat, opened the bag, and draped the coat over Heather's shoulders. Both watched as the Captain grabbed a stainless-steel aerosol container from one of the many shelves that lined the room's walls. In spite of the many other labeled containers on the shelves, the Captain grabbed the only one without any markings or labels.

"The Captain and I are willing to help you, but you're going to have to put your neck on the line. You're the one that's going to cure Hans," David told Heather as the Captain walked towards them with the small container in his right hand.

"This contains the retrovirus." The Captain handed Heather the aerosol container. Heather cautiously took it with both hands and looked up at the Captain without saying a word.

"Will you be seeing Hans tonight?" the Captain asked Heather as she continued looking straight at him.

"No, not tonight, not till tomorrow. He has an apartment in Potsdam. That's where I'm meeting him tomorrow."

"Good. This is what I want you to do. You take this capsule, open it, and dissolve the power into Hans' favorite drink. It will not knock him out but will make him very sleepy. He's a smart man. I don't want him to suspect that you've put something in his drink, so the dosage is very low. But once he goes to bed, I guarantee you he'll be out for several hours. Once you know that he's definitely asleep, remove this pin from the top of the container, just like a grenade, and set it on top of a dresser or whatever. The container will automatically start to dispense the retrovirus within ten seconds, so make sure you're out of the room by then, unless you want to be cured as well," the Captain said.

CHAPTER 43

Hans and the Captain sat at a sidewalk café on the Champs-Elysées. The noisy avenue was as busy as ever. The sun was setting, and the Parisian lights were starting to bloom.

"Let's cut to the chase, Captain. Do you still think David will not release the retrovirus?"

"He hasn't picked up the phone and called me to tell me what his latest intentions are, but I'm sure he will. We're the best of buddies; he tells me everything."

"Don't fuck with me, Captain. I sure would hate to see anything happen to your son." Hans looked into the crowded sidewalk. "You were pretty forceful when you were trying to convince Warren that David was not going to release the retrovirus. Do you want to take a look at the video I took of you guys chatting away at the pub."

"That's how I felt then, but why does it matter, anyway? I thought you wanted me to delay the release of the retrovirus by five days," the Captain said.

"I want the release delayed, not cancelled."

"Ok," the Captain replied.

"Warren should be here in a few minutes, so listen carefully. When I start talking, I want you to play along. But don't agree with everything I say; put up a fuss now and then. Warren is too smart. He'll know we're fucking with him if you agree with everything I say."

Warren arrived later than expected, but he had a good excuse. A kid ran up to him at the train station and tried stealing his laptop computer. A police officer heard Warren's call for help and immediately ran towards him. The kid dropped the laptop, ran through the hundreds of passengers, but stopped and surrendered when he saw other officers join the chase. He was arrested and taken to jail. This created a problem for Warren because he was forced to go to the Paris police station and file an official complaint. The countless number of times he had to repeat the incident to the authorities didn't make for a timely arrival to his meeting.

"We need to get our hands on all of the research data," Hans explained. "If David decides not to release the retrovirus, we at least have the data to start all over again. It might take us a year to duplicate the data and produce the retrovirus, but at least we'll be able to release it on our own. And getting back to the point you made about betraying David, I don't agree with you, Warren. We've done everything he has requested of us, especially you and the Captain. All I'm saying is that we make sure he goes through with the release," Hans said.

"No, Hans, you can't say that," Warren yelled at Hans. "We sure as hell are betraying David! No getting around it, you asshole. It's his intellectual property. You know that the racist gene data, retrovirus data, and everything else doesn't belong to us. We just can't take it and pretend it's ours. We have signed contracts, and these contracts specifically address intellectual property, specifically saying that our discoveries belong to him."

"Warren is right, Hans, we have signed contracts," the Captain said as he pointed at Warren.

"Listen to me, Captain." Hans said. "I know you and Warren have signed contracts. Do you honestly believe that contracts mean anything at a time like this? You both know that releasing the retrovirus is bigger than anything we can imagine. If David thought of your discovery as intellectual property, why hasn't he applied for a patent? He hasn't because this is bigger than any damn patent. I get the point you guys are trying to make, and under normal circumstances I would agree, but there's nothing ordinary about our situation. We need to work together. Neither of you two has a problem with the plan, so why not proceed with it? Does it really matter who releases the retrovirus? We've given many years of our lives to this project, but none more than the two of you. You guys have as much ownership of this project as David. It's about implementing the plan; it's not about David any longer."

"I don't care what you say, Hans, I don't want any part of this. You're asking us to deceive David. You want us to go around his back. I don't want any part of this shit. Meeting here in Paris without his knowledge is bad enough," the Captain said.

"Will you listen to me, both of you?" Hans asked. "We're not deceiving or betraying David. I just don't believe David can do such a thing! Tell me, Captain, you know David better than anybody at this table. Do you think David can go through with his own plan?"

"It doesn't matter what I think or believe, Hans. My job is done. I've completed my research. I'm a scientist! I'm not a policymaker or damn politician. It's not my job to decide. If David were to ask me, I would certainly tell him he has to go through with his plan, but don't forget, Hans, it's David's plan not ours."

"Nobody is saying anything different," Hans agreed. "This is David's plan, and all I'm proposing is that we keep a copy of the data we've mentioned. That's all I'm saying—keep a copy of all equations, formulas, all the stuff you guys are familiar with. We are just buying insurance in case David chickens out. If he goes through with his plan, then this whole conversation is moot and life goes on. Life without racism."

"Let's keep looking at other options. Maybe there's another way to tackle this problem," the Captain said.

"We don't have time to look at other options," Hans told the Captain.

"Fuck you, Hans!" Warren yelled at Hans. "You're accustomed to playing mind games, we're not. We're scientists. We don't sit around trying to guess at things, like trying to figure out what David may or may not do. The Captain made the discoveries, I'll soon be done with my work, and that's it. It's not for us to decide the project's ultimate fate."

"Ok, I'm willing to compromise. We don't have to decide the project's fate now. Let's just keep a copy of all the data on my laptop. Just like I said earlier," Hans reminded them.

"Why do we have to keep a copy of all of our work on your laptop, Hans?" Warren demanded. "Anyway, because of the protocol, only a simultaneous download that includes your laptop could go undetected."

"That's it, Warren! Your idea will work. Simultaneous downloads, that's it! The information on your computer and the Captain's will be downloaded to the computers aboard the *Milagro*. Once this happens the information on both of your computers will automatically be deleted, is that correct, Warren?" Hans asked.

Warren nodded.

"My laptop is not scheduled to be downloaded," Hans continued. "As far as David is concerned, there's nothing worth downloading. If Warren says that a simultaneous download will hide the fact that I'm also receiving the data, then I say that's our plan."

"I need time to think this over," Warren said without answering Hans.

"Don't you fucking understand, Warren? We're out of time!" Hans shouted.

"I want to talk to the Captain in private. I don't know if my answer is going to be yes, but at least I haven't said no," Warren told Hans.

"Ok, Warren, have it your way." Hans got up from the table and walked in the direction of the Arc de Triomphe.

CHAPTER 44

"You're such a good liar, Hans. I bet you convinced yourself you were really part of David's team. You're probably starting to believe you're the group's most loyal member," Moe said.

Moe sat behind a desk. The dark room hid his face. Hans was here to let Moe in on his plan to obtain the data.

"Last time we met was out on the North Sea. Now we meet in this rundown apartment in Monte Carlo. Don't you think it's time we had a meeting where I can at least see your face?"

"It's not important for you to know who I am. What's important is that you deliver the goods. Now about the meeting with the Captain and Warren, you said everything went well, is that correct?"

"Yes, that's correct," Hans said.

"How do you plan to get me the encrypted racist gene data?" Moe asked.

"Actually, it was Warren that came up with the plan, and this is how it's going to work: There will be a simultaneous download of the data from the Captain's computers at his lab to the *Milagro* and to my laptop as well. It is at this point that we will finally get our hands on the data. At this point, my men will be aboard the *Milagro* retrieving the vaccine. I have instructed them to destroy the *Milagro*'s computers on their way out, which means we will be the only ones in the world with a complete copy of the research data. That's why you have to make sure you're in complete control of my laptop once I give it to you. And as you have ordered, my men will also kill the Captain on their way out. Warren will already be dead—I put enough poison in the gum to kill an elephant."

"Sorry the Captain had to go, but I'm offering his life as a pilon to my clients," said Moe.

"What the fuck does *pilon* mean?" Hans asked.

"Never mind, it's none of your business."

"Whatever. Now don't forget: I'll be with David and the Race Group members at David's villa, getting ourselves ready to go down to the marina for the *Milagro*'s auction. I won't be around to help you if anything goes wrong, but trust me, everything is going to work out fine. The download will begin an hour before the auction. You'll be in possession of my laptop by then, so be ready. Trust me, everything is going to work out fine."

"I don't trust anybody, Hans, especially people like you."

Moe was still worried about the marina's depth, in spite of Hans' assurances that the marina had been dredged to meet the mini-sub's requirements. His $20 billion fee would disappear forever if the mini-subs ran aground. The depth had been measured at low tide…or had it? He remembered the Hubble telescope and the one-millimeter spacing mistake. "Fuck, I need to give my mind a rest," Moe told himself.

"What's David like nowadays?" Moe asked.

"What do you mean *nowadays*? Do you know him?"

"Of course not! How the fuck would I know him?"

"Don't know, you tell me," Hans countered.

"I always make it a point to keep track of people with money. I read a story about him in the Robb Report. However, that was over fourteen years ago. I was wondering if he was still going strong."

"Funny you remember it was fourteen years ago. Most people would say fifteen years or ten years or twenty, but you said fourteen. Why is that?"

"What are you now, a fucking psychoanalyst?" Moe answered.

"What can I say about David? He's ok, I guess. I mean, fuck, I don't know. He doesn't get personal very often. He always wants to talk about science, about the future. He's always talking about how the singularity is near. He always finds a way to bring it up," Hans said while trying to exit.

"Does he say why he likes science so much? Fuck, if he likes science so much, why isn't he a damn scientist?" Moe asked.

"Good question. Next time I see him I'll tell him there's a stranger who wants to know why he's not a fucking scientist."

"Fuck you, Hans."

"Hell, you're asking me fucking questions I don't give a shit about."

"You like science too, Hans, so don't pretend you and David don't have anything in common. I know your educational background."

"I didn't think you were interested in my science conversations with David."

"I keep wondering why David decided to go after the racist gene," said Moe. "Why spend all this money on a wild goose chase. The bastard got lucky and things worked out for him, but why go through all that trouble? He could as easily gotten involved in politics and helped pass laws against discrimination."

"Those laws already exist in your country. Based on your accent, I assume you're an American. The U.S. has all kinds of laws against discrimination. As a matter of fact, they gave one of those laws a name, it's called a racially motivated crimes law, hate crime laws, whatever."

"If he thinks racism can be eliminated via science, why didn't he go to an established science lab and get it done there? Would've been a lot cheaper," Moe said.

"Yeah, right."

"Well then you tell me, Hans. Why did he choose to do it in secret? I still don't understand why a biological or genetic approach. People can be educated about the evils of racism. People can change."

"If you say so," Hans said. "Now can I get the hell out of here?"

CHAPTER 45

Warren sat by himself, drinking coffee at the Weston Palace Hotel's Starbucks, trying to stay awake. The anxiety of having to secretly meet with the Captain in Madrid had kept him awake throughout the late-night flight. Warren was still struggling with his decision to cooperate with Hans and his betrayal of David.

The barista called out, "Soy nonfat latte for David is ready at the bar." A medium-framed man stood and walked towards the barista. Warren noticed a familiar figure, but the glare off the glass window prevented him from identifying the man. The man got his latte and walked in Warren's direction. The glare disappeared, and into sight came David's face.

A startled Warren jumped from his chair. "What the hell are you doing here? You scared the shit out of me."

"Same as you, waiting for the Captain." David sat as he answered Warren. "We're going to have one big, happy meeting, just the three of us. Calm down, Warren, you look as if you just saw a ghost."

David had called for the emergency meeting with the Captain and Warren while on business in Madrid. He specifically instructed the Captain not to tell Warren anything about the meeting other than to tell him to catch the next flight from Monaco to Madrid. The emergency meeting was also causing the Captain much anguish because he was starting to think that he could possibly be the target at the emergency meeting. Even before David called for David's emergency meeting, the Captain was having a difficult time reconciling his betrayal of David. With only five days left before the scheduled release of the retrovirus, the Captain considered coming clean with David but decided against it. His son's life was paramount.

"It's obvious you're not surprised to see me. Care to tell me what's going on?" Warren asked.

"Sure I'll tell you what's going on, Warren. I know you and the Captain have agreed to work with Hans. You guys decided to include Hans' laptop during the simultaneous download. You guys decided to give Hans a copy of my research data. Yes, Warren, it's my research data. It belongs to me. But don't worry, I know how conniving Hans can be. As a matter of fact, as soon as the Captain gets here, I'll share with you guys just how conniving Hans can be. I know you and the Captain both want to make sure I release the retrovirus. But don't worry, I'm not pissed off at you. As a matter of fact, I couldn't have planned it any better—that is, getting Hans to believe you're in bed with him."

"So you're not here to tell me I'm off the team or that you're having me done away with?" Warren asked.

"If that were the case I would have gotten rid of you some time ago. I learned of your complicity with Hans the moment it happened. The Captain told me of the meeting immediately after it took place. He told me that Hans wanted to make sure that he had a copy of all of the racist gene data, retrovirus, and everything else we've worked on for the past ten years. Hans' goal was to convince you guys that he was looking out after the best interest of the project, that he wanted to make sure that the retrovirus would be released in case I changed my mind."

"You're damn right," Warren jumped in. "Hans convinced me you were not going to go through with the plan. On top of that, the Captain had similar reservations not long before we met with Hans," Warren said.

"What reservations?" David asked.

"I'm sorry, David. But I agreed to secretly meet with the Captain at the pub down the road from the Pines Inn. It was during that meeting that the Captain told me that he wasn't totally convinced that you were going to release the retrovirus."

"Why would he think that?"

"Because he said that the retrovirus was ready to be released years ago. But you insisted on finding a reversal process, reversing the altered racist gene to its original state, before proceeding with the release of the retrovirus. In other words, a way of reactivating and reintroducing the racist gene back into our DNA. This didn't make sense to the Captain. He likened it to eradicating the AIDS virus only to find a way of reintroducing it back into society. He couldn't see the logic in your directive.

"The Captain started to believe that to you this whole business of finding and destroying the racist gene was nothing more than one big experiment. That's what he was afraid of, that his discovery would go down in history as a mere academic exercise. I was flabbergasted by his words. I couldn't believe his interpretation of your directive. So after I got over my anger at his words, I assured him that he had a right to be concerned about the retrovirus' release but that his fears were unfounded. I told him that as a scientist he should totally understand your position relative to the discovery of a reversal process. I assured him that the only reason you demanded he find a reversal process for the genetically altered racist gene was because of the possibility of unintended consequences. Told the Captain that if anything went awry, the situation could be corrected. Anyway, I think he finally accepted the fact that you were just trying to cover your ass in case things turned to shit."

"I wish he had come to me with his concerns," David said.

"I'm sorry I lost my bearing. I'm sorry I allowed myself to be duped."

"Don't blame yourself. He's excellent at manipulating people. He's been doing this all of his life. I know he led you to believe that only he was capable of releasing the retrovirus and..." David was interrupted in mid sentence.

"Looks like you gentlemen are having a serious conversation. Maybe it's best I don't interrupt," the Captain said.

"Have a seat, Captain, we were just catching up," David continued, "and letting Warren know that there aren't any hard feelings, that everything is ok. That being said, we need to get down to business. I know Hans tried convincing you that he was on your side, that he wants to eliminate racism as much as you, Warren. But he's been lying. There's something you need to know. Hans is plotting to steal all of our research data."

"And you were going to tell me, ah, when?" Warren asked sarcastically.

"You know how this business works, Warren. Everybody is on a need-to-know basis, including you. Nothing personal, Warren, that's just the nature of the business we're in. But things have changed, and you now need to know," David told Warren.

"I'm listening," Warren said.

David and the Captain proceeded to tell Warren about Heather. How David and the Captain had met at her request. That she didn't have details but knew that Hans was being paid millions of dollars to steal the racist gene data. Warren couldn't believe what he was hearing, especially the part of Heather using the retrovirus on Hans while he slept.

"I have something to tell you guys," David addressed both men. "I've been very busy since I found out about Hans' intentions. I had to shell out a lot of money, but I got my money's worth. My sources, both in and out of the CIA, got back to me, and this is what I found out. Hans is the person responsible for the bombing at the Captain's hideout in Granada. Hans went to Granada because he had come across information pertaining to the racist gene. He also knew that the Captain was meeting with an American in Granada, but that's all he knew. Hans tried to flush the Captain and me out of the Captain's hideout, but it didn't work. He left Granada without having gained any new knowledge. But one other thing before I continue," David said.

The Captain panicked. He was positive that David was about to tell him he knew about the vaccine. Betraying David, his only true friend for the past ten years, was tearing him apart. The Captain tried to appease his inner demons by telling David about his and Warren's collusion with Hans in reference to the simultaneous downloads, but it wasn't working. The last remaining hope for the Captain was that the retrovirus would change Hans' nefarious intentions.

"I found out that Hans was also responsible for the attempted burglary at Pines Inn. If not for the helicopter crashing, who knows if he might have succeeded, Captain," David continued.

"I've never trusted the son of a bitch!" the Captain yelled out.

"I'm sorry, guys. I should have never hired Hans. I should have known better. I can't believe I was so gullible, can't believe I allowed myself to be set up so easily," David said.

"Set you up?" Warren asked.

"Yes, he set me up. After leaving Granada emptyhanded, Hans returns to Berlin and intensified his efforts at finding out more about the racist gene. He started to monitor the Captain's every move. Hans was on the Captain's tail every time he made his midnight runs to Potsdam."

"Why were you going to Potsdam, Captain?" Warren asked.

"He went there periodically to drop off his latest research data so that it could be stored in secured computers." David didn't let the Captain answer.

"And just like in Granada," David continued, "Hans wanted to know who the Captain was meeting with in Potsdam. After several tries at breaking into the warehouse, the same warehouse he saw the Captain entering during his midnight runs to Potsdam, Hans gave up. He turned to his German intelligence buddies for help, and this is what he did. Hans had them plant a fictitious story in the local Berlin newspaper detailing the apprehension of a CIA operative during an attempted break-in at a local warehouse in Potsdam. Television networks around the world jumped on the story and ran with it without verifying any of the sources. The broadcasts showed pictures of the warehouse where the American spy was allegedly captured. Does this look familiar to you, Captain?" David handed the Captain a picture of the warehouse in Potsdam.

"That's your warehouse!" the Captain exclaimed.

"Sure is," David responded. "I watched as the CIA's Deputy Director denied the story, saying that no American, whether government employee or not, had been captured. I know they always deny everything, so it only intensified my curiosity. Hans knew it was an American that was behind the racist gene research—he knew this when he set off the bomb at Granada—but he had yet to figure out the American's identity. His assumption was spot-on. He assumed that the American behind the Captain and his genetic research also owned the warehouse. He also assumed that as soon as the American found out that a CIA agent had been apprehended at his warehouse he was is going to investigate the situation. In doing so, the American would expose himself.

"Hans is a very smart man. He figured out everything correctly. He read me like a book. I immediately reacted and started snooping around. I wanted to know why the hell a CIA agent was trying to get into one of my warehouses, especially the one containing the computers with the racist gene data. I should have listened to my instincts because for a moment I did have a feeling that I was being baited. But I overruled them because if the story of the CIA operative being apprehended at my warehouse was true I had some very serious problems. So in spite of the possibility that I was being set up, I proceeded. I sought out some of my resources and asked them if they knew anything about a CIA operative being apprehended in Potsdam. Well, wouldn't you know it, I was unwittingly taking my questions to Hans' damn rogue agents. Hell, how was I to know that they were working with Hans. Anyway, they immediately reported back to Hans and, bingo, he had me. He now knew who I was.

"Hans is either the luckiest person on earth or the smartest because he just sat and waited, waited for me to take the next step. And he knew exactly what my next step would be after the helicopter crash at the Pines Inn. I decided to revamp my security division and go in search of the best person to head my new security team. Hans pounced at the opportunity. His network of operatives in the intelligence community made sure Hans' resume was at the top when I started my search. I hired him. I was now sleeping with the enemy. Of course, his resume conveniently left out the years he served as a Stasi Officer. In any case, I created this problem, and I intend to fix it," David concluded.

"It's our problem as well, David. No sense crying over spilt milk. We have a major crisis on our hands and we need to deal with it. And it's going to take the three of us to handle it," Warren said.

"There's no doubt that we have to stop Hans from stealing the data, but our bigger challenge is to find out who is behind Hans."

"Why do you say that, David?" Warren asked. "Isn't foiling the theft of our data good enough? Let's just get rid of Hans. It's as simple as that."

"No, Warren, foiling the theft is not good enough. Getting rid of Hans is only a temporary solution. Whoever is after our data is not going to give up. They will merely find a different way of stealing our data. That's why I have to find out why they want it so bad. Heather told us that a person that goes by the name of Moe has been communicating with Hans. I need to find him."

"We don't have time for any of this drama. We've worked on this project for many years, and we can't afford to be sidetracked. We need to concentrate on the mission before us. I say we get rid of Hans!" Warren looked at David.

"We're not going there, Warren. We're not going to have Hans killed. That's a direct order. Do you understand?"

"I don't want to kill anybody, either. I'm not a murderer, but he is about to kill your project, David. We're so close to getting rid of racism. Why would we ever let Hans get in the way? We have to put an end to this shit," Warren said as he got up and went outside to smoke a cigarette.

A battle of wills started to erupt between David and Warren. Warren explained that his plan would also address David's strategy. If Hans were eliminated, Warren reasoned, Moe would have to come out of hiding to continue where Hans left off. Or perhaps come after David to avenge Hans' assassination. In either case, Moe would surface.

David strongly disagreed with Warren's calculations. David held to his belief that if Hans were eliminated, it would have the opposite effect. Moe would never surface because Hans' assassination would signal that he had been compromised. Moe might also wish to remain underground, not wanting to meet the same fate as Hans.

After his quick cigarette break, Warren rejoined David and the Captain.

"Ok guys, I've come up with a new plan," Warren said as he sat down.

"No, Warren. We're sticking to the plan I laid out. We're leaving Hans alone, giving him enough rope to hang himself or to at least lead us to Moe. And don't forget, Warren, Heather already has a small canister of the retrovirus that she intends to use on Hans to neutralize him. The racist bastard will soon cease to exist. And don't forget, we're to proceed with the simultaneous download on the day of the *Milagro's* auction. With luck, these efforts will lead us to Moe."

"Why are you so hung up on finding Moe, whoever the hell he is? I say we take Hans out now."

The Captain's participation in the conversation became more muted as their meeting progressed. The Captain reminisced about his childhood years as Warren and David argued about how to proceed with Hans. He sat there, totally appreciating the unquantifiable love his parents must have had for him when they left him with the Mueller family, never to return. *I, too, have to save my son,* the Captain told himself. *I'll do whatever it takes to keep my son alive.*

"I'll tell you why I'm so hung up on finding Moe. I need to find him because I don't think Hans is being paid millions of dollars to steal a historical document. The racist gene research data became obsolete the moment we discovered the gene. Why would anybody care how we discovered the racist gene?" David asked.

"Well, then tell me, what is Hans being paid for if not for the data?" Warren countered.

"You know, Warren, I wish I had an answer."

"Care to guess?" Warren asked.

"My guess is that things have evolved, their strategy has evolved, the reason for the planned theft has changed. I believe that before we made the discovery, they—whoever they are—wanted to either beat us to the punch in finding the racist gene. Or they wanted to prevent us from discovering the gene. Hans knows all about the discovery, so it leads me to believe that these two scenarios I presented are no longer valid. They can't prevent us from discovering something we already discovered, nor can they beat us to the punch. So why is Hans hanging around? Why hasn't Moe extricated Hans from his assignment? Why are they insisting on stealing our data? It's all about misdirection, I tell you. It's all about misdirection," David insisted.

CHAPTER 46

David had monitored the dredging of the marina from his villa high atop the highest point in the area. He kept an eye on the dredging because he was concerned that it would not be completed in time for the *Milagro's* auction. With the dredging now complete, a new concern surfaced. After his meeting with Warren and the Captain in Madrid, David rushed back home to Monaco. He knew the world of yachting and knew the draft of most luxury yachts, in particular the *Milagro's*. Combining this knowledge with the depth of the recently-dredged marina caused much consternation for David.

David yelled into his cell phone: "I've already checked my results three times. I'm sending you the raw data. You run the numbers. Of course I'm sending them on a secure line. I'm telling you the marina has been dredged eight feet deeper than necessary. I can't believe the Monaco Yacht Club is paying 3½ million euros extra to have the damn thing dredged deeper than necessary. There's no yacht in the world that requires such depth. Yes, I know it had to be dredged, but not eight feet deeper than necessary. Of course I asked," David continued yelling. "They told me it needs to be dredged every five years. Find out if it was dredged five years ago. You need to find out what's going on. Find out every little detail. We need to be suspicious of everything that takes place in that damn marina."

David tended to several other phone calls while waiting for Hans to arrive from Amsterdam. The Captain, Warren, and the Race

Group members were all starting to arrive in Monaco. Their final meeting was quickly approaching. There was no turning back. The last and final trial experiment was taking place this very moment. There would be no more trials.

"Has Hans boarded the plane yet?" David spoke into the phone.

"He's on his way," the answer came from Amsterdam.

Shortly after passing through security, Hans felt that he was being followed. He didn't know if it was paranoia, but he needed to find out for certain. Hans used his honed counterintelligence techniques to test his suspicions. All doubt was removed. He was being tailed. Hans' pursuer looked very ordinary, nothing unusual, nothing stood out. Just a typical traveler, carrying two bags that read "Tulip Bulbs" in bold red letters, along with a picture of red blooming tulips. The bags were just like the ones many tourists were carrying. Every gift shop at the Amsterdam Airport sells tulip bulbs—last minute souvenirs, one more gift for the folks at home. Hans proceeded to the first-class lounge reception desk. While standing in line, he intentionally dropped his boarding pass. The automatic door opened and a sudden gust blew the boarding pass toward the back of the queue. His pursuer was now in front of him. The man with the tulip bags presented his passport at the reception desk. Hans noticed it was not an American passport.

Hans reclined into the comfortable sofa, not worried about falling asleep, knowing that travelers flying first class were always personally notified of departing flights. Closing his eyes and relaxing was not possible. He was too worried about the simultaneous downloads. Hans left the first-class lounge and walked to the nearest bar, forgoing the free drinks at the first-class lounge. The bar was busy, standing-room only, except for one bar stool. He hurried towards it but immediately rushed out when he saw the two tulip bulb bags lying on the stool.

After an uneventful flight, he deplaned in Monaco. Hans was handed his suit coat by Rachel, the prettiest of the flight attendants. In the middle of a flirtatious conversation with Rachel, he overheard the other flight attendant telling an exiting passenger, "Sir, sir, you forgot these," handing him the tulip bags.

"Oh, thank you, but you must be mistaken. They're not mine," the gentleman replied.

Hans couldn't figure out why his pursuer denied ownership of the tulip bags. Hans stood in line, waiting to board a taxi. His pursuer stood within feet of him, also waiting to board a taxi but with no luggage. This is really getting strange, thought Hans. He had distinctly overheard the agent at the first-class lounge telling the man that his luggage had been accidentally sent ahead on another flight. He had been told his luggage would await him in Monaco. Hans felt his blood pressure rising.

Calm down, he repeated to himself. *It's probably one of David's men who wants to make sure I don't make contact with anyone outside the group. If I'm being tailed because of my work with David, then so be it. Otherwise, I'm in deep shit. I feel like somebody's out to fuck me. Who in the hell can it be?* Hans felt like contacting Moe, but he knew that would be a big mistake because David could be listening in. David and the Race Group owned the satellite that carried Hans' telephone signals.

Hans switched cabs twice in efforts to evade his pursuer, but it didn't do any good. He was still being followed. Hans continued on his way, sitting in the back seat of a taxi trying to make sense of his situation. The taxi driver appeared to be a Middle Easterner who could barely make himself understood in French. *Look at this guy.* Hans' mind started to wander. *He left his country to come here and work as a taxi driver. Aren't there any jobs in his native country?*

Hans noticed on the car's sun visor pictures of three children, two boys and one girl. *Damn, something has to be done about this broken-down immigration system. The only thing these immigration laws do is break up families. I don't understand how somebody can leave their kids behind. What makes somebody do that, leave their families behind? I'm sure his wife misses him. Hope he's able to send her money to support the kids. Although I don't think this guy makes much money as a*

*taxi driver. Taxi drivers make most of their money from tips. Better make
sure I tip him well. I wonder when he'll see his family again. Poor guy,
sometimes it's just the color of your skin that determines your fate. What in
the hell is wrong with me? I can't believe what I was just thinking. Fuck,
I have to stop thinking like this. I need to stay focused on my assignment.*

Once Hans checked into his hotel, he had a taxi take him to the
marina where David's yacht was being prepared for a party that night.
Chefs were busy loading the fare that would please the most discriminating palates. Cases of champagne were delivered and immediately
taken to the wine cellar. Hans was ready to board the yacht when he
realized he had made a mistake—he was supposed to meet David at
his villa.

"Have you told me everything, Hans? Try to remember, damn
it. Think, think hard. Is there anything else you can tell me about
the stranger that followed you here?" David insisted. "God damn it,
Hans, you know the magnitude of this project. How could you have
been so stupid and careless to allow somebody to follow you? Were
there any other people that you might not have noticed? Think, Hans,
did anyone accidentally bump into you or try to talk to you? I've spent
a good part of my life on this project and there's no way I'm going
to let you fuck it up. Tell me, is there a reason why someone would
want you followed, especially by somebody as good as you say? Think,
Hans. Why are you being followed?"

"I don't know. At first I thought it was one of your men keeping
tabs on me," Hans said.

"Did he follow you to the hotel?" asked David.

"I don't know, but I wouldn't doubt that he got there before me.
If he knew my travel schedule, I'm sure he knows where I'm staying,"
Hans said as he continued thinking about his situation.

"I'm so fed up with you right now. Go back to the damn hotel,
and don't leave your room until I send for you."

"Before I leave there is something very important I need to
tell you."

"What is it this time?"

"I need to warn you about Warren," Hans said.

"What the hell are you talking about, warning me about Warren? What's there to warn me about, Hans?"

"You've put me in charge of security and I intend to do my job. I'm here to inform you that I have very serious concerns regarding Warren," Hans said.

"Hurry up and get to the point. Every time you start with so many disclaimers I just get suspicious of you." David glared at Hans.

"Ok, ok... sorry I didn't tell you any sooner, but I've kept a close eye on everybody lately. Warren in particular."

"Why Warren?" David asked.

"Because he's young, he's vulnerable," Hans answered.

"Forget your theories on youth. Will you get to the point of why you need to warn me about Warren?" David demanded.

"My security detail told me that Warren had boxes and boxes of sophisticated computer equipment sent from your warehouse here in Monaco to the airport several days ago. The computer equipment in the boxes belongs to you. David, he's stealing from you. The boxes were loaded onto a private transport jet and the plane doesn't depart until Warren arrives and boards the plane. I decided to have him followed and catch him in the act.

"He flew to a remote village in the Himalayas and landed on a private airstrip at night. Can you believe that? A night landing in the Himalayas. What can be so secretive that you are willing to risk a night landing? We had to abandon our chase; none of our pilots are qualified nor certified to land where he landed. Hell, there's only a handful of pilots in the world that are certified to land at that airstrip. Not being able to land, I don't know who he met with or who he delivered the computer equipment to. I know he can't afford a private charter, so he must be getting help from somebody," Hans told David.

"You've taken valuable time of mine to tell me shit I already know. I can't believe you Hans. You've involved yourself in something that's none of your business. If you had asked, I would have informed you that Warren's partner had friends, monks that live up in the Himalayas. He had promised them computers and computer equipment before he was murdered. Warren felt a need to go through with his partner's promise. So he came to me and asked if I would be willing to make the equipment available. I said yes.

"I also made a transport jet available. The private airstrip belongs to the Race Group and our soon-to-be patented avionics allow us to land anywhere, anytime. Anyway, keeping the promise alive was important to Warren, almost like a pilgrimage. So if you have nothing else to tell me, please leave. I have things to do," David said.

"Anything else? Is there something I can do between now and tomorrow morning?" Hans asked.

"No. Now leave, I have a party to get ready for," David said.

David picked up his phone and called the Captain as soon as Hans left his villa. David wanted to know if the retrovirus was starting to have an impact on Hans. The Captain replied that Hans had been observed since deplaning in Monaco. The observations were showing that the retrovirus was not having the intended consequences on Hans. The Captain said that the driver of the taxi that took Hans from the airport to the hotel had been interviewed. The driver told the interviewer that Hans was acting weird. Said that Hans acted very respectful during the early part of the trip but that by the end of the trip Hans insulted him with racial slurs.

CHAPTER 47

Catherine sat out on the terrace with her Maltese on her lap, gazing at the sea of yachts moored at the Monaco Marina far below. She looked so at ease as she gently stroked her dog's back. Through one of the villa's windows, she could see David at his desk, busily going over last-minute details in preparation for the retrovirus release. It had been several years since David had brought Catherine into his confidence and shared with her his dream of eliminating racism.

At first, David wasn't sure if he had made the right decision by telling her. But now, any doubts he may have had were gone. Catherine had proven to be his most ardent supporter.

"Thought you had stood me up," Catherine told David as he walked out onto the terrace. "I've been out here for almost an hour waiting for you to finish your last-minute details. You and your details, David. You're always making sure everything is perfect," Catherine said as she reached up and kissed him. "I guess that's why you're so successful," she added.

"Here we are and nothing to do. Can you believe this? We've been working like crazy for so many years, and now there's nothing to do. Everything is set and ready to go," David said as he filled his wine glass with sparkling water.

"Is it, David? Is everything set and ready to go? Is your personal life ready to go?"

"What is that supposed to mean?" David asked.

"Your personal life, David. You haven't spent too much time thinking about what you're going to do with your life after the *Milagro*'s auction. We've fallen in love during a time of war, your war on racism. I can't help but think of how many soldiers left girlfriends behind when the war ended, about how many hearts were broken when it came time for the soldiers to return home. Will you ever tell your ex-wife why you left her?"

"You've picked a most inopportune time to talk about such matters. I'm in the middle of my masterpiece. I'm in the middle of making the most important decision of my life—hell, the most important decision made in human history—and you choose to talk about my ex-wife. I can't believe you would go there."

"You're going to have to tell her the truth sooner or later, David. But for now, I agree, my timing wasn't good. So let's get back to business. The Race Group and everybody around this project has placed the decision for the release of the retrovirus squarely on you. This is not something that was imposed on you, David. You asked for it. You demanded that you be in charge of every detail of this project from the very beginning. You told the group that the racist gene project would not proceed if you were not allowed to make every call. They gave you complete autonomy, including complete autonomy over the release of the retrovirus."

David reached across the table and gently put his hand over hers.

"I know it's my decision to make, but what if it were yours? Would you do it?"

"Oh, David. You're asking a lot from me. I so much would like to be able to answer your question, but I can't. And even if I were to answer your question, it would only be a hypothetical for me."

"Warren is here, Mr. Lorca," David's butler interrupted.

"Good, have him join us out here."

Warren walked out to the terrace and was greeted by the barking dog. The dog quieted down as soon as she noticed it was Warren.

D. G. HERNÁNDEZ

"Glad you could join us for a drink, but no smoking, Warren. No smoking at my villa."

"I know, I brought an extra package of gum," Warren laughed as he leaned down and gave Catherine a kiss.

"You know, Warren, we've spent so much time together, but we haven't had many times to just sit and relax. But I promise that we'll have plenty of time to let our hair down in a few days."

Catherine and Warren caught up on some of the details about the auction and subsequent travel arrangements. After the auction, the Captain and Warren were to board a private plane and fly to San Antonio, Texas. There they would relax for a couple of days and then, under the cover of darkness, cross the border into Mexico. David had two new travel trailers waiting for them at Warren's former residence. From there, the two men would navigate the *Milagro* around the world by means of remote control.

"The Captain will not be joining us tonight; seems he's not feeling well," Warren reported. "But I think he is mostly tired and not sick. Instead of asking me to leave his hotel room so he could go to bed, he just kept talking. He started to get introspective, reviewing his involvement in this project for the past so many years et cetera. But then he changed gears on me, and that's when I started to feel sorry for him."

"Really? How so?" Catherine asked.

"He told me he was positive he had a son. You guys should have seen his proud face when he told me about having a son. He said he felt so bad that he hadn't been there for his son. Said he would do just about anything to make up for his failure as a father. He was sounding so weird, though. I mean, he was so sure he had a son. He spoke in the present tense; there was no doubt in his mind he had a son. For a moment I thought he was going to pull out a picture of his son from his wallet. I didn't know how to respond to his babbling about having a son, so I simply told him that he would have made a great father."

"Poor Captain," Catherine said. "I guess the pressure is getting to him."

"I still haven't made up my mind," David said abruptly. "I told you from the beginning that I wasn't going to decide until the last minute, and I intend to keep my word."

David had assured his team that he was positive he would release the retrovirus but had never been able to definitively convince himself that he would. He was torn, having to unilaterally make a decision that would change the world forever was more than he could bear. The words *who died and made me king?* kept reverberating in his mind. Yet he knew he could never live with himself if he did nothing to improve the lives of billions of people around the world. And for billions of people not yet born.

The closer the deadline for the release of the retrovirus approached, the more intense his inner conflict became. David wrestled with the better angels of his nature, and sleepless nights became routine. When he did manage to sleep, he would wake up in the middle of the night, sweating profusely. In his dreams, he would hear the better angels tell him, *Do it, David. Do it.* In his dreams, David stood high above the *Milagro*'s flybridge, clutching a sword in his right hand, ready to unleash its powerful might against racism. His body jerked as he fought racism with sword in hand. He would suddenly find himself awake, his right hand firmly clenched.

David pushed his chair back and got up from the table. He pursed his lips as he walked towards the terrace's stone rails. He leaned over the rail and observed the beautiful lights in the distant marina. With his back to Catherine and Warren, he started to tell them, "Many years ago, the best scientific minds in the world came together and joined forces to extinguish a powerful evil. They didn't have the time to let evil run its course. They couldn't wait for evolution to solve the problem. Time was of the essence."

"And time is of the essence, David," Warren jumped in. "You must act. You can't deliberate forever. You mentioned scientists coming together to rid the world of evil. I know you're talking about the Manhattan Project. You make a good comparison, David. Our project and the Manhattan Project definitely have similarities. Both were driven by science and technology. Secrecy was a major component in both—not even Vice President Harry Truman knew of the atomic bomb's development. But the most obvious, maybe not-so-obvious, similarity is that when the scientists were finished with their work, it was up to somebody else to make the decision. I know it's your decision to make, David, but I say go through with it. Release the retrovirus. You cannot let our work go to waste. Trust your instincts. This project is ten years old; we've had plenty of time to raise objections. We've debated the merits of going through with your plan hundreds of times. There were nights that we didn't sleep. Morning would arrive and we were still going over all the pros and cons of our project.

"And we always arrived at the same conclusion," Warren continued. "Racism is a heinous disease that must be cured. We have found the cure, and it must be used. Yes, David, there are similarities between the Manhattan Project and ours. However, there is one very major difference: you're not the President of the United States. You don't have a cabinet to lean on, to support your war against racism. You didn't have Congress to fund your research or pass legislation mandating the eradication of racism. Don't get me wrong, there's probably a majority of people that would support you, but you can't openly ask them for their support." Warren's voice tapered off.

"I never thought we'd get this far this fast," David said. "I know it's odd for me to say, but I was hoping that it would take longer to make our discovery. I was hoping the extra time would get me out of having to make the decision. Throughout these past years, I've been torn with the thought of having to make a unilateral decision. I've always wondered how our presidents feel when they send young kids to die in war. At what point does a president's mind become numb to the realities of war? When does war become a chess game in their minds? I can't imagine the sleepless nights our presidents have endured on their way to war."

"Our retrovirus doesn't kill people," Catherine said. "All it kills is racism, David."

David came back to the table and sat down. Catherine and Warren looked at each other and then both looked at David.

"Racism is meaningless until it becomes personal," David said introspectively.

Catherine and Warren knew better than to ask David what he meant by that. David's response was always the same: "Think about it; you'll figure it out."

"See you guys later," David told Catherine and Warren as he ran from the table and into the house. "Call Brent and tell him to get the jet ready. I have a trip to make. I have an announcement to make," they overheard David tell his butler.

CHAPTER 48

David landed at San Antonio International airport at five in the morning. Brent and his copilot waited at the hangar while David drove to see his daughter.

David stood motionless in the pouring rain, looking into his daughter's eyes, trying to come up with the right words, words he had been in search of for fifteen years. He didn't know if he was doing the right thing, but it was something he had to do. In the dimness of the early dawn hours, her face and eyes were barely visible. Her long hair, full of curls, came to life in his cloudy eyes. The raindrops on his face were salty as they mixed with his tears. The rivulets flowed on both of their faces, but David could see only his daughter's. He had seen these tears of pain before, tears a father never wants to see, when she was only fourteen.

The relentless rain pounded the thousands of headstones at Sunset Cemetery that September morning. He stood alone in the dark. It was too early for anybody else to visit the cemetery that Monday morning. That's the way he wanted it, just him and his daughter. He couldn't afford to have anybody hear what he was about to tell her. He reached out and touched her face, the marble was cold. The sculptors in Carrara, Italy, had captured her beautiful smile even though they had never met her.

"I'm sorry I could not ease your pain that afternoon," David said, "the day your spirit was severed. I felt so helpless. There are no prosthetics for a severed spirit. I had never experienced such inadequacy as I did that afternoon. I couldn't even offer you a band-aid. I felt so helpless, because I was helpless.

"I'll never forget your words, nor do I want to forget them. "I lost the election" you told me as I drove you home from school that hot afternoon. I knew you had lost the election before you told me. The gallant tears that flowed down your beautiful face as you stoically looked straight ahead gave you away. You tried hiding your tears, but I could see them out of the corner of my eye. While not exactly easy, I knew that as a father I could come up with the right words to make you feel better. I knew I could offer comforting words. I was prepared to explain to you that winning wasn't the most important thing in life. I was prepared to talk about the many positive things that come from defeat—you know, all the usual clichés. I readied myself to act fatherly, to offer the usual fatherly advice. But suddenly my world was turned upside down by what you said next. 'I lost because some girls were telling other students not to vote for me because I was Mexican,' you gently told me.

"Your quietly uttered words nearly burst my ear drums. Your quietly uttered words rang louder than an exploding bomb, an exploding bomb that shattered my heart. I wanted to offer comforting words, but all I could say was, 'I'm glad you have experienced racism all on your own. I didn't have to tell you about it; now you know it exists. You see, Sarah Frances, I never told you about racism because I didn't want to prejudice your mind. I didn't want to poison your pure mind, an innocent mind.'"

David shook, startled by the sudden and blinding ray of lightning. The thunder pierced his ears as the rain became more intense. "If only I could have taken your pain away, if only I could have taken your place, I would have done so on instinct. Do you still feel the pain of injustice, the pain that no child should ever feel? I couldn't protect you then, and now it's too late. But it's not too late for me to help others.

"I know you would never want anybody else to feel the pain you felt that day. I remember the countless times you showed compassion towards strangers, regardless of their ethnicity. I know that is why it was so painful for you to hear, 'don't vote for her because she is Mexican.' It must have been so difficult for you to understand the concept of racism because I never taught it to you. Patrick Moynihan, a U.S. Senator from New York, once said about President's Kennedy's assassination, 'We'll laugh again. We'll just never be young again.' I saw your beautiful smile and heard your laughter many times after that fateful day. But you were never young again.

"I promise you, Sarah Frances. In two days, racism will be gone forever. It is then that I will release the retrovirus that will heal the world of this heinous disease forever. This I promise you, my dear daughter, my dear Sarah Frances."

CHAPTER 48

Monaco
David's Villa
September 15, 2015

The morning sun rose over the horizon, casting a blinding brilliance as it reflected off the coastal waters. Not having slept all night, David gladly welcomed the day's first light. The Race Group members were starting to arrive at David's villa for their last meeting. No more meetings after today. Any future communications, if necessary, would be channeled through their private satellites.

"This is it, guys. Tomorrow we make history," David said after welcoming his fellow Race Group members to his villa.

"Yes!" the Race Group members cheered. David had finally told them of his decision.

"I don't think that ten years ago anyone in this room would have predicted our success. It was a massive undertaking with countless risks and obstacles along the way, but we prevailed. All of us in this room have dedicated our lives to this project, and I think I speak for all of you when I say I'm glad we did it and we have no regrets. There are but a few moments in history that a select few have been called on to change the world, and I feel very honored, just like you, that we answered the call. If you believe in fate, then you can say it was fate that chose us to do its handiwork. We didn't push fate back and say, 'I'm too busy making money so please call on someone else.' We didn't tell fate that it was crazy, that it was asking too much of us. We weren't chosen because we were the smartest or the brightest people

286   D. G. HERNÁNDEZ

on earth, but rather fate chose us because it knew we wouldn't run away. And this is the one thing we should be most proud of: we didn't run from the clarion call."

The Captain, Hans, and Warren sat next to each other at the table among David and the rest of the Race Group members. The meeting had just begun, and Hans already needed a cigarette break, but that was not an option. David had chastised him the last time he had excused himself to go outside and smoke a cigarette.

"After tomorrow, some of us here will never see each other again. But before tomorrow comes, I want you to meet but three of the hundreds, if not thousands, of people who have made our project a success. I want you to meet these guys," David said. "I've kept them in the background and hidden from you guys for security reasons. But I brought them here today so you can meet them and to afford you an opportunity to thank them. These gentlemen have gone beyond the call of duty. I can honestly say that this has never been a job to them. They bought into our mission and as such have as much ownership of what will soon take place as any of us Race Group members. The Captain's discovery is very worthy of a Nobel Prize. However, we know that this will never happen because all of us here have taken an oath of secrecy. The principals that have undertaken this mission will forever remain anonymous."

David introduced Hans to the group.

"Gentleman, amazing things happen when there is the will," Hans stated. "Your work and commitment to making our world a better place inspires me and I congratulate you. But more to the point of why I'm here today, David approached me several years ago and asked if I was interested in working on a project that he could not fully describe because of security reasons. He told me that it was a highly scientific undertaking, that the science would be cutting-edge, that so-called futuristic technologies would become realities under our watch. My one and only job has been providing security, and I'm here to tell you that our project has not been compromised in any form or fashion. Tomorrow we will start to download all of the discoveries from the Pines Inn laboratories to the *Milagro*'s computers, where they will remain for eternity. You will be the only ones to access the information. Only you, the Race Group members, will have access to any of the data. You will be issued a one-time key pad that will enable you to decipher any encrypted information. Good luck gentlemen," Hans said.

The Captain was introduced to the Race Group by David. "What you gentlemen have accomplished is totally unbelievable," the Captain told the group. "I know you want to give me the credit, but I couldn't have done it without your vast resources. You decided to seek a scientific answer to a social ill. Your timing was perfect because this could not have happened twenty years ago. I know I've made an important discovery, but it doesn't compare to what you are going to accomplish tomorrow. You will singlehandedly rid the world of racism. Your willingness to release the retrovirus tomorrow is greater than any discovery I have made. It takes guts to do something like this, and you know it because you have gone through hell in making your decision. People talk of wanting to do the right thing, but that's all they do, talk. You in this room will be remembered and talked about for thousands of years. If Achilles were here, he would agree. He used his sword, you have used genetic engineering.

"Oh, one more thing," the Captain said before taking his seat. "Can I please have two more minutes of your time to explain my discovery?"

"I'd love to hear it Captain," Rosalind told him. "Take as much time as you need."

"Specifically I want to talk about the human trials that we've conducted. We've conducted them in various parts of the world, testing them on different races. They all proved successful. I decided to conduct one last experiment before this meeting a couple of days ago. I decided to conduct this last experiment aboard an airplane. The first challenge of this trial was to bring the canisters containing the retrovirus onto the airplane without notice, so we placed them inside two tulip bulb bags we had snuck in through one of the vendors. Very common for people to buy tulip bulbs at the airport in Amsterdam and bring them on board the airplane. This was a viable plan because at this point the passengers have already gone through the security gates.

"What was also unique about this last trial is that it involved only one individual. That's right, I said one individual. Immediately after takeoff, my researchers on board the airplane went to the lavatories and planted the hidden canisters of the retroviruses below the paper towel dispensers. One in each of the several lavatories throughout the plane. We didn't know which lavatory the individual would perhaps use, so we had them all covered. Within minutes after hiding the canisters, our subject walked into the forward cabin lavatory. The retrovirus was remotely released from the canister while our subject used the restroom. The results from this last trial are still pending, but there is absolutely no reason to believe that it will be any different than all the other successful trials. In a few minutes, David will introduce to you the subject who unwittingly participated in our last human trial."

It has to be me. Hans suddenly realized he had been part of the Captain's experiment. Of those present in the room, he knew he was the only one that had taken a flight from Amsterdam.

David called on Warren to address the group.

"My primary assignment was to develop software for a quantum computer. As all of you know, this is a thing of the very far and distant future," Warren said.

Some of the group's members looked at each other in disbelief. They instantly realized that David had not briefed Warren on the group's quantum computer project.

"If anybody asked about my research I would tell them that some crazy people were paying me to develop theoretical software for a theoretical computer. However, one of my real assignments was to establish a communication system, a system using quantum encryption.

All of you in this room are familiar with quantum mechanics, so I don't find it necessary to go over the details. But I do want to brief you on how things are going to work in reference to the storage of the racist gene data, retrovirus data, and other sensitive information. None of you have been briefed on this, so please pay close attention.

"The data will be transferred from a lab at the Pines Inn to the *Milagro*. Once aboard the *Milagro*, it will undergo an additional layer of quantum encryption. After this additional layer of encryption, the data will leave the *Milagro* and be beamed to one of our several satellites. Let me point out that the data will automatically be deleted from the broadcasting computers once it has finished transferring. In other words, none of our research data and related secrets will remain on Earth. All of the research results, discoveries, and implementation policies will be stored many miles above this room. The information cannot be accessed physically unless you go into space and retrieve the satellite. If anyone ever tries to retrieve the satellite without the quantum encrypted password, it will self-destruct and the information will be lost forever—well, perhaps not. David will brief you on that, but I will tell you that in case of sabotage the satellite will automatically transfer all information to another location," Warren continued.

"My second assignment was to undertake computer modeling of world trends in reference to racism. I have had my results verified by independent sources. I wanted to make sure they were not tainted by personal bias. The results are not encouraging. The results contradict common opinion. Racism is not going away," Warren said.

David's mind was too preoccupied with so many things to pay much attention to Warren's report.

"Mr. Lorca." David's personal attendant knocked on the door. "May I come in? It's important."

"Come in."

"Sir, our security detail at the marina wants me to inform you that the *Milagro*'s underwater alarm system keeps going off. Seems a mini submarine company is showcasing its newest mini-sub and is giving free underwater tours to prospective customers. They have six subs total, at least four of them are always underwater. The problem is that every time the alarms are activated, many of the onboard systems shut down."

"Have them shut down the ventral alarm systems, but that's it. I want all other alarm systems to stay active," David instructed.

David was about to expose Hans when he was interrupted by his assistant, so he took a few seconds to reorganize his thoughts. David walked over and stood behind Hans while addressing the group.

"Just a few more details before I introduce our last human trial subject."

Hans started to panic but didn't know what to do. Running out the door was not possible. David's security detail would subdue him easily. Pulling out his weapon and starting to shoot was not an option either; he had checked his gun at the front gate when he arrived at the villa.

"Warren mentioned a second ago that there might be an additional place where our secrets will be stored," David continued. "I decided to make the *Milagro* that second place. The satellites will bounce back the information to the *Milagro* with, yes, an additional layer of quantum encryption.

"After tomorrow, the *Milagro* will be known throughout the world. It will circle the world, releasing the retrovirus at every port of call. The retrovirus will self-replicate and spread from one person to another until every man, woman, and child in the world is cured of racism. Our secret will not be stored in some cave, waiting for Indiana Jones to retrieve it. Our secret will be on constant display for the world to see," David said.

David and the other people in the room were startled when the villa's sirens suddenly started blaring throughout the compound, bringing panic and fear to everyone. They all jumped to their feet and started running toward the villa's safe room. The alarm's sirens continued to blare. Men with drawn weapons broke through the locked doors before any of the people could reach the safe room. David's guests panicked, but their fears quickly abated when they realized the armed men were David's personal security detail responding to the alarm. Through the bullet-proof glass windows overlooking the villa's garden, everyone could see commando-looking mercenaries holding a woman to the ground. Their assault weapons were aimed at her, ready to unleash their fury.

One of the commandos searched the helpless woman as she lay with her face to the ground, unable to breath as three of the commandos held her down with their boots on her back. She futilely tried moving her head, but it was no use, one of the commandos had his foot on the back of her head. Extreme hypoxia was taking place. The commandos continued to restrain the seemingly lifeless woman, even though she was no longer a threat. The woman gasped, trying to get oxygen into her lungs as she was dragged towards the house. Her clothes were ragged, torn by the razor-sharp glass shards atop the villa's perimeter walls. Blood was dripping from her face, arms, and legs. The approaching woman's face came into focus. Hans jumped to his feet.

"Get your fucking hands off her, you motherfuckers," Hans yelled at the commandos as they dragged Heather's limp body into the villa.

"Get me the emergency backpack from behind my desk," David yelled out at his butler.

David was handed the backpack within seconds. David's personal physician was immediately summoned, but he was at least five minutes away. Heather needed immediate medical attention, so David took over.

"You idiots, you're supposed to take care of me, not kill a defenseless woman," David said as he gently lifted her head and held an oxygen mask to her face.

"Heather, Heather..." Hans cried out. "What are you doing here? Can you hear me? What are you doing here? How did you find me? Breathe, baby...breathe, baby...breathe. Fuck, this can't be happening. Why did you have to come looking for me? I love you, Heather. Can you hear me, Heather? I love you." Hans desperately watched the motionless Heather, inches from her face, as if wanting to share the oxygen mask.

"That's it, Heather, breathe, take deep breaths, that's it," David told Heather. "What are you doing here?"

Hans noticed David's familiarity with Heather but was too focused on making sure she was ok to ask any questions.

Slowly Heather started moving her fingers as if trying to touch something that wasn't there. She reached for the oxygen mask and yanked it off her face.

"Heather, Heather you're alive!" Hans yelled with tears in his eyes. "I love you. I'll always love you."

"I love you too, Hans. That's why you have to let me help you. Please, Hans, please let me help you. It's not too late. You can put an end to this. You have to tell us who Moe is," Heather whispered between breaths.

Hans tried saying something as he reached for his throat. He desperately looked at David, not able to say a word. Heather sat up and grabbed Hans, trying to find out what was wrong. She kept shaking him, trying to get him to say something. David grabbed a pillow from the sofa and put it under Hans' head as he laid on the floor. Heather removed the oxygen mask that hung around her neck and quickly placed it on Hans. It was only there for two seconds before Hans regained enough strength to move it away from his mouth.

"The Captain switched…switched…" Hans' words were barely audible.

"The Captain what?" David yelled at Hans. "Is the Captain in danger? What did you say? Try saying it again."

Hans shook his head.

David's doctor rushed in at that very moment. Excusing himself for not being able to get on the scene any sooner, he was confused when he saw Hans laying on the floor. He thought he had been summoned to help a woman.

"I'm sorry, I thought it was a woman," the doctor said as he rushed towards Hans. "Looks like he's having a heart attack."

The doctor tried to save Hans' life, but it didn't do any good. Hans had suffered a massive heart attack.

"Has he suffered any previous heart attacks?" the doctor asked David as he reached into Hans' suit coat pocket.

"Not that I know of, but I doubt it because he's always been in excellent shape."

"Well, this will do it," the doctor said as he pulled out a pack of cigarettes and two empty gum wrappers.

David gently helped Heather to her feet, pulling her away from Hans. Unable to hold herself upright, she sat down on a nearby settee.

"Did I screw things up when I released the retrovirus? Did I do something wrong?" Heather asked.

"There's no way to make a mistake. You either release it or you don't," David answered.

"Do you think that the virus didn't really take effect because he had been sick?" Heather asked.

"Hans has been sick?" a startled David asked. "He didn't appear sick at all. You saw how he fought my security team."

"I saw Hans wipe something from his shoulder a couple of days ago. When I asked what he was doing, he said he was wiping off a drop of blood left from the flu shot he had just received."

CHAPTER 49

David finished his last interview with the reporter for the *San Antonio Chronicle* and decided to walk up to his villa. He wanted to be alone and without any interruptions so he could concentrate on his most important and immediate problem: how were he and his team going to be attacked? But better yet, when were they going to be attacked? David knew that his attackers had but a few hours left to carry out their operation. David remembered the Captain's warnings, "Powerful forces are going to come after you with all they've got." David was convinced that he was already on an assassin's crosshairs as he walked up to his villa. "If anybody is to be killed, I hope it's me and nobody else. This was all my idea, and I'm the one that got them involved. So here I am. I'm not hiding; you know where to find me," he spoke out loud as he climbed the steep road in solitude.

David called the Captain and Warren several times as he made his way up to his villa. Both men reassured David that they were ready to release the retrovirus at exactly eighteen hundred hours, just as he had instructed them. They also added that there were no unusual or suspicious activities taking place anywhere near the *Milagro*. David directed them to keep him posted on an hourly basis.

It's misdirection, David kept repeating to himself as he kept putting one foot in front of the other, climbing up the steep switchbacks. As convinced of misdirection as he was, he couldn't figure out the true direction of his adversaries. *What are they really after?*

The steep climb left David drenched in perspiration, dehydrated, and nauseated. It was still three-and-a-half hours before the *Milagro's* auction. Exactly three-and-a-half hours before the release of the retrovirus and the beginning of the end of racism.

David showered and tried to take a nap, but it was futile. His brain was working too hard, no time to relax.

Startled by a sudden ring, David spilled his hot coffee on his leg. Ignoring the pain, he reached for his satellite phone.

"Yes, this is David. Who's calling?"

"We need to meet immediately," said the person on the phone.

"Who is this?" asked David again.

"Don't ask questions, just do as I say. Look out your window, Can you see the car just outside your gate?"

"Yes, I see it," David answered.

"I want you to walk down and meet it. The driver will let you in and bring you to me."

The car's windows suddenly became opaque the moment David stepped in, making it impossible for David to see where he was being taken. The car was very normal on the outside, but its interior was opulent. The rear compartment where he sat was separated from the front by a mahogany-paneled wall. The driver had no view of the passengers. *I'm sure there's a hidden camera looking at me, though*, David said to himself. The large armrest had a built-in panel with electronic displays and a touch screen that was only available in sophisticated communication systems. David was familiar with the equipment. One of his friends had designed it; there was none better. One of the cabinet doors was labeled "defibrillator." The seats' leather was immaculate, almost pure white in color, with not a scratch to be found. *The leather must have come from cattle raised at high altitudes; mosquitoes don't live at high altitudes. Why is the exterior so simple yet the interior so ostentatious?* David couldn't help but think of the Alhambra.

A television screen displayed stock market activity. At present those being broadcast were the European markets. Bach's six un-accompanied cello suites were playing on the car's sound system. Though David couldn't detect the speakers, the car's acoustics were perfect. There was one framed piece of art hanging on the right side. *Must be an expensive piece of art*, thought David. As his eyes focused on it, he couldn't help but laugh. It was a framed ribbon just like the ones little kids get when they do something special in school. The faded red ribbon with gold lettering read, "Second Place."

The car stopped and the windows cleared. David looked up and saw a pretentious Mediterranean-style house. David looked around, trying to orient himself, trying to figure out where exactly the short drive had taken him. The privacy wall around the house prevented David from determining his location. He could hear a cacophony of voices and, in the distance, the sound of a speedboat traveling from his left to his right. With only these clues to go by, he figured he was very close to the marina and the *Milagro*. Two husky men opened the car door and yanked David out. With his hands up in the air, David was searched. His satellite phone was immediately confiscated. The larger of the two men put his handgun to David's back and ordered him to walk in front of them. They led him into the house, walked down a spacious corridor that led to the library, and sat him down across from a large desk. The library's high wood ceiling had intri-cately carved figurines of all sizes and shapes. Leather-bound books filled the countless shelves that rose to within a few feet of the ceiling.

David heard footsteps on the travertine floor, gradually get-ting louder until they suddenly stopped. Through the beveled glass French doors, David saw a tall and muscular man. The man's neatly trimmed beard was beginning to gray, just like his full set of hair. David couldn't tell by the man's skin color if he was Egyptian, Iranian, or perhaps Mexican.

"Welcome, David. Haven't seen you in ages," were the stranger's first words.

The stranger's face now came into full view.

"Do I know you?" David asked. "You say you haven't seen me in ages. Is it possible you are mistaking me for somebody else? Because I have never seen you before. But that's not what we're here for, is it? You didn't bring me here to talk about having met before. I'm here because this has something to do with Hans and somebody named Moe. Which I hope is you because that's the only reason I agreed to get in the car and come here."

"I am Moe," the man said as he lit his cigar. Its aroma immediately filled the room, so let's get down to business."

"Are you so scared of me that you need these two armed men behind me?" David asked as he turned his head around to look at the two burly men. "I prefer we talk in private."

"Sorry, David, they stay."

David found himself in the situation he had hoped would never happen. He was about to be killed before seeing his dream become a reality. He desperately looked around, wanting to run out of the room. But the only exit was blocked by the armed men. Jumping out through one of the many closed windows was not an option, either. The house sat on the edge of a cliff overlooking the marina.

"You look like you just saw a ghost, David. Maybe we should get our business out of the way, and then you can be on your way, in one piece."

"I have every intention of leaving in one piece."

"Good, very good. So here's the deal," Moe said. "You deposit $10 billion, one billion into ten separate accounts. Once I verify that the deposits have been made, I'll release control of your computers and you'll have your discovery back in your possession. But before I forget, let me mention one very important detail: my men are aboard the *Milagro* at this very moment. And there's absolutely nothing you can do about it, unless you can get through those two guys behind you."

"You're lying," David stood up and pounded on Moe's desk. "The *Milagro* is impenetrable."

"I think you're the one's that's lying," Moe motioned for David to get back in his seat. "Have you forgotten about the ventral airlock door? When I found out about the ventral airlock, I immediately knew how I was going to penetrate the *Milagro*—mini submarines. My men entered the *Milagro* through the ventral airlock door about five minutes ago. By now they should have subdued Warren and the Captain and gained control of the computers—which as you know, contain the racist gene research data. This shouldn't scare you since you have probably figured out that the data is worthless. What should be alarming to you is that by having control of the computers, I have control over the release of the retrovirus, which is not going to take place today. If all goes as planned, you should be getting a call from the Captain," Moe pointed at David's satellite phone that now lay on his desk.

"He is going to tell you that he cannot release the retrovirus because it has been contaminated. The Captain will also tell you that he needs five days to decontaminate the retrovirus. I couldn't rely on you believing him and staying away from the *Milagro,* so I decided to buy some insurance. That's why you're here. You are now my hostage. We rely on computers for everything nowadays, David, which is very unfortunate for you at this moment. You have this wonderful discovery aboard the *Milagro,* but it's totally useless because I'm in control of your computers—well, it's actually my men that are now in control. You're so close to realizing your dream, David. Think of the many years of hard work that will go down the drain if you don't get to release the retrovirus. So pay up, and just like that you'll be back in business," Moe said.

Moe was positive David would pay the $10 billion, and just like that, he would realize a $10 billion windfall without incurring any additional costs.

"Now that I know your name, may I address you personally, by your first name?"

"Why of course."

"Fuck you, Moe! I'm not paying you shit, you hear that?"

As he directed his angry words at Moe, David kept thinking, *Are there others? He asked for ten billion, so are there ten people involved? He said "Haven't seen you in many years." Where did he see me? When exactly did he see me?* David searched his memory bank but came up empty.

"It's already five o'clock, one hour before show time. I'm sure the crowd is anxiously awaiting your arrival, probably wondering why you're not already there. Look out the window, David, look at the thousands of people gathered for the *Milagro's* auction. You're the man of the hour, David. Too bad you won't be showing up for your own party."

"We'll see about that," David started to get up but quickly changed his mind.

"If you say so, but in the meantime, you need to get busy and call your Race Group buddies and tell them you're being held hostage. Tell them the amount of the ransom, and tell them you need the money within the hour. You billionaires can get things done in a hurry when there's a will. And make sure you tell them that my men are already aboard the *Milagro*. This might add a little incentive for them to move quickly."

David used Moe's desk phone to call Rosalind and tell her what was taking place. He spoke as calmly as possible, not wanting to reveal his overwhelming fear. David didn't know anything about Moe, but he did know that he could not trust him. *I know he's going to kill me the moment he gets his $10 billion. I hope Rosalind realizes this and doesn't wire the money to any of Moe's offshore bank accounts.*

"What did your female friend have to say? Is she getting the money ready?" Moe asked.

"I'm sure you have somebody listening in on my conversation. Why don't you ask them?"

"Have it your way, but we're down to thirty minutes. I have all the time in the world, but you don't."

The antique grandfather clock in the library with its metronomic rhythm beat loudly in the silent room. David sat stoically across the desk from Moe, looking directly at him. Moe busied himself with his cigar without a whisper of a word, getting it perfectly cut and ready to be lit. The room was so quiet David could hear himself breathe. Moe picked up his gold cigar lighter, put his thumb on the spark wheel, looked around the room for a moment, and then quickly pushed down on the wheel. Suddenly a concussive sound wave hit the house, shattering many of the windows and spraying the room with shards of glass. The startled men ran toward the windows and saw an inferno, flames rising into the sky from the marina.

"The *Milagro* has exploded," David yelled out, terrified as he looked out the window. The *Milagro*'s bridge was engulfed in flames as it slowly sank into the shallow marina. Soon the last evidence of the majestic yacht would be gone.

David looked in disbelief as he saw people running away from the explosion. Others were not so lucky; their torn bodies were savagely strewn about. Moe yelled at his men, telling them to run down to the marina and find out what happened.

"Sir, you have James Morgan on the line," Moe's scared butler rushed into the library and yelled out.

Moe shook his head and signaled with his hand for David to leave. Then he abruptly changed his mind, "Wait, don't leave yet. There's something I need to tell you before I excuse you."

"Sir, Mr. Morgan insists you take his call now," Moe's butler yelled.

"I've always regretted not selling you the M&Ms for a nickel. Now leave before Morgan comes after you."

In disbelief but without saying a word, David ran down to the marina as fast as he could, hoping the Captain and Warren had miraculously survived, but he knew better. Nothing could have survived the horrific explosion. The traffic was paralyzed by hundreds of people running away from the marina. Emergency vehicles were unable to get to the injured because of the gridlock. Their sirens blared in vain.

David ran past the police barricade that had been set up to keep people away from the raging fires that were destroying other yachts close to the *Milagro*. He escaped a policeman's grasp and continued running toward the site were the *Milagro* once proudly stood. David arrived just in time to see the *Milagro*'s stern, the yacht's last vestige, slowly sink into the flaming waters. He stood watching his dream come to an abrupt ending when suddenly the stern exploded, sending David several feet into the the the air. Medical personnel rushed towards the unconscious and seriously injured David. Blood immediately soaked his clothes from the many wounds. Blood also flowed from his nose and ears.

The following morning, David woke up and found himself in the intensive care unit. His ex-wife, son, and daughter were at his side.

His son opened his laptop computer and turned it around so that David could read the words on the screen. In bold letters it read:

The Captain and Warren are missing. Both are presumed dead.

CHAPTER 50

"**W**here in the hell am I?" the dazed Captain mumbled.

The Captain lay on the hard frozen snow high in the Himalayas. He and Warren had parachuted from a transport plane onto a tiny piece of flat terrain—at least that had been the plan. Warren's parachute didn't completely open, causing him to miss the target by a wide margin, but he still managed to land safely. The Captain's landing was perfect. His many years of skydiving had paid off. Several hours had passed since the drop, and the plummeting temperatures were taking their toll on the Captain. The brightness of the full moon allowed Warren to locate the landing site and reunite with the Captain.

"Where in the hell are we, Warren?" the Captain asked as he saw Warren approaching.

"Get up, Captain. We've got to get out of here, do you hear me? We've got to get out of here. With this fucking full moon we can be seen from miles away."

The Captain looked up at Warren but didn't answer. The transport plane pilot warned them that they needed to get away from the clearing as soon as they landed because his radar showed that a small jet was following them. Their radar-jamming device made sure that the trailing jet's radar didn't see them parachute, but once on the ground, they could be spotted from the air. Warren picked up the Captain by his shoulders and dragged him from the clearing. They both hid behind a series of small snow-covered boulders. Warren removed the Captain's parachute, rolled it up, and placed it inside a large backpack.

"What are we doing here, Warren? What's going on?" the Captain asked repeatedly, barely able to speak.

"I'll tell you as soon as I get to our hideout. Come on, Captain, get up. It's about six hundred meters up the mountain, so let's hurry before the sun comes up."

With great effort, Warren helped the Captain walk further up the mountain. In exchange for the computer equipment, the grateful monks revealed to Warren a secret cave their ancestors had found centuries before. At first, the monks had considered it a sacred site, but the cave had since been abandoned. Warren had read about the sacred place, but no Westerner had ever actually seen it. Warren swore that he would come back someday and revisit the sacred place. He just didn't know it would be so soon.

"Ok, I get it, we're in this hole on the side of a mountain, but will you tell me what's going on?" the Captain asked.

"You really can't remember how we got here or why we're here?" Warren asked.

"No, I don't remember. That's why I'm asking."

"Do you remember jumping out of the plane?"

"No, Warren. I don't remember. I remember you, David, the discovery. I remember the years of research, but that's it. I kind of remember you and me walking to the *Milagro* and entering it after passing through the eye scanner security device, I remember that too. But after that I don't remember a damn thing."

Warren stared at the Captain and tried to come up with an idea as to what was happening to him. He held his finger in front of the Captain's eyes and asked him to follow it; the Captain's vision was fine.

"I can't believe you don't remember. Did you hit your head when you landed?" Warren asked.

"I don't know, Warren. I just told you, I don't remember a fuck-ing thing. I don't feel any bumps on my head, but I guess I wouldn't have any because I was wearing my helmet when you found me," the Captain said.

"Maybe you're suffering from TGA." Warren said.

"What the fuck is that?"

"Transient global amnesia. That means that your memory is a little fucked up, but you'll come out of it in no time."

"You're a computer guy, how would you know that?"

"Came across it while I was researching Alzheimer's. My dad's been diagnosed with the damn disease."

"Forget about my fucking memory loss and tell me what we're doing here."

"You said the last thing you remember is walking to the *Milagro,* so let's start there." Warren said.

"Good. Let's start there," the Captain said.

"So yesterday morning you and I walk to the *Milagro,* go through security, and wait for the eight o'clock delivery of the retrovirus. I finish unloading it, the lab technician takes over, and I then join you in the control room. You're watching me as I go about encrypting the racist gene data, the retrovirus data, and all of your experiments' results. You seem a bit jumpy; you keep asking me why I'm taking so long. You keep repeating the protocol for the release of the retrovirus. I tell you to shut up, that I have to concentrate on my work, but you just keep yapping. So I tune you out.

"But suddenly you shut up and we both look at each other when we hear a faint noise from the lower deck. We both know that the technician handling the retrovirus has finished and left the *Milagro,* meaning we should be the only ones on board. We can now distinctly hear voices, but it's too late. Two armed men wearing SWAT-type uniforms and pointing guns at us enter the control room. One of them yells at you to stand by the handrail so he can handcuff you to it. As soon as you start heading towards the handrail, I pull out my gun and point it at them. When he sees my gun, he puts his arm around your neck and puts his gun to your head. The guy that's closest to me tells me to drop my weapon and to hand over the vaccines. 'What vaccines? You mean *retrovirus*, you idiot. You don't even know the fucking name of what you're here to steal,' I yell at him.'"

"He said vaccines?"

"Yeah, and then he said, 'Ask the Captain. He knows what I'm talking about.' As he said this, he turned around to look at you. I jumped at the opportunity and shot."

"Did you hit him?"

"I hit him in the back of his head. I killed him."

"Holy shit!" the Captain exclaimed.

"The guy with his gun to your head starts shooting at me as he runs towards me. I duck behind the mainframe, positive that I'm about to die. He keeps shooting in my direction but hits the mainframe instead of me. The loud ring of the shots is gone and all I hear is *click, click, click*. He's run out of bullets. I crawl from behind the mainframe and shoot him as he reaches for another gun from his leg holster. He bends over and falls on the floor, but he's still breathing.

"I start removing the hard drives from the computers. I toss them to you and tell you to put them in my backpack as I continue removing the last one. No sooner do I toss the last hard drive to you when the mainframe explodes, knocks me off my feet. I get back on my feet but now see that all shit is breaking loose. Electrical wires are popping all over the control room, igniting fires all over the place. The whole fucking control room is now engulfed in flames. We start running up the stairs to the upper deck, but it too is on fire. So we head down to the lower deck and the ventral airlock hatch. But before we even enter the chamber, we see through the open door that a mini-sub is docked to the outer chamber of the hatch.

"We both look at each other, knowing that the sub is our only escape, but neither of us knows how to pilot the fucking sub. We see the fire coming down to the lower deck and realize we're dead. But before the fire reaches us, you figure out how to detach the sub from the hatch and we make our escape."

"Does David know we're here?" the Captain asked.

"Are you serious? Nobody could have survived the explosion," Warren told the Captain.

"What explosion?"

"The *Milagro* blew up. Don't you remember when we thought the mini-sub had hit something as we made our escape. We didn't hit anything. What we felt was the shock wave from the exploding *Milagro*.

"You try to call David, but his phone is dead. You and I agree that there's a strong possibility that David has been killed. Without direction from David, we take matters into our own hands. Our first priority is to not get killed. Second, we know we need to get the hell out of Monte Carlo. Getting out of the mini-sub is easy, but we have nowhere to go, nowhere to hide. And as crazy as it sounds, I use your telephone to call the pilot of a transport plane that is in the process of taking off to make a drop in the Himalayas. I tell you that it's our only escape but we have to hurry. You cuss at me and tell me that we'll both get killed if we jump out of a plane over the Himalayas. I remind you that you were an ace skydiver in your youth and that it's like riding a bike; you never forget. You tell me that you'll get on the plane but you sure as hell aren't going to parachute."

"Now how in the fuck did you know about the transport plane?"

"Because I had already made one delivery of computer equipment to the local monks and had scheduled one more delivery, on the same day as the *Milagro*'s auction. It's a long story; I'll tell you the rest later. But anyway, you did parachute, and here we are."

"Do you think David is alive?"

"I sure as hell hope so, Captain. But if he's alive, there's no way we are going to contact him, at least not for a long time."

"If the explosion was as bad as you say, then you're right, everybody has to assume we're dead. Which means there's nobody looking for us, especially up here. This will buy us time to plan our next step. What that may be I don't have a clue."

Warren left the Captain alone the following night and hiked

all night to get to the monastery. The monks were ecstatic at seeing Warren again. As hurriedly as possible, Warren told them of his and the Captain's situation. The monks immediately responded by providing food, water, and other supplies to the two fugitives. The monks agreed to provide for them indefinitely, for as long as they stayed hidden.

For the first few weeks of their existence in the cave, both men slept a lot. In spite of living in such cramped and close quarters, both men kept to themselves. Their conversations were few and far between.

"I know I'm old, but this is weird. One minute I'm a brilliant geneticist, and the next I can't remember shit. I know you said this whatever-you-called-it doesn't last long. I hope you're right."

"It doesn't last long, Captain. Trust me."

"Hey, Warren. When we were aboard the *Milagro* and the guy with his gun to my head said to hand over the vaccines, did I say anything?"

"No, why would you?" Warren asked.

"I need to tell you something in case we don't survive, in case we don't make it."

"I know it seems like we've been here for ages, but don't worry. We're going to make it out of here soon. And in one piece."

"Yeah, yeah, I guess you're right."

The Captain retreated and didn't say a word for the rest of the day. But by nighttime, he had to say what he had to say. He had to get it off his chest.

"I've been working with Hans."

"Why, you lying son of a bitch. You fucking piece of shit."

"It's not what you think, Warren."

"Really? Then tell me, Captain. What should I think?"

"It has to do with the theft of the racist gene data. Hans and the guy named Moe were initially set on stealing the data, destroying it, and killing all of us. You, me, and David. They had clients that were hell-bent on preserving racism so they were willing to pay top dollar to get rid of the data and us. But things changed. Things changed when they found out we had not only discovered the racist gene but how to eliminate it from our DNA. Moe, who I later found out is the brains behind the operation, figured out that it was more profitable to him if we released the virus."

"This doesn't make sense. One minute they want to kill us and destroy the racist gene data, and the next minute they want to rid the world of racism."

"You weren't listening carefully. They wanted to destroy everything before they knew of the retrovirus. When they learned of the retrovirus and how it could enter our DNA and disable the racist gene, they were ready to give up the fight. But Moe came up with a brilliant idea: to profit from racism by getting rid of racism throughout the world except for a select few. The only way to accomplish this is by inoculating those you wish to be immune to the retrovirus. So Hans came to me and threatened that if I didn't come up with a vaccine he would kill my son."

"So you do have a son."

"Yes, and this is where I have to tell you something else. I lied to David on another matter. Hell, I lied to you as well. I lied when I said I had discovered a reversal process. I never did."

"Fuck, Captain, how could you have lied about such an important thing? The reversal process was just as important as finding the racist gene. And you lied about it?"

"I've told you all along, I didn't believe David would release the retrovirus without having a reversal process, so I lied. Now, will you let me finish?"

"Go ahead and finish. As far as I know it's probably another lie!"

"Towards the end, when I had given up on finding the reversal process, I started working on developing a vaccine that would work against the retrovirus. It was just an experiment on my part. I wasn't interested in inoculating myself or any of you. I was just keeping my mind occupied because I didn't want to think about my lying to David. So when Hans came to me and asked me to develop the vaccine, I already had it. I told him that it was going to take time for me to develop it.

"I used that time to tweak the vaccine. I tweaked it so that the vaccine required a booster shot three days after the first dose in order for it to be fully effective against the retrovirus. Yes, Warren, the vaccine was useless if the recipient didn't receive a booster shot. I'm positive the young kid Hans brought in to verify my vaccine noticed it required a booster shot. But to this day I can't figure out why he didn't say a thing."

"Why you lying son of a bitch. I love you, Captain."

"One more thing. Remember the two empty gum wrappers that were found in Hans' coat pocket when the doctor pronounced him dead? The gum in those empty wrappers was meant for you. They were laced with cyanide. I switched the sticks of gum when Hans turned around to go to the sink. The poor sucker killed himself.

"Oh, and one more thing—I promise, the last thing. Do you know why Hans was a racist up until the end? He was accidentally inoculated in my lab by me, by sheer accident. I dropped a beaker that contained several dosages of the vaccine on the floor, and some of it splashed in Hans' eyes and on his face. And that did it. From then on he was immune to the retrovirus. He injected himself later with some of the tweaked vaccine he took from me, but it didn't matter, he was already immune to the virus with the real vaccine."

The Captain smiled, laid his head up against the wall, and looked up as if gazing at the stars, and quietly said, "Goodnight, Brishen."

"What did you say?"

"I was telling my son goodnight."

"But you said *Brishen*."

"That's his name, same as mine. It means *born in the rain*."

The Captain closed his eyes.

ACKNOWLEDGEMENTS

I am deeply appreciative of the many people who have influenced my life and who have enabled me in writing this novel. I thank my wife, Stella who has steadfastly supported me in writing The Milagro Affair, offering me valuable advice after diligently reading my countless rewrites. And I especially thank her for her patience while teaching me how to type as I wrote the Milagro Affair.

I thank my friends and fellow Lanier High School graduates, Professors Ignacio Garcia and Rafael Castillo, for their support and encouragement throughout the many revisions of The Milagro Affair.

I am also deeply indebted to my friend, Dr. Ken Maverick, who came to my support during the editorial process. Dr. Maverick's assistance proved pivotal in bringing The Milagro Affair to publication.

I always envisioned The Milagro Affair's cover to be explosive and I thank Ms. Abby Gonzales for having brought my vision to life. Abby took my preliminary renderings, mixed them with her artistic talents and gave me the cover that embodies my novel.

Brent Boller, my friend and mentor, I thank you. There were many times that I felt like sleeping in and not making it to Starbucks at five in the morning but I knew I had to be there to discuss my latest rewrite with you. I could hardly wait to tell you how I was making Hans a more disgusting character or making the Captain a more complex individual. I was always anxious to tell you about David Lorca's life in the barrio and about his inner conflict as he decides whether to release the retrovirus or not. I thank you, Brent, for your listening skills, for your editorial contributions but best of all I thank you for your friendship.

Printed in the United States
By Bookmasters